D1267239

LEST DARKNESS FALL

AND RELATED STORIES

CLASSIC SCIENCE FICTION AT PHOENIX PICK

Dark Universe by Daniel F. Galouye
The Long Tomorrow by Leigh Bracket
The Best of Edmond Hamilton edited by Leigh Brackett
The Time Machine by H. G Wells
The World Beyond the Hill by Alexei and Cory Panshin

www.PhoenixPick.com
Sign up for free ebooks

LEST DARKNESS FALL

L. SPRAGUE DE CAMP

Afterword by Alexei & Cory Panshin

AND RELATED STORIES

FREDERIK POHL
S. M. STIRLING
DAVID DRAKE

an imprint of

ARC MANOR

Rockville, Maryland

Lest Darkness Fall (in a shorter version) appeared in the December 1939 issue of *Unknown*. Copyright © 1939 by Street & smith Publications Inc. *Lest Darkness Fall* Copyright © 1941 by Henry Holt and Company. Copyright © 1949, 1977, 1996 by L. Sprague de Camp. Reprinted by permission of the author's estate and the estate's agents, The Spectrum Literary Agency.

Afterword, "L. Sprague de Camp's Great Leap of Imagination" is adapted from *The World Beyond the Hill*. Copyright © 1989 by Alexei and Cory Panshin. Reprinted by permission of the authors.

"The Deadly Mission of of Phineas Snodgrass" first appeared in *Galaxy Magazine*. Copyright © 1962 by Galaxy Publishing Corporation. Reprinted by permission of the author and the author's agents, Curtis Brown, Ltd.

"The Apotheosis of Martin Padway" first appeared in *The Enchanter Completed*. Copyright © S. M. Stirling 2005. Reprinted by permission of the author and the author's agents Scovil Galen Gosh Literary Agency.

To Bring the Light Copyright © 1996 by David Drake. Reprinted by permission of the author.

All rights reserved. This book may not be copied or reproduced, in whole or in part, by any means, electronic, mechanical or otherwise without written permission from the publisher except by a reviewer who may quote brief passages in a review.

Tarikian, TARK Classic Fiction, Arc Manor, Arc Manor Classic Reprints, Phoenix Pick, Phoenix Rider and logos associated with those imprints are trademarks or registered trademarks of Arc Manor Publishers, Rockville, Maryland. All other trademarks and trademarked names are properties of their respective owners.

This book is presented as is, without any warranties (implied or otherwise) as to the accuracy of the production, text or translation.

Phoenix Pick Hardcover Edition, November 2017

ISBN: 978-1-61242-226-8

Published in Paper and Ebook Formats by Phoenix Pick
an imprint of Arc Manor
P. O. Box 10339
Rockville, MD 20849-0339
www.ArcManor.com

Publisher's Acknowledgement

An edition like this, with multiple stories from multiple authors, written over a span of about sixty years, is not possible without the cooperation of many people. Our appreciation goes out to:

The Managers of the Estate of L. Sprague de Camp
David Drake
Frederik Pohl
Elizabeth Anne Hull (for her gracious follow-ups)
S. M. Stirling
Alexei & Cory Panshin
Mitchell Waters and Mark McCloud of *Curtis Brown, Ltd.*
Russell Galen and Ann Behar of *Scovil Galen Gosh Literary Agency*
Eleanor Wood of the *Spectrum Literary Agency* (without whom this project would never have gotten off the ground)

Contents

LEST DARKNESS FALL

L. SPRAGUE DE CAMP

To Catherine

♈

CHAPTER I

Tancredi took his hands off the wheel again and waved them. "—so I envy you, Dr. Padway. Here in Rome we have still some work to do. But *pah!* It is all filling in little gaps. Nothing big, nothing new. And restoration work. Building contractor's work. Again, *pah!*"

"Professor Tancredi," said Martin Padway patiently, "as I said, I am not a doctor. I hope to be one soon, if I can get a thesis out of this Lebanon dig." Being himself the most cautious of drivers, his knuckles were white from gripping the side of the little Fiat, and his right foot ached from trying to shove it through the floor boards.

Tancredi snatched the wheel in time to avoid a lordly Isotta by the thickness of a razor blade. The Isotta went its way thinking dark thoughts. "Oh, what is the difference? Here everybody is a doc-tor, whether he is or not, if you understand me. And such a smart young man as you—What was I talking about?"

"That depends." Padway closed his eyes as a pedestrian just escaped destruction. "You were talking about Etruscan inscriptions, and then about the nature of time, and then about Roman archaeol—"

"Ah, yes, the nature of time. This is just a silly idea of mine, you understand. I was saying all these people who just disappear, they have slipped back down the suitcase."

"The what?"

"The trunk, I mean. The trunk of the tree of time. When they stop slipping, they are back in some former time. But as soon as they do anything, they change all subsequent history."

"Sounds like a paradox," said Padway.

"No-o. The trunk continues to exist. But a new branch starts out where they come to rest. It has to, otherwise we would all disappear, because history would have changed and our parents might not have met."

"That's a thought," said Padway. "It's bad enough knowing the sun might become a nova, but if we're also likely to vanish because somebody has gone back to the twelfth century and stirred things up—"

"No. That has never happened. We have never vanished, that is. You see, doc-tor? We continue to exist, but another history has been started. Perhaps there are many such, all existing somewhere. Maybe, they aren't much different from ours. Maybe the man comes to rest in the middle of the ocean. So what? The fish eat him, and things go on as before. Or they think he is mad, and shut him up or kill him. Again, not much difference. But suppose he becomes a king or a *duce*? What then?

"*Presto*, we have a new history! History is a four-dimensional web. It is a tough web. But it has weak points. The junction places—the focal points, one might say—are weak. The backslipping, if it happens, would happen at these places."

"What do you mean by focal points?" asked Padway. It sounded to him like polysyllabic nonsense.

"Oh, places like Rome, where the world-lines of many famous events intersect. Or Istanbul. Or Babylon. You remember that archaeologist, Skrzetuski, who disappeared at Babylon in 1936?"

"I thought he was killed by some Arab holdup men."

"Ah. They never found his body! Now, Rome may soon again be the intersection point of great events. That means the web is weakening again here."

"I hope they don't bomb the Forum," said Padway.

"Oh, nothing like that. There will be no more great wars; everybody knows it is too dangerous. But let us not talk politics. The web, as I say, is tough. If a man did slip back, it would take a terrible lot of work to distort it. Like a fly in a spider web that fills a room."

"Pleasant thought," said Padway.

"Is it not, though?" Tancredi turned to grin at him, then trod frantically on the brake. The Italian leaned out and showered a pedestrian with curses.

He turned back to Padway. "Are you coming to my house for dinner tomorrow?"

"Wh-what? Why yes, I'll be glad to. I'm sailing next—"

"*Si, si.* I will show you the equations I have worked out. Energy must be conserved, even in changing one's time. But nothing of this to my colleagues, please. You understand." The sallow little man took his hands off the wheel to wag both forefingers at Padway. "It is a harmless eccentricity. But one's professional reputation must not suffer."

"*Eek!*" said Padway.

Tancredi jammed on the brake and skidded to a stop behind a truck halted at the intersection of the Via del Mare and the Piazza Aracoeli. "What was I talking about?" he asked.

"Harmless eccentricities," said Padway. He felt like adding that Professor Tancredi's driving ranked among his less harmless ones. But the man had been very kind to him.

"Ah, yes. Things get out, and people talk. Archaeologists talk even worse than most people. Are you married?"

"What?" Padway felt he should have gotten used to this sort of thing by now. He hadn't. "Why—yes."

"Good. Bring your wife along. Then you see some real Italian cooking, not this spaghetti-and-meat-balls stuff."

"She's back in Chicago." Padway didn't feel like explaining that he and his wife had been separated for over a year.

He could see, now, that it hadn't been entirely Betty's fault. To a person of her background and tastes he must have seemed pretty impossible: a man who danced badly, refused to play bridge, and whose idea of fun was to get a few similar creatures in for an evening of heavy talk on the future of capitalism and the love life of the bullfrog. At first she had been thrilled by the idea of traveling in far places, but one taste of living in a tent and watching her husband mutter over the inscriptions on potsherds had cured that.

And he wasn't much to look at—rather small, with outsize nose and ears and a diffident manner. At college they had called him Mouse Padway. Oh, well, a man in exploratory work was a fool to marry, anyway. Just look at the divorce rate among them—anthropologists, paleontologists, and such—

"Could you drop me at the Pantheon?" he asked. "I've never examined it closely, and it's just a couple of blocks to my hotel."

"Yes, doc-tor, though I am afraid you will get wet. It looks like rain, does it not?"

"That's all right. This coat will shed water."

Tancredi shrugged. They bucketed down the Corso Vittorio Emanuele and screeched around the corner into the Via Cestari. Padway got out at the Piazza del Pantheon, and Tancredi departed, waving both arms and shouting: "Tomorrow at eight, then? *Si*, fine."

Padway looked at the building for a few minutes. He had always thought it a very ugly one, with the Corinthian front stuck on the brick rotunda. Of course that great concrete dome had taken some engineering, considering when it had been erected. Then he had to jump to avoid being spattered as a man in a military uniform tore by on a motorcycle.

Padway walked over to the portico, round which clustered men engaged in the national sport of loitering. One of the things that he liked about Italy was that here he was, by comparison, a fairly tall man. Thunder rumbled behind him, and a raindrop struck his hand. He began to take long steps. Even if his trench coat would shed water, he didn't want his new twelve-thousand-lire Borsalino soaked. He liked that hat.

His reflections were cut off in their prime by the grand-daddy of all lightning flashes, which struck the Piazza to his right. The pavement dropped out from under him like a trapdoor.

His feet seemed to be dangling over nothing. He could not see anything for the reddish-purple after-images in his retinas. The thunder rolled on and on.

It was a most disconcerting feeling, hanging in the midst of nothing. There was no uprush of air as in falling down a shaft. He felt somewhat as Alice must have felt on her leisurely fall down the rabbit-hole, except that his senses gave him no clear information as to what was happening. He could not even guess how fast it was happening.

Then something hard smacked his soles. He almost fell. The impact was about as strong as that resulting from a two-foot fall. As he staggered by he hit his shin on something. He said "Ouch!"

His retinas cleared. He was standing in the depression caused by the drop of a roughly circular piece of pavement.

The rain was coming down hard, now. He climbed out of the pit and ran under the portico of the Pantheon. It was so dark that the lights in the building ought to have been switched on. They were not.

Padway saw something curious: the red brick of the rotunda was covered by slabs of marble facing. That, he thought, was one of the restoration jobs that Tancredi had been complaining about.

Padway's eyes glided indifferently over the nearest of the loafers. They switched back again sharply. The man, instead of coat and pants, was wearing a dirty white woolen tunic.

It was odd. But if the man wanted to wear such a getup, it was none of Padway's business.

The gloom was brightening a little. Now Padway's eyes began to dance from person to person. They were all wearing tunics. Some had come under the portico to get out of the rain. These also wore tunics, sometimes with poncholike cloaks over them.

A few of them stared at Padway without much curiosity. He and they were still staring when the shower let up a few minutes later. Padway knew fear.

The tunics alone would not have frightened him. A single incongruous fact might have a rational if recondite explanation. But everywhere he looked more of these facts crowded in on him. He could not concisely notice them all at once.

The concrete sidewalk had been replaced by slabs of slate.

There were still buildings around the Piazza, but they were not the same buildings. Over the lower ones Padway could see that the Senate House and the Ministry of Communications—both fairly conspicuous objects—were missing.

The sounds were different. The honk of taxi horns was absent. There were no taxis to honk. Instead, two oxcarts creaked slowly and shrilly down the via della Minerva.

Padway sniffed. The garlic-and-gasoline aroma of modern Rome had been replaced by a barnyard-and-backhouse symphony wherein the smell of horse was the strongest and also the most mentionable motif. Another ingredient was incense, wafting from the door of the Pantheon.

The sun came out. Padway stepped out into it. Yes, the portico still bore the inscription crediting the construction of the building to M. Agrippa.

Glancing around to see that he was not watched, Padway stepped up to one of the pillars and slammed his fist into it. It hurt.

"Hell," said Padway, looking at his bruised knuckles.

He thought, I'm not asleep. All this is too solid and consistent for a dream. There's nothing fantastic about the early afternoon sunshine and the beggars around the Piazza.

But if he was not asleep, what? He might be crazy...But that was a hypothesis difficult to build a sensible course of action on.

There was Tancredi's theory about slipping back in time. Had he slipped back, or had something happened to him to make him imagine he had? The time-travel idea did not appeal to Padway. It sounded metaphysical, and he was a hardened empiricist.

There was the possibility of amnesia. Suppose that flash of lightning had actually hit him and suppressed his memory up to that time; then suppose something had happened to jar it loose again...He would have a gap in his memory between the first lightning flash and his arrival in this archaistic copy of old Rome. All sorts of things might have happened in the meantime. He might have blundered into a movie set. Mussolini, having long secretly believed himself a reincarnation of Julius Caesar, might have decided to make his people adopt classical Roman costume.

It was an attractive theory. But the fact that he was wearing exactly the same clothes, and had the same things in his pockets as before the flash, exploded it.

He listened to the chatter of a couple of the loafers. Padway spoke fair, if pedantic, Italian. He could not quite get the substance of these men's talk. In the rush of syllables he would often catch a familiar sound-group, but never enough at one time. Their speech had the tantalizing pseudo familiarity of Plattdeutsch to an English-speaking person.

He thought of Latin. At once the loafers' speech became more familiar. They were not speaking classical Latin. But Padway found that if he took one of their sentences and matched it first against Italian and then against Latin, he could understand most of it.

He decided that they were speaking a late form of Vulgar Latin, rather more than halfway from the language of Cicero to that of Dante. He had never even tried to speak this hybrid. But by dredging his memory for his knowledge of sound changes, he could make a stab at it: *Omnia Gallia e devisa en parte trei, quaro una encolont Belge, alia...*

The two loafers had observed his eavesdropping. They frowned, lowered their voices, and moved off.

No, the hypothesis of delirium might be a tough one, but it offered fewer difficulties than that of the time-slip.

If he was imagining things, was he really standing in front of the Pantheon and imagining that the people were dressed and speaking in the manner of the period 300-900 A.D.? Or was he lying in a hospital bed recovering from near-electrocution and imagining he was in front of the Pantheon? In the former case he ought to find a policeman and have himself taken to a hospital. In the latter this would be waste motion. For safety's sake he had better assume the former.

No doubt one of these people was really a policeman complete with shiny hat. What did he mean "really"? Let Bertrand Russell and Alfred Korzybski worry about that. How to find...

A beggar had been whining at him for a couple of minutes. Padway gave such a perfect impression of deafness that the ragged little hunchback moved off. Now another man was speaking to him. On his left palm the man held a string of beads with a cross, all in a heap. Between his right thumb and forefinger he held the clasp of the string. He raised his right hand until the whole string hung from it, then lowered it back onto his left palm, then raised it again, talking all the while.

Whenever and however all this was, that gesture assured Padway that he was still in Italy.

Padway asked in Italian: "Could you tell me where I could find a policeman?"

The man stopped his sales talk, shrugged, and replied, "*Non compr' endo.*"

"Hey!" said Padway. The man paused. With great concentration Padway translated his request into what he hoped was Vulgar Latin.

The man thought, and said he didn't know.

Padway started to turn elsewhere. But the seller of beads called to another hawker: "*Marco!* The gentleman wants to find a police agent."

"The gentleman is brave. He is also crazy," replied Marco.

The bead-seller laughed. So did several people. Padway grinned a little; the people were human if not very helpful, He said: "Please, I—really—want—to—know."

The second hawker, who had a tray full of brass knick-knacks tied around his neck, shrugged. He rattled off a paragraph that Padway could not follow.

Padway slowly asked the bead-seller: "What did he say?"

"He said he didn't know," replied the bead-seller. "I don't know either."

Padway started to walk off. The bead-seller called after him: "Mister."

"Yes?"

"Did you mean an agent of the municipal prefect?"

"Yes."

"Marco, where can the gentleman find an agent of the municipal prefect?"

"I don't know," said Marco.

The bead-seller shrugged. "Sorry, I don't know either."

If this were twentieth-century Rome, there would be no difficulty about finding a cop. And not even Benny the Moose could make a whole city change its language. So he must be in (a) a movie set, (b) ancient Rome (the Tancredi hypothesis), or (c) a figment of his imagination.

He started walking. Talking was too much of a strain.

It was not long before any lingering hopes about a movie set were dashed by the discovery that this alleged ancient city stretched for miles in all directions, and that its street plan was quite different from that of modern Rome. Padway found his little pocket map nearly useless.

The signs on the shops were in intelligible classical Latin. The spelling had remained as in Caesar's time, if the pronunciation had not.

The streets were narrow, and for the most part not very crowded. The town had a drowsy, shabby-genteel, rundown personality, like that of Philadelphia.

At one relatively busy intersection Padway watched a man on a horse direct traffic. He would hold up a hand to stop an oxcart, and beckon a sedan chair across. The man wore a gaudily striped shirt and leather trousers. He looked like a central or northern European rather than an Italian.

Padway leaned against a wall, listening. A man would say a sentence just too fast for him to catch. It was like having your hook nibbled but never taken. By terrific concentration, Padway forced himself to think in Latin. He mixed his cases and numbers, but as long as he confined himself to simple sentences he did not have too much trouble with vocabulary.

A couple of small boys were watching him. When he looked at them they giggled and raced off.

It reminded Padway of those United States Government projects for the restoration of Colonial towns, like Williamsburg. But this looked like the real thing. No restoration included all the dirt and disease, the insults and altercations, that Padway had seen and heard in an hour's walk.

Only two hypotheses remained: delirium and time-slip. Delirium now seemed the less probable. He would act on the assumption that things were in fact what they seemed.

He couldn't stand there indefinitely. He'd have to ask questions and get himself oriented. The idea gave him gooseflesh. He had a phobia about accosting strangers. Twice he opened his mouth, but his glottis closed up tight with stage fright.

Come on, Padway, get a grip on yourself. "I beg your pardon, but could you tell me the date?"

The man addressed, a mild-looking person with a loaf of bread under his arm, stopped and looked blank. "*Qui' e'?* What is it?"

"I said, could you tell me the date?"

The man frowned. Was he going to be nasty? But all he said was, "*Non compr' endo.*" Padway tried again, speaking very slowly. The man repeated that he did not understand.

Padway fumbled for his date-book and pencil. He wrote his request on a page of the date-book, and held the thing up.

The man peered at it, moving his lips. His face cleared. "Oh, you want to know the *date?*" said he.

"*Sic,* the date."

The man rattled a long sentence at him. It might as well have been in Trabresh. Padway waved his hands despairingly, crying, "*Lento!*"

The man backed up and started over. "I said I understood you, and I thought it was October 9th, but I wasn't sure because I couldn't remember whether my mother's wedding anniversary came three days ago or four."

"What year?"

"What *year?*"

"*Sic*, what year?"

"Twelve eighty-eight *Anno Urbis Conditae.*"

It was Padway's turn to be puzzled. "Please, what is that in the Christian era?"

"You mean, how many years since the birth of Christ?"

"*Hoc ille*—that's right."

"Well, now—I don't know; five hundred and something. Better ask a priest, stranger."

"I will," said Padway. "Thank you."

"It's nothing," said the man, and went about his business. Padway's knees were weak, though the man hadn't bitten him, and had answered his question in a civil enough manner. But it sounded as though Padway, who was a peaceable man, had not picked a very peaceable period.

What was he to do? Well, what would any sensible man do under the circumstances? He'd have to find a place to sleep and a method of making a living. He was a little startled when he realized how quickly he had accepted the Tancredi theory as a working hypothesis.

He strolled up an alley to be out of sight and began going through his pockets. The roll of Italian bank notes would be about as useful as a broken five-cent mousetrap. No, even less; you might be able to fix a mousetrap. A book of American Express traveler's checks, a Roman street-car transfer, an Illinois driver's license, a leather case full of keys—all ditto. His pen, pencil, and lighter would be useful as long as ink, leads, and lighter fuel held out. His pocketknife and his watch would undoubtedly fetch good prices, but he wanted to hang onto them as long as he could.

He counted the fistful of small change. There were just twenty coins, beginning with four ten-lire silver cartwheels. They added up to forty-nine lire, eight centesimi, or about five dollars. The silver and bronze should be exchangeable. As for the nickel fifty-centesimo and twenty-centesimo pieces, he'd have to see. He started walking again.

He stopped before an establishment that advertised itself as that of S. Dentatus, goldsmith and money changer. He took a deep breath and went in.

S. Dentatus had a face rather like that of a frog. Padway laid out his change and said: "I...I should like to change this into local money, please." As usual he had to repeat the sentence to make himself understood.

S. Dentatus blinked at the coins. He picked them up, one by one, and scratched at them a little with a pointed instrument. "Where do these—you—come from?" he finally croaked.

"America."

"Never heard of it."

"It is a long way off."

"Hm-m-m. What are these made of? Tin?" The money changer indicated the four nickel coins.

"Nickel."

"What's that? Some funny metal they have in your country?"

"*Hoc ille.*"

"What's it worth?"

Padway thought for a second of trying to put a fantastically high value on the coins. While he was working up his courage, S. Dentatus interrupted his thoughts:

"It doesn't matter, because I wouldn't touch the stuff. There wouldn't be any market for it. But these other pieces—let's see—" He got out a balance and weighed the bronze coins, and then the silver coins. He pushed counters up and down the grooves of a little bronze abacus, and said: "They're worth just under one solidus. Give you a solidus even for them."

Padway didn't answer immediately. Eventually he'd have to take what was offered, as he hated the idea of bargaining and didn't know the values of the current money. But to save his face he had to appear to consider the offer carefully.

A man stepped up to the counter beside him. He was a heavy, ruddy man with a flaring brown mustache and his hair in a long or Ginger Rogers bob. He wore a linen blouse and long leather pants. He grinned at Padway, and reeled off: "*Ho, frijond, habais faurthei! Alai skalljans sind waidedjans.*"

Oh, Lord, another language! Padway answered: "I…I am sorry, but I do not understand."

The man's face fell a little; he dropped into Latin: "Sorry, thought you were from the Chersonese, from your clothes. I couldn't stand around and watch a fellow Goth swindled without saying anything, ha, ha!"

The Goth's loud, explosive laugh made Padway jump a little; he hoped nobody noticed. "I appreciate that. What is this stuff worth?"

"What has he offered you?" Padway told him. "Well," said the man, "even I can see that you're being hornswoggled. You give him a fair rate, Sextus, or I'll make you eat your own stock. That would be funny, ha, ha!"

S. Dentatus sighed resignedly. "Oh, very well, a solidus and a half. How am I to live, with you fellows interfering with legitimate business all the time? That would be, at the current rate of exchange, one solidus thirty-one sesterces."

"What is this about a rate of exchange?" asked Padway.

The Goth answered: "The gold-silver rate. Gold has been going down the last few months."

Padway said: "I think I will take it all in silver."

While Dentatus sourly counted out ninety-three sesterces, the Goth asked: "Where do you come from? Somewhere up in the Hunnish country?"

"No," said Padway, "a place farther than that, called America. You have never heard of it, have you?"

"No. Well now, that's interesting. I'm glad I met you, young fellow. It'll give me something to tell the wife about. She thinks I head for the nearest brothel every time I come to town, ha, ha!" He fumbled in his handbag and brought out a large gold ring and an unfaceted gem. "Sextus, this thing came out of its setting again. Fix it up, will you? And no substitutions, mind."

As they went out the Goth spoke to Padway in a lowered voice. "The real reason I'm glad to come to town is that somebody put a curse on my house."

"A curse? What kind of a curse?"

The Goth nodded solemnly. "A shortness-of-breath curse. When I'm home I can't breathe. I go around like this—" He gasped asthmatically. "But as soon as I get away from home I'm all right. And I think I know who did it."

"Who?"

"I foreclosed a couple of mortgages last year. I can't prove anything against the former owners, *but*—" He winked ponderously at Padway.

"Tell me," said Padway, "do you keep animals in your house?"

"Couple of dogs. There's the stock, of course, but we don't let them in the house. Though a shoat got in yesterday and ran away with one of my shoes. Had to chase it all over the damned farm. I must have been a sight, ha, ha!"

"Well," said Padway, "try keeping the dogs outside all the time and having your place well swept every day. That might stop your—uh—wheezing."

"Now, that's interesting. You really think it would?"

"I do not know. Some people get the shortness of breath from dog hairs. Try it for a couple of months and see."

"I still think it's a curse, young fellow, but I'll try your scheme. I've tried everything from a couple of Greek physicians to one of St. Ignatius' teeth, and none of them works." He hesitated. "If you don't mind, what were you in your own country?"

Padway thought quickly, then remembered the few acres he owned in down-state Illinois. "I had a farm," he said.

"That's fine," roared the Goth, clapping Padway on the back with staggering force. I'm a friendly soul but I don't want to get mixed up with people too far above or below my own class, ha, ha! My name is Nevitta; Nevitta Gummund's son. If you're passing up the Flaminian Way sometime, drop in. My place is about eight miles north of here."

"Thanks. My name is Martin Padway. Where would be a good place to rent a room?"

"That depends. If I didn't want to spend too much money I'd pick a place farther down the river. Plenty of boarding houses over toward the Viminal Hill. Say, I'm in no hurry; I'll help you look." He whistled sharply and called: "*Hermann, hiri her!*"

Hermann, who was dressed much like his master, got up off the curb and trotted down the street leading two horses, his leather pants making a distinctive *flop-flop* as he ran.

Nevitta set out a brisk walk, Hermann leading the horses behind. Nevitta said: "What did you say your name was?"

"Martin Padway—Martinus is good enough." (Padway properly pronounced it Mart*ee*no.)

Padway did not want to impose on Nevitta's good nature, but he wanted the most useful information he could get. He thought a minute, then asked: "Could you give me the names of a few people in Rome, lawyers and physicians and such, to go to when I need them?"

"Sure. If you want a lawyer specializing in cases involving foreigners, Valerius Mummius is your man. His office is alongside of the Aemilian Basilica. For a physician try my friend Leo Vekkos. He's a good fellow as Greeks go. But personally I think the relic of a good Arian saint like Asterius is as effective as all their herbs and potations."

"It probably is at that," said Padway. He wrote the names and addresses in his date-book. "How about a banker?"

"I don't have much truck with them; hate the idea of getting in debt. But if you want the name of one, there's Thomasus the Syrian, near the Aemilian Bridge. Keep your eyes open if you deal with him."

"Why, isn't he honest?"

"Thomasus? Sure he's honest. You just have to watch him, that's all.

Here, this looks like a place you could stay." Nevitta pounded on the door, which was opened by a frowsy superintendent.

This man had a room, yes. It was small and ill-lighted. It smelled. But then so did all of Rome. The superintendent wanted seven sesterces a day.

"Offer him half," said Nevitta to Padway in a stage whisper.

Padway did. The superintendent acted as bored by the ensuing haggling as Padway was. Padway got the room for five sesterces.

Nevitta squeezed Padway's hand in his large red paw. "Don't forget, Martinus, come see me some time. I always like to hear a man who speaks Latin with a worse accent than mine, ha, ha!" He and Hermann mounted and trotted off.

Padway hated to see them go. But Nevitta had his own business to tend to. Padway watched the stocky figure round a corner, then entered the gloomy, creaking boarding house.

CHAPTER II

Padway awoke early with a bad taste in his mouth, and a stomach that seemed to have some grasshopper in its ancestry. Perhaps that was the dinner he'd eaten—not bad, but unfamiliar—consisting mainly of stew smothered in leeks. The restaurateur must have wondered when Padway made plucking motions at the table top; he was unthinkingly trying to pick up a knife and fork that weren't there.

One might very well sleep badly the first night on a bed consisting merely of a straw-stuffed mattress. And it had cost him an extra sesterce a day, too. An itch made him pull up his undershirt. Sure enough, a row of red spots on his midriff showed that he had not, after all, slept alone.

He got up and washed with the soap he had bought the previous evening. He had been pleasantly surprised to find that soap had already been invented. But when he broke a piece off the cake, which resembled a slightly decayed pumpkin pie, he found that the inside was soft and gooey because of incomplete potash-soda metathesis. Moreover, the soap was so alkaline that the thought he might as well have cleaned his hands and face by sandpapering.

Then he made a determined effort to shave with olive oil and a sixth-century razor. The process was so painful that he wondered if it mightn't be better to let nature take its course.

He was in a tight fix, he knew. His money would last about a week—with care, perhaps a little longer.

If a man knew he was going to be whisked back into the past, he would load himself down with all sorts of useful junk in preparation, an encyclopedia, texts on metallurgy, mathematics, and medicine, a slide rule, and so forth. And a gun, with plenty of ammunition.

But Padway had no gun, no encyclopedia, nothing but what an ordinary twentieth-century man carries in his pockets. Oh, a little more, because he'd been traveling at the time: such useful things as the traveler's checks, a hopelessly anachronistic street map, and his passport.

And he had his wits. He'd need them.

The problem was to find a way of using his twentieth-century knowledge that would support him without getting him into trouble. You couldn't, for example, set out to build an automobile. It would take several lifetimes to collect the necessary materials, and several more to learn how to handle them and to worry them into the proper form. Not to mention the question of fuel.

The air was fairly warm, and he thought of leaving his hat and vest in the room. But the door had the simplest kind of ward lock, with a bronze key big enough to be presented by a mayor to a visiting dignitary. Padway was sure he could pick the lock with a knife blade. So he took all his clothes along. He went back to the same restaurant for breakfast. The place had a sign over the counter reading, "RELIGIOUS ARGUMENTS NOT ALLOWED." Padway asked the proprietor how to get to the address of Thomasus the Syrian.

The man said: "You follow along Long Street down to the Arch of Constantine, and then New Street to the Julian Basilica, and then you turn left onto Tuscan Street, and—" and so on.

Padway made him repeat it twice. Even so, it took most of the morning to find his objective. His walk took him past the Forum area, full of temples, most of whose columns had been removed for use in the five big and thirty-odd little churches scattered around the city. The temples looked pathetic, like a Park Avenue doorman bereft of his pants.

At the sight of the Ulpian Library, Padway had to suppress an urge to say to hell with his present errand. He loved burrowing into libraries, and he definitely did not love the idea of bearding a strange banker in a strange land with a strange proposition. In fact, the idea scared him silly, but his was the kind of courage that shows itself best when its owner is about to collapse from blue funk. So he grimly kept on toward the Tiber.

Thomasus hung out in a shabby two-story building. The Negro at the door—probably a slave—ushered Padway into what he would have called a living room. Presently the banker appeared. Thomasus was a paunchy, bald man with a cataract on his left eye. He gathered his shabby robe about him, sat down, and said: "Well, young man?"

"I"—Padway swallowed and started again—"I'm interested in a loan."

"How much?"

"I don't know yet. I want to start a business, and I'll have to investigate prices and things first."

"You want to start a new business? In Rome? *Hm-m-m.*" Thomasus rubbed his hands together. "What security can you give?"

"None at all."

"*What?*"

"I said, none at all. You'd just have to take a chance on me."

"But…but, my dear sir, don't you know anybody in town?"

"I know a Gothic farmer named Nevitta Gummund's son. He sent me hither."

"Oh, yes, Nevitta. I know him slightly. Would he go your note?"

Padway thought. Nevitta, despite his expansive gestures, had impressed him as being pretty close where money was concerned. "No," he said, "I don't think he would."

Thomasus rolled his eyes upward. "Do You hear that, God? He comes in here, a barbarian who hardly knows Latin, and admits that he has no security and no guarantors, and still he expects me to lend him money! Did You ever hear the like?"

"I think I can make you change your mind," said Padway.

Thomasus shook his head and made clucking noises. "You certainly have plenty of self-confidence, young man; I admit as much. What did you say your name was?" Padway told him what he had told Nevitta. "All right, what's your scheme?"

"As you correctly inferred," said Padway, hoping he was showing the right mixture of dignity and cordiality, "I'm a foreigner. I just arrived from a place called America. That's a long way off, and naturally it has a lot of customs and features different from those of Rome. Now, if you could back me in the manufacture of some of our commodities that are not known here—"

"Ai!" yelped Thomasus, throwing up his hands. "Did You hear that, God? He doesn't want me to back him in some well-known business. Oh, no. He wants me to start some newfangled line that nobody ever heard of! I couldn't think of such a thing, Martinus. What was it you had in mind?"

"Well, we have a drink made from wine, called brandy, that ought to go well."

"No, I couldn't consider it. Though I admit that Rome needs manufacturing establishments badly. When the capital was moved to Ravenna all revenue from Imperial salaries was cut off, which is why the population has shrunk so the last century. The town is badly located, and hasn't any real reason for being any more. But you can't get anybody to do anything about it. King Thiudahad spends his time writing Latin verse. Poetry! But no, young man, I couldn't put money into a wild project for making some weird barbarian drink."

Padway's knowledge of sixth-century history was beginning to come back to him. He said: "Speaking of Thiudahad, has Queen Amalaswentha been murdered yet?"

"Why"—Thomasus looked sharply at Padway with his good eye—"yes, she has." That meant that Justinian, the "Roman" emperor of Constantinople, would soon begin his disastrously successful effort to reconquer Italy for the Empire. "But why did you put your question that way?"

Padway asked. "Do—do you mind if I sit down?"

Thomasus said he didn't. Padway almost collapsed into a chair. His knees were weak. Up to now his adventure had seemed like a complicated and difficult masquerade party. His own question about the murder of Queen Amalaswentha had brought home to him all at once the fearful hazards of life in this world.

Thomasus repeated: "I asked why, young sir, you put your question that way?"

"What way?" asked Padway innocently. He saw where he'd made a slip.

"You asked whether she had been murdered *yet*. That sounds as though you had known ahead of time that she would be killed. Are you a soothsayer?"

There were no flies on Thomasus. Padway remembered Nevitta's advice to keep his eyes open.

He shrugged. "Not exactly. I heard before I came here that there had been trouble between the two Gothic sovereigns, and that Thiudahad would put his co-ruler out of the way if he had a chance. I—uh—just wondered how it came out, that's all."

"Yes," said the Syrian. "It was a shame. She was quite a woman. Good-looking, too, though she was in her forties. They caught her in her bath last summer and held her head under. Personally I think Thiudahad's wife Gudelinda put the old jelly-fish up to it. He wouldn't have nerve enough by himself."

"Maybe she was jealous," said Padway. "Now, about the manufacture of that barbarian drink, as you call it—"

"What? *You* are a stubborn fellow. It's absolutely out of the question, though. You have to be careful, doing business here in Rome. It's not like a growing town. Now, if this were Constantinople—" he sighed. "You can really make money in the East. But I don't care to live there, with Justinian making life exciting for the heretics, as he calls them. What's your religion, by the way?"

"What's yours? Not that it makes any difference to me."

"Nestorian."

"Well," said Padway carefully, "I'm what we call a Congregationalist." (It was not really true, but he guessed an agnostic would hardly be popular in this theology-mad world.) "That's the nearest thing we have to Nestorianism in my country. But about the manufacture of brandy—"

"Nothing doing, young man. Absolutely not. How much equipment would you need to start?"

"Oh, a big copper kettle and a lot of copper tubing, and a stock of wine for the raw material. It wouldn't have to be good wine. And I could get started quicker with a couple of men to help me."

"I'm afraid it's too much of a gamble. I'm sorry."

"Look here, Thomasus, if I show you how you can halve the time it takes you to do your accounts, would you be interested?"

"You mean you're a mathematical genius or something?"

"No, but I have a system I can teach your clerks."

Thomasus closed his eyes like some Levantine Buddha. "Well—if you don't want more than fifty solidi—"

"All business is a gamble, you know."

"That's the trouble with it. But—I'll do it, *if* your accounting system is as good as you say it is."

"How about interest?" asked Padway.

"Three per cent."

Padway was startled. Then he asked. "Three per cent per what?"

"Per month, of course."

"Too much."

"Well, what do you expect?"

"In my country six per cent per year is considered fairly high."

"You mean you expect *me* to lend you money at that rate? *Ai!* Did You hear that, God? Young man, you ought to go live among the wild Saxons, to teach them something about piracy. But I like you, so I'll make it twenty-five per year."

"Still too much. I might consider seven and a half."

"You're being ridiculous. I wouldn't consider less than twenty for a minute."

"No. Nine per cent, perhaps."

"I'm not even interested. Too bad; it would have been nice to do business with you. Fifteen."

"That's out, Thomasus. Nine and a half."

"Did You hear that, God? He wants me to make him a present of my business! Go away, Martinus. You're wasting your time here. I couldn't possibly come down any more. Twelve and a half. That's absolutely the bottom."

"Ten."

"Don't you understand Latin? I said that was the bottom. Good day; I'm glad to have met you." When Padway got up, the banker sucked his breath through his teeth as though he had been wounded unto death, and rasped: "Eleven."

"Ten and a half."

"Would you mind showing your teeth? My word, they are human after all. I thought maybe they were shark's teeth. Oh, very well. This sentimental generosity of mine will be my ruin yet. And now let's see that accounting system of yours."

An hour later three chagrined clerks sat in a row and regarded Padway with expressions of, respectively, wonderment, apprehension, and active hatred. Padway had just finished doing a simple piece of long division with Arabic numerals at the time when the three clerks, using Roman numerals, had barely gotten started on the interminable trial-and-error process that their system required. Padway translated his answers back into Roman, wrote it out on his tablet, and handed the tablet to Thomasus.

"There you are," he said. "Have one of the boys check it by multiplying the divisor by the quotient. You might as well call them off their job; they'll be at it all night."

The middle-aged clerk, the one with the hostile expression, copied down the figures and began checking grimly. When after a long time he finished, he threw down his stylus. "That man's a sorcerer of some sort," he growled. "He does the operations in his head, and puts down all those silly marks just to fool us."

"Not at all," said Padway urbanely. "I can teach you to do the same."

"What? *Me* take lessons from a long-trousered barbarian? I—" he started to say more, but Thomasus cut him off by saying that he'd do as he was told, and no back talk. "Is that so?" sneered the man. "I'm a free Roman citizen, and I've been keeping books for twenty years. I guess I know my business. If you want a man to use that heathen system, go buy yourself some cringing Greek slave. I'm through!"

"Now see what you've done!" cried Thomasus when the clerk had taken his coat off the peg and marched out. "I shall have to hire another man, and with this labor shortage—"

"That's all right," soothed Padway. "These two boys will be able to do all the work of three easily, once they learn American arithmetic. And that isn't all; we have something called double-entry bookkeeping, which enables you to tell any time how you stand financially, and to catch errors—"

"Do You hear that, God? He wants to turn the whole banking business upside down! Please, dear sir, one thing at a time; or you'll drive us mad! I'll grant your loan, I'll help you buy your equipment. Only don't spring any more of your revolutionary methods just now!" He continued more calmly: "What's that bracelet I see you looking at from time to time?"

Padway extended his wrist. "It's a portable sundial, of sorts. We call it a watch."

"A *vatcha*, hm? It looks like magic. Are you sure you aren't a sorcerer after all?" He laughed nervously.

"No," said Padway. "It's a simple mechanical device, like a—a water clock."

"Ah. I see. But why a pointer to show sixtieths of an hour? Surely nobody in his right mind would want to know the time as closely as that?"

"We find it useful."

"Oh, well, other lands, other customs. How about giving my boys a lesson in your American arithmetic now? Just to assure us that it is as good as you claim."

"All right. Give me a tablet." Padway scratched the numerals 1 to 9 in the wax, and explained them. "Now," he said, "this is the important part." He drew a circle. "This is our character meaning *nothing*."

The younger clerk scratched his head. "You mean it's a symbol without meaning? What would be the use of that?"

"I didn't say it was without meaning. It means nil, zero—what you have left when you take two away from two."

The older clerk looked skeptical. "It doesn't make sense to me. What is the use of a symbol for what does not exist?"

"You have a *word* for it, haven't you? Several words, in fact. And you find them useful, don't you?"

"I suppose so," said the older clerk. "But we don't use *nothing* in our calculations. Whoever heard of figuring the interest on a loan at no per cent? Or renting a house for no weeks?"

"Maybe," grinned the younger clerk, "the honorable sir can tell us how to make a profit on no sales—"

Padway snapped: "And we'll get through this explanation sooner with no interruptions. You'll learn the reason for the zero symbol soon enough."

It took an hour to cover the elements of addition. Then Padway said the clerks had had enough for one day; they should practice addition for a while every day until they could do it faster than by Roman numerals. Actually he was worn out. He was naturally a quick speaker, and to have to plod syllable by syllable through this foul language almost drove him crazy.

"Very ingenious, Martinus," wheezed the banker. "And. now for the details of that loan. Of course you weren't serious in setting such an absurdly low figure as ten and a half percent—"

"What? You're damn right I was serious! And you agreed—"

"Now, Martinus. What I meant was that *after* my clerks had learned your system, if it was as good as you claimed, I'd consider lending you money at that rate. But meanwhile you can't expect me to give you my—"

Padway jumped up. "You—you wielder of a—oh, hell, what's Latin for *chisel?* If you won't—"

"Don't be hasty, my young friend. After all, you've given my boys their start; they can go alone from there if need be. So you might as well—"

"All right, you just let them try to go on from there. I'll find another banker and teach his clerks properly. Subtraction, multiplication, div—"

"*Ai!*" yelped Thomasus. "You can't go spreading this secret all over Rome! It wouldn't be fair to me!"

"Oh, can't I? Just watch. I could even make a pretty good living teaching it. If you think—"

"Now, now, let's not lose our tempers. Let's remember Christ's teachings about patience. I'll make a special concession because you're just starting out in business…"

Padway got his loan at ten and a half. He agreed grudgingly not to reveal his arithmetic elsewhere until the first loan was paid off.

Padway bought a copper kettle at what he would have called a junk shop. But nobody had ever heard of copper tubing. After he and Thomasus had exhausted the secondhand metal shops between the latter's house and the warehouse district at the south end of town, he started in on coppersmith's places. The coppersmiths had never heard of copper tubing, either. A couple of them offered to try to turn out some, but at astronomical prices.

"Martinus!" wailed the banker. "We've walked at least five miles, and my feet are giving out. Wouldn't lead pipe do just as well? You can get all you want of that."

"It would do fine except for one thing," said Padway, "we'd probably poison our customers. And that *might* give the business a bad name, you know."

"Well, I don't see that you're getting anywhere as it is."

Padway thought a minute while Thomasus and Ajax, the Negro slave, who was carrying the kettle, watched him. "If I could hire a man who was generally handy with tools, and had some metal-working experience, I could show him how to make copper tubing. How do you go about hiring people here?"

"You don't," said Thomasus. "It just happens. You could buy a slave— but you haven't enough money. I shouldn't care to put up the price of a good slave into your venture. And it takes a skilled foreman to get enough work out of a slave to make him a profitable investment."

Padway said, "How would it be to put a sign in front of your place, stating that a position is open?"

"What?" squawked the banker. "Do You hear that, God? First he seduces my money away from me on this wild plan. Now he wants to plaster my house with signs! Is there no limit—"

"Now, Thomasus, don't get excited. It won't be a big sign, and it'll be very artistic. I'll paint it myself. You want me to succeed, don't you?"

"It won't work, I tell you. Most workmen can't read. And I won't have you demean yourself by manual labor that way. It's ridiculous; I won't consider it. About how big a sign did you have in mind?"

Padway dragged himself to bed right after dinner. There was no way, as far as he knew, of getting back to his own time. Never again would he know the pleasures of the *American Journal of Archaeology*, of Mickey Mouse, of flush toilets, of speaking the simple, rich, sensitive English language...

Padway hired his man the third day after his first meeting with Thomasus the Syrian. The man was a dark, cocky little Sicilian named Hannibal Scipio.

Padway had meanwhile taken a short lease on a tumble-down house on the Quirinal, and collected such equipment and personal effects as he thought he would need. He bought a short-sleeved tunic to wear over his pants, with the idea of making himself less conspicuous. Adults seldom paid much attention to him in this motley town, but he was tired of having small boys follow him through the streets. He did, however, insist on having ample pockets sewn into the tunic, despite the tailor's shocked protests at ruining a good, stylish garment with this heathen innovation.

He whittled a mandrel out of wood and showed Hannibal Scipio how to bend the copper stripping around it. Hannibal claimed to know all that was necessary about soldering. But when Padway tried to bend the tubing into shape for his still, the seams popped open with the greatest of ease.

After that Hannibal was a little less cocky—for a while.

Padway approached the great day of his first distillation with some apprehension. According to Tancredi's ideas this was a new branch of the tree of time. But mightn't the professor have been wrong, so that, as soon as Padway did anything drastic enough to affect all subsequent history, he would make the birth of Martin Padway in 1908 impossible, and disappear?

"Shouldn't there be an incantation or something?" asked Thomasus the Syrian.

"No," said Padway. "As I've already said three times, this isn't magic." Looking around though, he could see how some mumbo-jumbo might have been appropriate: running his first large batch off at night in a creaky old house, illuminated by flickering oil lamps, in the presence of only Thomasus, Hannibal Scipio, and Ajax. All three looked apprehensive, and the Negro seemed all teeth and eyeballs. He stared at the still as if he expected it to start producing demons in carload lots any minute.

"It takes a long time, doesn't it?" said Thomasus, rubbing his pudgy hands together nervously. His good eye glittered at the nozzle from which drop after yellow drop slowly dripped.

"I think that's enough," said Padway. "We'll get mostly water if we continue the run." He directed Hannibal to remove the kettle and poured the contents of the receiving flask into a bottle. "I'd better try it first," he said. He poured out a little into a cup, sniffed, and took a swallow. It was definitely not good brandy. But it would do.

"Have some?" he said to the banker.

"Give some to Ajax first."

Ajax backed away, holding his hands in front of him, yellow palms out. "No, please, master—"

He seemed so alarmed that Thomasus did not insist. "Hannibal, how about you?"

"Oh, no," said Hannibal. "Meaning no disrespect, but I've got a delicate stomach. The least little thing upsets it. And if you're all through, I'd like to go home. I didn't sleep well last night." He yawned theatrically. Padway let him go, and took another swallow.

"Well," said Thomasus, "if you're sure it won't hurt me, I might take just a little." He took just a little, then coughed violently, spilling a few drops from the cup. "Good God, man, what are your insides made of? That's volcano juice!" As his coughing subsided, a saintlike expression appeared. "It does warm you up nicely inside, though, doesn't it?" He screwed up his face and his courage, and finished the cup in one gulp.

"Hey," said Padway. "Go easy. That isn't wine."

"Oh, don't worry about me. Nothing makes me drunk."

Padway got out another cup and sat down. "Maybe you can tell me one thing that I haven't got straight yet. In my country we reckon years from the birth of Christ. When I asked a man, the day I arrived, what year it was, he said 1288 after the founding of the city. Now, can you tell me how many years before Christ Rome was founded? I've forgotten."

Thomasus took another slug of brandy and thought. "Seven hundred and fifty-four—no, 753. That means that this is the year of our Lord 535. That's the system the church uses. The Goths say the second year of Thiudahad's reign, and the Byzantines the first year of the consulship of Flavius Belisarius. Or the somethingth year of Justinian *imperium*. I can see how it might confuse you." He drank some more. "This is a wonderful invention, isn't it?" He held his cup up and turned it this way and that. "Let's have some more. I think you'll make a success, Martinus."

"Thanks. I hope so."

"Wonderful invention. Course it'll be a success. Couldn't help being a success. A big success. Are You listening, God? Well, make sure my friend Martinus has a big success.

"I know a successful man when I see him, Martinus. Been picking them for years. That's how I'm such a success in the banking business. Success—success—let's drink to success. Beautiful success. Gorgeous success.

"I know what, Martinus. Let's go some place. Don't like drinking to success in this old ruin. You know, atmosphere. Some place where there's music. How much brandy have you got left? Good, bring the bottle along."

The joint was in the theater district on the north side of the Capitoline. The "music" was furnished by a young woman who twanged a harp and sang songs in Calabrian dialect, which the cash customers seemed to find very funny.

"Let's drink to—" Thomasus started to say "success" for the thirtieth time, but changed his mind. "Say, Martinus, we'd better buy some of this lousy wine, or he'll have us thrown out. How does this stuff mix with wine?" At Padway's expression, he said: "Don't worry, Martinus, old friend, this is on me. Haven't made a night of it in years. You know, family man." He winked and snapped his fingers for the waiter. When he had finally gotten through his little ceremony, he said: "Just a minute, Martinus, old friend, I see a man who owes me money. I'll be right back." He waddled unsteadily across the room.

A man at the next table asked Padway suddenly: "What's that stuff you and old one-eye have been drinking, friend?"

"Oh, just a foreign drink called brandy," said Padway uneasily.

"That's right, you're a foreigner, aren't you? I can tell by your accent." He screwed up his face, and then said: "I know; you're a Persian. I know a Persian accent."

"Not exactly," said Padway. "Farther away than that."

"That so? How do you like Rome?" The man had very large and very black eyebrows.

"Fine, so far," said Padway.

"Well, you haven't seen anything," said the man. "It hasn't been the same since the Goths came." He lowered his voice conspiratorially: "Mark my words, it won't be like this always, either!"

"You don't like the Goths?"

"No! Not with the persecution we have to put up with!"

"Persecution?" Padway raised his eyebrows.

"Religious persecution. We won't stand for it forever."

"I thought the Goths let everybody worship as they pleased."

"That's just it! We Orthodox are forced to stand around and watch Arians and Monophysites and Nestorians and Jews going about their business unmolested, as if they owned the country. If that isn't persecution, I'd like to know what is!"

"You mean that you're persecuted because the heretics and such are not?"

"Certainly, isn't that obvious? We won't stand—What's your religion, by the way?"

"Well," said Padway, "I'm what in my country is called a Congregationalist That's the nearest thing to Orthodoxy that we have."

"*Hm-m-m.* We'll make a good Catholic out of you, perhaps. So long as you're not one of these Maronites or Nestorians—"

"What's that about Nestorians?" said Thomasus, who had returned unobserved. "We who have the only logical view of the nature of the Son—that He was a man in whom the Father indwelt—"

"Nonsense!" snapped Eyebrows. "That's what you expect of half-baked amateur theologians. Our view—that of the dual nature of the Son—has been irrefutably shown—"

"Hear that, God? As if one person could have more than one nature—"

"You're all crazy!" rumbled a tall, sad-looking man with thin yellow hair, watery blue eyes, and a heavy accent. "We Arians abhor theological controversy, being sensible men. But if you want a sensible view of the nature of the Son—"

"You're a Goth?" barked Eyebrows tensely.

37

"No, I'm a Vandal, exiled from Africa. But as I was saying"—he began counting on his fingers—"either the Son was a man, or He was a god, or He was something in between. Well, now, we admit He wasn't a man. And there's only one God, so He wasn't a god. So He must have been—"

About that time things began to happen too fast for Padway to follow them all at once. Eyebrows jumped up and began yelling like one possessed. Padway couldn't follow him, except to note that the term "infamous heretics" occurred about once per sentence. Yellow Hair roared back at him, and other men began shouting from various parts of the room: "Eat him up, barbarian!" "This is an Orthodox country, and those who don't like it can go back where they—" "Damned nonsense about dual natures! We Monophysites—" "I'm a Jacobite, and I can lick any man in the place!" "Let's throw all the heretics out!" "I'm a Eunomian, and I can lick any *two* men in the place!"

Padway saw something coming and ducked, the mug missed his head by an inch and a half. When he looked up the room was a blur of action. Eyebrows was holding the self-styled Jacobite by the hair and punching his face; Yellow Hair was swinging four feet of bench around his head and howling a Vandal battle song. Padway hit one champion of Orthodoxy in the middle; his place was immediately taken by another who hit Padway in the middle. Then they were overborne by a rush of men.

As Padway struggled up through the pile of kicking, yelling humanity, like a swimmer striking for the surface, somebody got hold of his foot and tried to bite it off. As Padway was still wearing a pair of massive and practically indestructible English walking shoes, the biter got nowhere. So he shifted his attack to Padway's ankle. Padway yelped with pain, yanked his foot free, and kicked the biter in the face. The face yielded a little, and Padway wondered whether he'd broken a nose or a few teeth. He hoped he had.

The heretics seemed to be in a minority, that shrank as its members were beaten down and cast forth into darkness. Padway's eye caught the gleam of a knife blade and he thought it was well past his bedtime. Not being a religious man, he had no desire to be whittled up in the cause of the single, dual, or any other nature of Christ. He located Thomasus the Syrian under a table. When he tried to drag him out, the banker shrieked with terror and hugged the table leg as if it were a woman and he a sailor who had been six months at sea. Padway finally got him untangled.

The yellow-haired Vandal was still swinging his bench. Padway shouted at him. The man couldn't have understood in the uproar, but his attention was attracted, and when Padway pointed at the door he got the idea. In a few seconds he had cleared a path. The three stumbled out, pushed through the crowd that was beginning to gather outside, and ran. A yell behind them made them run faster, until they realized that it was Ajax, and slowed down to let him catch up.

They finally sat down on a park bench on the edge of the Field of Mars, only a few blocks from the Pantheon, where Padway had his first sight of post-Imperial Rome. Thomasus, when he got his breath, said: "Martinus, why did you let me drink so much of that heathen drink? Oh, my head! If I hadn't been drunk, I'd have had more sense than to start a theological argument."

"I tried to slow you down," said Padway mildly, "but you—"

"I know, I know. But you should have prevented me from drinking so much, forcibly if necessary. My head! What will my wife say? I never want to see that lousy barbarian drink again! What did you do with the bottle, by the way?"

"It got lost in the scuffle. But there wasn't much left in it anyway." Padway turned to the Vandal. "I guess I owe you some thanks for getting us out of there so quickly."

The man pulled his drooping mustache. "I was glad to do it, friend. Religious argument is no occupation for decent people. Permit me; my name is Fritharik Staifan's son." He spoke slowly, fumbling for words occasionally. "Once I was counted a man of noble family. Now I am merely a poor wanderer. Life holds nothing for me any more." Padway saw a tear glistening in the moonlight.

"You said you were a Vandal?"

Fritharik sighed like a vacuum cleaner. "Yes, mine was one of the finest estates in Carthage, before the Greeks came. When King Gelimer ran away, and our army scattered, I escaped to Spain, and thence I came hither last year."

"What are you doing now?"

"Alas, I am not doing anything now. I had a job as bodyguard to a Roman patrician until last week. Think of it—a noble Vandal serving as bodyguard! But my employer got set on the idea of converting me to Orthodoxy. That," said Fritharik with dignity, "I would not allow. So here I am. When my money is gone, I don't know what will become of me. Perhaps I will kill myself. Nobody would care." He sighed some more, then said: "You aren't looking for a good, reliable bodyguard, are you?"

"Not just now," said Padway, "but I may be in a few weeks. Do you think you can postpone your suicide until then?"

"I don't know. It depends on how my money holds out. I have no sense about money. Being of noble birth, I never needed any. I don't know whether you'll ever see me alive again." He wiped his eyes on his sleeve.

"Oh, for heaven's sake," said Thomasus, "there are plenty of things you could do."

"No," said Fritharik tragically. "You wouldn't understand, friend. There are considerations of honor. And anyway, what has life to offer me? Did you say you might be able to take me on later?" he asked Padway. Padway said yes, and gave him his address. "Very well, friend, I shall probably be in a nameless lonely grave before two weeks have passed. But if not, I'll be around."

CHAPTER III

A t the end of the week, Padway was gratified not only by the fact that he had not vanished into thin air, and by the appearance of the row of bottles on the shelf, but by the state of his finances. Counting the five solidi for the first month's rent on the house, the six more that had gone into his apparatus, and Hannibal's wages and his own living expenses, he still had over thirty of his fifty borrowed solidi left. The first two items wouldn't recur for a couple of weeks, anyway.

"How much are you going to charge for that stuff?" asked Thomasus.

Padway thought. "It's a luxury article, obviously. If we can get some of the better-class restaurants to stock it, I don't see why we shouldn't get two solidi per bottle. At least until somebody discovers our secret and begins competing with us."

Thomasus rubbed his hands together. "At that rate, you could practically pay back your loan with the proceeds of the first week's sales. But I'm in no hurry; it might be better to reinvest them in the business. We'll see how things turn out. I think I know the restaurant we should start with."

Padway experienced a twinge of dread at the idea of trying to sell the restaurateur the idea. He was not a born salesman, and he knew it.

He asked: "How should I go about getting him to buy some of the stuff? I'm not very familiar with your Roman business methods."

"That's all right. He won't refuse, because he owes me money, and he's behind in his interest payments. I'll introduce you."

It came about as the banker had said. The restaurant owner, a puffy man named Gaius Attalus, glowered a bit at first. The entrepreneur fed him a little brandy by way of a sample, and he warmed up. Thomasus had to ask God whether He was listening only twice before Attalus agreed to Padway's price for half a dozen bottles.

Padway, who had been suffering from one of his periodic fits of depression all morning, glowed visibly as they emerged from the restaurant, his pockets pleasantly heavy with gold.

"I think," said Thomasus, "you had better hire that Vandal chap, if you're going to have money around the house. And I'd spend some of it on a good strong box."

So when Hannibal Scipio told Padway "There's a tall, gloomy-looking bird outside who says you said to come see you," he had the Vandal sent in and hired him almost at once.

When Padway asked Fritharik what he proposed to do his bodyguarding with, Fritharik looked embarrassed, chewed his mustache, and finally said: "I had a fine sword, but I hocked it to keep alive. It was all that stood between me and a nameless grave. Perhaps I shall end in one yet," he sighed.

"Stop thinking about graves for a while," snapped Padway, "and tell me how much you need to get your sword back."

"Forty solidi."

"*Whew!* Is it made of solid gold, or what?"

"No. But it's good Damascus steel, and has gems in the handle. It was all that I saved from my beautiful estate in Africa. You have no idea what a fine place I had—"

"Now, now!" said Padway. "For heaven's sake don't start crying! Here's five solidi; go buy yourself the best sword you can with that. I'm taking it out of your salary. If you want to save up to get this bejeweled cheese knife of yours back, that's your business." So Fritharik departed, and shortly thereafter reappeared with a secondhand sword clanking at his side.

"It's the best I could do for the money," he explained. "The dealer claimed it was Damascus work, but you can tell that the Damascus marks on the blade are fakes. This local steel is soft, but I suppose it will have to do. When I had my beautiful estate in Africa, the finest steel was none too good." He sighed gustily.

Padway examined the sword, which was a typical sixth-century *spatha* with a broad single-edged thirty-inch blade. It was, in fact, much like a Scotch broadsword without the fancy knuckle-guard. He also noticed that Fritharik Staifan's son, though as mournful as ever, stood straighter and walked with a more determined stride when wearing the sword. He must, Padway thought, feel practically naked without it.

"Can you cook?" Padway asked Fritharik.

"You hired me as a bodyguard, not as a housemaid, my lord Martinus. I have my dignity."

"Oh, nonsense, old man. I've been doing my own cooking, but it takes too much of my time. If I don't mind, you shouldn't. Now, can you cook?"

Fritharik pulled his mustache. "Well—yes."

"What, for instance?"

"I can do a steak. I can fry bacon."

"What else?"

"Nothing else. That is all I ever had occasion to do. Good red meat is the food for a warrior. I can't stomach these greens the Italians eat."

Padway sighed. He resigned himself to living on an unbalanced diet until—well, why not? He could at least inquire into the costs of domestic help.

Thomasus found a serving-wench for him who would cook, clean house, and make beds for an absurdly low wage. The wench was named Julia. She came from Apulia and talked dialect. She was about twenty, dark, stocky, and gave promise of developing tremendous heft in later years. She wore a single shapeless garment and padded about the house on large bare feet. Now and then she cracked a joke too rapidly for Padway to follow and shook with peals of laughter. She worked hard, but Padway had to teach her his ideas from the ground up. The first time he fumigated his house he almost frightened her out of her wits. The smell of sulphur dioxide sent her racing out the door shrieking that Satanas had come.

Padway decided to knock off on his fifth Sunday in Rome. For almost a month he had been working all day and most of the night, helping Hannibal to run the still, clean it, and unload casks of wine; and seeing restaurateurs who had received inquiries from their customers about this remarkable new drink.

In an economy of scarcity, he reflected, you didn't have to turn handsprings finding customers, once your commodity caught on. He was meditating striking Thomasus for a loan to build another still. This time he'd build a set of rolls and roll his own copper sheeting out of round stock, instead of trying to patch together this irregular hand-hammered stuff.

Just now, though, he was heartily sick of the business. He wanted fun, which to him meant the Ulpian Library. As he looked in the mirror, he thought he hadn't changed much inside. He disliked barging in on strangers and bargaining as much as ever. But outside none of his former friends would have known him. He had grown a short reddish beard. This was partly because he had never in his other life shaved with a guardless razor, and it gave him the jitters to do so; and partly because he had always secretly coveted a beard, to balance his oversized nose.

He wore another new tunic, a Byzantine-style thing with ballooning sleeves. The trousers of his tweed suit gave an incongruous effect, but he didn't fancy the short pants of the country, with winter coming on. He also wore a cloak, which was nothing but a big square blanket with a hole in the middle to put his head through. He had hired an old woman to make him socks and underwear.

Altogether he was pretty well pleased with himself. He admitted he had been lucky in finding Thomasus; the Syrian had been an enormous help to him.

He approached the library with much the same visceral tingle that a lover gets from the imminence of a meeting with his beloved. Nor was he disappointed. He felt like shouting when a brief nosing about the shelves showed him Berosus' *Chaldean History*, the complete works of Livius, Tacitus' *History of the Conquest of Britain*, and Cassiodorus' recently published *Gothic History* complete. Here was stuff for which more than one twentieth-century historian or archaeologist would cheerfully commit murder.

For a few minutes he simply dithered, like the proverbial ass between two haystacks. Then he decided that Cassiodorus would have the most valuable information to impart, as it dealt with an environment in which he himself was living. So he lugged the big volumes out and set to work. It was hard work, too, even for a man who knew Latin. The books were written in a semi-cursive minuscule hand with all the words run together. The incredibly wordy and affected style of the writer didn't bother him as it would have if he had been reading English; he was after facts.

"Excuse me, sir," said the librarian, "but is that tall barbarian with the yellow mustache your man?"

"I suppose so," said Padway. "What is it?"

"He's gone to sleep in the Oriental section, and he's snoring so that the readers are complaining."

"I'll tend to him," said Padway.

He went over and awakened Fritharik. "Can't you read?" he asked.

"No," said Fritharik quite simply. "Why should I? When I had my beautiful estate in Africa, there was no occasion—"

"Yes, I know all about your beautiful estate, old man. But you'll have to learn to read, or else do your snoring outside."

Fritharik went out somewhat huffily, muttering in his own East-German dialect. Padway's guess was that he was calling reading a sissy accomplishment.

When Padway got back to his table, he found an elderly Italian dressed with simple elegance going through his Cassiodorus. The man looked up and said: "I'm sorry; were you reading these?"

"That's all right," said Padway. "I wasn't reading all of them. If you're not using the first volume..."

"Certainly, certainly, my dear young man. I ought to warn you, though, to be careful to put it back in its proper place. Scylla cheated of her prey by Jason has no fury like that of our esteemed librarian when people misplace his books. And what, may I ask, do you think of the work of our illustrious pretorian prefect?"

"That depends," said Padway judiciously. "He has a lot of facts you can't get elsewhere. But I prefer my facts straight."

"How do you mean?"

"I mean with less flowery rhetoric."

"Oh, but my dear, dear young man! Here we moderns have at last produced a historian to rank with the great Livius, and you say you don't like—" He glanced up, lowered his voice, and leaned forward. "Just consider the delicate imagery, the glorious erudition! Such style! Such wit!"

"That's just the trouble. You can't give me Polybius, or even Julius Caesar—"

"Julius Caesar! Why everybody knows *he* couldn't write! They use his *Gallic War* as an elementary Latin text for foreigners! All very well for the skin-clad barbarian, who through the gloomy fastnesses of the northern forests pursues the sanguinary boar and horrid bear. But for cultivated men like ourselves—I ask you, my dear young man! Oh"—he looked embarrassed—"you will understand that in my remarks on foreigners I meant nothing personal. I perceive that you are an outlander, despite your obvious breeding and erudition. Are you by any chance from the fabled land of Hind, with its pearl-decked maidens and its elephants?"

"No, farther away than that," said Padway. He knew he had flushed a literary Roman patrician, of the sort who couldn't ask you to pass the butter without wrapping the request in three puns, four mythological illusions, and a dissertation on the manufacture of butter in ancient Crete. "A place called America. I doubt whether I should ever return, though."

"Ah, how right you are! Why should one live anywhere but in Rome if one can? But perhaps you can tell me of the wonders of far-off China, with its gold-paved streets!"

"I can tell you a little about it," said Padway cautiously. "For one thing, the streets aren't gold-paved. In fact they're mostly not paved at all."

"How disappointing! But I daresay that a truthful traveler returning from heaven would pronounce its wonders grossly overrated. We must get together, my excellent young sir. I am Cornelius Anicius."

Evidently, Padway thought, he was expected to know who Cornelius Anicius was. He introduced himself. Ah, he thought, enter romance. A pretty slim dark girl approached, addressed Anicius as "Father," and said that she had not been able to find the Sabellian edition of Persius Flaccus.

"Somebody is using it, no doubt," said Anicius. "Martinus, this is my daughter Dorothea. A veritable pearl from King Khusrau's headdress of a daughter, though I as her father may be prejudiced." The girl smiled sweetly at Padway and excused herself.

Anicius asked: "And now, my dear young man, what is your occupation?"

Without thinking, Padway said he was in business.

"Indeed? What sort of business?"

Padway told him. The patrician froze up as he digested the information. He was still polite and smiling, but with a smile of a different sort.

"Well, well, that's interesting. Very interesting. I daresay you'll make a good financial success of your business." He spoke the sentence with a slight difficulty, like a Y.M.C.A. secretary talking about the facts of life. "I suppose we aren't to blame for the callings wherein God stations us. But it's too bad you haven't tried the public service. That is the only way to rise above one's class, and an intelligent young man like you deserves to do so. And now, if you'll excuse me, I'll do some reading."

Padway had been hoping for an invitation to Anicius' house. But now that Anicius knew him to be a mere vulgar manufacturer, no invitation would be forthcoming. Padway looked at his watch; it was nearly lunch time. He went out and awoke Fritharik.

The Vandal yawned. "Find all the books you wanted, Martinus? I was just dreaming of my beautiful estate—"

"To hell with—" barked Padway, then shut his mouth.

"What?" said Fritharik. "Can't I even dream about the time I was rich and respected? That's not very—"

"Nothing, nothing. I didn't mean you."

"I'm glad of that. My one consolation nowadays is my memories. But what are you so angry at, Martinus? You look as if you could bite nails in two." When there was no answer, he went on: "It must have been something in those books. I'm glad I never learned to read. You get all worked up over things that happened long ago. I'd rather dream about my beaut—oop! I'm sorry, boss; I won't mention it again."

Padway and Thomasus the Syrian sat, along with several hundred naked Romans, in the steam room of the Baths of Diocletian. The banker looked around and leered: "I hear that in the old days they let the women into these baths, too. Right mixed in with the men. Of course that was in pagan times; there's nothing like that now."

"Christian morality, no doubt," said Padway dryly.

"Yes" chuckled Thomasus. "We moderns are *such* a moral people. You know what the Empress Theodora used to complain about?"

"Yes," said Padway, and told Thomasus what the empress used to complain about.

"Damn it!" cried Thomasus. "Every time I have a dirty story, either you've heard it, or you know a better one."

Padway didn't see fit to tell the banker that he had read that bit of dirt in a book that hadn't yet been written, namely, the *Anecdotes* by Procopius of Caesarea.

Thomasus went on: "I've got a letter from my cousin Antiochus in Naples. He's in the shipping business. He has news from Constantinople." He paused impressively. "War."

"Between us and the Empire?"

"Between the Goths and the Empire, anyway. They've been carrying on mysterious dickerings ever since Amalaswentha was killed. Thiudahad has tried to duck responsibility for the murder, but I think our old poet-king has come to the end of his rope."

Padway said: "Watch Dalmatia and Sicily. Before the end of the year—" He stopped.

"Doing a bit of soothsaying?"

"No, just an opinion."

The good eye sparkled at Padway through the steam, very black and very intelligent. "Martinus, just who are you?"

"What do you mean?"

"Oh, there's something about you—I don't know how to put it—not just your funny way of putting things. You produce the most astonishing bits of knowledge, like a magician pulling rabbits out of his cap. And when I try to pump you about your own country or how you came hither, you change the subject."

"Well—" said Padway, wondering just how big a lie to risk. Then he thought of the perfect answer—a truthful one that Thomasus would be sure to misconstrue. "You see, I left my own country in a great hurry."

"Oh. For reasons of health, eh? I don't blame you for being cagy in that case." Thomasus winked.

When they were walking up Long Street toward Padway's house, Thomasus asked how the business was. Padway told him: "Pretty good.

The new still will be ready next week. And I sold some copper strip to a merchant leaving for Spain. Right now I'm waiting for the murder."

"The *murder?*"

"Yes, Fritharik and Hannibal Scipio didn't get along. Hannibal's been cockier than ever since he's had a couple of men under him. He rides Fritharik."

"*Rides* him?"

"American vernacular, literally translated. Meaning that he subjects him to constant and subtle ridicule and insult. By the way, I'm going to pay off your loan when we get home."

"Entirely?"

"That's right. The money's in the strong box waiting for you."

"Splendid, my dear Martinus! But won't you need another?"

"I'm not sure," said Padway, who was sure that he would. "I was thinking of expanding my distillery."

"That's a great idea. Of course now that you're established we'll put our loans on a business basis—"

"Meaning?" said Padway.

"Meaning that the rate of interest will have to be adjusted. The normal rate, you know, is much higher—"

"Ha, ha," said Padway. "That's what I thought you had in mind. But now that you know the business is a sure one, you can afford to give me a lower rate."

"*Ai*, Martinus, that's absurd! Is that any way to treat me after all I've done for you?"

"You don't have to lend it if you don't want to. There are other bankers who'd be glad to learn American arithmetic—"

"Listen to him, God! It's robbery! It's extortion! I'll never give in! Go to your other bankers, see if I care!"

Three blocks of argument brought the interest rate down to ten per cent, which Thomasus said was cutting his own heart out and burning it on the altar of friendship.

When Padway had spoken of an impending murder, he had neither been passing off hindsight as foresight, nor trying to be literally prophetic. He was more astonished than Thomasus, when they entered his big workshop, to find Fritharik and Hannibal glaring like a couple of dogs who dislike each other's smell. Hannibal's two assistants were looking on with their backs to the door; thus nobody saw the newcomers.

Hannibal snarled: "What do you mean, you big cotton-head? You lie around all day, too lazy to turn over, and then you dare criticize me—"

"All I said," growled the Vandal in his clumsy, deliberate Latin, "was that the next time I caught you, I'd report it. Well I did, and I'm going to."

"I'll slit your lousy throat if you do!" yelled Hannibal.

Fritharik cast a short but pungent aspersion on the Sicilian's sex life. Hannibal whipped out a dagger and lunged at Fritharik. He moved with rattlesnake speed, but he used the instinctive but tactically unsound overhand stab. Fritharik, who was unarmed, caught his wrist with a smack of flesh on flesh, then lost it as Hannibal dug his point into the Vandal's forearm.

When Hannibal swung his arm up for another stab, Padway arrived and caught his arm. He hauled the little man away from his opponent, and immediately had to hang on for dear life to keep from being stabbed himself. Hannibal was shrieking in Sicilian patois and foaming a little at the mouth. Padway saw that he wanted to kill him. He jerked his face back as the dirty fingernails of Hannibal's left hand raked his nose, which was a target hard to miss.

Then there was a thump, and Hannibal collapsed, dropping his dagger. Padway let him slide to the floor, and saw that Nerva, the older of the two assistants, was holding a stool by one leg. It had all happened so quickly that Fritharik was just bending over to pick up a short piece of board for a weapon, and Thomasus and Carbo, the other workman, were still standing just inside the door.

Padway said to Nerva: "I think you're the man for my next foreman. What's this about, Fritharik?"

Fritharik didn't answer, he stalked toward the unconscious Hannibal with plain and fancy murder in his face.

"That's enough, Fritharik!" said Padway sharply. "No more rough stuff, or you're fired, too!" He planted himself in front of the intended victim. "What was he doing?"

The Vandal came to himself. "He was stealing bits of copper from stock and selling them. I tried to get him to stop without telling you; you know how it is if your fellow employees think you're spying on them. Please, boss, let me have one whack at him. I may be a poor exile, but no little Greek catamite—"

Padway refused permission. Thomasus suggested swearing out a complaint and having Hannibal arrested; Padway said no, he didn't want to get mixed up with the law. He did allow Fritharik to send Hannibal, when the Sicilian came to, out the front door with a mighty kick in the fundament. Exit villain, sneering, thought Padway as he watched the ex-foreman slink off.

Fritharik said: "I think that was a mistake, Martinus. I could have sunk his body in the Tiber without anybody's knowing. He'll make trouble for us."

Padway suspected that the last statement was correct. But he merely said: "We'd better bind your arm up. Your whole sleeve is blood-soaked. Julia, get a strip of linen and boil it. Yes, *boil* it!"

CHAPTER IV

Padway had resolved not to let anything distract him from the task of assuring himself a livelihood. Until that was accomplished, he didn't intend to stick his neck out by springing gunpowder or the law of gravitation on the unsuspecting Romans.

But the banker's war talk reminded him that he was, after all, living in a political and cultural as well as an economic world. He had never, in his other life, paid more attention to current events than he had to. And in post-Imperial Rome, with no newspapers or electrical communication, it was even easier to forget about things outside one's immediate orbit.

He was living in the twilight of western classical civilization. The Age of Faith, better known as the Dark Ages, was closing down. Europe would be in darkness, from a scientific and technological aspect, for nearly a thousand years. That aspect was, to Padway's naturally prejudiced mind, the most, if not the only, important aspect of a civilization. Of course, the people among whom he was living had no conception of what was happening to them. The process was too slow to observe directly, even over the span of a life-time. They took their environment for granted, and even bragged about their modernity.

So what? Could one man change the course of history to the extent of preventing this interregnum? One man had changed the course of history before. Maybe. A Carlylean would say yes. A Tolstoyan or Marxist would say no; the environment fixes the pattern of a man's accomplishments and throws up the man to fit that pattern. Tancredi had expressed it differently by calling history a tough web, which would take a huge effort to distort.

How would one man go about it? Invention was the mainspring of technological development. But even in his own time, the lot of the professional inventor had been hard, without the handicap of a powerful and suspicious ecclesiasticism. And how much could he accomplish by simply "inventing," even if he escaped the unwelcome attentions of the pious? The arts of distilling and metal rolling were launched, no doubt, and so were Arabic numerals. But there was so much to be done, and only one lifetime to do it in.

What then? Business? He was already in it; the upper classes were contemptuous of it; and he was not naturally a businessman, though he could hold his own well enough in competition with these sixth-century yaps. Politics? In an age when victory went to the sharpest knife, and no moral rules of conduct were observable? *Br-r-r-r!*

How to prevent darkness from falling?

The Empire might have been together longer if it had had better means of communication. But the Empire, at least in the west, was hopelessly smashed, with Italy, Gaul, and Spain under the muscular thumbs of their barbarian "garrisons."

The answer was *Rapid communication and the multiple record*—that is, printing. Not even the most diligently destructive barbarian can extirpate the written word from a culture wherein the *minimum* edition of most books is fifteen hundred copies. There are just too many books.

So he would be a printer. The web might be tough, but maybe it had never been attacked by a Martin Padway.

"Good morning, my dear Martinus," said Thomasus. "How is the copper-rolling business?"

"So-so. The local smiths are pretty well stocked with strip, and not many of the shippers are interested in paying my prices for such a heavy commodity. But I think I'll clean up that last note in a few weeks."

"I'm glad to hear that. What will you do then?"

"That's what I came to see you about. Who's publishing books in Rome now?"

"Books? Books? Nobody, unless you count the copyists who replace worn-out copies for the libraries. There are a couple of bookstores down in the Agiletum, but their stock is all imported. The last man who tried to run a publishing business in Rome went broke years ago. Not enough demand, and not enough good authors. You're not thinking of going into it, I hope?"

"Yes, I am. I'll make money at it, too."

"What? You're crazy, Martinus. Don't consider it. I don't want to see you go broke after making such a fine start."

"I shan't go broke. But I'll need some capital to start."

"What? Another loan? But I've just told you that nobody can make money publishing in Rome. It's a proven fact. I won't lend you an as on such a harebrained scheme. How much do you think you'd need?"

"About five hundred solidi."

"*Ai, ai!* You've gone mad, my boy! What would you need such a lot for? All you have to do is buy or hire a couple of scribes—"

Padway grinned. "Oh, no. That's the point. It takes a scribe months to copy out a work like Cassiodorus' *Gothic History* by hand, and that's only one copy. No wonder a work like that costs fifty solidi per copy! I can build a machine that will turn out five hundred or a thousand copies in a few weeks, to retail for five or ten solidi. But it will take time and money to build the machine and teach an operator how to run it."

"But that's real money! God, are You listening? Well, please make my misguided young friend listen to reason! For the last time, Martinus, I won't consider it! How does the machine work?"

If Padway had known the travail that was in store for him, he might have been less confident about the possibilities of starting a printshop in a world that knew neither printing presses, type, printer's ink, nor paper. Writing ink was available, and so was papyrus. But it didn't take Padway long to decide that these would be impractical for his purposes.

His press, seemingly the most formidable job, proved the easiest. A carpenter down in the warehouse district promised to knock one together for him in a few weeks, though he manifested a not unnatural curiosity as to what Padway proposed to do with the contraption. Padway wouldn't tell him.

"It's not like any press I ever saw," said the man. "It doesn't look like a felt press. I know! You're the city's new executioner, and this is a newfangled torture instrument! Why didn't you want to tell me, boss? It's a perfectly respectable trade! But say, how about giving me a pass to the torture chamber the first time you use it? I want to be sure my work holds up, you know!"

For a bed they used a piece sawn off the top of a section of a broken marble column and mounted on wheels. All Padway's instincts revolted at this use of a monument of antiquity, but he consoled himself with the thought that one column mattered less than the art of printing.

For type, he contracted with a seal cutter to cut him a set of brass types. He had, at first, been appalled to discover that he would need ten to twelve thousand of the little things, since he could hardly build a type-casting machine, and would therefore have to print directly from the types. He had hoped to be able to print in Greek and Gothic as well as in Latin, but the Latin types alone set him back a round two hundred solidi. And the first sample set that the seal cutter ran off had the letters facing the wrong way and had to be melted up again. The type was what a twentieth-century printer would have called fourteen-point Gothic, and an engraver would have called sans-serif. With such big type he would not be able to get much copy on a page, but it would at least, he hoped, be legible.

Padway shrank from the idea of making his own paper. He had only a hazy idea of how it was done, except that it was a complicated process. Papyrus was too glossy and brittle, and the supply in Rome was meager and uncertain.

There remained vellum. Padway found that one of the tanneries across the Tiber turned out small quantities as a side line. It was made from the skins of sheep and goats by extensive scraping, washing, stretching, and paring. The price seemed reasonable. Padway rather staggered the owner of the tannery by ordering a thousand sheets at one crack.

He was fortunate in knowing that printer's ink was based on linseed oil and lampblack. It was no great trick to buy a bag of flaxseed and run it through a set of rolls like those he used for copper rolling, and to rig up a contraption consisting of an oil lamp, a water-filled bowl suspended and revolved over it, and a scraper for removing the lampblack. The only thing wrong with the resulting ink was that it wouldn't print. That is, it either made no impression or came off the type in shapeless gobs.

Padway was getting nervous about his finances; his five hundred solidi were getting low, and this seemed a cruel joke. His air of discouragement became so obvious that he caught his workers remarking on it behind their hands. But he grimly set out to experiment on his ink. Sure enough, he found that with a little soap in it, it would work fairly well.

In the middle of February Nevitta Gummund's son wandered in through the raw drizzle. When Fritharik showed him in, the Goth slapped Padway on the back so hard as to send him halfway across the room. "Well, well!" he bellowed. "Somebody gave me some of that terrific drink you've been selling, and I remembered your name. So I thought I'd look you up. Say, you got yourself well established in record time, for a stranger. Pretty smart young man, eh? Ha, ha!"

"Would you like to look around?" invited Padway. "Only I'll have to ask you to keep my methods confidential. There's no law here protecting ideas, so I have to keep my things secret until I'm ready to make them public property."

"Sure, you can trust me. I wouldn't understand how your devices work anyhow."

In the machine shop Nevitta was fascinated by a crude wire-drawing machine that Padway had rigged up. "Isn't that pretty?" he said, picking up the roll of brass wire. "I'd like to buy some for my wife. It would make nice bracelets and earrings."

Padway hadn't anticipated that use of his products, but said he would have some ready in a week.

"Where do you get your power?" asked Nevitta.

Padway showed him the work-horse in the back yard walking around a shaft in the rain.

"Shouldn't think a horse would be efficient," said the Goth. "You could get a lot more power out of a couple of husky slaves. That is, if your driver knew his whip. Ha, ha!"

"Oh, no," said Padway. "Not this horse. Notice anything peculiar about his harness?"

"Well, yes, it *is* peculiar. But I don't know what's wrong with it."

"It's that collar over his neck. You people make your horses pull against a strap around the throat. Every time he pulls, the strap cuts into his windpipe and shuts off the poor animal's breath. That collar puts the load on his shoulders. If you were going to pull a load, you wouldn't hitch a rope around your neck to pull it with, would you?"

"Well," said Nevitta dubiously, "maybe you're right. I've been using my kind of harness for a long time, and I don't know that I'd care to change."

Padway shrugged. "Any time you want one of these outfits, you can get it from Metellus the Saddler on the Appian Way. He made this to my specifications. I'm not making them myself; I have too much else to do."

Here Padway leaned against the doorframe and closed his eyes.

"Aren't you feeling well?" asked Nevitta in alarm.

"No. My head weighs as much as the dome of the Pantheon. I think I'm going to bed."

"Oh, my word, I'll help you. Where's that man of mine? *Hermann!*" When Hermann appeared, Nevitta rattled a sentence of Gothic at him wherein Padway caught the name of Leo Vekkos.

Padway protested: "I don't want a physician—"

"Nonsense, my boy, it's no trouble. You were right about keeping the dogs outside. It cured my wheezes. So I'm glad to help you."

Padway feared the ministrations of a sixth-century physician more than he feared the grippe with which he was coming down. He did not know how to refuse gracefully. Nevitta and Fritharik got him to bed with rough efficiency.

Fritharik said: "It looks to me like a clear case of elf-shot."

"What?" croaked Padway.

"Elf-shot. The elves have shot you. I know, because I had it once in Africa. A Vandal physician cured me by drawing out the invisible darts of the elves. When they become visible they are little arrowheads made of chipped flint."

"Look," said Padway, "I know what's wrong with me. If everybody will let me alone, I'll get well in a week or ten days."

"We couldn't think of that!" cried Nevitta and Fritharik together. While they were arguing, Hermann arrived with a sallow, black-bearded, sensitive-looking man.

Leo Vekkos opened his bag. Padway got a glimpse into the bag, and shuddered. It contained a couple of books, an assortment of weeds, and several small bottles holding organs of what had probably been small mammals.

"Now then, excellent Martinus," said Vekkos, "let me see your tongue. Say ah." The physician felt Padway's forehead, poked his chest and stomach, and asked him intelligent-sounding questions about his condition.

"This is a common condition in winter," said Vekkos in a didactic tone. "It is something of a mystery. Some hold it to be an excess of blood in the head, which causes that stuffy feeling whereof you complain. Others assert that it is an excess of black bile. I hold the view that it is caused by the conflict of the natural spirits of the liver with the animal spirits of the nervous system. The defeat of the animal spirits naturally reacts on the respiratory system—"

"It's nothing but a bad cold—" said Padway.

Vekkos ignored him. "—since the lungs and throat are under their control. The best cure for you is to rouse the vital spirits of the heart to put the natural spirits in their place." He began fishing weeds out of the bag.

"How about elf-shot?" asked Fritharik.

"What?"

Fritharik explained the medical doctrine of his people.

Vekkos smiled. "My good man, there is nothing in Galen about elf-shot. Nor in Celsus. Nor in Asclepiades. So I cannot take you seriously—"

"Then you don't know much about doctoring," growled Fritharik.

"Really," snapped Vekkos. "Who is the physician?"

"Stop squabbling, or you'll make me worse," grumbled Padway. "What are you going to do to me?"

Vekkos held up a bunch of weeds. "Have these herbs stewed and drink a cupful every three hours. They include a mild purgative, to draw off the black bile through the bowels in case there should be an excess."

"Which is the purgative?" asked Padway.

Vekkos pulled it out. Padway's thin arm shot out and grabbed the weed. "I just want to keep this separate from the rest, if you don't mind."

Vekkos humored him, told him to keep warm and stay in bed, and departed. Nevitta and Hermann went with him.

"Calls himself a physician," grumbled Fritharik, "and never heard of elf-shot."

"Get Julia," said Padway.

When the girl came, she set up a great to-do: "Oh, generous master, whatever is wrong with you? I'll get Father Narcissus—"

"No, you won't," said Padway. He broke off a small part of the purgative weed and handed it to her. "Boil this in a kettle of water, and bring me a cup of the water." He handed her the rest of the bunch of greenery. "And throw these out. Somewhere where the medicine man won't see them."

A slight laxative should be just the thing, he thought. If they would only leave him alone...

Next morning his head was less thick, but he felt very tired. He slept until eleven, when he was wakened by Julia. With Julia was a dignified man wearing an ordinary civilian cloak over a long white tunic with tight sleeves. Padway guessed that he was Father Narcissus by his tonsure.

"My son," said the priest. "I am sorry to see that the Devil had set his henchmen on you. This virtuous young woman besought my spiritual aid..."

Padway resisted a desire to tell Father Narcissus where to go. His one constant principle was to avoid trouble with the Church.

"I have not seen you at the Church of the Angel Gabriel," continued Father Narcissus. "You are one of us, though, I hope?"

"American rite," mumbled Padway.

The priest was puzzled by this. But he went on. "I know that you have consulted the physician Vekkos. How much better it is to put your trust in God, compared to whose power these bleeders and stewers of herbs are impotent! We shall start with a few prayers...."

Padway lived through it. Then Julia appeared stirring something.

"Don't be alarmed," said the priest. "This is one cure that never fails. Dust from the tomb of St. Nereus, mixed with water."

There was nothing obviously lethal about the combination, so Padway drank it. Father Narcissus asked conversationally: "You are not, then, from Padua?"

Fritharik put his head in. "That so-called physician is here again."

"Tell him just a moment," said Padway. God, he was tired. "Thanks a lot,

Father. It's nice to have seen you."

The priest went out, shaking his head over the blindness of mortals who trusted in *materia medica*.

Vekkos came in with an accusing look. Padway said: "Don't blame me. The girl brought him."

Vekkos sighed. "We physicians spend our lives in hard scientific study, and then we have to compete with these allied miracle-workers. Well, how's my patient today?"

While he was still examining Padway, Thomasus the Syrian appeared. The banker waited around nervously until the Greek left. Then Thomasus said: "I came as soon as I heard you were sick, Martinus. Prayers and medicines are all very well, but we don't want to miss any bets. My colleague, Ebenezer the Jew, knows a man, one of his own sect named Jeconias of Naples, who is pretty good at curative magic. A lot of these magicians are frauds; I don't believe in them for a minute. But this man has done some remarkable—"

"I don't want him," groaned Padway. "I'll be all right if everybody will stop trying to cure me..."

"I brought him along, Martinus. Now do be reasonable. He won't hurt you. And I couldn't afford to have you die with those notes outstanding—of course that's not the only consideration; I'm fond of you personally..."

Padway felt like one in the grip of a nightmare. The more he protested, the more quacks they sicked on him.

Jeconias of Naples was a little fat man with a bouncing manner, more like a high-pressure salesman than the conventional picture of a magician.

He chanted: "Now, just leave everything to me, excellent Martinus. Here's a little cantrip that'll scare off the weaker spirits." He pulled out a piece of papyrus and read off something in an unknown language. "There, that didn't hurt, did it? Just leave it all to old Jeconias. He knows what he's doing. Now we'll put this charm under the bed, so-o-o! There, don't you feel better already? Now we'll cast your horoscope. If you'll give me the date and hour of your birth..."

How the hell, thought Padway, could he explain to this damned little quack that he was going to be born 1,373 years hence? He threw his reserve to the winds. He heaved himself up in bed and shouted feebly: "Presumptions slave, know you not that I am one of the hereditary custodians of the Seal of Solomon? That I can shuffle your silly planets around the sky with a word, and put out the sun with a sentence? And you talk of casting *my* horoscope?"

The magician's eyes were popping. "I—I'm sorry, sir, I didn't know..."

"Shemkhamphoras!" yelled Padway. "Ashtaroth! Baâl-Marduk! St. Frigidaire! Tippecanoe and Tyler too! Begone, worm! One word from you of my true identity, and I'll strike you down with the foulest form of leprosy! Your eyeballs will rot, your fingers will drop off joint by joint—" But Jeconias was already out the door. Padway could hear him negotiate the first half of the stairway three steps at a time, roll head over heels the rest of the way, and race out of the front door.

Padway chuckled. He told Fritharik, who had been attracted by the noise: "You park yourself at the door with your sword, and say that Vekkos has given orders to let nobody see me. And I mean *nobody*. Even if the Holy Ghost shows up, keep him out."

Fritharik did as ordered. Then he craned his neck around the doorframe. "Excellent boss! I found a Goth who knows the theory of elf-shot. Shall I have him come up and—"

Padway pulled the covers over his head.

It was now April, 536. Sicily had fallen to General Belisarius in December. Padway had heard this weeks after it happened. Except for business errands, he had hardly been outside his house in four months in his desperate anxiety to get his press going. And except for his workers and his business contacts he knew practically nobody in Rome, though he had a speaking acquaintance with the librarians and two of Thomasus' banker friends, Ebenezer the Jew and Vardan the Armenian.

The day the press was finally ready he called his workers together and said: "I suppose you know that this is likely to be an important day for us. Fritharik will give each of you a small bottle of brandy to take home when you leave. And the first man who drops a hammer or anything on those little brass letters gets fired. I hope none of you do, because you've done a good job and I'm proud of you. That's all."

"Well, well," said Thomasus, "that's splendid. I always knew you'd get your machine to run. Said so right from the start. What are you going to print? The *Gothic History?* That would flatter the pretorian prefect, no doubt."

"No. That would take months to run off, especially as my men are new at the job. I'm starting off with a little alphabet book. You know, A is for *asinus* (ass), B is for *braccae* (breeches), and so on."

"That sounds like a good idea. But, Martinus, can't you let your men handle it, and take a rest? You look as if you haven't had a good night's sleep in months."

"I haven't, to tell the truth. But I can't leave; every time something goes wrong I have to be there to fix it. And I've got to find outlets for this first book. Schoolmasters and such people. I have to do everything myself, sooner or later. Also, I have an idea for another kind of publication."

"What? Don't tell me you're going to start another wild scheme—"

"Now, now, don't get excited, Thomasus. This is a weekly booklet of news."

"Listen, Martinus, don't overreach yourself. You'll get the scribes' guild down on you. As it is, I wish you'd tell me more about yourself. You're the town's great mystery, you know. Everybody asks about you."

"You just tell them I'm the most uninteresting bore you ever met in your life."

There were only a little over a hundred free-lance scribes in Rome. Padway disarmed any hostility they might have had for him by the curious expedient of enlisting them as reporters. He made a standing offer of a couple of sesterces per story for acceptable accounts of news items.

When he came to assemble the copy for his first issue, he found that some drastic censorship was necessary. For instance, one story read:

Our depraved and licentious city governor, Count Honorius, was seen early Wednesday morning being pursued down Broad Way by a young woman with a butcher's cleaver. Because this cowardly wretch was not encumbered by a decent minimum of clothing, he outdistanced his pursuer. This is the fourth time in a month that the wicked and corrupt count has created a scandal by his conduct with women. It is rumored that King Thiudahad will be petitioned to remove him by a committee of the outraged fathers of daughters whom he has dishonored. It is to be hoped that the next time the diabolical count is chased with a cleaver, his pursuer will catch him.

Somebody, thought Padway, doesn't *like* our illustrious count. He didn't know Honorius, but whether the story was true or not, there was no free-press clause in the Italian constitutions between Padway and the city's torture chambers.

So the first eight-page issue said nothing about young women with cleavers. It had a lot of relatively innocuous news items, one short poem contributed by a scribe who fancied himself a second Ovid, an editorial by Padway in which he said briefly that he hoped the Romans would find his paper useful, and a short article—also by Padway—on the nature and habits of the elephant.

Padway turned the crackling sheepskin pages of the proof copy, was proud of himself and his men, a pride not much diminished by the immediate discovery of a number of glaring typographical errors. One of these, in a story about a Roman mortally wounded by robbers on High Path a few nights back, had the unfortunate effect of turning a harmless word into an obscene one. Oh, well, with only two hundred and fifty copies he could have somebody go through them and correct the error with pen and ink.

Still, he could not help being a little awed by the importance of Martin Padway in this world. But for pure good luck, it might have been he who had been fatally stabbed on High Path—and behold, no printing press, none of the inventions he might yet introduce, until the slow natural process of technical development prepared the way for them. Not that he deserved too much credit—Gutenberg ought to have some for the press, for instance.

Padway called his paper *Tempora Romae* and offered it at ten sesterces, about the equivalent of fifty cents. He was surprised when not only did the first issue sell out, but Fritharik was busy for three days turning away from his door people who wanted copies that were not to be had.

A few scribes dropped in every day with more news items. One of them, a plump cheerful-looking fellow about Padway's age, handed in a story beginning:

The blood of an innocent man has been sacrificed to the lusts of our vile monster of a city governor, Count Honorius.

Reliable sources have revealed that Q. Aurelius Galba, crucified on a charge of murder last week, was the husband of a wife who had long been adulterously coveted by our villainous count. At Galba's trial there was much comment among the spectators on the flimsiness of the evidence...

∞∞∞∞

"Hey!" said Padway. "Aren't you the man who handed in that other story about Honorius and a cleaver?"

"That's right," said the scribe. "I wondered why you didn't publish it."

"How long do you think I'd be allowed to run my paper without interference if I did?"

"Oh, I never thought of that."

"Well, remember next time. I can't use this story either. But don't let it discourage you. It's well done; a lead sentence and everything. How do you get all this information?"

The man grinned. "I hear things. And what I don't hear, my wife does. She has women friends who get together for games of backgammon, and they talk."

"It's too bad I don't dare run a gossip column," said Padway. "But you would seem to have the makings of a newspaper man. What's your name?"

"George Menandrus."

"That's Greek, isn't it?"

"My parents were Greek; I am Roman."

"All right, George, keep in touch with me. Some day I may want to hire an assistant to help run the thing."

Padway confidently visited the tanner to place another order for vellum.

"When will you want it?" said the tanner. Padway told him in four days.

"That's impossible. I might have fifty sheets for you in that time. They'll cost you five times as much apiece as the first ones."

Padway gasped. "In God's name, why?"

"You practically cleaned out Rome's supply with that first order," said the tanner. "All of our stock, and all the rest that was floating around, which I went out and bought up for you. There aren't enough skins left in the whole city to make a hundred sheets. And making vellum takes time, you know. If you buy up the last fifty sheets, it will be weeks before you can prepare another large batch."

Padway asked: "If you expanded your plant, do you suppose you could eventually get up to a capacity of two thousand a week?"

The tanner shook his head. "I should not want to spend the money to expand in such a risky business. And, if I did, there wouldn't be enough animals in Central Italy to supply such a demand."

Padway recognized when he was licked. Vellum was essentially a by-product of the sheep-and-goat industry. Therefore a sudden increase in demand would skyrocket the price without much increasing the output. Though the Romans knew next to nothing of economics, the law of supply and demand worked here just the same.

It would have to be paper after all. And his second edition was going to be very, very late.

For paper, he got hold of a felter and told him that he wanted him to chop up a few pounds of white cloth and make them into the thinnest felt that anybody had ever heard of. The felter dutifully produced a sheet of what looked like exceptionally thick and fuzzy blotting paper. Padway patiently insisted on finer breaking up of the cloth, on a brief boiling before felting, and on pressing after. As he went out of the shop he saw the felter tap his forehead significantly. But after many trials the man presented him with a paper not much worse for writing than a twentieth-century paper towel.

Then came the heartbreaking part. A drop of ink applied to this paper spread out with the alacrity of a picnic party that has discovered a rattlesnake in their midst. So Padway told the felter to make up ten more sheets, and into the mush from which each was made to introduce one common substance—soap, olive oil, and so forth. At this point the felter threatened to quit, and had to be appeased by a raise in price. Padway was vastly relieved to discover that a little clay mixed with the pulp made all the difference between a fair writing paper and an impossible one.

By the time Padway's second issue had been sold out, he had ceased to worry about the possibility of running out of paper. But another thought moved into the vacated worrying compartment in his mind: What should he do when the Gothic War really got going? In his own history it had raged for twenty years up and down Italy. Nearly every important town had been besieged or captured at least once. Rome itself would be practically depopulated by sieges, famine, and pestilence. If he lived long enough he might see the Lombard invasion and the near-extinction of Italian civilization. All this would interfere dreadfully with his plans.

He tried to shake off the mood. Probably the weather was responsible; it had rained steadily for two days. Everything in the house was dank. The only way to cure that would be to build a fire, and the air was too warm for that already. So Padway sat and looked out at the leaden landscape.

He was surprised when Fritharik brought in Thomasus' colleague, Ebenezer the Jew. Ebenezer was a frail-looking, kindly oldster with a long white beard. Padway found him distressingly pious; when he ate with the other bankers he did not eat at all, to put it Irishly, for fear of transgressing one of the innumerable rules of his sect.

Ebenezer took his cloak off over his head and asked: "Where can I put this where it won't drip, excellent Martinus? Ah. Thank you. I was this way on business, and I thought I'd look your place over, if I may. It must be interesting, from Thomasus' accounts." He wrung the water from his beard.

Padway was glad of something to take his mind off the ominous future. He showed the old man around.

Ebenezer looked at him from under bushy white eyebrows. "Ah. Now I can believe that you are from a far country. From another world, almost. Take that system of arithmetic of yours; it has changed our whole concept of banking—"

"What?" cried Padway. "What do you know about it?"

"Why," said Ebenezer, "Thomasus sold the secret to Vardan and me. I thought you knew that."

"He *did?* How much?"

"A hundred and fifty solidi apiece. Didn't you—"

Padway growled a resounding Latin oath, grabbed his hat and cloak, and started for the door.

"Where are you going, Martinus?" said Ebenezer in alarm.

"I'm going to tell that cutthroat what I think of him!" snapped Padway. "And then I'm going to—"

"Did Thomasus promise you not to reveal the secret? I cannot believe that he violated—"

Padway stopped with his hand on the door handle. Now that he thought, the Syrian had never agreed not to tell anybody about Arabic numerals. Padway had taken it for granted that he would not want to do so. But if Thomasus got pressed for ready cash, there was no legal impediment to his selling or giving the knowledge to whom he pleased.

As Padway got his anger under control, he saw that he had not really lost anything, since his original intention had been to spread Arabic numerals far and wide. What really peeved him was that Thomasus should chisel such a handsome sum out of the science without even offering Padway a cut. It was like Thomasus. He was all right, but as Nevitta had said you had to watch him.

When Padway did appear at Thomasus' house, later that day, he had Fritharik with him. Fritharik was carrying a strong box. The box was nicely heavy with gold.

"Martinus," cried Thomasus, a little appalled, "do you really want to pay off all your loans? Where did you get all this money?"

"You heard me," grinned Padway. "Here's an accounting of principal and interest. I'm tired of paying ten per cent when I can get the same for seven and a half."

"What? Where can you get any such absurd rate?"

"From your esteemed colleague, Ebenezer. Here's a copy of the new note."

"Well, I must say I wouldn't have expected that of Ebenezer. If all this is true, I suppose I could meet his rate."

"You'll have to better it, after what you made from selling my arithmetic."

"Now, Martinus, what I did was strictly legal—"

"Didn't say it wasn't."

"Oh, very well. I suppose God planned it this way. I'll give you seven and four tenths."

Padway laughed scornfully.

"Seven, then. But that's the lowest, absolutely, positively, finally."

When Padway had received his old notes, a receipt for the old loans, and a copy of the new note, Thomasus asked him, "How did you get Ebenezer to offer you such an unheard-of figure?"

Padway smiled. "I told him that he could have had the secret of the new arithmetic from me for the asking."

ooooo

Padway's next effort was a clock. He was going to begin with the simplest design possible: a weight on the end of a rope, a ratchet, a train of gears, the hand and dial from a battered old clepsydra or water clock he picked up secondhand, a pendulum, and an escapement. One by one he assembled these parts—all but the last.

He had not supposed there was anything so difficult about making an escapement. He could take the back cover off his wrist-watch and see the escapement-wheel there, jerking its merry way around. He did not want to take his watch apart for fear of never getting it together again. Besides, the parts thereof were too small to reproduce accurately.

But he could *see* the damned thing; why couldn't he make a large one? The workmen turned out several wheels, and the little tongs to go with them. Padway filed and scraped and bent. But they would not work. The tongs caught the teeth of the wheels and stuck fast. Or they did not catch at all, so that the shaft on which the rope was wound unwound itself all at once. Padway at last got one of the contraptions adjusted so that if you swung the pendulum with your hand, the tongs would let the escapement-wheel revolve one tooth at a time. Fine. But the clock would not run under its own power. Take your hand off the pendulum, and it made a couple of half-hearted swings and stopped.

Padway said to hell with it. He'd come back to it some day when he had more time and better tools and instruments. He stowed the mess of cog-wheels in a corner of his cellar. Perhaps, he thought, this failure had been a good thing, to keep him from getting an exaggerated idea of his own cleverness.

Nevitta popped in again. "All over your sickness, Martinus? Fine; I knew you had a sound constitution. How about coming out to the Flaminian racetrack with me now and losing a few solidi? Then come on up to the farm overnight."

"I'd like to a lot. But I have to put the *Times* to bed this afternoon."

"Put to bed?" queried Nevitta.

Padway explained.

65

Nevitta said: "I see. Ha, ha, I thought you had a girl friend named Tempora. Tomorrow for supper, then."

"How shall I get there?"

"You haven't a saddle horse? I'll send Hermann down with one tomorrow afternoon. But mind, I don't want to get him back with wings growing out of his shoulders!"

"It might attract attention," said Padway solemnly. "And you'd have a hell of a time catching him if he didn't want to be bridled."

So the next afternoon Padway, in a new pair of rawhide Byzantine jack boots, set out with Hermann up the Flaminian Way. The Roman Campagna, he noted, was still fairly prosperous farming country. He wondered how long it would take for it to become the desolate, malarial plain of the Middle Ages.

"How were the races?" he asked.

Hermann, it seemed, knew very little Latin, though that little was still better than Padway's Gothic. "Oh, my boss…he terrible angry. He talk… you know…hot sport. But hate lose money. Lose fifty sesterces on horse. Make noise like…you know…lion with gutache."

At the farmhouse Padway met Nevitta's wife, a pleasant, plump woman who spoke no Latin, and his eldest son, Dagalaif, a Gothic *scaio*, or marshal, home on vacation. Supper fully bore out the stories that Padway had heard about Gothic appetites. He was agreeably surprised to drink some fairly good beer, after the bilgewater that went by that name in Rome.

"I've got some wine, if you prefer it," said Nevitta.

"Thanks, but I'm getting a little tired of Italian wine. The Roman writers talk a lot about their different kinds, but it all tastes alike to me."

"That's the way I feel. If you really *want* some, I have some perfumed Greek wine."

Padway shuddered.

Nevitta grinned. "That's the way I feel. Any man who'd put perfume in his liquor probably swishes when he walks. I only keep the stuff for my Greek friends, like Leo Vekkos. Reminds me, I must tell him about your cure for my wheezes by having me put the dogs out. He'll figure out some fancy theory full of long words to explain it."

Dagalaif spoke up: "Say, Martinus, maybe you have inside information on how the war will go."

Padway shrugged. "All I know is what everybody else knows. I haven't a private wire—I mean a private channel of information to heaven. If you want a guess, I'd say that Belisarius would invade Bruttium this summer and besiege Naples about August. He won't have a large force, but he'll be infernally hard to beat."

Dagalaif said: "Huh! We'll let him up all right. A handful of Greeks won't get very far against the united Gothic nation."

"That's what the Vandals thought," answered Padway dryly.

"*Aiw*," said Dagalaif. "But we won't make the mistakes the Vandals made."

"I don't know, son," said Nevitta. "It seems to me we are making them already—or others just as bad. This king of ours—all he's good for is hornswoggling his neighbors out of land and writing Latin poetry. And digging around in libraries. It would be better if we had an illiterate one, like Theoderik. Of course," he added apologetically, "I admit I can read and write. My old man came from Pannonia with Theoderik, and he was always talking about the sacred duty of the Goths to preserve Roman civilization from savages like the Franks. He was determined that I would have a Latin education if it killed me. I admit I've found my education useful. But in the next few months it'll be more important for our leader to know how to lead a charge than to say *amo-amas-amat*."

CHAPTER V

Padway returned to Rome in the best of humor. Nevitta was the first person, besides Thomasus the Syrian, who had asked him to his house. And Padway, despite his somewhat cool exterior, was a sociable fellow at heart. He was, in fact, so elated that he dismounted and handed the reins of the borrowed horse to Hermann without noticing the three tough-looking parties leaning against the new fence in front of the old house on Long Street.

When he headed for the gate, the largest of the three, a black-bearded man, stepped in front of him. The man was holding a sheet of paper—real paper, no doubt from the felter to whom Padway had taught the art—in front of him and reading out loud to himself:—"medium height, brown hair and eyes, large nose, short beard. Speaks with an accent." He looked up sharply. "Are you Martinus Paduei?"

"*Sic. Quis est?*"

"You're under arrest. Will you come along quietly?"

"*What?* Who—What for—"

"Order of the municipal prefect. Sorcery."

"But…but—*Hey!* You can't—"

"I said *quietly.*"

The other two men had moved up on each side of Padway, and each took an arm and started to walk him along the street. When he resisted, a short bludgeon appeared in the hand of one. Padway looked around frantically. Hermann was already out of sight. Fritharik was not to be seen; no doubt he was snoring as usual. Padway filled his lungs to shout; the man on his right tightened his grip and raised the bludgeon threateningly. Padway didn't shout.

They marched him down the Argiletum to the old jail below the

Record Office on the Capitoline. He was still in somewhat of a daze as the clerk demanded his name, age, and address. All he could think of was that he had heard somewhere that you were entitled to telephone your lawyer before being locked up. And that information seemed hardly useful in the present circumstances.

A small, snapping Italian who had been lounging on a bench got up. "What's this, a sorcery case involving a foreigner? Sounds like a national case to me,"

"Oh, no, it isn't," said the clerk. "You national officers have authority in Rome only in mixed Roman-Gothic cases. This man isn't a Goth; says he's an American, whatever that is."

"Yes, it is! Read your regulations. The pretorian prefect's office has jurisdiction in all capital cases involving foreigners. If you have a sorcery complaint, you turn it and the prisoner over to us. Come on, now." The little man moved possessively toward Padway. Padway did not like the use of the term "capital cases."

The clerk said: "Don't be a fool. Think you're going to drag him clear up to Ravenna for interrogation? We've got a perfectly good torture chamber here."

"I'm only doing my duty," snapped the state policeman. He grabbed Padway's arm and started to haul him toward the door. "Come along now, sorcerer. We'll show you some real, up-to-date torture at Ravenna. These Roman cops don't know anything."

"*Christus!* Are you crazy?" yelled the clerk. He jumped up and grabbed Padway's other arm; so did the black-bearded man who had arrested him. The state policemen pulled and so did the other two.

"Hey!" yelled Padway. But the assorted functionaries were too engrossed in their tug-of-war to notice.

The state policeman shouted in a painfully penetrating voice: "Justinius, run and tell the adjutant prefect that these municipal scum are trying to withhold a prisoner from us!" A man ran out the door.

Another door opened, and a fat, sleepy-looking man came in. "What's this?" he squeaked.

The clerk and the municipal policeman straightened up to attention, releasing Padway. The state policeman immediately resumed hauling him toward the door; the local cops abandoned their etiquette and grabbed him again. They all shouted at once at the fat man. Padway gathered that he was the municipal *commentariensius*, or police chief.

At that two more municipal policemen came in with a thin, ragged prisoner. They entered into the dispute with true Italian fervor, which meant using both hands. The ragged prisoner promptly darted out the door; his captors didn't notice his absence for a full minute.

They then began shouting at each other. "What did you let him go for?" "You brass-bound idiot, you're the one who let him go!"

The man called Justinius came back with an elegant person who announced himself as the *corniculatis*, or adjutant prefect. This individual waved a perfumed handkerchief at the struggling group and said: "Let him go, you chaps. Yes, you, too, Sulla." (This was the state policeman.) "There won't be anything left of him to interrogate if you keep that up."

From the way the others in the now-crowded room quieted, Padway guessed that the adjutant prefect was a pretty big shot.

The adjutant prefect asked a few questions, then said: "I'm sorry, my dear old *commentariensius*, but I'm afraid he's our man."

"Not yet he isn't," squeaked the chief. "You fellows can't just walk in here and grab a prisoner any time you feel like it. It would mean my job to let you have him."

The adjutant prefect yawned. "Dear, dear, you're *such* a bore. You forget that I represent the pretorian prefect, who represents the king, and if I order you to hand the prisoner over, you hand him over and that's the end of it. I so order you, now."

"Go ahead and order. You'll have to take him by force, and I've got more force than you have." The chief beamed Billikenlike and twiddled his thumbs. "Clodianus, go fetch our illustrious city governor, if he's not too busy. We'll see whether we have authority over our own jail." The clerk departed. "Of course," the chief continued, "we *might* use Solomon's method."

"You mean cut him in two?" asked the adjutant prefect.

"That's it. Lord Jesus, that would be funny, wouldn't it? Ho, ho, ho, ho, ho!" The chief laughed shrilly until the tears ran down his face. "Would you prefer the head end or the legs end? Ho, ho, ho, ho, ho!" He rocked on his seat.

The other municipal officers dutifully laughed, also; the adjutant prefect permitted himself a wan, bored smile. Padway thought the chief's humor in questionable taste.

Eventually the clerk returned with the city governor. Count Honorius wore a tunic with the two purple stripes of a Roman senator, and walked with such a carefully measured tread that Padway wondered if his footsteps hadn't been laid out ahead of time with chalk marks. He had a square jaw and all the warmth of expression of a snapping turtle.

"What," he asked in a voice like a steel file, "is this all about? Quick, now, I'm a busy man." As he spoke, the little wattle under his jaw wobbled in a way that reminded Padway more than ever of a snapper.

The chief and the adjutant prefect gave their versions. The clerk dragged out a couple of law books; the three executive officers put their heads together and talked in low tones, turning pages rapidly and pointing to passages.

Finally the adjutant prefect gave in. He yawned elaborately. "Oh, well, it would be a dreadful bore to have to drag him up to Ravenna, anyway. Especially as the mosquito season will be starting there shortly. Glad to have seen you, my lord count." He bowed to Honorius, nodded casually to the chief, and departed.

Honorius said: "Now that we have him, what's to be done with him? Let's see that complaint."

The clerk dug out a paper and gave it to the count.

"*Hm-m-m.* '—and furthermore, that the said Martinus Paduei did most wickedly and feloniously consort with the Evil One, who taught him the diabolical arts of magic wherewith he has been jeopardizing the welfare of the citizens of the city of Rome—signed, Hannibal Scipio of Palermo.' Wasn't this Hannibal Scipio a former associate of yours or something?"

"Yes, my lord count," said Padway, and explaining the circumstances of his parting with his foreman. "If it's my printing press that he's referring to, I can easily show that it's a simple mechanical device, no more magical than one of your water clocks."

"*Hm-m-m,*" said Honorius, "that may or may not be true." He looked through narrowed eyes at Padway. "These new enterprises of yours have prospered pretty well, haven't they?" His faint smile reminded Padway of a fox dreaming of unguarded henroosts.

"Yes and no, my lord. I have made a little money, but I've put most of it back in the business. So I haven't more cash than I need for day-to-day expenses."

"Too bad," said Honorius. "It looks as though we'd have to let the case go through."

Padway was getting more and more nervous under that penetrating scrutiny, but he put up a bold front. "Oh, my lord, I don't think you have a case. If I may say so, it would be most unfortunate for your dignity to let the case come to trial."

"So? I'm afraid my good man, that you don't know what expert interrogators we have. You'll have admitted all sorts of things by the time they finish…ah…questioning you."

"Um-m-m. My lord, I said I didn't have much *cash*. But I have an idea that might interest you."

"That's better. Lutetius, may I use your private office?"

Without waiting for an answer, Honorius marched to the office, jerking his head to Padway to follow. The chief looked after them sourly, obviously resenting the loss of his share of the swag.

In the chief's office, Honorius turned to Padway. "You weren't proposing to bribe your governor by chance, were you?" he asked coldly.

"Well…uh…not exactly—"

The count shot his head forward. "How much?" he snapped. "And what's it in—jewels?"

Padway sighed with relief. "Please, my lord, not so fast, It'll take a bit of explaining."

"Your explanation had better be good."

"It's this way, my lord: I'm just a poor stranger in Rome, and naturally I have to depend on my wits for a living. The only really valuable thing I have is those wits. But, with reasonably kind treatment, they can be made to pay a handsome return."

"Get to the point, young man."

"You have a law against limited-liability corporations in other than public enterprises, haven't you?"

Honorius rubbed his chin. "We did have once. I don't know what its status is, now that the senate's authority is limited to the city. I don't think the Goths have made any regulations on that subject. Why?"

"Well if you can get the senate to pass an amendment to the old law—I don't think it would be necessary, but it would look better—I could show you how you and a few other deserving senators could benefit handsomely from the organization and operation of such a company."

Honorius stiffened. "Young man, that's a miserable sort of offer. You ought to know that the dignity of a patrician forbids him to engage in trade."

"You wouldn't engage in it, my lord. You'd be the stockholders."

"We'd be the what?"

Padway explained the operation of a stock corporation.

Honorius rubbed his chin again. "Yes, I see where something might be made of that plan. What sort of company did you have in mind?"

"A company for the transmission of information over long distances much more rapidly than a messenger can travel. In my country they'd call it a semaphore telegraph. The company gets its revenue from tolls on private messages. Of course, it wouldn't hurt if you could get a subsidy from the royal treasury, on the ground that the institution was valuable for national defense."

Honorius thought awhile. Then he said: "I won't commit myself now; I shall have to think about the matter and sound out my friends. In the meantime, you will, of course, remain in Lutetius' custody here."

Padway grinned. "My lord count, your daughter is getting married next week, isn't she?"

"What of it?"

"You want a nice write-up of the wedding in my paper, don't you? A list of distinguished guests, a wood-cut picture of the bride, and so forth."

"Hm-m-m. I shouldn't mind that; no."

"Well, then, you better not hold me, or I shan't be able to get the paper out. It would be a pity if such a gala event missed the news because the publisher was in jail at the time."

Honorius rubbed his chin and smiled thinly. "For a barbarian, you're not as stupid as one would expect. I'll have you released."

"Many thanks, my lord. I might add that I shall be able to write much more glowing paragraphs after that complaint has been dismissed. We creative workers, you know—"

When Padway was out of earshot of the jail, he indulged in a long "*Whew!*" He was sweating, and not with the heat, either. It was a good thing that none of the officials noticed how near he had been to collapse from sheer terror. The prospect of a stand-up fight wouldn't have bothered him more than most young men. But torture...

As soon as he had put his establishment in order, he went into a huddle with Thomasus. He was properly prepared when the procession of five sedan chairs, bearing Honorius and four other senators, crawled up Long Street to his place. The senators seemed not only willing but eager to lay their money on the line, especially after they saw the beautiful stock certificates that Padway had printed. But they didn't seem to have quite Padway's idea of how to run a corporation.

One of them poked him in the ribs and grinned. "My dear Martinus, you're not *really* going to put up those silly signal towers and things?"

"Well," said Padway cautiously, "that was the idea."

The senator winked. "Oh, I understand that you'll have to put up a couple to fool the middle class, so we can sell our stock at a profit. But *we* know it's all a fake, don't we? You couldn't make anything with your signaling scheme in a thousand years."

Padway didn't bother to argue with him. He also didn't bother to explain the true object of having Thomasus the Syrian, Ebenezer the Jew, and Vardan the Armenian each take eighteen per cent of the stock. The senators might have been interested in knowing that these three bankers had agreed ahead of time to hold their stock and vote as Padway instructed, thereby giving him, with fifty-four per cent of the stock, complete control of the corporation.

Padway had every intention of making his telegraph company a success, starting with a line of towers from Naples to Rome to Ravenna, and tying its operation in with that of his paper. He soon ran into an elementary difficulty: If he wanted to keep his expenses down to somewhere within sight of income, he needed telescopes, to make possible a wide spacing of the towers. Telescopes meant lenses. Where in the world was there a lens or a man who could make one? True, there was a story about Nero's emerald lorgnette…

Padway went to see Sextus Dentatus, the froglike goldsmith who had changed his lire to sesterces. Dentatus croaked directions to the establishment of one Florianus the Glazier.

Florianus was a light-haired man with a drooping mustache and a nasal accent. He came to the front of his dark little shop smelling strongly of wine. Yes, he had owned his own glass factory once, at Cologne. But business was bad for the Rhineland glass industry; the uncertainties of life under the Franks, you know, my sir. He had gone broke. Now he made a precarious living mending windows and such.

Padway explained what he wanted, paid a little on account, and left him. When he went back on the promised day, Florianus flapped his hands as if he were trying to take off. "A thousand pardons, my sir! It has been hard to buy up the necessary cullet. But a few days more, I pray you. And if I could have a little more money on account—times are hard—I am poor—"

On Padway's third visit he found Florianus drunk. When Padway shook him, all the man could do was mumble Gallo-romance at him, which Padway did not understand. Padway went to the back of the shop. There was no sign of tools or materials for making lenses.

Padway left in disgust. The nearest real glass industry was at Puteoli, near Naples. It would take forever to get anything done by correspondence.

Padway called in George Menandrus and hired him as editor of the paper. For several days he talked himself hoarse and Menandrus deaf on How to Be an Editor. Then, with a sinking heart, he left for Naples. He experienced the famous canal-boat ride celebrated by Horace, and found it quite as bad as alleged.

Vesuvius was not smoking. But Puteoli, on the little strip of level ground between the extinct crater of Solfatara and the sea, was. Padway and Fritharik sought out the place recommended by Dentatus. This was one of the largest and smokiest of the glass factories.

Padway asked the doorman for Andronicus, the proprietor. Andronicus was a short, brawny man covered with soot. When Padway told who he was, Andronicus cried: "Ah! Fine! Come, gentlemen, I have just the thing."

They followed him into his private inferno. The vestibule, which was also the office, was lined with shelves. The shelves were covered with glassware. Andronicus picked up a vase. "Ah! Look! Such clearness! You couldn't get whiter glass from Alexandria! Only two solidi!"

Padway said: "I didn't come for a vase, my dear sir. I want—"

"No vase? No vase? Ah! Here is the thing." He picked up another vase. "Look! The shape! Such, purity of line! It reminds you—"

"I said I didn't want to buy a vase. I want—"

"It reminds you of a beautiful woman! Of love!" Andronicus kissed his fingertips.

"I want some small pieces of glass, made specially—"

"Beads? Of course, gentlemen. Look." The glass manufacturer scooped up a handful of beads. "Look at the color! Emerald, turquoise, everything!" He picked up another bunch. "See here, the faces of the twelve apostles, one on each bead—"

"Not beads—"

"A beaker, then! Here is one. Look, it has the Holy Family in high relief—"

"Jesus!" yelled Padway. "Will you listen?"

When Andronicus let Padway explain what he wanted, the Neapolitan said: "Of course! Fine! I've seen ornaments shaped like that. I'll rough them out tonight, and have them ready day after tomorrow—"

"That won't quite do," said Padway. "These have to have an exactly spherical surface. You grind a concave against a convex with—what's your word for *emery*? The stuff you use in rough grinding? Some *naxium* to true them off…"

Padway and Fritharik went on to Naples and put up at the house of Thomasus' cousin, Antiochus the Shipper. Their welcome was less than cordial. It transpired that Antiochus was fanatically Orthodox. He loathed his cousin's Nestorianism. His pointed remarks about heretics made his guests so uncomfortable that they moved out on the third day. They took lodgings at an inn whose lack of sanitation distressed Padway's cleanly soul.

Each morning they rode out to Puteoli to see how the lenses were coming. Andronicus invariably tried to sell them a ton of glass junk.

When they left for Rome, Padway had a dozen lenses, half plano-convex and half plano-concave. He was skeptical about the possibility of making a telescope by holding a pair of lenses in line with his eye and judging the distances. It worked, though.

The most practical combination proved to be a concave lens for the eyepiece with a convex one about thirty inches in front of it. The glass had bubbles, and the image was somewhat distorted. But Padway's telescope, crude as it was, would make a two-to-one difference in the number of signal towers required.

About then, the paper ran its first advertisement. Thomasus had had to turn the screw on one of his debtors to make him buy space. The ad read:

DO YOU WANT A GLAMOROUS FUNERAL?

Go to meet your Maker in style! With one of our funerals to look forward to, you will hardly mind dying!

Don't imperil your chances of salvation with a bungled burial! Our experts have handled some of the noblest corpses in Rome.

Arrangements made with the priesthood of any sect. Special rates for heretics. Appropriately doleful music furnished at slight extra cost.

John the Egyptian, Genteel Undertaker, Near the Viminal Gate

CHAPTER VI

Junianus, construction manager of the Roman Telegraph Co., panted into Padway's office. He said: "Work"—stopped to get his breath, and started again—"work on the third tower on the Naples line was stopped this morning by a squad of soldiers from the Rome garrison. I asked them what the devil was up, and they said they didn't know; they just had orders to stop construction. What, most excellent boss, are you going to do about it?"

So the Goths objected? That meant seeing their higher-ups. Padway winced at the idea of getting involved any further in politics. He sighed. "I'll see Liuderis, I suppose."

The commander of the Rome garrison was a big, portly Goth with the bushiest white whiskers Padway had ever seen. His Latin was fair. But now and then he cocked a blue eye at the ceiling and moved his lips silently, as if praying; actually he was running through a declension or a conjugation for the right ending.

He said: "My good Martinus, there is a war on. You start erecting these...ah...mysterious towers without asking our permission. Some of your backers are patricians...ah...notorious for their pro-Greek sentiments. What are we to think? You should consider yourself lucky to have escaped arrest."

Padway protested: "I was hoping the army would find them useful for transmitting military information."

Liuderis shrugged. "I am merely a simple soldier doing my duty. I do not understand these...ah...devices. Perhaps they will work as you say. But I could not take the...ah...responsibility for permitting them."

"Then you won't withdraw your order?"

"No. If you want permission, you will have to see the king."

"But, my dear sir, I can't spare the time to go running up to Ravenna—"

Another shrug. "All one to me, my good Martinus. I know my duty."

Padway tried guile. "You certainly do, it seems. If I were the king, I couldn't ask for a more faithful soldier."

"You flatterer!" But Liuderis grinned, pleased. "I regret that I cannot grant your little request."

"What's the latest war news?"

Liuderis frowned. "Not very—But then I should be careful what I say. You are a more dangerous person than you look, I am sure."

"You can trust me. I'm pro-Gothic."

"Yes?" Liuderis was silent while the wheels turned. Then: "What is your religion?"

Padway was expecting that. "Congregationalist. That's the nearest thing to Arianism we have in my country."

"Ah, then perhaps you are as you say. The news is not good, what little there is. There is nobody in Bruttium but a small force under the king's son-in-law, Evermuth. And our good king—" He shrugged again, this time hopelessly.

"Now look here, most excellent Liuderis, won't you withdraw that order? I'll write Thiudahad at once asking his permission."

"No, my good Martinus, I cannot. You get the permission first. And you had better go in person, if you want action."

Thus it came about that Padway found himself, quite against his wishes, trotting an elderly saddle horse across the Apennines toward the Adriatic. Fritharik had been delighted at first to get any kind of a horse between his knees. Before they had gone very far his tone changed.

"Boss," he grumbled, "I'm not an educated man. But I know horseflesh. I always claimed that a good horse was a good investment." He added darkly: "If we are attacked by brigands, we'll have no chance with those poor old wrecks. Not that I fear death, or brigands either. But it would be sad for a Vandal knight to end in a nameless grave in one of these lonely valleys. When I was a noble in Africa—"

"We aren't running a racing stable," snapped Padway. At Fritharik's hurt look he was sorry he had spoken sharply. "Never mind, old man, we'll be able to afford good horses some day. Only right now I feel as if I had a pantsful of ants."

Brazilian army ants, he added to himself. He had done almost no riding since his arrival in old Rome, and not a great deal in his former life. By the time they reached Spoleto he felt as if he could neither sit nor stand, but would have to spend the rest of his life in a sort of semi-squat, like a rheumatic chimpanzee.

They approached Ravenna at dusk on the fourth day. The City in the Mist sat dimly astride the thirty-mile causeway that divided the Adriatic from the vast marshy lagoons to the west. A faint sunbeam lighted the gilded church domes. The church bells bonged, and the frogs in the lagoons fell silent; then resumed their croaking. Padway thought that anyone who visited this strange city would always be haunted by the bong of the bells, the croak of the frogs, and the thin, merciless song of the mosquitoes.

Padway decided that the chief usher, like Poo-Bah, had been born sneering. "My good man," said this being, "I couldn't possibly give you an audience with our lord king for three weeks at least."

Three weeks! In that time half of Padway's assorted machines would have broken down, and his men would be running in useless circles trying to fix them. Menandrus, who was inclined to be reckless with money, especially other people's, would have run the paper into bankruptcy. This impasse required thought. Padway straightened his aching legs and started to leave.

The Italian immediately lost some of his top-loftiness. "But," he cried in honest amazement, "didn't you bring any *money?*"

Of course, Padway thought, he should have known that the man hadn't meant what he'd said. "What's your schedule of rates?"

The usher, quite seriously, began counting on his fingers. "Well, for twenty solidi I could give you your audience tomorrow. For the day after tomorrow, ten solidi is my usual rate; but that's Sunday, so I'm offering interviews on Monday at seven and a half. For one week in advance, two solidi. For two weeks—"

Padway interrupted to offer a five-solidi bribe for a Monday interview, and finally got it at that price plus a small bottle of brandy. The usher said: "You'll be expected to have a present for the king, too, you know."

"I know," said Padway wearily. He showed the usher a small leather case. "I'll present it personally."

Thiudahad Tharasmund's son, King of the Ostrogoths and Italians; Commander in Chief of the Armies of Italy, Illyria, and Southern Gaul; Premier Prince of the Amal Clan; Count of Tuscany; Illustrious Patrician; *ex-officio* President of the Circus; et cetera, et cetera, was about Padway's height, thin to gauntness, and had a small gray beard. He peered at his caller with watery gray eyes, and said in a reedy voice: "Come in, come in, my good man. What's *your* business? Oh, yes, Martinus Paduei. You're the publisher chap aren't you? Eh?" He spoke upper-class Latin without a trace of accent.

Padway bowed ceremoniously. "I am, my lord king. Before we discuss the business, I have—"

"Great thing, that book-making machine of yours. I've heard of it. Great thing for scholarship. You must see my man Cassiodorus. I'm sure he'd like you to publish his *Gothic History*. Great work. Deserves a wide circulation."

Padway waited patiently. "I have a small gift for you, my lord. A rather unusual—"

"Eh? Gift? By all means. Let's see it."

Padway took out the case and opened it.

Thiudahad piped: "Eh? What the devil is that?"

Padway explained the function of a magnifying glass. He didn't dwell on Thiudahad's notorious nearsightedness.

Thiudahad picked up a book and tried the glass on it. He squealed with delight. "Fine, my good Martinus. Shall I be able to read all I want without getting headaches?"

"I hope so, my lord. At least it should help. Now, about my business here—"

"Oh, yes, you want to see me about publishing Cassiodorus. I'll fetch him for you."

"No, my lord. It's about something else." He went on quickly before Thiudahad could interrupt again, telling him of his difficulty with Liuderis.

"Eh? I never bother my local military commanders. They know their business."

"But, my lord—" and Padway gave the king a little sales talk on the importance of the telegraph company.

"Eh? A money-making scheme, you say? If it's as good as all that, why wasn't I let in on it at the start?"

That rather jarred Padway. He said something vague about there not having been time. King Thiudahad wagged his head. "Still, that wasn't considerate of you, Martinus. It wasn't loyal. And if people aren't loyal to their king, where are we? If you deprive your king of an opportunity to make a little honest profit, I don't see why I should interfere with Liuderis on your account."

"Well, ahem, my lord, I did have an idea—"

"Not considerate at all. What were you saying? Come to the point, my good man, come to the point."

Padway resisted an impulse to strangle this exasperating little man. He beckoned Fritharik, who was standing statuesquely in the background. Fritharik produced a telescope, and Padway explained *its* functions....

"Yes, Yes? Very interesting, I'm sure. Thank you, Martinus. I will say that you bring your king original presents."

Padway gasped; he hadn't intended giving Thiudahad his best telescope. But it was too late now. He said: "I thought that if my lord king saw fit to…ah…ease matters with your excellent Liuderis, I could insure your undying fame in the world of scholarship."

"Eh? What's that? What do you know about scholarship? Oh, I forgot; you're a publisher. Something about Cassiodorus?"

Padway repressed a sigh. "No, my lord. *Not* Cassiodorus. How would you like the credit for revolutionizing men's idea about the solar system?"

"I don't believe in interfering with my local commanders, Martinus. Liuderis is an excellent man. Eh? What were you saying. Something about the solar system? What's that got to do with Liuderis?"

"Nothing, my lord." Padway repeated what he had said.

"Well, maybe I'd consider it. What is this theory of yours?"

Little by little Padway wormed from Thiudahad a promise of a free hand for the telegraph company, in return for bits of information about the Copernican hypothesis, instructions for the use of the telescope to see the moons of Jupiter, and a promise to publish a treatise on astronomy in Thiudahad's name.

At the end of an hour he grinned and said, "Well, my lord, we seem to be in agreement. There's just one more thing. This telescope would be a valuable instrument of warfare. If you wanted to equip your officers with them—"

"Eh? Warfare? You'll have to see Wittigis about that. He's my head general."

"Where's he?"

"Where? Oh, dear me, I don't know. Somewhere up north, I think. There's been a little invasion by the Allemans or somebody."

"When will he be back?"

"How should I know, my good Martinus? When he's driven out these Allemans or Burgunds or whoever they are."

"But, most excellent lord, if you'll pardon me, the war with the Imperialists is definitely on. I think it's important to get these telescopes into the hands of the army as soon as possible? We'd be prepared to supply them at a reasonable—"

"Now, Martinus," snapped the king peevishly, "don't try to tell me how to run my kingdom. You're as bad as my Royal Council. Always 'Why don't you do this?', 'Why don't you do that?' I trust my commanders; don't bother myself with details. I say you'll have to see Wittigis, and that settles it."

Thiudahad was obviously prepared to be mulish, so Padway said a few polite nothings, bowed, and withdrew.

CHAPTER VII

When Padway got back to Rome, his primary concern was to see how his paper was coming. The first issue that had been put out since his departure was all right. About the second, which had just been printed, Menandrus was mysteriously elated, hinting that he had a splendid surprise for his employer. He had. Padway glanced at a proof sheet, and his heart almost stopped. On the front page was a detailed account of the bribe which the new Pope, Silverius, had paid King Thiudahad to secure his election.

"Hell's bells!" cried Padway. "Haven't you any better sense than to print this, George?"

"Why?" asked Menandrus, crestfallen. "It's true, isn't it?"

"Of course, it's true! But you don't want us all hanged or burned at the stake, do you? The Church is already suspicious of us. Even if you find that a bishop is keeping twenty concubines, you're not to print a word of it."

Menandrus sniffled a little; he wiped away a tear and blew his nose on his tunic. "I'm sorry, excellent boss. I tried to please you; you have no idea how much trouble I went to to get the facts about that bribe. There *is* a bishop, too—not *twenty* concubines, but—"

"But we don't consider that news, for reasons of health. Thank heaven, no copies of this issue have gone out yet."

"Oh, but they have."

"*What?*" Padway's yell made a couple of workmen from the machine shop look in.

"Why, yes, John the Bookseller took the first hundred copies out just a minute ago."

John the Bookseller got the scare of his life when Padway, still dirty from days of travel, galloped down the street after him, dove off his horse, and grabbed his arm. Somebody set up a cry of "Thieves! Robbers! Help! Murder!" Padway found himself trying to explain to forty truculent citizens that everything was all right.

A Gothic soldier pushed through the crowd and asked what was going on here. A citizen pointed at Padway and shouted: "It's the fellow with the boots. I heard him say he'd cut the other man's throat if he didn't hand over his money!" So the Goth arrested Padway.

Padway kept his clutch on John the Bookseller, who was too frightened to speak. He went along quietly with the Goth until they were out of earshot of the crowd. Then he asked the soldier into a wineshop, treated him and John, and explained. The Goth was noncommittal, despite John's corroboration, until Padway tipped him liberally. Padway got his freedom and his precious papers. Then all he had to worry about was the fact that somebody had stolen his horse while he was in the Goth's custody.

Padway trudged back to his house with the papers under his arm. His household was properly sympathetic about the loss of the horse. Fritharik said: "There, illustrious boss, that piece of crow bait wasn't worth much anyhow."

Padway felt much better when he learned that the first leg of the telegraph ought to be completed in a week or ten days. He poured himself a stiff drink before dinner. After his strenuous day it made his head swim a little. He got Fritharik to join him in one of the latter's barbarian war-songs:

"*The black earth shakes*
As the heroes ride,
And the ravens blood-
Red sun will hide!
The lances dip
In a glittering wave,
And the coward turns
His gore to save..."

When Julia was late with the food, Padway gave her a playful spank. He was a little surprised at himself.

After dinner he was sleepy. He said to hell with the accounts and went upstairs to bed, leaving Fritharik already snoring on his mattress in front of the door. Padway would not have laid any long bets on Fritharik's ability to wake up when a burglar entered.

He had just started to undress when a knock startled him. He could not imagine…

"Fritharik?" he called.

"No. It's me."

He frowned and opened the door. The lamplight showed Julia from Apulia. She walked in with a swaying motion.

"What do you want, Julia?" asked Padway.

The stocky, black-haired girl looked at him in some surprise. "Why—uh—my lord wouldn't want me to say right out loud? That wouldn't be nice!"

"Huh?"

She giggled.

"Sorry," said Padway. "Wrong station. Off you go."

She looked baffled. "My—my master doesn't want me?"

"That's right. Not for that anyway."

Her mouth turned down. Two large tears appeared. "You don't like me? You don't think I'm nice?"

"I think you're a fine cook and a nice girl. Now out with you. Good night."

She stood solidly and began to sniffle. Then she sobbed. Her voice rose to a shrill wail: "Just because I'm from the country—you never looked at me—you never asked for me all this time—then tonight you were nice—I thought—I thought—boo-oo-oo…"

"Now, now…for heaven's sake stop crying! Here, sit down. I'll get you a drink."

She smacked her lips over the first swallow of diluted brandy. She wiped off the remaining tears. "Nice," she said. Everything was nice—*bonus*, *bona*, or *bonum*, as the case might be. "You are nice. Love is nice. Every man should have some love. Love—ah!" She made a serpentine movement remarkable in a person of her build.

Padway gulped. "Give me that drink," he said. "I need some too."

After a while. "Now," she said, "we make love?"

"Well—pretty soon. Yes, I guess we do." Padway hiccuped.

Padway frowned at Julia's large bare feet. "Just—*hic*—just a minute, my bounding hamadryad. Let's see those feet." The soles were black. "That won't do. Oh, it absolutely won't do, my lusty Amazon. The feet present an in-sur-insurmountable psychological obstacle."

"Huh?"

"They interpose a psychic barrier to the—*hic*—appropriately devout worship of Ashtaroth. We must have the pedal extremities—"

"I don't understand."

"Skip it; neither do I. What I mean is that we're going to wash your feet first."

"Is that a religion?"

"You might put it that way. Damn!" He knocked the ewer off its base, miraculously catching it on the way down. "Here we go, my Tritoness from the wine-dark, fish-swarming sea…"

She giggled. "You are the nicest man. You are a real gentleman. No man ever did *that* for me before…"

Padway blinked his eyes open. It all came back to him quickly enough. He tightened his muscles serratus. He felt fine. He prodded his conscience experimentally. It reacted not at all.

He moved carefully, for Julia was taking up two-thirds of his none-too-wide bed. He heaved himself on one elbow and looked at her. The movement uncovered her large breasts. Between them was a bit of iron, tied around her neck. This, she had told him, was a nail from the cross of St Andrew. And she would not put it off.

He smiled. To the list of mechanical inventions he meant to introduce he added a couple of items. But for the present, should he…

A small gray thing with six legs, not much larger than a pinhead, emerged from the hair under her armpit. Pale against her olive-brown skin, it crept with glacial slowness…

Padway shot out of bed. Face writhing with revulsion, he pulled his clothes on without taking time to wash. The room smelled. Rome must have blunted his sense of smell, or he'd have noticed it before.

Julia awoke as he was finishing. He threw a muttered good morning at her and tramped out.

He spent two hours in the public baths that day. The next night Julia's knock brought a harsh order to get away from his room and stay away. She began to wail. Padway snatched the door open. "One more squawk and you're fired!" he snapped, and slammed the door.

She was obedient but sulky. During the next few days he caught venomous glances from her; she was no actress.

The following Sunday he returned from the Ulpian Library to find a small crowd of men in front of his house. They were just standing and looking. Padway looked at the house and could see nothing out of order.

He asked a man: "What's funny about my house, stranger?"

The man looked at him silently. They all looked at him silently. They moved off in twos and threes. They began to walk fast, sometimes glancing back.

Monday morning two of the workmen failed to report. Nerva came to Padway and, after much clearing of the throat, said: "I thought you'd like to know, lordly Martinus. I went to mass at the Church of the Angel Gabriel yesterday as usual."

"Yes?" That Church was on Long Street four blocks from Padway's house.

"Father Narcissus preached a homily against sorcery. He talked about people who hired demons from Satanas and work strange devices. It was a very strong sermon. He sounded as if he might be thinking of you."

Padway worried. It might be coincidence, but he was pretty sure that Julia had gone to confessional and spilled the beans about fornicating with a magician. One sermon had sent the crowd to stare at the wizard's lair. A few more like that...

Padway feared a mob of religious enthusiasts more than anything on earth, no doubt because their mental processes were so utterly alien to his own.

He called Menandrus in and asked for information on Father Narcissus.

The information was discouraging from Padway's point of view. Father Narcissus was one of the most respected priests in Rome. He was upright, charitable, humane, and fearless. He was in deadly earnest twenty-four hours a day. And there was no breath of scandal about him, which fact by itself made him a distinguished cleric.

"George," said Padway, "didn't you once mention a bishop with concubines?"

Menandrus grinned slyly. "It's the Bishop of Bologna, sir. He's one of the Pope's cronies; spends more time at the Vatican than at his see. He has two women—at least, two that we know of. I have their names and everything. Everybody knows that a lot of bishops have one concubine, but two! I thought it would make a good story for the paper."

"It may yet. Write me up a story, George, about the Bishop of Bologna and his loves. Make it sensational, but accurate. Set it up and pull three or four galley proofs; then put the type away in a safe place."

It took Padway a week to gain an audience with the Bishop of Bologna, who was providentially in Rome. The bishop was a gorgeously dressed person with a beautiful, bloodless face. Padway suspected a highly convoluted brain behind that sweet, ascetic smile.

Padway kissed the bishop's hand, and they murmured pleasant nothings. Padway talked of the Church's wonderful work, and how he tried in his humble way to further it at every opportunity.

"For instance," he said, "—do you know of my weekly paper, reverend sir?"

"Yes, I read it with pleasure."

"Well, you know I have to keep a close watch on my boys, who are prone to err in their enthusiasm for news. I have tried to make the paper a clean sheet fit to enter any home, without scandal or libel. Though that sometimes meant I had to write most of an issue myself." He sighed. "Ah, sinful men! Would you believe it, reverend sir, that I have had to suppress stories of foul libel against members of the Holy Church? The most shocking of all came in recently." He took out one of the galley proofs. "I hardly dare show it to you, sir, lest your justified wrath at this filthy product of a disordered imagination should damn me to eternal flames."

The bishop squared his thin shoulders. "Let me see it, my son. A priest sees many dreadful things in his career. It takes a strong spirit to serve the Lord in these times."

Padway handed over the sheet. The bishop read it. A sad expression came over his angelic face. "Ah, poor weak mortals! They know not that they hurt themselves far more than the object of their calumny. It shows that we must have God's help at every turn lest we fall into sin. If you will tell me who wrote this, I will pray for him."

"A man named Marcus," said Padway. "I discharged him immediately, of course. I want nobody who is not prepared to co-operate with the Church to the full."

The bishop cleared his throat delicately. "I appreciate your righteous efforts," he said. "If there is some favor within my power—"

Padway told him about the good Father Narcissus, who was showing such a lamentable misunderstanding of Padway's enterprises...

Padway went to mass next Sunday. He sat well down in front, determined to face the thing out if Father Narcissus proved obdurate. He sang with the rest:

> *"Imminet, imminet,*
> *Recta remuneret.*
> *Aethera donet,*
> *Ille supremus!"*

He reflected that there was this good in Christianity: By its concepts of the Millennium and Judgment Day it accustomed people to looking forward in a way that the older religions did not, and so prepared their minds for the conceptions of organic evolution and scientific progress.

Father Narcissus began his sermon where he had left off a week before.

Sorcery was the most damnable of crimes; they should not suffer a witch to live, etc. Padway stiffened.

But, continued the good priest with a sour glance at Padway, we should not in our holy enthusiasm confuse the practitioner of black arts and the familiar of devils with the honest artisan who by his ingenious devices ameliorates our journey through this vale of tears. After all, Adam invented the plow and Noah the ocean-going ship. And this new art of machine writing would make it possible to spread the word of God among the heathen more effectively.

When Padway got home, he called in Julia and told her he would not need her any more. Julia from Apulia began to weep, softly at first, then more and more violently. "What kind of man are you? I give you love. I give you everything. But no, you think I am just a little country girl you can do anythingyouwantandthenyougettired…"The patois came with such machine-gun rapidity that Padway could no longer follow. When she began to shriek and tear her dress, Padway ungallantly threatened to have Fritharik throw her out bodily forthwith. She quieted.

The day after she left, Padway gave his house a personal going over to see whether anything had been stolen or broken. Under his bed he found a curious object: a bundle of chicken feathers tied with horsehair around what appeared to be a long-defunct mouse; the whole thing stiff with dried blood. Fritharik did not know what it was. But George Menandrus did; he turned a little pale and muttered: "A curse!"

He reluctantly informed Padway that this was a bad-luck charm peddled by one of the local wizards; the discharged housekeeper had undoubtedly left it there to bring Padway to an early and gruesome death. Menandrus himself wasn't too sure he wanted to keep on with his job. "Not that I really believe in curses, excellent sir, but with my family to support I can't take chances…"

A raise in pay disposed of Menandrus' qualms. Menandrus was disappointed that Padway didn't use the occasion to have Julia arrested and hanged for witchcraft. "Just think," he said, "it would put us on the right side of the Church, and it would make a wonderful story for the paper!"

Padway hired another housekeeper. This one was gray-haired, rather frail-looking, and depressingly virginal. That was why Padway took her.

He learned that Julia had gone to work for Ebenezer the Jew. He hoped that Julia would not try any of her specialties on Ebenezer. The old banker did not look as if he could stand much of them.

Padway told Thomasus: "We ought to get the first message from Naples over the telegraph any time now."

Thomasus rubbed his hands together: "You are a wonder, Martinus. Only I'm worried that you'll overreach yourself. The messengers of the Italian civil service are complaining that this invention will destroy their livelihood. Unfair competition, they say."

Padway shrugged. "We'll see. Maybe there'll be some war news."

Thomasus frowned. "That's another thing that's worrying me. Thiudahad hasn't done a thing about the defense of Italy. I'd hate to see the war carried as far north as Rome."

"I'll make you a bet," said Padway. "The king's son-in-law, Evermuth the Vandal, will desert to the Imperialists. One solidus."

"Done!" Almost at that moment Junianus, who had been put in charge of operations, came in with a paper. It was the first message, and it carried the news that Belisarius had landed at Reggio; that Evermuth had gone over to him; that the Imperialists were marching on Naples.

Padway grinned at the banker, whose jaw was sagging. "Sorry, old man, but I need that solidus. I'm saving up for a new horse."

"Do You hear that, God? Martinus, the next time I lay a bet with a magician, you can have me declared incompetent and a guardian appointed."

Two days later a messenger came in and told Padway that the king was in Rome, staying at the Palace of Tiberius, and that Padway's presence was desired. Padway thought that perhaps Thiudahad had reconsidered the telescope proposal. But no.

"My good Martinus," said Thiudahad, "I must ask you to discontinue the operation of your telegraph. At once."

"What? Why, my lord king?"

"You know what happened? Eh? That thing of yours spread the news of my son-in-law's good fort—his treachery all over Rome a few hours after it happened. Bad for morale. Encourages the pro-Greek element, and brings criticism on me. *Me.* So you'll please not operate it any more, at least during the war."

"But, my lord, I thought that your army would find it useful for—"

"Not another word about it, Martinus. I forbid it. Now, let me see. Dear me, there was something else I wanted to see you about. Oh, yes, my man Cassiodorus would like to meet you. You'll stay for lunch, won't you? Great scholar, Cassiodorus."

So Padway presently found himself bowing to the pretorian prefect, an elderly, rather saintly Italian. They were immediately deep in a discussion of historiography, literature, and the hazards of the publishing business.

Padway to his annoyance found that he was enjoying himself. He knew that he was abetting these spineless old dodderers in their criminal disregard of their country's defense. But—upsetting thought—he had enough of the unworldly intellectual in his own nature so that he couldn't help sympathizing with them. And he hadn't gone on an intellectual debauch of this kind since he'd arrived in old Rome.

"Illustrious Cassiodorus," he said, "perhaps you've noticed that in my paper I've been trying to teach the typesetter to distinguish between U and V, and also between I and J. That's a reform that's long been needed, don't you think?"

"Yes, yes, my excellent Martinus. The Emperor Claudius tried something of the sort. But which letter do you use for which sound in each case?"

Padway explained. He also told Cassiodorus of his plans for printing the paper, or at least part of it, in Vulgar Latin. At that Cassiodorus held up his hands in mild horror.

"Excellent Martinus! These wretched dialects that pass for Latin nowadays? What would Ovid say if he heard them? What would Virgil say? What would any of the ancient masters say?"

"As they were a bit before our time," grinned Padway, "I'm afraid we shall never know. But I will assert that even in their day the final s's and m's had been dropped from ordinary pronunciation. And in any event, the pronunciation and grammar have changed too far from the classical models ever to be changed back again. So if we want our new instrument for the dissemination of literature to be useful, we shall have to adopt a spelling that more or less agrees with the spoken language. Otherwise people won't bother to learn it. To begin with, we shall have to add a half dozen new letters to the alphabet. For instance—"

When Padway left, hours later, he had at least made an effort to bring the conversation around to measures for prosecuting the war. It had been useless, but his conscience was salved.

Padway was surprised, though he shouldn't have been, at the effect of the news of his acquaintance with the king and the prefect. Well-born Romans called on him, and he was even asked to a couple of very dull dinners that began at four P.M. and lasted most of the night.

As he listened to the windy conversation and the windier speeches, he thought that a twentieth-century after-dinner speaker could have taken lessons in high-flown, meaningless rhetoric from these people. From the slightly nervous way that his hosts introduced him around, he gathered that they still regarded him as something of a monster, but a well-behaved monster whom it might be useful to know.

Even Cornelius Anicius looked him up and issued the long-coveted invitation to his house. He did not apologize for the slight snub in the library, but his deferential manner suggested that he remembered it.

Padway swallowed his pride and accepted. He thought it foolish to judge Anicius by his own standards. And he wanted another look at the pretty brunette.

When the time came, he got up from his desk, washed his hands, and told Fritharik to come along.

Fritharik said, scandalized: "You are going to *walk* to this Roman gentleman's house?"

"Sure. It's only a couple of miles. Do us good."

"Oh, most respectable boss, you can't! It isn't done! I know; I worked for such a patrician once. You should have a sedan chair, or at least a horse."

"Nonsense. Anyway, we've got only one saddle-horse. You don't want to walk while I ride, do you?"

"N-no-not that I mind walking; but it would look funny for a gentleman's free retainer like me to go afoot like a slave on a formal occasion."

Damn this etiquette, thought Padway.

Fritharik said hopefully: "Of course there's the workhorse. He's a good-looking animal; one might almost mistake him for a heavy cavalry horse."

"But I don't want the boys in the shop to lose a couple of hours' production just because of some damned piece of face-saving—"

Padway rode the work-horse. Fritharik rode the remaining bony saddle-horse.

Padway was shown into a big room whose ornamentation reminded him of the late Victorian gewgaw culture. Through a closed door he could hear Anicius' voice coming through in rolling pentameters:

> "Rome, the warrior-goddess, her seat had taken,
> With breast uncovered, a mural crown on her head.
> Behind, from under her spacious helmet escaping,
> The hair of her plumed head flowed over her back.
> Modest her mien, but sternness her beauty makes awesome.
> Of purple hue is her robe, with fang-like clasp;
> Under her bosom a jewel her mantle gathers.
> A vast and glowing shield her side supports,
> Whereon, in stout metal cast, the cave of Rhea—"

The servant had sneaked through the door and whispered. Anicius broke off his declamation and popped out with a book under his arm. He cried: "My dear Martinus! I crave your pardon; I was rehearsing a speech I am to give tomorrow." He tapped the book under his arm and smiled guiltily. "It will not be a strictly original speech; but you won't betray me, will you?"

"Of course not. I heard some of it through the door."

"You did? What did you think of it?"

"I thought your delivery was excellent." Padway resisted a temptation to add: "But what does it *mean?*" Such a question about a piece of post-Roman rhetoric would, he realized, be both futile and tactless.

"You did?" cried Anicius. "Splendid! I am greatly gratified! I shall be as nervous tomorrow as Cadmus when the dragon's teeth began to sprout, but the approval of one competent critic in advance will fortify me. And now I'll leave you to Dorothea's mercy while I finish this. You will not take offense, I hope? Splendid! Oh, daughter!"

Dorothea appeared and exchanged courtesies. She took Padway out in the garden while Anicius went back to his plagiarism of Sidonius.

Dorothea said: "You should hear father some time. He takes you back to the time when Rome really was the mistress of the world. If restoring the power of Rome could be done by fine talk, father and his friends would have restored it long ago."

It was hot in the garden, with the heat of an Italian June. Bees buzzed.

Padway said: "What kind of flower do you call that?"

She told him. He was hot. And he was tired of strain and responsibility and ruthless effort. He wanted to be young and foolish for a change.

He asked her more questions about flowers—trivial questions about unimportant matters.

She answered prettily, bending over the flowers to remove a bug now and then. She was hot too. There were little beads of sweat on her upper lip. Her thin dress stuck to her in places. Padway admired the places. She was standing close to him, talking with grave good humor about flowers and about the bugs and blights that beset them. To kiss her, all he had to do was reach and lean forward a bit. He could hear his blood in his ears. The way she smiled up at him might almost be considered an invitation.

But Padway made no move. While he hesitated his mind clicked off reasons: (a) He didn't know how she'd take it, and shouldn't presume on the strength of a mere friendly smile; (b) if she resented it, as she very likely would, there might be repercussions of incalculable scope; (c) if he made love to her, what would she think he was after? He didn't want a mistress—not that Dorothea Anicius would be willing to become such—and he was not, as far as he knew, in need of a wife; (d) he was in a sense already married…

So, he thought, you wanted to be young and foolish a few minutes ago, eh, Martin, my boy? You can't; it's too late; you'll always stop to figure things out rationally, as you've been doing just now. Might as well resign yourself to being a calculating adult, especially as you can't do anything about it.

But it made him a little sad that he would never be one of those impetuous fellows—usually described as tall and handsome—who take one look at a girl, know her to be their destined mate, and sweep her into their arms. He let Dorothea do most of the talking as they wandered back into the house to dinner with Cornelius Anicius and Anicius' oratory. Padway, watching Dorothea as she preceded him, felt slightly disgusted with himself for having let Julia invade his bed.

They sat down—or rather stretched themselves out on the couches, as Anicius insisted on eating in the good old Roman style, to Padway's acute discomfort. Anicius had a look in his eye that Padway found vaguely familiar.

Padway learned that the look was that of a man who is writing or is about to write a book. Anicius explained: "Ah, the degenerate times we live in, excellent Martinus! The lyre of Orpheus sounds but faintly; Calliope veils her face; blithe Thalia is mute; the hymns of our Holy Church have drowned Euterpe's sweet strains. Yet a few of us strive to hold high the torch of poetry while swimming the Hellespont of barbarism and hoeing the garden of culture."

"Quite a feat," said Padway, squirming in a vain effort to find a comfortable position.

"Yes, we persist despite Herculean discouragements. For instance, you will not consider me forward in submitting to your publisher's eagle-bright scrutiny a little book of verses." He produced a sheaf of papyrus. "Some of them are not really bad, though I their unworthy author say so."

"I should be very much interested," said Padway, smiling with effort. "As for publication, however, I should warn you that I'm contracted for three books by your excellent colleagues already. And between the paper and my schoolbook, it will be some weeks before I can print them."

"Oh," said Anicius with a drooping inflection.

"The Illustrious Trajanus Herodius, the Distinguished John Leontius, and the Respectable Felix Avitus. All epic poems. Because of market conditions these gentlemen have undertaken the financial responsibility of publication."

"Meaning—ah?"

"Meaning that they pay cash in advance, and get the whole price of their books when sold, subject to bookseller's discounts. Of course, distinguished sir, if the book is really good, the author doesn't have to worry about getting back his cost of publication."

"Yes, yes, excellent Martinus, I see. What chances do you think my little creation would have?"

"I'd have to see it first."

"So you would. I'll read some of it now, to give you the idea." Anicius sat up. He held the papyrus in one hand and made noble gestures with the other:

"Mars with his thunderous trumpet his lord acclaims,
The youthful Jupiter, new to his throne ascended,
Above the stars by all-wise Nature placed.
The lesser deities their sire worship,
To ancient sovereignty with pomp succeeding—"

"Father," interrupted Dorothea, "your food's getting cold."

"What? Oh, so it is, child."

"And," continued Dorothea, "I think you ought to write some good Christian sentiment sometime, instead of all that pagan superstition."

Anicius signed. "If you ever have a daughter, Martinus, marry her off early, before she develops the critical faculty."

In August Naples fell to General Belisarius. Thiudahad had done nothing to help the town except seize the families of the small Gothic garrison to insure their fidelity. The only vigorous defense of the city was made by the Neapolitan Jews. These, having heard of Justinian's religious complexes, knew what treatment to expect under Imperial rule.

Padway heard the news with a sick feeling. There was so much that he could do for them if they'd only let him alone. And it would take such a little accident to snuff him out—one of the normal accidents of warfare, like that which happened to Archimedes. In this age civilians who got in the way of belligerent armies would be given the good old rough and ruthless treatment to which the military of his own twentieth century, after a brief hundred and fifty years of relatively humane forbearance, had seemed to be returning.

Fritharik announced that a party of Goths wanted to look Padway's place over. He added in his sepulchral voice: "Thiudegiskel's with them. You know, the king's son. Watch out for him, excellent boss. He makes trouble."

There were six of them, all young, and they tramped into the house wearing swords, which was not good manners by the standards of the times. Thiudegiskel was a handsome, blond young man who had inherited his father's high-pitched voice.

He stared at Padway, like something in a zoo, and said: "I've wanted to see your place ever since I heard you and the old man were mumbling over manuscripts together. I'm a curious chap, you know, active-minded. What the devil are all these silly machines for?"

Padway did some explaining, while the prince's companions made remarks about his personal appearance in Gothic, under the mistaken impression that he couldn't understand them.

"Ah, yes," said Thiudegiskel, interrupting one of the explanations. "I think that's all I'm interested in here. Now, let's see that bookmaking machine."

Padway showed him the presses.

"Oh, yes, I understand. Really a simple thing, isn't it? I could have invented it myself. All very well for those who like it. Though I can read and write and all that. Better than most people, in fact. But I never cared for it. Dull business, not suited to a healthy man like me."

"No doubt, no doubt, my lord," said Padway. He hoped that the red rage he was feeling didn't show in his face.

"Say, Willimer," said Thiudegiskel, "you remember that tradesman we had fun with last winter? He looked something like this Martinus person. Same big nose."

Willimer roared with laughter. "Do I remember it! *Guths in himinam!* I'll never forget the way he looked when we told him we were going to baptize him in the Tiber, with rocks tied to him so the angels couldn't carry him off! But the funniest thing was when some soldiers from the garrison arrested us for assault!"

Thiudegiskel said to Padway, between guffaws: "You ought to have been there, Martinus. You should have seen old Liuderis' face when he found out who we were! We made him grovel, I can tell you. I've always regretted that I missed the flogging of those soldiers who pinched us. That's one thing about me; I can appreciate the humor of things like that."

"Would you like to see anything more, my lord?" asked Padway, his face wooden.

"Oh, I don't know—Say, what are all those packing cases for?"

"Some stuff just arrived for our machines, my lord, and we haven't gotten around to burning the cases," Padway lied.

Thiudegiskel grinned good-naturedly. "Trying to fool me, huh? I know what you're up to. You're going to sneak your stuff out of Rome before Belisarius gets here, aren't you? That's one thing about me; I can see through little tricks like that. Well, can't say I blame you. Though it sounds as though you had inside information on how the war will go." He examined a new brass telescope on a workbench. "This is an interesting little device. I'll take it along, if you don't mind."

That was too much even for Padway's monumental prudence. "No, my lord, I'm sorry, but I need that in my business."

Thiudegiskel's eyes were round with astonishment. "Huh? You mean I can't have it?"

"That, my lord, is it."

"Well...uh...uh...if you're going to take that attitude, I'll pay for it."

"It isn't for sale."

Thiudegiskel's neck turned slowly pink with embarrassment and anger. His five friends moved up behind him, their left hands resting on their sword hilts.

The one called Willimer said in a low tone: "I *think*, gentlemen, that our king's son has been insulted."

Thiudegiskel had laid the telescope on the bench. He reached out for it; Padway snatched it up and smacked the end of the tube meaningfully against his left palm. He knew that, even if he got out of this situation in one piece, he'd curse himself for a double-dyed knight-erranting idiot. But at the moment he was too furious to care.

The uncomfortable silence was broken by the shuffle of feet behind Padway; he saw the Goths' eyes shift from him. He glanced around. In the doorway was Fritharik, with his sword belt hitched around so the scabbard was in front, and Nerva, holding a three-foot length of bronze bar-stock. Behind them came the other workmen with an assortment of blunt instruments.

"It seems," said Thiudegiskel, "that these people have no manners whatever. We should give them a lesson. But I promised my old man to lay off fighting. That's one thing about me; I always keep my promises. Come along boys." They went.

"*Whew!*" said Padway. "You boys certainly saved my bacon. Thanks."

"Oh, it was nothing," said George Menandrus airily. "I'm rather sorry they didn't stay to fight it out. I'd have enjoyed smacking their thick skulls."

"You? *Honh!*" snorted Fritharik. "Boss, the first thing I saw when I started to round the men up was this fellow sneaking out the back door. You know how I changed his mind? I said I'd hang him with a rope made of his own guts if he didn't stick! And the others, I threatened to cut their heads off and stick them on the fence palings in front of the house." He contemplated infinite calamities for a few seconds, then added: "But it won't do any good, excellent Martinus. Those fellows will have it in for us, and they're pretty influential, naturally. They can get away with anything. We'll all end in nameless graves yet."

Padway struggled mightily to get the movable parts of his equipment packed for shipment to Florence. As far as he could remember his Procopius, Florence had not been besieged or sacked in Justinian's Gothic War, at least in the early part.

But the job was not half done when eight soldiers from the garrison descended on him and told him he was under arrest. He was getting rather used to arrest by now, so he calmly gave his foremen and editor orders about getting the equipment moved and set up, and about seeing Thomasus and trying to get in touch with him. Then he went along.

On the way he offered to stand the Goths drinks. They accepted quickly. In the wineshop he got the commander aside to suggest a little bribe to let him go. The Goth seemed to accept, and pocketed a solidus. Then when Padway, his mind full of plans for shaving his beard, getting a horse, and galloping off to Florence, broached the subject of his release, the Goth looked at him with an air of pained surprise.

"Why, most distinguished Martinus, I couldn't think of letting you go! Our commander-in-chief, the noble Liuderis, is a man of stern and rigid principles. If my men talked, he'd hear about it, and he'd break me sure. Of course I appreciate your little *gift*, and I'll try to put in a good word for you."

Padway said nothing, but he made a resolve that it would be a long day before he put in a good word for this officer.

CHAPTER VIII

Liuderis blew out his snowy whiskers and explained: "I am sorry you deceived me, Martinus. I never thought a true Arian would stoop to...ah...conniving with these pro-Greek Italians to let a swarm of Orthodox fanatics into Italy."

"Who says so?" asked Padway, more annoyed than apprehensive.

"No less a person than the...ah...noble Thiudegiskel. He told how when he visited your house, you not only insulted and reviled him, but boasted of your connections with the Imperialists. His companions corroborated him. They said you had inside information about a plan for betraying Rome, and that you were planning to move your effects elsewhere to escape any disturbances. When my men arrested you, they found that you were in fact about to move."

"My dear sir!" said Padway in exasperation. "Don't you think I have *any* brains? If I were in on some plot of some sort, do you think I would go around telling the world about it?"

Liuderis shrugged. "I would not know. I am only doing my duty, which is to hold you for questioning about this secret plan. Take him away, Sigifrith."

Padway hid a shudder at the word "questioning." If this honest blockhead got set on an idea, he'd have a swell chance of talking him out of it.

The Goths had set up a prison camp at the north end of the city, between the Flaminian Way and the Tiber. Two sides of the camp were formed by a hastily erected fence, and the remaining two by the Wall of Aurelian. Padway found that two Roman patricians had preceded him in custody; both said they had been arrested on suspicion of complicity in an Imperialist plot. Several more Romans arrived within a few hours.

The camp was no escape-proof masterpiece, but the Goths made the best of it. They kept a heavy guard around the fence and along the wall. They even had a squad camped across the Tiber, in case a prisoner got over the wall and tried to swim the river.

For three days Padway rusticated. He walked from one end of the camp to the other, and back, and forward, and back. When he got tired of walking he sat. When he got tired of sitting he walked. He talked a little with his fellow prisoners, but in a moody and abstracted manner.

He'd been a fool—well, at least he'd been badly mistaken—in supposing that he could carry out his plans with as little difficulty as in Chicago. This was a harsh, convulsive world; you had to take it into account, or you'd get caught in the gears sooner or later. Even the experts at political intrigue and uniformed banditry often came to a bad end. What chance would such a hopelessly unwarlike and unpolitical alien as himself have?

Well, what chance did he have anyway? He'd kept out of public affairs as much as possible, and here he was in a horrifying predicament as a result of a petty squabble over a brass telescope. He might just as well have gone adventuring up to the hilt. If he ever got out, he *would* go adventuring. He'd show 'em!

The fourth day failed to settle Padway's gnawing anxiety about his interrogation. The guards seemed excited about something. Padway tried to question them, but they rebuffed him. Listening to their muttering talk, he caught the word *folkmote*. That meant that the great meeting was about to be held near Terracina, at which the Goths would consider what to do about the loss of Naples.

Padway got into talk with one of the patrician prisoners.

"Bet you a solidus," he said, "that they depose Thiudahad and elect Wittigis king in his place."

The patrician, poor man, took him on.

Thomasus the Syrian arrived. He explained: "Nerva tried to get in to see you, but he couldn't afford a high enough bribe. How do they treat you?"

"Not badly. The food's not exactly good, but they give us plenty of it. What worries me is that Liuderis thinks I know all about some alleged conspiracy to betray Rome, and he may use drastic methods to try to get information out of me."

"Oh, that. There's a conspiracy afoot, all right. But I think you'll be safe for a few days anyway. Liuderis has gone off to a convention, and the Goths' affairs are all in confusion." He went on to report on the state of Padway's business. "We got the last case off this morning. Ebenezer the

Jew is going up to Florence in a couple of weeks. He'll look in and see that your foremen haven't run off with all your property."

"You mean to see *whether* they've run off with it. Any war news?"

"None, except that Naples suffered pretty badly. Belisarius' Huns got out of hand when the town was captured. But I suppose you know that. You can't tell me that you haven't some magical knowledge of the future."

"Maybe. Which side do you favor, Thomasus?"

"Me? Why—I haven't thought about it much, but I suppose I favor the Goths. These Italians haven't any more fight than a lot of rabbits, so the country can't be really independent. And if we have to be ruled by outsiders, the Goths have been a lot easier on us than Justinian's tax gatherers would be. Only my Orthodox friends can't be made to see it that way. Like my cousin, Antiochus, for instance. They become completely irrational when they get off on the subject of Arian heretics."

When Thomasus was ready to go, he asked Padway: "Is there anything I can bring you? I don't know what the guards will allow, but if there's something—"

Padway thought. "Yes," he said. "I'd like some painting equipment."

"Painting? You mean you're going to whitewash the Wall of Aurelian?"

"No; stuff for painting pictures. *You* know." Padway made motions.

"Oh, *that* kind of painting. Sure. It'll pass the time."

Padway wanted to get on top of the wall, to give the camp a proper looking-over for ways of escape. So when Thomasus brought his painting supplies he applied to the commander of the guards, a surly fellow named Hrotheigs, for permission. Hrotheigs took one look, and spoke one word: "*Ni!*"

Padway masked his annoyance and retired to ponder on How to Win Friends. He spent the better part of the day experimenting with his equipment, which was a bit puzzling to one unaccustomed to it. A fellow prisoner explained that you coated one of the thin boards with wax, painted in water color on this surface, and then warmed the board until the wax became soft enough to absorb the pigment. It was ticklish business; if you overheated the board, the wax melted and the colors ran.

Padway was not a professional artist by any means. But an archaeologist has to know something about drawing and painting in the exercise of his profession. So the next day Padway felt confident enough to ask Hrotheigs if he would like his portrait painted.

The Goth for the first time looked almost pleased. "*Could* you make a picture of me? I mean, one for me to keep?"

"Try to, excellent captain. I don't know how good it'll be. You may end up looking like Satanas with a gutache."

"Huh? Like whom? Oh, I see! Haw! Haw! Haw! You *are* a funny fellow."

So Padway painted a picture. As far as he could see, it looked as much like any black-bearded ruffian as it did like Hrotheigs. But the Goth was delighted, asserting that it was his spit and image. The second time he made no objections to Padway's climbing the wall to paint landscapes from the top, merely detailing a guard to keep close to him at all times.

Saying that he had to pick the best vantage point for painting, Padway walked up and down the wall the length of the camp. At the north end, where the wall turned east toward the Flaminian Gate, the ground outside sloped down for a few yards to a recess in the river bank—a small pool full of water lilies.

He was digesting this information when his attention was attracted to the camp. A couple of guards were bringing in a prisoner in rich Gothic clothes who was not co-operating. Padway recognized Thiudegiskel, the king's precious son. This was too interesting. Padway went down the ladder.

"*Hails,*" he said. "Hello."

Thiudegiskel was squatting disconsolately by himself. He was somewhat disheveled, and his face had been badly bruised. Both eyes would soon be swollen shut. The Roman patricians were grinning unsympathetically at him.

He looked up. "Oh, it's you," he said. Most of the arrogance seemed to have been let out of him, like air out of a punctured balloon.

"I didn't expect to run into you here," said Padway. "You look like you had a hard time of it."

"*Unh.*" Thiudegiskel moved his joints painfully. "A couple of those soldiers we had flogged for arresting us got hold of me." Surprisingly, he grinned, showing a broken front tooth. "Can't say I blame them much. That's one thing about me; I can always see the other fellow's point of view."

"What are you in for?"

"Hadn't you heard? I'm not the king's son any more. Or rather my old man isn't king. The convention deposed him and elected that fathead Wittigis. So Fathead has me locked up so I can't make trouble."

"*Tsk, tsk.* Too bad."

Thiudegiskel grinned painfully again. "Don't try to tell me *you're* sorry for me. I'm not that stupid. But say, maybe you can tell me what sort of treatment to expect, and whom to bribe, and so on."

Padway gave the young man a few pointers on getting on with the guards, then asked: "Where's Thiudahad now?"

"I don't know. The last I'd heard he'd gone up to Tivoli to get away from the heat. But he was supposed to come back down here this week. Some piece of literary research he's working on."

Between what Padway remembered of the history of the time and the information he had recently picked up, he had a good picture of the course of events. Thiudahad had been kicked out. The new king, Wittigis, would put up a loyal and determined resistance. The result would be worse than no resistance at all as far as Italy was concerned. He could not beat the Imperialists, having no brains to speak of. He would begin his campaign with the fatal mistake of marching off to Ravenna, leaving Rome with only its normal garrison.

Neither could the Imperialists beat him with their slender forces except by years of destructive campaigning. Anything, from Padway's point of view, was preferable to a long war. If the Imperialists did win, their conquest would prove ephemeral. Justinian should not be blamed too much; he would require supernatural foresight to foresee all this. That was the point: Padway *did* have such foresight. So wasn't it up to him to do something about it?

Padway had no violent prejudices in favor either of Gothic or of Imperial rule. Neither side had a political setup for which he could feel enthusiasm. Liberal capitalism and socialist democracy both had good points, but he did not think there was the remotest chance of establishing either one definitively in the sixth-century world.

If the Goths were lazy and ignorant, the Greeks were rapacious and venal. Yet these two were the best rulers available. The sixth-century Italian was too hopelessly unmilitary to stand on his own feet, and he was supinely aware of the fact.

On the whole the Gothic regime had not had an ill effect. The Goths enforced tolerance on a people whose idea of religious liberty was freedom to hang, drown, or burn all members of sects other than their own. And the Goths looked on the peninsula as a pleasant home to be protected and preserved. This was a more benign attitude than could be expected of a savage like the Meroving monarch, Theudebert of Austrasia, or an insatiable grafter like Justinian's quartermaster-general, John of Cappadocia.

Suppose, then, he decided to work for a quick victory by the Goths instead of a quick victory for the Imperialists. How could the Gothic regime be succored? It would do no good for him to try to persuade the Goths to get rid of Wittigis. If the Gothic king, whoever he was, could be induced to take Padway's advice, something might be done. But old Thiudahad, worthless as he was by himself, *might* be managed.

A plan began to form in Padway's mind. He wished he'd told Thomasus to hurry back sooner. To keep darkness from falling—

When Thomasus did appear, Padway told him: "I want a couple of pounds of sulphur, mixed with olive oil to form a paste, and some candles. And forty feet of light rope, strong enough to support a man. Believe it or not, I got the idea from the voluptuous Julia. Remember how she acted when I fumigated the house?"

"Look here, Martinus, you're perfectly safe for the time being, so why don't you stay here instead of trying some crazy scheme of escaping?"

"Oh, I have reasons. The convention should break up today or tomorrow, from what I hear, and I've got to get out before it does."

"Listen to him! Just listen! Here I am, the best friend he has in Rome, and does he pay attention to my advice? No! He wants to break out of the camp, and maybe get an arrow through the kidney for his pains, and then go get mixed up with Gothic politics. Did you ever hear the like? Martinus, you haven't some wild idea of getting yourself elected king of the Goths, have you? Because it won't work. You have to be—"

"I know," grinned Padway. "You have to be a Goth of the noble family of the Amalings. That's why I'm in such a hurry to get out. You want the business saved so you'll get your loans back, don't you?"

"But how on earth am I going to smuggle those things in? The guards watch pretty closely."

"Bring the sulphur paste in a container at the bottom of a food basket. If they open it, say it's something my physician ordered. Better coach Vekkos to corroborate. And for the rope—let's see—I know, go to my tailor and get a green cloak like mine. Have him fasten the rope inside around the edges, lightly, so it can be ripped out quickly. Then, when you come in, lay your cloak alongside mine, and pick mine up when you go."

"Martinus, that's a crazy plan. I'll get caught sure, and what will become of my family? No, you'd better do as I say. I can't risk innocent persons' futures. What time would you want me to come around with the rope and things?"

Padway sat on the Wall of Aurelian in the bright morning sunshine. He affected to be much interested in the Tomb of Hadrian down river on the other side. The guard who was detailed to him, one Aiulf, looked over his shoulder. Padway appreciated Aiulf's interest, but he sometimes wished the Goth's beard was less long and bristly. It was a disconcerting thing to have crawling over your shoulder, and down your shirt front when you were trying to get the color just right.

"You see," he explained in halting Gothic, "I hold the brush out and look past it at the thing I am painting, and mark its apparent length and height off on the brush with my thumb. That is how I keep everything in proper proportion."

"I see," said Aiulf in equally bad Latin—both were having a little language practice. "But suppose you want to paint a small picture—how would you say—with a lot of things in it just the same? The measurements on the brush would all be too large, would they not?" Aiulf, for a camp guard, was not at all stupid.

Padway's attention was actually on things other than the Tomb. He was covertly watching all the guards, and his little pile of belongings. All the prisoners did that, for obvious reasons. But Padway's interest was special. He was wondering when the candle concealed in the food basket would burn down to the sulphur paste. He had apparently had a lot of trouble that morning getting his brazier going; actually he had been setting up his little infernal machine. He also couldn't help stealing an occasional nervous glance at the soldiers across the river, and at the lily-covered pool behind him.

Aiulf grew tired of watching and retired a few steps. The guard sat down on his little stool, took up his flutelike instrument and started to play faint moaning notes. The thing sounded like a banshee lost in a rain barrel, and never failed to give Padway the slithering creeps. But he valued Aiulf's good will too much to protest.

He worked and worked, and still his contraption showed no signs of life. The candle must have gone out; it would surely have burned down to the sulphur by now. Or the sulphur had failed to light. It would soon be time for lunch. If they called him down off the wall, it would arouse suspicion for him to say he wasn't hungry. Perhaps.

Aiulf stopped his moaning for an instant. "What is the matter with your ear, Martinus? You keep rubbing it."

"Just an itch," replied Padway. He didn't say that fingering his ear lobe was a symptom of shrieking nervousness. He kept on painting. One result of his attempt, he thought, would be the lousiest picture of a tomb ever painted by an amateur artist.

As he gave up hope, his nerves steadied, The sulphur hadn't lit, and that was that. He'd try again tomorrow...

Below, in the camp, a prisoner coughed; then another. Then they were all coughing. Fragments of talk floated up: "What the devil—" "Must be the tanneries—" "Can't be, they're two or three miles from here—" "That's burning sulphur, by all the saints—" "Maybe the Devil is paying us a call—" People moved around; the coughing increased; the guards trailed into the camp. Somebody located the source of the fumes and kicked Padway's pile. Instantly a square yard was covered with yellow mush over which little blue flames danced. There were strangled shouts. A thin wisp of blue smoke crawled up through the still air. The guards on the wall, including Aiulf, hurried to the ladder and down.

Padway had planned his course so carefully in his mind that he went through it almost unconscious of the individual acts. Over his brazier were two little pots of molten wax, both already pigmented. He plunged his hands into the scalding stuff and smeared his face and beard with dark green wax. It hardened almost instantly. With his fingers he then smeared three large circles of yellow wax from the other pot over the green.

Then, as if he were just strolling, he walked up to the angle of the wall, squatted down out of sight of those in the camp, ripped the rope out of the lining of his cloak, and slipped a bight over a projection at the corner of the wall. A last glance across the river showed that the soldiers over there had not, apparently, noticed anything, though they could have heard the commotion inside the wall if they had listened. Padway lowered himself down the north face of the wall, hand over hand.

He flipped the rope down after him. As he did so, a flash of sunlight on his wrist made him curse silently. His watch would be ruined by prolonged soaking; he should have thought to give it to Thomasus. He saw a loose stone in the wall. He pulled it out, wrapped the watch in his handkerchief, put it in the hole, and replaced the stone. It took only a few seconds, but he knew he was being insanely foolish to risk the loss of time for the sake of the watch. On the other hand, being the kind of person he was, he just could not ruin the watch knowingly.

He trotted down the slope to the pond. He did not throw himself in, but walked carefully out to where it was a couple of feet deep. He sat down in the dark water, like a man getting into an over-hot tub bath, and stretched out on his back among the pond lilies until only his nose and eyes were above water. He moved the water plants around until they hid him pretty thoroughly. For the rest, he had to rely on the green of his cloak and his bizarre facial camouflage for concealment. He waited, listening, to his own heart and the murmur from over the wall.

He did not have long to wait. There were shouts, the blowing of whistles, the pounding of large Gothic feet on the top of the wall. The guards waved to the soldiers across the river. Padway didn't dare turn his head far enough to see, but he could imagine a rowboat's being put out.

"*Ailôe*! The fiend seems to have vanished into thin air—"

"He's hiding somewhere, you idiot! Search, search! Get the horses out!"

Padway lay still while guards searched around the base of the wall and poked swords into bushes barely big enough to hide a Sealyham. He lay still while a small fish maddeningly investigated his left ear. He lay still, his eyes almost closed, while a couple of Goths walked around the pond and stared hard at it and him, hardly thirty feet from them. He lay still while a Goth on a horse rode splashing through the pond, actually passing within fifteen feet of him. He lay still through the whole long afternoon, while the sounds of search and pursuit rose and ebbed, and finally faded away completely.

Nevitta Gummund's son was justifiably startled when a man rose from the shadows of the bushes that lined the driveway to his house and called him by name. He had just ridden up to the farm. Hermann, in tow as usual, had his sword halfway out before Martin Padway identified himself.

He explained: "I got here a couple of hours ago, and wanted to borrow a horse. Your people said you were away at the convention, but that you'd be back sometime tonight. So I've been waiting." He went on to tell briefly of his imprisonment and escape.

The Goth bellowed. "Ha! Ha! You mean to say, ha! ha! that you lay in the pond all day, right under the noses of the guards, with your face painted up like a damned flower? Ha! ha! Christ, that's the best thing I ever heard!" He dismounted. "Come on in the house and tell me more about it. *Whew*, you certainly look like a frog pond, old friend!" Later, he said more seriously: "I'd like to trust you, Martinus. By all accounts, you're a pretty reliable young man, in spite of your funny foreign ways. But how do I *know* that Liuderis wasn't right? There *is* something queer about you, you know. People say you can foresee the future, but try to hide the fact. And, some of those machines of yours do smell a little bit of magic."

"I'll tell you," said Padway thoughtfully. "I can see a little bit in the future. Don't blame me; I just happen to have that power. Satanas has nothing to do with it. That is, I can sometimes see what will happen *if* people are allowed to do what they intend to. If I use my knowledge to intervene, that changes the future, so my vision isn't true any more.

"In this case, I know that Wittigis will lose the war. And will lose in the worst possible way—at the end of years of fighting which will completely devastate Italy. Not his fault. He's simply built that way. The last thing I want is to see the country ruined; it would spoil a lot of plans I have. So I propose to intervene and change the natural course of events. The results may be better; they could hardly be worse."

Nevitta frowned. "You mean you're going to try to defeat the Goths quickly. I don't think I could agree to such—"

"No. I propose to win your war for you. If I can."

CHAPTER IX

Padway wasn't mistaken, and if Procopius' history had not lied, Thiudahad ought to pass along the Flaminian Way within the next twenty-four hours in his panicky flight to Vienna. All the way, Padway had asked people whether the king had passed that way. All said no.

Now, on the outskirts of Narnia, he was as far north as he dared go. The Flaminian Way forked at this point, and he had no way of knowing whether Thiudahad would take the new road or the old. So he and Hermann made themselves easy by the side of the road and listened to their horses cropping grass. Padway looked at his companion with a bilious eye. Hermann had taken much too much beer aboard at Ocriculum.

To Padway's questions and his instructions about taking turns at watching the road, he merely grinned idiotically and said, "*Ja, ja!*" He had finally gone to sleep in the middle of a sentence, and no amount of shaking would arouse him.

Padway walked up and down in the shade, listening to Hermann's snores and trying to think. He had not slept since the previous day, and here that whiskery slob was taking the ease that he, Padway, needed badly. Maybe he should have grabbed a couple of hours at Nevitta's—but if he'd once gotten to sleep nothing short of an earthquake would have gotten him up. His stomach was jumpy; he had no appetite; and this accursed sixth-century world didn't even have coffee to lighten the weights that dragged down the eyelids.

Suppose Thiudahad didn't show up? Or suppose he went roundabout, by the Salarian Way? Or suppose he'd already passed? Time after time he'd tensed himself as dust appeared down the road, only to have it materialize as a farmer driving an oxcart, or a trader slouching along on a mule, or a small half-naked boy driving goats.

Could his, Padway's, influence have changed Thiudahad's plans so that his course of action would be different from what it should have been? Padway saw his influence as a set of ripples spreading over a pool. By the mere fact of having known him, the lives of people like Thomasus and Fritharik had already been changed radically from what they would have been if he'd never appeared in Rome.

But Thiudahad had only seen him twice, and nothing very drastic had happened either time. Thiudahad's course in time and space might have been altered, but only very slightly. The other higher-up Goths, such as King Wittigis, ought not to have been affected at all. Some of them might have read his paper. But few of them were literary and many were plain illiterate.

Tancredi had been right about the fact that this was an entirely new branch of the tree of time, as he called it. The things that Padway had done so far, while only a fraction of what he hoped to do, couldn't help but change history somewhat. Yet he had not vanished into thin air, as he should have if this was the same history that had produced him in the year 1908 A.D.

He glanced at his wrist, and remembered that his watch was cached in the Wall of Aurelian. He hoped he'd get a chance to recover it some day, and that it would be in running order when he did.

That new bit of dust down the road was probably another damned cow or flock of sheep. No, it was a man on a horse. Probably some fat Narnian burgher. He was in a hurry, whoever he was. Padway's ears caught the blowing of a hard-ridden mount; then he recognized Thiudahad.

"Hermann!" he yelled.

"*Akhkhkhkhkhkhg,*" snored Hermann. Padway ran over and hit the Goth with his boot. Hermann said: "*Akhkhkhkhg. Akhkhkhkhg. Meina luibs— guhhg. Akhkhkhg.*"

Padway gave up; the ex-king would be up to them in an instant. He swung aboard his horse and trotted out into the road with his arm up. "*Hai,* Thiudahad! My lord!"

Thiudahad kicked his horse and hauled on the reins at the same time, apparently undecided whether to stop, try to run with Padway, or turn around the way he had come. The exhausted animal thereupon put his head down and bucked.

Waters of the Nar showed blue between Thiudahad and his horse for a second; he came down on the saddle with a thump and clutched it frantically. His face was white with terror and covered with dust.

Padway leaned over and gathered up the reins. "Calm yourself, my lord," he said.

"Who…who…what—Oh, it's the publisher. What's your name? Don't tell me; I know it. Why are you stopping—We've got to get to Ravenna…Ravenna—"

"Calm yourself. You'd never reach Ravenna alive."

"What do you mean? Are you out to murder me, too?"

"Not at all. But, as you may have heard, I have some small talent reading the future."

"Oh, dear, yes, I've heard. What's…what's my future? Don't tell me I'm going to be killed! *Please* don't tell me that, excellent Martinus. I don't want to die. If they'll just let me live I won't bother anybody again, ever." The little gray-bearded man fairly gibbered with fright.

"If you'll keep still for a few minutes, I'll tell you what I can. Do you remember when, for a consideration, you swindled a noble Goth out of a beautiful heiress who had been promised to him in marriage?"

"Oh, dear me. That would be Optaris Winithar's son, wouldn't it? Only don't say 'swindled,' excellent Martinus. Merely…ah…exerted my influence on the side of the man. But why?"

"Wittigis gave Optaris a commission to hunt you down and kill you. He's following you now, riding day and night. If you continue toward Ravenna, this Optaris will catch up with you before you get there, pull you off your horse, and cut your throat—like this, *khh!*" Padway clutched his own throat with one hand, tilted up his chin, and drew a finger across his Adam's apple.

Thiudahad covered his face with his hands. "What'll I do? What'll I do? If I could get to Ravenna, I have friends there—"

"That's what *you* think. I know better."

"But isn't there anything? I mean, is Optaris fated to kill me no matter what I do? Can't we hide?"

"Perhaps, My prophecy is good only if you try to carry out your original plan."

"Well, we'll hide, then."

"All right, just as soon as I get this fellow awake." Padway indicated Hermann.

"Why wait for him? Why not just leave him?"

"He works for a friend of mine. He was supposed to take care of me, but it's turned out the other way around." They dismounted, and Padway resumed his efforts to arouse Hermann.

Thiudahad sat down on the grass and moaned: "Such ingratitude! And

I was such a good king—"

"Sure," said Padway acidly, "except for breaking your oath to Amalaswentha not to interfere in public affairs, and then having her murdered—"

"But you don't understand, excellent Martinus. She had our noblest patriot, Count Tulum, murdered, along with those other two friends of her son Athalarik—"

"—and intervening—for a consideration, again—in the last Papal election; offering to sell Italy to Justinian in return for an estate near Constantinople and an annuity—"

"*What?* How did you know—I mean it's a lie!"

"I know lots of things. To continue: neglecting the defense of Italy; failing to relieve Naples—"

"Oh, dear me. You don't understand, I tell you. I hate all this military business. I admit I'm no soldier; I'm a scholar. So I leave it to my generals. That's only sensible, isn't it?"

"As events have proved—no."

"Oh, dear. Nobody understands me," moaned Thiudahad. "I'll tell you, Martinus, why I did nothing about Naples. I knew it was no use. I had gone to a Jewish magician, Jeconias of Naples, who has a great reputation for successful prophecy. Everybody knows the Jews are good at that. This man took thirty hogs, and put ten in each of three pens. One pen was labeled 'Goths,' one 'Italians,' and one 'Imperialists.' He starved them for some weeks. We found that all the 'Goths' had died; that the 'Italians' were some of them dead, and the rest had lost their hair; but the 'Imperialists' were doing fine. So we knew the Goths were bound to lose. In that case, why sacrifice a lot of brave boys' lives to no effect?"

"Bunk," said Padway. "My prophecies are as good as that fat faker's any day. Ask my friends. But any prophecy is good only as long as you follow your original plans. If you follow yours, you'll get your throat cut like one of your magical hogs. If you want to live, you'll do as I say and like it."

"What? Now, look here, Martinus, even if I'm not king anymore, I'm of noble birth, and I won't be dictated to—"

"Suit yourself." Padway rose and walked toward his horse. I'll ride down the road a way. When I meet Optaris, I'll tell him where to find you."

"*Eek!* Don't do that! I'll do what you say! I'll do anything, only don't let that awful man catch me!"

"All right. If you obey orders, I may even be able to get you back your kingship. But it'll be purely nominal this time, understand." Padway didn't miss the crafty gleam in Thiudahad's eyes. Then the eyes shifted past

Padway.

"Here he comes! It's the murderer, Optaris!" he squealed.

Padway spun around. Sure enough, a burly Goth was poking up the road toward them. This was a fine state of affairs, thought Padway. He'd wasted so much time talking that the pursuer had caught up with them. He should have had a few hours' leeway still; but there the man was. What to do; what to do?

He had no weapon but a knife designed for cutting steaks rather than human throats. Thiudahad had no sword, either.

Padway, brought up in a world of Thompson submachine-guns, swords seemed silly weapons, always catching you between the knees. So it had never occurred to him to form the habit of toting one. He realized his error as his eye caught one flash of Optaris' blade. The Goth leaned forward and kicked his horse straight at them.

Thiudahad stood rooted to the spot, trembling violently and making little meowing sounds of terror. He wet his dry lips and squealed one word over and over: "*Armaio!* Mercy!" Optaris grinned through his beard and swung his right arm up.

At the last instant Padway dived at the ex-king and tackled him, rolling him out of the way of Optaris' horse. He scrambled up as Optaris reined in furiously, the animal's hoofs kicking dust forward as they braked. Thiudahad got up, too, and bolted for the shelter of the trees. With a yell of rage Optaris jumped to the ground and took after him. Meantime, Padway had had a rush of brains to the head. He bent over Hermann, who was beginning to revive, tore Hermann's sword out of the scabbard, and sprinted to cut off Optaris. It wasn't necessary. Optaris saw him coming and started for him, evidently preferring to settle with Padway before the latter could take him in flank.

Now Padway cursed himself for all kinds of a fool. He had only the crudest theoretical knowledge of fencing, and no tactical experience whatever. The heavy Gothic broadsword was unfamiliar and uncomfortable in his sweaty hand. He could see the whites of Optaris' eyes as the Goth trotted up to him, took his measure, shifted his weight, and whipped his sword, arm up for a back-hand slash.

Padway's parry was more instinctive than designed. The blades met with a great clang, and Padway's borrowed sword went sailing away, end over end, into the woods. Quick as a flash Optaris struck again, but met only air and swung himself halfway around. If Padway was an incompetent fencer, there was nothing the matter with his legs. He sprinted after his sword, found it, and kept right on running with Optaris panting heavily after him. He'd been a minor quarter-mile star in college; if he could run the legs off Optaris maybe the odds would be nearer even when they finally—*umph!* He tripped over a root and sprawled on his face.

Somehow he rolled over and got to his feet before Optaris came up to him. And, somehow, he got himself between Optaris and a pair of big oaks that grew too close together to be squeezed between. So there was nothing for him to do but stand and take it. As the Goth chumped forward and swung his sword over his head, Padway, in a last despairing gesture, thrust as far as he could at Optaris' exposed chest, more with the idea of keeping the man off than of hurting him.

Now, Optaris was an able fighter. But the sword-play of his age was entirely with the edge. Nobody had ever worked a simple stop thrust on him. So it was no fault of his that in his effort to get within cutting distance of Padway he spitted himself neatly on the outthrust blade. His own slash faltered and ended against one of the oaks, The Goth gasped, tried to breathe, and his thick legs slowly sagged. He fell, pulling the sword out of his body. His hands clawed at the dirt, and a great river of blood ran from his mouth.

When Thiudahad and Hermann came up they found Padway vomiting quietly against a tree trunk. He barely heard their congratulations.

He was reacting to his first homicide with a combination of humane revulsion and buck fever. He was too sensible to blame himself much, but he was still no mere thoughtless adventurer to take a killing lightly. To save Thiudahad's worthless neck, he had killed one who was probably a better man, who had a legitimate grudge against the ex-king, and who had never harmed Padway. If he could only have talked to Optaris, or have wounded him slightly…But that was water over the dam; the man was as dead as one of John the Egyptian's customers. The living presented a more immediate problem.

He said to Thiudahad: "We'd better disguise you. If you're recognized, Wittigis will send another of your friends around to call. Better take that beard off first. It's too bad you already have your hair cut short, Roman style."

"Maybe," said Hermann, "could cut him off nose. Then nobody recognize."

"Oh!" cried Thiudahad, clutching the member indicated. "Oh, dear me! You wouldn't *really* disfigure me that way, most excellent, most noble Martinus?"

"Not if you behave yourself, my lord. And your clothes are entirely too fancy. Hermann, could I trust you to go into Narnia and buy an Italian peasant's Sunday-go-to-church outfit?"

"*Ja, ja,* you give me *silubr.* I go."

"What?" squeaked Thiudahad. "I will not get myself up in such an absurd costume! A prince of the Amalings has his dignity—"

Padway looked at him narrowly and felt the edge of Hermann's sword. He said silkily: "Then, my lord, you *do* prefer the loss of your nose? No? I thought not. Give Hermann a couple of solidi. We'll make a prosperous farmer of you. How are you on Umbrian dialect?"

CHAPTER X

L iuderis Oskar's son, commander of the garrison of the city of Rome, looked out of his office window gloomily at the gray September skies. The world had been turning upside down too often for this simple, loyal soul. First Thiudahad is deposed and Wittigis elected king. Then Wittigis, by some mysterious process, convinces himself and the other Gothic leaders that the way to deal with the redoubtable Belisarius is to run off to Ravenna, leaving an inadequate garrison in Rome. And now it transpires that the citizens are becoming dissatisfied; worse, that his troops are afraid to try to hold the city against the Greeks; worse yet, that Pope Silverius, blandly violating his oaths to Wittigis on the ground that the king is a heretic, has been corresponding with Belisarius with the object of arranging a bloodless surrender of the city.

But all these shocks were mild compared to that which he got when the two callers announced by his orderly turned out to be Martin Padway and ex-King Thiudahad, whom he recognized immediately despite his clean-shaven state. He simply sat, stared, and blew out his whiskers. "You!" he said. "You!"

"Yes, us," said Padway mildly. "You know Thiudahad, King of the Ostrogoths and Italians, I believe. And you know me. I'm the king's new quaestor, by the way." (That meant he was a combination of secretary, legal draftsman, and ghost writer.)

"But...but we have another king! You two are supposed to have prices on your heads or something."

"Oh, that," smiled Padway negligently. "The Royal Council was a little hasty in its action as we hope to show them in time. We'll explain—"

"But where have you been? And how did you escape from my camp? And what are you doing here?"

"One thing at a time, please, excellent Liuderis. First, we've been up at Florence collecting a few supplies for the campaign. Second—"

"What campaign?"

"—second, I have ways of getting out of camps denied to ordinary men. Third, we're here to lead your troops against the Greeks and destroy them."

"You are mad, both of you! I shall have you locked up until—"

"Now, now, wait until you hear us. Do you know of my…ah…little gifts for seeing the future results of men's actions?"

"Unh, I *have* heard things. But if you think you can seduce me away from my duty by some wild tale—"

"Exactly, my dear sir. The king will tell you how I foresaw Optaris' unfortunate attempt on his life, and how I used my knowledge to thwart Optaris' plans. If you insist, I can produce more evidence.

"For instance, I can tell you that you'll get no help from Ravenna. That Belisarius will march up the Latin Way in November. That the Pope will persuade your garrison to march away before they arrive. And that *you* will remain at your post, and be captured and sent to Constantinople."

Liuderis gasped. "Are you in league with Satanas? Or perhaps you are the Devil himself? I have not told a soul of my determination to stay if my garrison leaves, and yet you know of it."

Padway smiled. "No such luck, excellent Liuderis. Just an ordinary flesh-and-blood man who happens to have a few special gifts. Moreover, Wittigis will eventually lose his war, though only after years of destructive fighting. That is, all these things will happen unless you change your plans."

It took an hour of talk to wear Liuderis down to the point where he asked: "Well, what plans for operations against the Greeks did you have in mind?"

Padway replied: "We know they'll come by the Latin Way, so there's no point in leaving Terracina garrisoned. And we know about when they'll come. Counting the Terracina garrison, about how many men could you collect by the end of next month?"

Liuderis blew out his whiskers and thought. "If I called in the men from Formia—six thousand, perhaps seven. About half and half archers and lancers. That is, assuming that King Wittigis did not hear of it and interfere. But news travels slowly."

"If I could show you how you'd have a pretty good chance against the Greeks, would you lead them out?"

"I do not know. I should have to think. Perhaps. If as you say our king—excuse me, noble Thiudahad, I mean the *other* king—is bound to be defeated, it might be worth taking a chance on. What would you do?"

"Belisarius has about ten thousand men," replied Padway. "He'll leave two thousand to garrison Naples and other southern towns. He'll still out-number us a little. I notice that your brave Wittigis ran off when he had twenty thousand available."

Liuderis shrugged and looked embarrassed. "It is true, that was not a wise move. But he expects many thousands more from Gaul and Dalmatia."

"Have your men had any practice at night attacks?" asked Padway.

"Night attacks? You mean to assault the enemy at *night?* No. I never heard of such a proceeding. Battles are always fought in the daytime. A night attack does not sound very practical to me. How would you keep control of your men?"

"That's just the point. Nobody ever heard of the Goths making a night attack, so it ought to have some chance of success. But it'll require special training. First, you'll have to throw out patrols on the roads leading north, to turn back people who might carry the news to Ravenna. And I need a couple of good catapult engineers. I don't want to depend entirely on the books in the libraries for my artillery. If none of your troops knows anything about catapults, we ought to be able to dredge up a Roman or two who does. And you might appoint me to your staff—you don't have staffs? Then it's time you started—at a reasonable salary—"

Padway lay on a hilltop near Fregellae and watched the Imperialists through a telescope. He was surprised that Belisarius, as the foremost soldier in his age, hadn't thrown scouts out farther, but, then this was 536. His advance party consisted of a few hundred mounted Huns and Moors, who galloped about, pushing up side roads a few hundred yards and racing back. Then came two thousand of the famous *cataphracti* or cuirassiers, trotting in orderly formation. The low, cold sun glittered on the scales of their armor. Their standard was a blown-up leather serpent writhing from the top of a long pole, like a balloon from Macy's Thanksgiving Day parade.

These were the best and certainly the most versatile soldiers in the world, and everybody was afraid of them. Padway, watching their cloaks and scarves flutter behind them, didn't feel too confident himself. Then came three thousand Isaurian archers marching afoot, and finally two thousand more cuirassiers.

Liuderis, at Padway's elbow, said: "That is some sort of signal. *Ja*, I believe they are going to camp there. How did you know they would pick that spot, Martinus?"

"Simple. You remember that little device I had on the wheel of that wagon? That measures distance. I measured the distances along the road.

Knowing their normal day's march and the point they started from, the rest was easy."

"*Tsk, tsk,* wonderful. How do you think of all those things?" Liuderis' big, trustful eyes reminded Padway of those of a St. Bernard. "Shall I have the engineers set up Brunhilde now?"

"Not yet. When the sun sets we'll measure the distance to the camp."

"How will you do that without being seen?"

"I'll show you when the time comes. Meanwhile make sure that the boys keep quiet and out of sight."

Liuderis frowned. "They will not like having to eat a cold supper. If we do not watch them, somebody will surely start a fire."

Padway sighed. He'd had plenty of sad experience with the temperamental and undisciplined Goths. One minute they were as excited as small boys over the plans of Mysterious Martinus, as they called him; the next day they were growling on the edge of mutiny about the enforcement of some petty regulation. Since Padway felt that it wouldn't do for him to order them around directly, poor Liuderis had to take it.

The Byzantines set up their camp with orderly promptitude. Those, Padway thought, were real soldiers. You could accomplish something with men like that to command. It would be a long time before the Goths attained such a smooth perfection of movement. The Goths were still obsessed with childish, slam-bang ideas of warfare.

Witness the grumbling that had greeted Padway's requisition of a squad for engineers. Running catapults was a sassy job, inconsistent with knightly honor. And well-born lancers fight on foot like a lot or serfs? Perish the thought! Padway had seduced them away from their beloved horses by an ingenious method: He, or rather Liuderis at his suggestion, formed a company of pikemen, loudly announcing that only that the best men would be admitted, and that furthermore candidates would be made to *pay* for admission. Padway explained that there was no type of troop wherein morale and discipline were as vital as in heavy infantry, because one man flinching from a cavalry charge might break the line of spears and let the enemy in.

It was getting too dark for his telescope to be useful. He could make out the general's standard in front of a big tent. Perhaps Belisarius was one of those little figures around it. If he had a machine-gun—but he didn't have, and never would. You needed machines to make a machine-gun, and machines to make those machines, and so on. If he ever got a workable muzzle-loading musket he'd be doing well.

The standard no doubt bore the letters S. P. Q. R.—the Senate and the People of Rome. An army of Hunnish, Moorish, and Anatolian mercenaries, commanded by a Thracian Slav who worked for a Dalmatian autocrat who reigned in Constantinople and didn't even rule the city of Rome, called himself the Army of the Roman Republic and saw nothing funny in the act.

Padway got up, grunting at the weight of his shirt of scale mail. He wished a lot of things, such as that he'd had time to train some mounted archers. They were the only troops who could really deal on even terms with the deadly Byzantine cuirassiers. But he'd have to hope that darkness would nullify the Imperialists' advantage in missile fire.

He superintended the driving of a stake into the ground and paced off the base of a triangle. With a little geometry he figured the quarter-mile distance that was Brunhilde's range, and ordered the big catapult set up. The thing required eleven wagon-loads of lumber, even though it was not of record size. Padway hovered around his engineers nervously, jumping and hissing reprimands when somebody dropped a piece of wood,

Snatches of song came from the camp. Apparently Padway's scheme of leaving a wagon-load of brandy where foragers would be sure to find it had had results, despite Belisarius' well-known strictness with drunken soldiers.

The bags of sulphur paste were brought out. Padway looked at his watch, which he had recovered from the hole in the wall. It was nearly midnight, though he'd have sworn the job hadn't taken over an hour.

"All ready?" he asked. "Light the first bag." The oil-soaked rags were lit. The bag was placed in the sling. Padway himself pulled the lanyard. *Wht-bam!* said Brunhilde. The bag did a fiery parabola. Padway raced up the little knoll that masked his position. He missed seeing the bag land in the camp. But the drunken songs ended, instead there was a growing buzz as of a nest of irritated hornets. Behind him whips cracked and ropes creaked in the dark, as the horses heaved on the block-and-tackle he'd rigged up for quick recocking. *Wht-bam!* The fuse came out of the second bag in midair, so that it continued its course to the camp unseen and harmless. Never mind, another would follow in a few seconds. Another did. The buzz was louder, and broken by clear, high-pitched commands. *Wht-bam!*

"Liuderis!" Padway called. "Give your signal!"

Over in the camp the horse lines began to scream. The horses didn't like the sulphur dioxide. Good; maybe the Imperialist cavalry would be immobilized. Under the other noises Padway heard the clank and shuffle of the Goths, getting under way. Something in the camp was burning brightly. Its light showed a company of Goths on Padway's right picking their way over the broken, weed-covered ground. Their big round shields were painted white for recognition, and every man had a wet rag tied over his nose. Padway thought they ought to be able to frighten the Imperialists if they couldn't do anything else. On all sides the night was alive with the little orange twinkle of firelight on helmets, scale skirts, and sword blades.

As the Goths closed in, the noise increased tenfold, with the addition of organized battle yells, the flat snap of bowstrings, and finally the blacksmith's symphony of metal on metal. Padway could see "his" men, black against the fires, grow smaller and then drop out of sight into the camp ditch. Then there was only a confused blur of movement and a great din as the attackers scrambled up the other side—invisible until they popped up into the firelight again—and mixed it with the defenders.

One of the engineers called to say that that was all the sulphur bags, and what should they do now? "Stand by for further orders," replied Padway.

"But, captain, can't we go fight? We're missing all the fun!"

"*Ni*, you can't! You're the only engineer corps west of the Adriatic that's worth a damn, and I won't have you getting yourselves killed off!"

"Huh!" said a voice in the dark. "This is a cowardly way of doing, standing back here. Let's go, boys. To hell with Mysterious Martinus!" And before Padway could do anything, the twenty-odd catapult men trotted off toward the fires.

Padway angrily called for his horse and rode off to find Liuderis. The commander was sitting his horse in front of a solid mass of lancers. The firelight picked out their helms and faces and shoulders, and the forest of vertical lances. They looked like something out of a Wagnerian opera.

Padway asked: "Has there been any sign of a sortie yet?"

"No."

"There will be, if I know Belisarius. Who's going to lead this troop?"

"I am."

"Oh, lord! I thought I explained why the commander should—"

"I know, Martinus," said Liuderis firmly. "You have lots of ideas. But you're young. I'm an old soldier, you know. Honor requires that I lead my men. Look, isn't something doing in the camp?"

True enough, the Imperial cavalry was coming out. Belisarius had, despite his difficulties, managed to collect a body of manageable horses and cuirassiers to ride them. As they watched, this group thundered out the main gate, the Gothic infantry scattering in all directions before them. Liuderis shouted, and the mass of Gothic knights clattered off, picking up speed as they went. Padway saw the Imperialists swing widely to take the attacking foe in the rear, and then Liuderis' men hid them. He heard the crash as the forces met, and then everything was dark confusion for a few minutes.

Little by little the noise died. Padway wondered just what had happened. He felt silly, sitting alone on his horse a quarter mile from all the action. Theoretically, he was where the staff, the reserves, and the artillery ought to be. But there were no reserves, their one catapult stood deserted off in the dark somewhere, and the artillerists and staff were exchanging sword strokes with the Imperialists up front.

With a few mental disparagements of sixth-century ideas of warfare, Padway trotted toward the camp. He came across a Goth quite peacefully tying up his shin with a piece torn from his tunic, another who clutched his stomach and moaned, and a corpse. Then he found a considerable body of dismounted Imperial cuirassiers standing weaponless.

"What are you doing?" he asked.

One replied: "We're prisoners. There were some Goths supposed to be guarding us, but they were angry at missing the looting, so they went off to the camp."

"What became of Belisarius?"

"Here he is." The prisoner indicated a man sitting on the ground with his head in his hands. "A Goth hit him on the head and stunned him. He's just coming to. Do you know what will be done with us, noble sir?"

"Nothing very drastic, I imagine. You fellows wait here until I send somebody for you." Padway rode on toward the camp. Soldiers were strange people, he thought. With Belisarius to lead them and a fair chance to use their famous bow-plus-lance tactics, the *cataphracti* could lick thrice their number of any other troops. Now, because their leader had been conked on the head, they were as meek as lambs.

There were more corpses and wounded near the camp, and a few riderless horses calmly grazing. In the camp itself were Imperial soldiers, Isaurians and Moors and Huns, standing around in little clumps, holding bits of clothing to their noses against the reek of sulphur fumes. Goths ran hither and thither among them looking for movable property worth stealing.

Padway dismounted and asked a couple of the looters where Liuderis was. They said they didn't know, and went on about their business. He found an officer he knew, Gaina by name. Gaina was squatting by a corpse and weeping. He turned a streaked, bearded face up to Padway.

"Liuderis is dead," he said between sobs. "He was killed in the mêlée when we struck the Greek cavalry."

"Who's that?" Padway indicated the corpse.

"My younger brother."

"I'm sorry. But won't you come with me and get things organized? There are a hundred cuirassiers out there with nobody guarding them. If they come to their senses they'll make a break—"

"No, I will stay with my little brother. You go on, Martinus. You can take care of things." Gaina dissolved in fresh tears.

Padway hunted until he found another officer, Gudareths, who seemed to have some sort of wits about him. At least, he was making frantic efforts to round up a few troopers to guard the surrendered Imperialists. The minute he turned his back on his men, they melted off into the general confusion of the camp.

Padway grabbed him. "Forget them," he snapped. "Liuderis is dead, I hear, but Belisarius is alive. If we don't nab him—"

So they took a handful of Goths in tow and walked back to where the Imperial general still sat among his men. They moved the lesser prisoners away, and set several men to guard Belisarius. Then they put a solid hour rounding up troopers and prisoners and getting them into some sort of order.

Gudareths, a small, cheerful man, talked continually: "That was some charge, some charge. Never saw a better, even in the battle against the Gepids on the Danube. We took them in flank, neatest thing you ever saw. The Greek general fought like a wild man, until I hit him over the head. Broke my sword, it did. Best stroke I ever made, by God. Even harder than the time I cut off that Bulgarian Hun's head, five years ago. Oh, yes, I've killed hundreds of enemies in my time. Thousands, even. I'm sorry for the poor devils. I'm not really a bloodthirsty fellow, but they will try to stand up against me. Say, where were you during the charge?" He looked sharply at Padway, like an accusatory chipmunk.

"I was supposed to be running the artillery. But my men ran off to join the fight. And by the time I arrived it was all over."

"*Aiw*, no doubt, no doubt. Like one time when I was in a battle with the Burgunds. My orders kept me out of the thick until it was nearly over. Of course, when I arrived I must have killed at least twenty—"

The train of troops and prisoners headed north on the Latin Way. Padway, still a little bewildered to find himself in command of the Gothic army, simply by virtue of having taken over Liuderis' responsibilities on the night of confusion, rode near the front. The best are always the first to go, he thought sadly, remembering the simple, honest old Santa Claus who lay dead in one of the wagons in the rear, and thinking of the mean and treacherous little king whom he had to manage when he got back to Rome.

Belisarius, jogging along beside him, was even less cheerful. The Imperial general was a surprisingly young man, in his middle thirties, tall and a bit stout, with gray eyes and curly brown beard. His Slavic ancestry showed in his wide cheek bones.

He said gravely: "Excellent Martinus, I ought to thank you for the consideration you showed my wife. You went out of your way to make her comfortable on this sad journey."

"Quite all right, illustrious Belisarius. Maybe you'll capture me some day."

"That seems hardly likely, after this fiasco. By the way, if I may ask, just what are you? I hear you called Mysterious Martinus! You're no Goth, nor yet an Italian, by your speech."

Padway gave his impressively vague formula about America.

"Really? They must be a people skilled in war, these Americans. I knew when the fight started that I wasn't dealing with any barbarian commander. The timing was much too good, especially on that cavalry charge. *Phew!* I can still smell that damnable sulphur!"

Padway saw no point in explaining that his previous military experience consisted of one year of R.O.T.C. in a Chicago high school. He asked: "How would you like the idea of coming over to our side? We need a good general, and as Thiudahad's quaestor I'll have my hands full otherwise."

Belisarius frowned. "No, I swore an oath to Justinian."

"So you did. But as you'll probably hear, I can sometimes see a little into the future. And I can tell you that the more faithful you are to Justinian, the meaner and more ungrateful he'll be to you. He'll—"

"I said no!" said Belisarius sternly. "You can do what you like with me. But the word of Belisarius is not to be questioned."

Padway argued some more. But, remembering his Procopius, he had little hope of shaking the Thracian's stern rectitude. Belisarius was a fine fellow, but his rigid virtue made him a slightly uncomfortable companion. He asked: "Where's your secretary, Procopius of Caesarea?"

"I don't know. He was in southern Italy, and supposedly on his way to join us."

"Good. We'll gather him in. We shall need a competent historian."

Belisarius' eyes widened. "How do you know about the histories he's collecting notes for? I thought he'd told nobody but me."

"Oh, I have ways. That's why they call me Mysterious Martinus."

They marched into Rome by the Latin Gate, north past the Circus Maximus and the Colosseum, and up the Quirinal Valley to the Old Viminal Gate and the Pretorian Camp.

Here Padway gave orders to encamp the prisoners, and told Gudareths to set a guard over them. That was obvious enough. Then he found himself in the midst of a crowd of officers looking at him expectantly. He could not think what orders to give next.

He rubbed his ear lobe for a few seconds, then took the captive Belisarius aside, "Say, illustrious general," he said in a low voice, "what in hell do I do next? This military business isn't my proper trade."

There was a hint of amusement in Belisarius' broad and usually solemn face. He answered: "Call out your paymaster and have him pay the men's wages. Better give them a little bonus for winning the battle. Detail an officer to round up some physicians to tend the wounded; at least I don't suppose a barbarian army like this has its own medical corps. There ought to be a man whose duty it is to check the rolls. Find out about it. I hear the commander of the Rome garrison was killed. Appoint a man in his place, and have the garrison returned to barracks. Tell the commanders of the other contingents to find what lodging they can for their men. If they are to board at private houses, say the owners will be compensated at standard rates. You can find those out later. But you ought to make a speech."

"*Me* make a speech?" hissed Padway in horror. "My Gothic is lousy—"

"That's part of the business, you know. Tell them what good soldiers they are. Make it short. They won't listen very closely anyway."

CHAPTER XI

After some searching Padway located Thiudahad in the Arian Library. The little man was barricaded behind a huge load of books. Four bodyguards sprawled on a table, a bench, and the floor, snoring thunderously. The librarian was glaring at them with a look compounded of hydrofluoric acid and cobra venom, but did not dare protest.

Thiudahad looked up blearily. "Oh, yes, it's the publisher fellow. Martinus, isn't it?"

"That's right, my lord. I might add that I'm your new quaestor."

"What? What? Who told you so?"

"You did. You appointed me."

"Oh, dear me, so I did. Silly of me. When I get engrossed in books I really don't know what's going on. Let's see, you and Liuderis were going to fight the Imperialists, weren't you?"

"*Hoc ille*, my lord. It's all over."

"Really? I suppose you sold out to Belisarius, didn't you? I hope you arranged for an estate and an annuity from Justinian for me."

"It wasn't necessary, my lord. We won."

"*What?*"

Padway gave a résumé of the last three days' events. "And you'd better get to bed early tonight, my lord. We're leaving in the morning for Florence."

"Florence? Why, in heaven's name?"

"We're on our way to intercept your generals, Asinar and Grippas. They're coming back from Dalmatia, having been ordered out by the Imperial general, Constantianus. If we can catch them before they get to Ravenna and learn about Wittigis, we might be able to get your crown back."

Thiudahad sighed. "Yes, I suppose we ought to. But how did you know that Asinar and Grippas were coming home?"

"Trade secret, my lord. I've also sent a force of two thousand to reoccupy Naples. It's held by General Herodianus with a mere three hundred, so there shouldn't be much trouble."

Thiudahad narrowed his watery eyes. "You do get things done, Martinus. If you can deliver that vile usurper Wittigis into my hands—*aaah!* I'll send clear to Constantinople for a torturer, if I can't find one ingenious enough in Italy!"

Padway did not answer that one, having his own plans for Wittigis. He said instead: "I have a pleasant surprise for you. The pay chests of the Imperial army—"

"Yes?" Thiudahad's eyes gleamed. "They're mine, of course. Very considerate of you, excellent Martinus."

"Well, I did have to dip into them a little to pay our troops and clear up the army's bills. But you'll find the rest an agreeable addition to the royal purse. I'll be waiting for you at home."

Padway neglected to state that he had sequestered over half the remainder and deposited the money with Thomasus. Who owns the pay chests of a captured army, especially when the captor is a volunteer theoretically serving one of two rival kings, was a question that the legal science of the time was hardly equipped to decide. In any event Padway was sure he could make better use of the money than Thiudahad. I'm becoming quite a hardened criminal, he thought with pride.

Padway rode up to Cornelius Anicius' home. Its rhetorical owner was out at the baths, but Dorothea came out. Padway had to admit that it made him feel pretty good to sit on a powerful horse in a (to him) romantic get-up, with cloak and boots and all, and report to one of the prettier girls of Rome on his success.

She said: "You know, Martinus, father was silly at first about your social standing. But after all you've done he's forgotten about that. Of course he is not enthusiastic about Gothic rule. But he much prefers Thiudahad, who *is* a scholar, to that savage Wittigis."

"I'm glad of that. I like your old man."

"Everybody's talking about you now. They call you 'Mysterious Martinus.'"

"I know. Absurd, isn't it?"

"Yes. You never seemed very mysterious to me, in spite of your foreign background."

"That's great. You're not afraid of me, are you?"

"Not in the least. If you made a deal with Satanas as some people hint,

I'm sure the Devil got the worst of it." They laughed. She added: "It's nearly dinner time. Won't you stay? Father will be back any time."

"I'm sorry, but I can't possibly. We're off to the wars again tomorrow."

As he rode off, he thought: If I *should change* my mind about the expediency of marriage, I'd know where to begin. She's attractive and pleasant, and has what passes for a good education here...

Padway made one more attempt to shake Belisarius, but without success. He did, however, enlist five hundred of the Imperial cuirassiers as a personal guard. His share of the Imperialist loot would suffice to pay them for some weeks. After that he'd see.

The trip to Florence was anything but pleasant. It rained most of the way, with intermittent snow squalls as they climbed toward the City of Flowers. Being in a hurry, Padway took only cavalry.

In Florence he sent his officers around to buy warmer clothes for the troops, and looked in on his business. It seemed to be surviving, though Fritharik said: "I don't trust any of them, excellent boss. I'm sure the foreman and this George Menandrus have been stealing, though I can't prove it. I don't understand all this writing and figuring. If you leave them alone long enough they'll steal everything, and then where'll we be? Out in the cold, headed for a pair of nameless graves."

"We'll see," said Padway. He called in the treasurer, Proclus Proclus, and asked to see the books. Proclus Proclus instantly looked apprehensive, but he got the books. Padway waded into the figures. They were all nice and neat, since he himself had taught the treasurer double-entry bookkeeping. All his employees were astounded to hear Padway burst into a shout of laughter.

"What...what is it, noble sir?" asked Proclus Proclus.

"Why, you poor fool, didn't you realize that with my system of bookkeeping, your little thefts would stick up in the accounts like a sore toe? Look here: thirty solidi last month, and nine solidi and some sesterces only last week. You might just as well have left a signed receipt every time you stole something!"

"What...what are you going to do to me?"

"Well—I *ought* to have you jailed and flogged." Padway was silent for a while and watched Proclus Proclus squirm. "But I hate to have your family suffer. And I certainly oughtn't to keep you on, after this. But I'm pretty busy, and I can't take the time to train a new treasurer to keep books in a civilized manner. So I'll just take a third of your salary until these little *borrowings* of yours are paid back."

"Thank you, thank you kindly, sir. But just to be fair—George Menandrus ought to pay a share of it, too. He—"

"Liar!" shouted the editor.

"Liar yourself! Look, I can prove it. Here's an item for one solidus, November 10th. And on November 11th George shows up with a pair of new shoes and a bracelet. I know where he bought them. On the 15th—"

"How about it, George?" asked Padway.

Menandrus finally confessed, though he insisted that the thefts were merely temporary borrowings to tide him over until pay day.

Padway divided the total liability between the two of them. He warned them sternly against recidivism. Then he left a set of plans with the foreman for new machines and metal-working processes, including plans for a machine for spinning copper plate into bowls. The intelligent Nerva caught on immediately.

As Padway was leaving, Fritharik asked him: "Can't I go with you, excellent Martinus? It's very dull here in Florence. And you need somebody to take care of you. I've saved up almost enough to get my jeweled sword back, and if you'll let—"

"No, old man. I'm sorry, but I've got to have *one* person I can trust here. When this damned war and politics is over, we'll see."

Fritharik sighed gustily. "Oh, very well, if you insist. But I hate to think of your going around unprotected with all these treacherous Greeks and Italians and Goths. You'll end in an unmarked grave yet, I fear."

They shivered and skidded over the icy Apennines to Bologna. Padway resolved to have his men's horses shod if he could ever get a few days to spare—stirrups had been invented but not horseshoes. From Bologna to Padua—still largely in ruins from its destruction by Attila's Huns—the road was no longer the splendid stone-paved affair they had been traveling on, but a track in the mud. However, the weather turned almost springlike, which was something.

At Padua they found they had missed the Dalmatian force by one day. Thiudahad wanted to halt. "Martinus," he whined, "you've dragged my old bones all over northern Italy, and nearly frozen me to death. That's not considerate. You do owe your king some consideration, don't you?"

Padway repressed his irritation with some effort. "My lord, *do* you or *don't* you want your crown back?"

So poor Thiudahad had to go along. By hard riding they caught up with the Dalmatian army halfway to Atria. They heaved past thousands and thousands of Goths, afoot and horsemen. There must have been well over fifty thousand of them. All these big, tough-looking men had skedaddled at the mere thought that Count Constantianus was approaching.

The count had had only a small force, but Padway was the only one present who knew that, and his source of information was not strictly kosher. The Goths cheered Thiudahad and Padway's Gothic lancers, and stared and muttered at the five hundred cuirassiers. Padway had made his guard don Gothic helmets and Italian military cloaks in lieu of the spiked steel helmets and burnoose-like mantels they had worn. But still their lean chins, tight pants, and high yellow boots made them sufficiently different to arouse suspicion.

Padway found the two commanders up near the head of the column. Asinar was tall and Grippas was short, but otherwise both were just a couple of middle-aged and bewhiskered barbarians. They respectfully saluted Thiudahad, who seemed to move slightly from so much latent force. Thiudahad introduced Padway as his new prefect—no, he meant his new quaestor.

Asinar said to Padway: "In Padua we heard a rumor that war and usurpation had been going on in Italy. Just what is the news, anyway?"

Padway was for once thankful that his telegraph hadn't been operating that far north. He laughed scornfully. "Oh, our lord General Wittigis got a brainstorm a couple of weeks ago. He put himself up in Ravenna, where the Greeks couldn't kill him, and had himself proclaimed king. We've cleaned up the Greeks, and are on our way to settle with Wittigis now. These boys will be a help." All of which was rather unjust to Wittigis.

Padway wondered whether there'd be anything left of his character after a few years in this mendacious atmosphere. The two Gothic generals accepted his statement without comment. Padway decided quickly that neither of them could be called very bright.

They marched into Ravenna at noon the day after next. The mists were so thick about the northern causeway that a man had to precede the leading horsemen on foot to keep them from spattering off into the marsh.

There was some alarm in Ravenna when the force appeared in the fog. Padway and Thiudahad prudently kept quiet as Asinar and Grippas identified themselves. As a result, most of the huge force was in the city before somebody noticed the little gray man with Padway. Immediately there were shouts and runnings to and fro.

Presently a Goth in a rich red cloak ran out to the head of the column. He shouted: "What the devil's going on here? Have you captured Thiudahad, or is it the other way around?"

Asinar and Grippas sat on their horses and said: "Uh…well…that is—"

Padway spurred up front and asked: "Who are you, my dear sir?"

"If it's any of your business, I'm Unilas Wiljarith's son, general of our lord Wittigis, King of the Goths and Italians. Now who are *you?*"

Padway grinned and replied smoothly: "I'm delighted to know you, General Unilas. I'm Martin Paduei, quaestor to old lord Thiudahad, King of the Goths and Italians. Now that we know each other—"

"But, you fool, there isn't any King Thiudahad! He was deposed! We've got a new king! Or hadn't you heard about it?"

"Oh, I've heard lots of things. But, my excellent Unilas, before you make any more rude remarks, consider that we—that is to say King Thiudahad—have over sixty thousand troops in Ravenna, whereas you have about twelve thousand. You don't want any unnecessary unpleasantness, do you?"

"Why, you impudent...you...uh...did you say *sixty* thousand?"

"Maybe seventy; I haven't counted them."

"Oh. That's different."

"I thought you'd see it that way."

"What are you going to do?"

"Well, if you can tell where *General* Wittigis is, I thought we might pay him a call."

"He's getting married today. I think he ought to be on his way to St. Vitalis' Church about now."

"You mean he hasn't married Mathaswentha yet?"

"No. There was some delay in getting his divorce."

"Quick, how do you get to St. Vitalis' Church?"

Padway hadn't hoped to be in time to interfere with Wittigis' attempt to engraft himself on the Amal family tree by his forcible marriage of the late Queen Amalaswentha's daughter. But this was too good an opportunity to let slip.

Unilas pointed out a dome flanked by two towers. Padway shouted to his guard and kicked his horse into a canter. The five hundred men galloped after, spattering unfortunate pedestrians with mud. They thundered across a bridge over one of Ravenna's canals, the stench from which fully lived up to its reputation, and up to the door of St. Vitalis' Church.

There were a score of guards at the door, through which organ music wafted faintly. The guards brought their spears up to "poise."

Padway reined in and turned to the commander of his guard, a Macedonian named Achilleus. "Cover them," he snapped.

There was a quick, concerted movement among the cuirassiers, who had been sorting themselves into a semicircle in front of the church door. The next instant the guards were looking at a hundred stiff Byzantine bows drawn to the cheek. "*Nu*," said Padway in Gothic, "if you boys will put your stickers down and your hands up, we have an appointment—oh, that's better. Much better." He slid off his horse. "Achilleus, give me a troop. Then surround the church, and keep those in in and those out out until I finish with Wittigis."

He marched into St. Vitalis' Church with a hundred cuirassiers at his heels. The organ music died with a wail, and people turned to look at him. It took his eyes a few seconds to become accustomed to the gloom.

In the center of the huge octagon was a pickle-faced Arian bishop, and three people stood before him. One was a big man in a long, rich robe, with a crown on his dark graying hair: King Wittigis. Another was a tallish girl with a strawberries-and-cream complexion and her hair in thick golden braids: the princess Mathaswentha. The third was an ordinary Gothic soldier, somewhat cleaned up, who stood beside the bride and held her arm behind her back. The audience was a handful of Gothic nobles and their ladies.

Padway walked very purposefully down the aisle, *thump, thump, thump.* People squirmed and rustled in their seats and murmured: "The Greeks! The Greeks are in Ravenna!"

The bishop spoke up: "Young man, what is the meaning of this intrusion?"

"You'll soon learn, my lord bishop. Since when has the Arian faith countenanced the taking of a woman to wife against her will?"

"What's that? Who is being taken against her will? What business is this wedding of yours? Who are you, who dares interrupt—"

Padway laughed his most irritating laugh. "One question at a time, please. I'm Martinus Paduei, quaestor to King Thiudahad. Ravenna is in our hands, and prudent persons will comport themselves accordingly. As for the wedding, it isn't normally necessary to assign a man to twist the bride's arm to make sure she gives the right answers. You don't want to marry this man, do you, my lady?"

Mathaswentha jerked her arm away from the soldier, who had been relaxing his grip. She made a fist and punched him in the nose with enough force to rock his head back on its hinges. Then she swung at Wittigis, who dodged back. "You beast!" she cried. "I'll claw your eyes—"

The bishop grabbed her arm. "Calm yourself, my daughter! Please! In the house of God—"

King Wittigis had been blinking at Padway, gradually soaking in the news. Mathaswentha's attack shocked him out of his lethargy. He growled: "You're trying to tell me that the miserable pen pusher, Thiudahad, has taken the town? *My* town?"

"That, my lord, is the general idea. I fear you'll have to give up your idea of becoming an Amaling and ruling the Goths. But we'll—"

Wittigis' face had been turning darker and darker red. Now he burst into a shocking roar. "You swine!" he yelled. "You think I'll hand over my crown and bride peaceably? By Jesus, I'll see you in the hottest hell first!" As he spoke he whipped out his sword and ran heavily at Padway, his gold-embroidered robe flapping.

Padway was not entirely taken by surprise. He got his own sword out and parried Wittigis' terrific downward cut easily enough, though the force of the blow almost disarmed him. Then he found himself chest to chest with the Goth, hugging the barrel torso and chewing Wittigis' pepper-and-salt beard. He tried to shout to his men, but it was like trying to talk with a mouth full of shredded wheat.

He spat out, it seemed, half a bale of the stuff. "Grab...*gffth*...*pffth*... grab him, boys! Don't hurt him!"

That was easier said than done. Wittigis struggled like a captive gorilla, even when five men were hanging onto him, and he bellowed and foamed all the while. The Gothic gentlemen were standing up, some with hands on their sword hilts, but in a hopeless minority, none seemed anxious to die for his king just then. Wittigis began to sob between roars.

"Tie him up until he cools off," said Padway unfeelingly. "My lord bishop, may I trouble you for pen and paper?"

The bishop looked bleakly at Padway, and called a sexton, who led Padway to a room off the vestibule. Here he sat down and wrote:

Martinus Paduei to Thomasus the Syrian. Greetings:

My dear Thomasus: I am sending you with this letter the person of Wittigis, former King of the Goths and Italians. His escort has orders to deliver him to your house secretly, so forgive me for any alarm they cause you if they get you out of bed.

As I remember, we have a telegraph tower under construction on the Flaminian Way near Helvillum. Please arrange to have a chamber constructed in the earth underneath this tower and fitted up as an apartment forthwith. Incarcerate Wittigis therein with an adequate guard. Have him made as comfortable as possible, as I judge him a man of moody temperament, and I do not wish him to harm himself.

The utmost secrecy is to be observed at all times. That should not be too difficult, as this tower is in a wild stretch of country. It would be advisable to have Wittigis delivered to the tower by guards other than those who take him to Rome, and to have him guarded by men who speak neither Latin nor Gothic. They shall release their prisoner only on my order, delivered either in person or via the telegraph, or without orders in the event of my imprisonment or death.

With best regards,

Martinus Paduei.

Padway said to Wittigis: "I'm sorry to have to treat you so roughly, my lord. I would not have interfered if I hadn't known it was necessary to save Italy."

Wittigis had relapsed into morose taciturnity. He glared silently.

Padway continued: "I'm really doing you a favor, you know. If Thiudahad got hold of you, you would die—slowly."

There was still no reply.

"Oh, well, take him away boys. Wrap him up so the people won't recognize him, and use the back streets."

Thiudahad peered moistly at Padway. "Marvelous, marvelous, my dear Martinus. The Royal Council accepted the inevitable. The only trouble is that the evil usurper had my crown altered to fit his big head; I'll have to alter it back. Now I can devote my time to some real scholarly research. Let's see—there was something else I wanted to ask you. Oh, yes, what did you do with Wittigis?"

Padway put on a benign smile. "He's out of your reach, my lord king."

"You mean you killed him? Now, that's too bad! Most inconsiderate of you, Martinus. I told you I'd promised myself a nice long session with him in the torture chambers—"

"No, he's alive. Very much so."

"What? What? Then produce him, at once!"

Padway shook his head. "He's where you'll never find him. You see, I figured it would be foolish to waste a good spare king. If anything happened to you, I might need one in a hurry."

"You're insubordinate, young man! I won't stand for it! You'll do as your king orders you, or else—"

Padway grinned, shaking his head. "No, my lord. Nobody shall hurt Wittigis. And you'd better not get rough with me, either. His guards have orders to release him if anything happens to me. He doesn't like you any better than you like him. You can figure the rest out for yourself."

"You devil!" spat the king venomously. "Why, oh, why did I ever let you save my life? I haven't had a moment's peace since. You might have a little consideration for an old man," he whined. "Let's see, what was I talking about?"

"Perhaps," said Padway, "about the new book we're going to get out in our joint names. It has a perfectly splendid theory, about the mutual attraction of masses. Accounts for the movements of the heavenly bodies, and all sorts of things. It's called the law of gravitation."

"Really? Now, that's most interesting, Martinus, most interesting. It would spread my fame as a philosopher to the ends of the earth, wouldn't it?"

Padway asked Unilas if Wittigis' nephew Urias was in Ravenna. Unilas said yes, and sent a man to hunt him up.

Urias was big and dark like his uncle. He arrived scowling defiance. "Well, Mysterious Martinus, now that you've overthrown my uncle by trickery, what are you going to do with me?"

"Not a thing," said Padway. "Unless you force me to."

"Aren't you having a purge of my uncle's family?"

"No. I'm not even purging your uncle. In strict confidence, I'm hiding Wittigis to keep Thiudahad from harming him."

"Really? Can I believe that?"

"Sure. I'll even get a letter from him, testifying to the good treatment he's getting."

"Letters can be produced by torture."

"Not with Wittigis. For all your uncle's faults, I think you will agree that he's a stubborn chap."

Urias relaxed visibly. "That's something. Yes, if that's true, perhaps you have some decency, after all."

"Now to get down to business. How do you feel about working for us—that is, nominally for Thiudahad but actually for me?"

Urias stiffened. "Out of the question. I'm resigning my commission, of course. I won't take any action disloyal to my uncle."

"I'm sorry to hear that. I need a good man to command the reoccupation of Dalmatia."

Urias shook his head stubbornly. "It's a question of loyalty. I've never gone back on my plighted word yet."

Padway sighed. "You're as bad as Belisarius. The few trustworthy and able men in the world won't work with me because of previous obligations. So I have to struggle along with crooks and dimwits."

Darkness seemed to want to fall by mere inertia—

CHAPTER XII

Little by little Ravenna's nonce population flowed away, like trickles of water from a wet sponge on a tile floor. A big trickle flowed north, as fifty thousand Goths marched back toward Dalmatia. Padway prayed that Asinar, who seemed to have little more glimmering of intelligence than Grippas, would not have another brainstorm and come rushing back to Italy before he'd accomplished anything.

Padway did not dare leave Italy long enough to take command of the campaign himself. He did what he could by sending some of his personal guard along to teach the Goths horse-archery tactics. Asinar might decide to ignore this newfangled nonsense as soon as he was out of sight. Or the cuirassiers might desert to Count Constantianus. Or—but there was no point in anticipating calamities.

Padway finally found time to pay his respects to Mathaswentha. He told himself that he was merely being polite and making a useful contact. But he knew that actually he didn't want to leave Ravenna without another look at the luscious wench.

The Gothic princess received him graciously. She spoke excellent Latin, in a rich contralto vibrant with good health. "I thank you, excellent Martinus, for saving me from that beast. I shall never be able to repay you properly."

They walked into her living room. Padway found that it was no effort at all to keep in step with her. But then; she was almost as tall as he was.

"It was very little, my lady," he said. "We just happened to arrive at an opportune time."

"Don't deprecate yourself, Martinus. I know a lot about you. It takes a real man to accomplish all you have. Especially when one considers that you arrived in Italy, a stranger, only a little over a year ago."

"I do what I must, princess. It may seem impressive to others, but to me it's more as if I had been forced into each action by circumstances, regardless of my intentions."

"A fatalistic doctrine, Martinus. I could almost believe that you're a pagan. Not that I'd mind."

Padway laughed. "Hardly. I understand that you can still find pagans if you hunt around the Italian hills."

"No doubt. I should like to visit some of the little villages some day. With a good guide, of course."

"I ought to be a pretty good guide, after the amount of running around I've done in the last couple of months."

"Would you take me? Be careful; I'll hold you to it, you know."

"That doesn't worry me any, princess. But it would have to be some day. At the present rate, God knows when I'll get time for anything but war and politics, neither of which is my proper trade."

"What is, then?"

"I was a gatherer of facts; a kind of historian of periods that had no history. I suppose you could call me a historical philosopher."

"You're a fascinating person, Martinus. I can see why they call you Mysterious. But if you don't like war and politics, why do you engage in them?"

"That would be hard to explain, my lady. In the course of my work in my own country, I had occasion to study the rise and fall of many civilizations. In looking around me here, I see many symptoms of a fall."

"Really? That's a strange thing to say. Of course, my own people, and barbarians like the Franks, have occupied most of the Western Empire. But they're not a danger to civilization. They protect it from the real wild men like the Bulgarian Huns and the Slavs. I can't think of a time when our western culture was more secure."

"You're entitled to your opinion, my lady," said Padway. "I merely put together such facts as I have, and draw what conclusions I can. Facts such as the decline in the population of Italy, despite the Gothic immigrations. And such things as the volume of shipping."

"Shipping? I never thought of measuring civilization *that* way. But in any event, that doesn't answer my question."

"*Triggws,* to use one of your own Gothic words. Well, I want to prevent the darkness of barbarism from falling over western Europe. It sounds conceited, the idea that one man could do anything like that. But I can try. One of the weaknesses of our present set-up is slow communication. So I promote the telegraph company. And because my backers are Roman patricians suspected of Graecophile leanings, I find myself in politics up to my neck. One thing leads to another, until today I'm practically running Italy."

Mathaswentha looked thoughtful. "I suppose the trouble with slow communication is that a general can revolt or an invader overrun the border weeks before the central government hears about it."

"Right. I can see you're your mother's daughter. If I wanted to patronize you, I should say that you had a man's mind."

She smiled. "On the contrary, I should be very much pleased. At least, if you mean a man like yourself. Most of the men around here—*bah!* Squalling infants, without one idea among them. When I marry, it must be to a man—shall we say both of thought and action?"

Padway met her eyes, and was aware that his heart had stepped up several beats per minute. "I hope you find him, princess."

"I may yet." She sat up straight and looked at him directly, almost defiantly, quite unconcerned with the inner confusion she was causing him. He noticed that sitting up straight didn't make her look any less desirable. On the contrary.

She continued: "That's one reason I'm so grateful to you for saving me from the beast. Of all these thick-headed ninnies he had the thickest head. What became of him, by the way? Don't pretend innocence, Martinus. Everybody knows your guards took him into the vestibule of the church, and then he apparently vanished."

"He's safe, I hope, both from our point of view and his."

"You mean you hid him? Death would have been safer yet."

"I had reasons for not wanting him killed."

"You did? I give you fair warning that if he ever falls into my hands, I shall not have such reasons."

"Aren't you a bit hard on poor old Wittigis? He was merely trying, in his own muddle-headed way, to defend the kingdom."

"Perhaps. But after that performance in the church I hate him." The gray eyes were cold as ice. "And when I hate, I don't do it halfway."

"So I see," said Padway dryly, jarred out of the pink fog for the moment. But then Mathaswentha smiled again, all curvesome and desirable woman. "You'll stay to dinner, of course? There will only be a few people, and they'll leave early."

"Why—" There were piles of work to be done that evening. And he needed to catch up on his sleep—a chronic condition with him. "Thank you, my lady, I shall be delighted."

By the third visit to Mathaswentha, Padway was saying to himself: There's a real woman. Ravishing good looks, forceful character, keen brain. The man who gets her will have one in a million. Why shouldn't I be the one? She seems to like me. With her to back me up, there's nothing I couldn't accomplish. Of course, she *is* a bit bloodthirsty. You wouldn't exactly describe her as a "sweet" girl. But that's the fault of the times, not of her. She'll settle down when she has a man of her own to do her fighting for her.

In other words, Padway was as thoroughly in love as such a rational and prudent man can ever be.

But how did one go about marrying a Gothic princess? You certainly didn't take her out in an automobile and kiss her lipstick off by way of a starter. Nor did you begin by knowing her in high school, the way he had known Betty. She was an orphan, so you couldn't approach her old man.

He supposed that the only thing to do was to bring the subject up a little at a time and see how she reacted.

He asked: "Mathaswentha, my dear, when you spoke of the kind of man you'd like to marry, did you have any other specifications in mind?"

She smiled at him, whereat the room swam slightly. "Curious, Martinus? I didn't have many, aside from those I mentioned. Of course he shouldn't be *too* much older than I, as Wittigis was."

"You wouldn't mind if he wasn't much taller than you?"

"No, unless he were a mere shrimp."

"You haven't any objections to large noses?"

She laughed a rich, throaty laugh. "Martinus, you *are* the funniest man. I suppose it's that you and I are different. I go directly for what I want, whether it's love, or revenge, or anything else."

"What do I do?"

"You walk all around it, and peer at it from every angle, and spend a week figuring out whether you want it badly enough to risk taking it." She added quickly. "Don't think I mind. I like you for it."

"I'm glad of that. But about noses—"

"Of *course* I don't mind! I think yours, for instance, is aristocratic-looking. Nor do I mind little red beards or wavy brown hair or any of the other features of an amazing young man named Martinus Paduei. That's what you were getting at, wasn't it?"

Padway knew a great relief. This marvelous woman went out of her way to ease your difficulties! "As a matter of fact it was, princess."

"You needn't be so frightfully respectful, Martinus. Anybody would know you are a foreigner, the way you meticulously use all the proper titles and epithets."

Padway grinned. "I don't like to take chances, as you know. Well, you see, now, it's this way. I—uh—was wondering—uh—if you don't dislike these—uh—characteristics, whether you couldn't learn to—uh—uh—"

"You don't by any chance mean love, do you?"

"Yes!" said Padway loudly.

"With practice I might."

"*Whew!*" said Padway mopping his forehead.

"I'd need teaching," said Mathaswentha, "I've lived a sheltered life, and know little of the world."

"I looked up the law," said Padway quickly, "and while there's an ordinance against marriage of Goths to Italians, there's nothing about Americans. So—"

Mathaswentha interrupted: "I could hear you better, dear Martinus, if you came closer."

Padway went over and sat down beside her. He began again: "The Edicts of Theoderik—"

She said softly: "I know the laws, Martinus. That is not what I need instruction in."

Padway suppressed his tendency to talk frantically of impersonal matters to cover emotional turmoil. He said, "My love, your first lesson will be this." He kissed her hand.

Her eyes were half closed, her mouth slightly open, and her breath was quick and shallow. She whispered: "Do the Americans, then, practice the art of kissing as we do?"

He gathered her in and applied the second lesson.

Mathaswentha opened her eyes, blinked, and shook her head. "That was a foolish question, my dear Martinus. The Americans are way ahead of us. What ideas you put in an innocent girl's head!" She laughed joyfully. Padway laughed too.

Padway said: "You've made me very happy, princess."

"You've made me happy, too, my prince. I thought I should never find anyone like you." She swayed into his arms again.

Mathaswentha sat up and straightened her hair. She said in a brisk, businesslike manner: "There are a lot of questions to settle before we decide anything finally. Wittigis, for instance."

"What about him?" Padway's happiness suddenly wasn't quite so complete.

"He'll have to be killed, naturally."

"Oh?"

"Don't 'oh' me, my dear. I warned you that I am no halfhearted hater. And Thiudahad, too."

"Why him?"

She straightened up, frowning. "He murdered my mother, didn't he? What more reason do you want? And eventually you will want to become king yourself—"

"No, I won't," said Padway.

"Not want to be king? Why, Martinus!"

"Not for me, my dear. Anyhow, I'm not an Amaling."

"As my husband you will be considered one."

"I still don't want—"

"Now, darling, you just *think* you don't. You will change your mind. While we are about it, there is that former serving-wench of yours, Julia I think her name is—"

"What about—what do you know about her?"

"Enough. We women hear everything sooner or later."

The little cold spot in Padway's stomach spread and spread. "But—but—"

"Now, Martinus, it's a small favor that your betrothed is asking. And don't think that a person like me would be jealous of a mere house-servant. But it would be a humiliation to me if she were living after our marriage. It needn't be a painful death—some quick poison..."

Padway's face was as blank as that of a renting agent at the mention of cockroaches. His mind was whirling. There seemed to be no end to Mathaswentha's lethal little plans. His underwear was damp with cold sweat.

He knew now that he was not in the least in love with Mathaswentha. Let some roaring Goth have this fierce blond Valkyr! He preferred a girl with less direct ideas of getting what she wanted. And no insurance man would give a policy on a member of the Amal clan, considering their dark and bloody past.

"Well?" said Mathaswentha.

"I was thinking," replied Padway. He did not say that he was thinking, frantically, how to get out of this fix.

"I just remembered," he said slowly, "I have a wife back in America."

"Oh. This is a fine time to think of *that*," she answered coldly.

"I haven't seen her for a long time."

"Well, then, there's a divorce, isn't there?"

"Not in my religion. We congregationalists believe there's a special compartment in hell for frying divorced persons."

"Martinus!" Her eyes were a pair of gray blow-torches. "You're afraid. You're trying to back out. No man shall ever do that to me and live to tell—"

"No, no, not at all!" cried Padway. "Nothing of the sort, my dear! I'd wade through rivers of blood to reach your side."

"*Hmmm.* A very pretty speech, Martinus Paduei. Do you use it on all the girls?"

"I mean it. I'm mad about you."

"Then why don't you act as if—"

"I'm devoted to you. It was stupid of me not to think of this obstacle sooner."

"Do you really love me?" She softened a little.

"Of course I do! I've never known anyone like you." The last sentence was truthful. "But facts are facts."

Mathaswentha rubbed her forehead, obviously struggling with conflicting emotions. She asked: "If you haven't seen her for so long, how do you know she's alive?"

"I don't. But I don't know that she isn't. You know how strict your laws are about bigamy. Edicts of Athalarik, Paragraph Six, I looked it up."

"You would," she said with some bitterness. "Does anyone else in Italy know about this American bitch of yours?"

"N-no—but—"

"Then aren't you being a bit silly, Martinus? What difference does it make, if she's on the other side of the earth?"

"Religion."

"Oh, the devil fly away with the priests! I'll handle the Arians when we're in power. For the Catholics, you have influence with the Bishop of Bologna, I hear, and that means with the Pope."

"I don't mean the churches. I mean my personal convictions."

"A practical fellow like you? Nonsense. You're using them as an excuse—"

Padway, seeing the fires about to flare up again, interrupted: "Now, Mathaswentha, you don't want to start a religious argument, do you? You let my creed alone and I'll say nothing against yours. Oh, I just thought of a solution."

"What?"

"I'll send a messenger to America to find out whether my wife is still alive."

"How long will that take?"

"Weeks. Months, perhaps. If you really love me you won't mind waiting."

"I'd wait," she said without enthusiasm. She looked up sharply. "Suppose your messenger finds the woman alive?"

"We'll worry about that when the time comes."

"Oh, no, we won't. We'll settle this now."

"Look, darling, don't you trust your future husband? Then—"

"Don't evade, Martinus. You're as slippery as a Byzantine lawyer."

"In that case, I suppose I'd take a chance on my immortal—"

"Oh, but, Martinus!" she cried cheerfully. "How stupid of me not to see the answer before! You shall instruct your messenger, if he finds her alive, to poison her! Such things can always be managed discreetly."

"That *is* an idea."

"It's the obvious idea! I'd prefer it to a mere divorce anyway, for the sake of my good name. Now all our worries are over." She hugged him with disconcerting violence.

"I suppose they are," said Padway with an utter lack of conviction. "Let's continue our lessons, dearest." He kissed her again, trying for a record this time.

She smiled up at him and sighed happily. "You shall never kiss anyone else, my love."

"I wouldn't think of it, princess."

"You'd better not," she said. "You will forgive me, dear boy, for getting a little upset just now. I am but an innocent young girl, with no knowledge of the world and no will of her own."

At least, thought Padway, he was not the only liar present. He stood up and pulled her to her feet. "I must go now. I'll send the messenger off the first thing. And tomorrow I leave for Rome."

"Oh, Martinus! You surely don't have to go. You just *think* you do—"

"No, really. State business, you know. I'll think of you all the way." He kissed her again. "Be brave, my dear. Smile, now."

She smiled a trifle tearfully and squeezed the breath out of him.

When Padway got back to his quarters, he hauled his orderly, an Armenian cuirassier, out of bed. "Put on your right boot," he ordered.

The man rubbed his eyes. "My *right* boot? Do I understand you, noble sir?"

"You do. Quickly, now." When the yellow rawhide boot was on, Padway turned his back to the orderly and bent over. He said over his shoulder, "You will give me a swift kick in the fundament, my good Tirdat."

Tirdat's mouth fell open. "*Kick my commander?*"

"You heard me the first time. Go ahead. Now."

Tirdat shuffled uneasily, but at Padway's glare he finally hauled off and let fly. The kick almost sent Padway sprawling. He straightened up, rubbing the spot. "Thank you, Tirdat. You may go back to bed." He started for the wash bowl to brush his teeth with a willow twig. (Must start the manufacture of real toothbrushes one of these days, he thought.) He felt much better.

But Padway did not get off to Rome the next day, or even the day after that. He began to learn that the position of king's quaestor was not just a nice well-paying job that let you order people around and do as you pleased. First Wakkis Thurumund's son, a Gothic noble of the Royal Council, came around with a rough draft of a proposed amendment to the law against horse stealing.

He explained: "Wittigis agreed to this revision of the law, but the counter-revolution took place before he had a chance to change it. So, excellent Martinus, it's up to you to discuss the matter with Thiudahad, put the amendment in proper legal language, and *try* to hold the king's attention long enough to get his signature." Wakkis grinned. "And may the saints help you if he's in a stubborn mood, my lad!"

Padway wondered what the devil to do; then he dug up Cassiodorus, who as head of the Italian Civil Service ought to know the ropes. The old scholar proved a great help, though Padway saw fit to edit some of the unnecessarily flowery phrases of the prefect's draft.

He asked Urias around for lunch. Urias came and was friendly enough, though still somewhat bitter about the treatment of his uncle Wittigis. Padway liked him. He thought, I can't hold out on Mathaswentha indefinitely. And I shan't dare take up with another girl while she looks on me as a suitor. But this fellow is big and good-looking, and he seems intelligent. If I could engineer a match—

He asked Urias whether he was married. Urias raised eyebrows. "No. Why?"

"I just wondered. What do you intend to do with yourself now?"

"I don't know. Go rusticate on my land in Picenum, I suppose. It'll be a dull life, after the soldiering I've been doing the past few years."

Padway asked casually: "Have you ever met the Princess Mathaswentha?"

"Not formally. I arrived in Ravenna only a few days ago for the wedding. I saw her in the church, of course, when you barged in. She's attractive, isn't she?"

"Quite so. She's a person worth knowing. If you like, I'll try to arrange a meeting."

Padway, as soon as Urias had gone, rushed around to Mathaswentha's house. He contrived to make his arrival look as unpremeditated as possible. He started to explain: "I've been delayed, my dear. I may not get off to Rome *ubb*—" Mathaswentha had slid her arms around his neck and stopped his little speech in the most effective manner. Padway didn't dare seem tepid, but that wasn't at all difficult. The only trouble was that it made coherent thought impossible at a time when he wanted all his craft. And the passionate wench seemed satisfied to stand in the vestibule and kiss him all afternoon.

She finally said: "Now, what were you saying, my dearest?"

Padway finished his statement. "So I thought I'd drop in for a moment." He laughed. "It's just as well I'm going to Rome; I shall never get any work done as long as I'm in the city with you. Do you know Wittigis' nephew Urias by the way?"

"No. And I'm not sure I want to. When we kill Wittigis, we shall naturally have to consider killing his nephews, too. I have a silly prejudice against murdering people I know socially."

"Oh, my dear, I think that's a mistake. He's a splendid young man; you'd really like him. He's one Goth with both brains and character; probably the only one."

"Well, I don't know—"

"And I need him in my business, only he's got scruples against working for me. I thought maybe you could work your flashing smile on him, to soften him up a bit."

"If you think I could really help you, perhaps—"

Thus the Gothic princess had Padway and Urias for company at dinner that night. Mathaswentha was pretty cool to Urias at first. But they drank a good deal of wine, and she unbent. Urias was good company. Presently they were all laughing uproariously at his imitation of a drunken Hun, and at Padway's hastily translated off-color stories. Padway taught the other two a Greek popular song that Tirdat, his orderly, had brought from Constantinople. If Padway hadn't been conscious of a small gnawing anxiety for the success of his various plots, he'd have said he was having the best time of his life.

CHAPTER XIII

Back in Rome, Padway went to see his captive Imperial generals. They were comfortably housed and seemed well enough pleased with their situation, though Belisarius was moody and abstracted. Enforced inactivity didn't sit well with the former commander-in-chief.

Padway asked him: "As you can learn easily enough, we shall soon have a powerful state here. Have you changed your mind about joining us?"

"No, my lord quaestor, I have not. An oath is an oath."

"Have you ever broken an oath in your life?"

"Not to my knowledge."

"If for any reason you should swear an oath to me, I suppose, you'd consider yourself as firmly bound by it as by the others, wouldn't you?"

"Naturally. But that's a ridiculous supposition."

"Perhaps. How would it be if I offered you parole and transportation back to Constantinople, on condition that you would never again bear arms against the kingdom of the Goths and Italians?"

"You're a crafty and resourceful man, Martinus. I thank you for the offer, but I couldn't square it with my oath to Justinian. Therefore I must decline."

Padway repeated his offer to the other generals. Constantianus, Perianus, and Bessas accepted at once. Padway's reasoning was as follows: These three were just fair-to-middling commanders. Justinian could get plenty more of this kind, so there was not much point in keeping them. Of course they'd violate their oaths as soon as they were out of his reach. But Belisarius was a real military genius; he mustn't be allowed to fight against the kingdom again. Either he'd have to come over, or give his parole—which he alone would keep—or be kept in detention.

On the other hand, Justinian's clever but slightly warped mind was unreasonably jealous of Belisarius' success and his somewhat stuffy virtue. When he learned that Belisarius had stayed behind in Rome rather than give a parole that he'd be expected to break, the emperor *might* be sufficiently annoyed to do something interesting.

Padway wrote:

King Thiudahad to the Emperor Justinian, Greetings.

Your serene highness: We send you with this letter the persons of your generals Constantianus, Perianus, and Bessas, under parole not to bear arms against us again. A similar parole was offered your general Belisarius, but he declined to accept it on grounds of his personal honor.

As continuation of this war seems unlikely to achieve any constructive result, we take the opportunity of stating the terms that we should consider reasonable for the establishment of enduring peace between us.

1. Imperial troops shall evacuate Sicily and Dalmatia forthwith.

2. An indemnity of one hundred thousand solidi in gold shall be paid us for damages done by your invading armies.

3. We shall agree never again to make war, one upon the other, without mutual consultation in advance. Details can be settled in due course.

4. We shall agree not to assist any third parties, by men, money, or munitions, which hereafter shall make war upon either of us.

5. We shall agree upon a commercial treaty to facilitate the exchange of goods between our respective realms.

This is of course a very rough outline, details of which would have to be settled by conference between our representatives. We think you will agree that these terms, or others very similar in intent, are the least that we could reasonably ask under the circumstances.

We shall anticipate the gracious favor of a reply at your serenity's earliest convenience.

by

Martinus Paduei, Quaestor.

When he saw who his visitor was, Thomasus got up with a grunt and waddled toward him, good eye sparkling and hand outstretched. "Martinus! It's good to see you again. How does it feel to be important?"

"Wearisome," said Padway, shaking hands vigorously. "What's the news?"

"News? News? Listen to that! He's been making most of the news in

Italy for the past two months, and he wants to know what the news is!"

"I mean about our little bird in a cage."

"Huh? Oh, you mean"—Thomasus looked around cautiously—"ex-King Wittigis? He was doing fine at last reports, though nobody's been able to get a civil word out of him. Listen, Martinus, of all the lousy tricks I ever heard of, springing the job of hiding him on me without warning was the worst. I'm sure God agrees with me, too. Those soldiers dragged me out of bed, and then I had them and their prisoner around the house for several days."

"I'm sorry, Thomasus. But you were the only man in Rome I felt I could trust absolutely."

"Oh, well, if you put it that way. But Wittigis was the worst grouch I ever saw. Nothing suited him."

"How's the telegraph company coming?"

"That's another thing. The Naples line is working regularly. But the lines to Ravenna and Florence won't be finished for a month, and until they are there's no chance of a profit. *And* the minority stockholders have discovered that they're a minority. You should have heard them howl! They're after your blood. At first Count Honorius was with them. He threatened to jail Vardan and Ebenezer and me if we didn't sell him—give him, practically—a controlling interest. But we learned he needed money worse than he needed the stock, and bought his from him. So the other patricians have to be satisfied with snubbing us when they pass us in the street."

"I'm going to start another paper as soon as I get time," said Padway. "There'll be two, one in Rome and one in Florence."

"Why one in Florence?"

"That's where our new capital's going to be."

"*What?*"

"Yes. It's better located than Rome with regard to roads and such, and it has a much better climate than Ravenna. In fact I can't think of a place that *hasn't* a better climate than Ravenna, hell included. I sold the idea to Cassiodorus, and between us we got Thiudahad to agree to move the administrative offices thither. If Thiudahad wants to hold court in the City of Fogs, Bogs and Frogs, that's his lookout. I'll be just as glad not to have him in my hair."

"In your hair? Oh, ho-ho-ho, you *are the* funniest fellow, Martinus. I wish I could say things the way you do. But all this activity takes my breath away. What else of revolutionary nature are you planning?"

"I'm going to try to start a school. We have a flock of teachers on the public payroll now, but all they know is grammar and rhetoric. I'm going to have things taught that really matter: mathematics, and the sciences, and medicine. I see where I shall have to write all the textbooks myself."

"Just one question, Martinus. When do you find time to sleep?"

Padway grinned wanly. "Mostly I don't. But if I can ever get out of all this political and military activity I hope to catch up. I don't really like it, but it's a necessary means to an end. The end is things like the telegraph and the presses. My politicking and soldiering may not make any difference a hundred years from now, but the other things will, I hope."

Padway started to go, then said: "Is Julia from Apulia still working for Ebenezer the Jew?"

"The last I heard she was. Why? Do you want her back?"

"God forbid. She's got to disappear from Rome."

"Why?"

"For her own safety. I can't tell you about it yet."

"But I thought you disliked her—"

"That doesn't mean I want her murdered. And my own hide may be in danger, too, unless we get her out of town."

"Oh, God, why didst Thou let me get involved with a politician? I don't know, Martinus; she's a free citizen..."

"How about your cousin in Naples, Antiochus? I'd made it worth his while to hire her at higher wages."

"Well, I—"

"Have her go to work for Antiochus under another name. Fix it up quietly, old man. If the news leaks out, we'll all be in the soup."

"Soup? Ha, ha. Very funny. I'll do what I can. Now, about that old six-month note of yours..."

Oh, dear, thought Padway, now it would begin again, Thomasus was easy enough to get on with most of the time. But he could not or would not conduct the simplest financial transactions without three hours of frantic haggling. Perhaps he enjoyed it. Padway did not.

Jogging along the road to Florence again, Padway regretted that he had not seen Dorothea while he was in Rome. He had not dared. That was one more reason for getting Mathaswentha married off quickly. Dorothea would be a much more suitable if less spectacular girl for *him*. Not that he was in love with her. But he probably would be if he saw enough of her, he thought somewhat cold-bloodedly.

But he had too much else to do now. If he could only get time to relax, to catch up on his sleep, to investigate the things that really interested him, to have a little fun! He liked fun as much as the next man, even if the next man would consider his ideas of fun peculiar.

But his sharp, conscientious mind goaded him on. He knew that his job rested on the unstable foundation of his influence over a senile, unpopular king. As long as Padway pleased them the Goths would not interfere, as they were accustomed to leaving civil administration in the hands of non-Goths. But when Thiudahad went? Padway had lots of hay to gather, and there were plenty of thunderheads sticking up over the barn.

In Florence Padway leased office space in the name of the government, and looked in on his own business. This time there were no irregularities in the accounts. Either there had been no more stealing, or the boys were getting cleverer at concealing it.

Fritharik renewed his plea to be allowed to come along, showing with much pride his jeweled sword, which he had redeemed and had sent up from Rome. The sword disappointed Padway, though he did not say so. The gems were merely polished, not cut; faceting had not been invented. But wearing it seemed to add inches to Fritharik's already imposing stature. Padway, somewhat against his better judgment, gave in. He appointed the competent and apparently honest Nerva his general manager.

They were snowed in by a late storm for two days crossing the mountains, and arrived in Ravenna still shivering. The town with its clammy atmosphere and its currents of intrigue depressed him, and the Mathaswentha problem made him nervous. He called on her and made some insincere love to her, which made him all the more anxious to get away. But there was lots of public business to be handled.

Urias announced that he was ready and willing to enter Padway's service. "Mathaswentha talked me into it," he said. "She's a wonderful woman, isn't she?"

"Certainly is," replied Padway. He thought he detected a faintly guilty and furtive air about the straightforward Urias when he spoke of the princess. He smiled to himself. "What I had in mind was setting up a regular military school for the Gothic officers, somewhat on the Byzantine model, with you in charge."

"What? Oh, my word, I hoped you'd have a command on the frontiers for me."

So, thought Padway, he wasn't the only one who disliked Ravenna. "No, my dear sir. This job has to be done for the sake of the kingdom. And I can't do it myself, because the Goths don't think any non-Goth knows anything about soldiering. On the other hand I need a literate and intelligent man to run the thing, and you're the only one in sight."

"But, most excellent Martinus, have you ever tried to teach a Gothic officer anything? I admit that an academy is needed, but—"

"I know. I know. Most of them can't read or write and look down on those who do. That's why I picked *you* for the job. You're respected, and if anybody can put sense into their heads you can." He grinned sympathetically. "I wouldn't have tried so hard to enlist your services if I'd had just an easy, everyday job in mind."

"Thanks. I see you know how to get people to do things for you."

Padway went on to tell Urias some of his ideas. How the Goths' great weakness was the lack of co-ordination between their mounted lancers and their foot archers; how they needed both reliable foot spearmen and mounted archers to have a well-rounded force. He also described the crossbow, the calthorp, and other military devices.

He said: "It takes five years to make a good long-bowman, whereas a recruit can learn to handle a crossbow in a few weeks.

"And if I can get some good steel workers, I'll show you a suit of plate armor that weighs only half as much as one of those scale-mail shirts, but gives better protection and allows fully as much freedom of action." He grinned. "You may expect grumbling at all these newfangled ideas from the more conservative Goths. So you'd better introduce them gradually. And remember, they're your ideas; I won't try to deprive you of the credit for them."

"I understand," grinned Urias. "So if anybody gets hanged for them, it'll be me and not you. Like that book on astronomy that came out in Thiudahad's name. It has every churchman from here to Persia sizzling. Poor old Thiudahad gets the blame, but I know you furnished the ideas and put him up to it. Very well, my mysterious friend, I'm game."

Padway himself was surprised when Urias appeared with a very respectable crossbow a few days later. Although the device was simple enough, and he'd furnished an adequate set of drawings for it, he knew from sad experience that to get a sixth-century artisan to make something he'd never seen before, you had to stand over him while he botched six attempts, and then make it yourself.

They spent an afternoon in the great pine wood east of the city shooting at marks. Fritharik proved uncannily accurate, though he affected to despise missile weapons as unworthy of a noble Vandal knight. "But," he said, "it is a remarkably easy thing to aim."

"Yes," replied Padway. "Among my people there's a legend about a crossbowman who offended a government official, and was compelled as punishment to shoot an apple off his son's head. He did so, without harming the boy."

When he got back, Padway learned that he had an appointment the next day with an envoy from the Franks. The envoy, one Count Hlodovik, was a tall, lantern-jawed man. Like most Franks he was clean-shaven except for the mustache. He was quite gorgeous in a red silk tunic, gold chains and bracelets, and a jeweled baldric. Padway privately thought that the knobby bare legs below his short pants detracted from his impressiveness. Moreover, Hlodovik was rather obviously suffering from a hangover.

"Mother of God, I'm thirsty," he said. "Will you please do something about that, friend quaestor, before we discuss business?" So Padway had some wine sent in. Hlodovik drank in deep gulps, "Ah! That's better. Now, friend quaestor, I may say that I don't think I've been very well treated here. The king would only see me for a wink of the eye; said you handle the business. Is that the proper reception for the envoy of King Theudebert, King Hildebert, and King Hlotokar? Not just *one* king, mind you; *three*."

"That's a lot of kings," said Padway, smiling pleasantly. "I am greatly impressed. But you mustn't take offense, my lord count. Our king is an old man, and he finds the press of public business hard to bear."

"So, *hrrmp*. We'll forget about it, then. But we shall not find the reason for my coming hither so easy to forget. Briefly, what became of that hundred and fifty thousand solidi that Wittigis promised my masters, King Theudebert, King Hildebert, and King Hlotokar if they wouldn't attack him while he was involved with the Greeks? Moreover, he ceded Provence to my masters, King Theudebert, King Hildebert, and King Hlotokar. Yet your general Sisigis has not evacuated Provence. When my masters sent a force to occupy it a few weeks ago, they were driven back and several were killed. You should know that the Franks, who are the bravest and proudest people on earth, will never submit to such treatment. What are you going to do about it?"

Padway answered: "*You*, my lord Hlodovik, should know that the acts of an unsuccessful usurper cannot bind the legitimate government. We intend to hold what we have. So you may inform your masters, King Theudebert, King Hildebert, and King Hlotokar, that there will be no payment and no evacuation."

"Do you really mean that?" Hlodovik seemed astonished. "Don't you know, young man, that the armies of the Franks could sweep the length of Italy, burning and ravaging, any time they wished? My masters, King Theudebert, King Hildebert, and King Hlotokar, are showing great forbearance and humanity by offering you a way out. Think carefully before you invite disaster."

"I have thought, my lord," replied Padway. "And I respectfully suggest that you and your masters do the same. Especially about a little military device that we are introducing. Would you like to see it demonstrated? The parade ground is only a step from here."

Padway had made the proper preparations in advance. When they arrived at the parade ground, Hlodovik weaving slightly all the way, they found Urias, Fritharik, the crossbow, and a supply of bolts. Padway's idea was to have Fritharik take a few demonstration shots at a target. But Fritharik and Urias had other ideas. The latter walked off fifty feet, turned, and placed an apple on his head. Fritharik cocked the crossbow, put a bolt in the groove, and raised the bow to his shoulder.

Padway was frozen speechless with horror. He didn't dare shout at the two idiots to desist for fear of losing face before the Frank. And if Urias was killed, he hated to think of the damage that would be done to his plans.

The crossbow snapped. There was a short *splush*, and fragments of apple flew about. Urias, grinning, picked pieces of apple out of his hair and walked back.

"Do you find the demonstration impressive, my lord?" Padway asked.

"Yes, quite," said Hlodovik. "Let's see that device. *Hm-m-m.* Of course, the brave Franks don't believe that any battle was ever won by a lot of silly arrows. But for hunting, now, this mightn't be bad. How does it work? I see; you pull the string back to here—"

While Fritharik was demonstrating the crossbow, Padway took Urias aside and told him, in a low tone, just what he thought of such a fool stunt. Urias tried to look serious, but couldn't help a faint, small-boy grin. Then there was another snap, and something whizzed between them, not a foot from Padway's face. They jumped and spun around. Hlodovik was holding the crossbow, a foolish look on his long face. "I didn't know it went off so easily," he said.

Fritharik lost his temper. "What are you trying to do, you drunken fool? Kill somebody—"

"What's that? *You* call me a fool? Why—" and the Frank's sword came halfway out of the scabbard.

Fritharik jumped back and grabbed his own sword hilt. Padway and Urias pounced on the two and grabbed their elbows.

"Calm yourself, my lord!" cried Padway. "It's nothing to start a fight over. I'll apologize personally."

The Frank merely got madder and tried to shake off Padway. "I'll teach that low-born bastard! My honor is insulted!" he shouted. Several Gothic soldiers loafing around the field looked up and trotted over. Hlodovik saw them coming and put his sword back, growling: "This is fine treatment for the representative of King Theudebert, King Hildebert, and King Hlotokar. Just wait till they hear of this."

Padway tried to mollify him, but Hlodovik merely grumped, and soon left Ravenna. Padway dispatched a warning to Sisigis to be on the lookout for a Frankish attack. His conscience bothered him a good deal. In a way he thought he ought to have tried to appease the Franks, as he hated the idea of being responsible for war. But he knew that that fierce and treacherous tribe would only take each concession as a sign of weakness. The time to stop the Franks was the first time.

Then another envoy arrived, this time from the Kutrigurs or Bulgarian Huns. The usher told Padway: "He's very dignified; doesn't speak any Latin or Gothic, so he uses an interpreter. Says he's a boyar, whatever that is."

"Show him in."

The Bulgarian envoy was a stocky, bowlegged man with high cheek bones, a fiercely upswept mustache, and a nose even bigger than Padway's. He wore a handsome furlined coat, baggy trousers, and a silk turban wound about his shaven skull, from the rear of which two black pigtails jutted absurdly. Despite the finery, Padway found reason to suspect that the man had never had a bath in his life. The interpreter was a small, nervous Thracian who hovered a pace to the Bulgar's left and rear.

The Bulgar clumped in, bowed stiffly, and did not offer to shake hands. Probably not done among the Huns, thought Padway. He bowed back and indicated a chair. He regretted having done so a moment later, when the Bulgar hiked his boots up on the upholstery and sat cross-legged. Then he began to speak, in a strangely musical tongue which Padway surmised was related to Turkish. He stopped every three or four words for the interpreter to translate. It ran something like this:

Envoy: (Twitter, twitter.)
Interpreter: I am the Boyar Karojan—
Envoy: (Twitter, twitter.)
Interpreter: The son of Chakir—
Envoy: (Twitter, twitter.)
Interpreter. Who was the son of Tardu—
Envoy: (Twitter, twitter.)
Interpreter: Envoy of Kardam—
Envoy: (Twitter, twitter.)

Interpreter: The son of Kapagan—
Envoy: (Twitter, twitter.)
Interpreter: And Great Khan of the Kutrigurs.

It was distracting to listen to, but not without a certain poetic grandeur. The Bulgar paused impassively at that point. Padway identified himself, and the duo began again:

"My master, the Great Khan—"
"Has received an offer from Justinian, Emperor of the Romans—"
"Of fifty thousand solidi—"
"To refrain from invading his dominions."
"If Thiudahad, King of the Goths—"
"Will make us a better offer—"
"We will ravage Thrace—"
"And leave the Gothic realm alone."
"If he does not—"
"We will take Justinian's gold—"
"And invade the Gothic territories—"
"Of Pannonia and Noricum."

Padway cleared this throat and began his reply, pausing for translation. This method had its advantages, he found. It gave him time to think.

"My master, Thiudahad, King of the Goths and Italians—"
"Authorizes me to say—"
'That he has better use for his money—"
"Than to bribe people not to attack him—"
"And that if the Kutrigurs think—"
"That they can invade our territory—"
"They are welcome to try—"
"But that we cannot guarantee them—"
"A very hospitable reception."
The envoy replied:
"Think man, on what you say."
"For the armies of the Kutrigurs—"
"Cover the Sarmatian steppe like locusts."
"The hoofbeats of their horses—"
"Are a mighty thunder."
"The flight of their arrows—"

"Darkens the sun."
"Where they have passed—"
"Not even grass will grow."
 Padway replied:
"Most excellent Karojan—"
"What you say may be true."
"But in spite of their thundering and sun-darkening—"
"The last time the Kutrigurs—"
"Assailed our land, a few years ago—"
"They got the pants beat off them."

As this was translated, the Bulgar looked puzzled for a moment. Then he turned red. Padway thought he was angry, but it soon appeared that he was trying to keep from laughing. He said between sputters:

"This time, man, it will be different."
"If any pants are lost—"
"They will be yours."
"How would this be?"
"You pay us sixty thousand—"
"In three installments—"
"Of twenty thousand each?"
 But Padway was immovable. The Bulgar finished:
"I shall inform my master—"
"Kardam, the Great Khan of the Kutrigurs—"
"Of your obduracy."
"For a reasonable bribe—"
"I am prepared to tell him—"
"Of the might of the Gothic arms—"
"In terms that shall dissuade him—"
"From his projected invasion."

Padway beat the Bulgar down to half the bribe he originally asked, and they parted on the best of terms. When he went around to his quarters he found Fritharik trying to wind a towel around his head.

The Vandal looked up with guilty embarrassment. "I was trying, excellent boss, to make a headgear like that of the Hunnish gentleman. It has style."

Padway had long since decided that Thiudahad was a pathological case. But lately the little king was showing more definite signs of mental failure. For instance, when Padway went to see about a new inheritance law, Thiudahad gravely listened to him explain the reasons that the Royal Council and Cassiodorus had agreed upon bringing the Gothic law more into line with the Roman.

Then he said: "When are you going to put out another book in my name, Martinus? Your name *is* Martinus, isn't it? Martinus Paduei, Martinus Paduei. Didn't I appoint you prefect or something? Dear me, I can't seem to remember anything. Now, what's this you want to see me about? Always business, business, business. I hate business. Scholarship is more important. Silly state papers. What is it, an order for an execution? I hope you're going to torture the rascal as he deserves. I can't understand this absurd prejudice of yours against torture. The people aren't happy unless they're terrified of their government. Let's see, what was I talking about?"

It was convenient in one way, as Thiudahad didn't bother him much. But it was awkward when the king simply refused to listen to him or to sign anything for a day at a time.

Then he found himself in a hot dispute with the paymaster-general of the Gothic army. The latter refused to put the Imperialist mercenaries whom Padway had captured on the rolls. Padway argued that the men were first-rate soldiers who seemed glad enough to serve the Italo-Gothic state, and that it would cost little more to enlist them than to continue to feed them as prisoners. The paymaster-general replied that national defense had been a prerogative of the Goths since the time of Theoderik, and the men in question were not, with some few exceptions, Goths. Q.E.D.

Each stubbornly maintained his point, so the dispute was carried to Thiudahad. The king listened to the argument with a specious air of wisdom.

Then he sent the paymaster-general away and told Padway: "Lots to be said on both sides, dear sir, lots to be said on both sides: Now, if I decide in your favor, I shall expect a suitable command for my son, Thiudegiskel."

Padway was horrified, though he tried not to show it. "But, my lord king, what military experience has Thiudegiskel had?"

"None; that's just the trouble. Spends all his time drinking and wenching with his wild young friends. He needs a bit of responsibility. Something good, consistent with the dignity of his birth."

Padway argued some more. But he didn't say that he couldn't imagine a worse commander than this self-conceited and arrogant puppy. Thiudahad was obstinate. "After all, Martinus, I'm king, am I not? You can't browbeat me and you can't frighten me with your Wittigis. Heh, heh I'll have a surprise for you one of these days. What was I talking about? Oh, yes. You do, I think, owe Thiudegiskel something for putting him in that horrid prison camp—"

"But *I* didn't put him in jail—"

"Don't interrupt, Martinus. It isn't considerate. Either you give him a command, or I decide in favor of the other man, what's-his-name. That is my final royal word."

So Padway gave in. Thiudegiskel was put in command of the Gothic forces in Calabria, where, Padway hoped, he wouldn't be able to do much harm. Later he had occasion to remember that hope.

Padway may seem rash to have incorporated such an alien element as the ex-Imperialists in the Italo-Gothic army. But in this age there was no such thing as nationalism in the modern sense. The ties that counted were those of religion and personal loyalty to a commander. Many of the Imperialists were Thracian Goths who had remained in the Balkans at that time of the migration under Theoderik. And some Italian Goths had served the Empire as mercenaries. They mixed with little prejudice on either side.

Then three things happened. General Sisigis sent word of suspicious activity among the Franks.

Padway got a letter from Thomasus, which told of an attempt on the life of ex-King Wittigis. The assassin had inexplicably sneaked into the dugout, where Wittigis, though slightly wounded in the process, had killed him with his bare hands. Nobody knew who the assassin was until Wittigis had declared, with many a bloodcurdling curse, that he recognized the man as an old-time secret agent of Thiudahad. Padway knew what that meant. Thiudahad had discovered Wittigis' whereabouts, and meant to put his rival out of the way. If he succeeded, he'd be prepared to defy Padway's management, or even to heave him out of his office. Or worse.

Finally Padway got a letter from Justinian. It read:

Flavius Anicius Justinian, Emperor of the Romans, to King Thiudahad, Greetings.

Our serenity's attention has been called to the terms which you propose for termination of the war between us.

We find these terms so absurd and unreasonable that our deigning to reply at all is an act of great condescension on our part. Our holy endeavor to recover for the Empire the provinces of western Europe, which belonged to our forebears and rightfully belong to us, will be carried through to a victorious conclusion.

As for our former general, Flavius Belisarius, his refusal of parole is an act of gross disloyalty, which we shall fittingly punish in due course. Meanwhile the illustrious Belisarius may consider himself free of all obligations to us. Nay more, we order him to place himself unreservedly under the orders of that infamous heretic and agent of the Evil One who calls himself Martinus of Padua, of whom we have heard.

We are confident that, between the incompetence and cowardice of Belisarius and the heavenly wrath that will attach to those who submit to the unclean touch of the diabolical Martinus, the doom of the Gothic kingdom will not be long delayed.

Padway realized, with a slightly sick feeling, that he had a lot to learn about diplomacy. His defiance of Justinian, and of the Frankish kings, and of the Bulgars, had each been justified, considered by itself. But he shouldn't have committed himself to taking them on all at once.

The thunderheads were piling up fast.

CHAPTER XIV

Padway dashed back to Rome and showed Justinian's letter to Belisarius. He thought he had seldom seen a more unhappy man than the stalwart Thracian.

"I don't know," was all Belisarius would say in answer to his questions. "I shall have to think."

Padway got an interview with Belisarius' wife, Antonina. He got along fine with this slim, vigorous redhead.

She said: "I told him repeatedly that he'd get nothing but ingratitude from Justinian. But you know how he is—reasonable about everything except what concerns his honor. The only thing that would make me hesitate is my friendship with the Empress Theodora. That's not a connection to be thrown over lightly. But after this letter—I'll do what I can, excellent Martinus."

Belisarius, to Padway's unconcealed delight, finally capitulated.

The immediate danger point seemed to be Provence. Padway's runner-collecting service had gathered a story of another bribe paid by Justinian to the Franks to attack the Goths. So Padway did some shuffling. Asinar, who had sat at Senia for months without the gumption to move against the Imperialists in Spalato, was ordered home. Sisigis, who if no genius was not obviously incompetent, was transferred to command of Asinar's Dalmatian army. And Belisarius was given command of Sisigis' forces in Gaul. Belisarius, before leaving for the North, asked Padway for all the information available about the Franks.

Padway explained: "Brave, treacherous, and stupid. They have nothing but unarmored infantry, who fight in a single deep column. They come whooping along, hurl a volley of throwing-axes and javelins, and close with the sword. If you can stop them by a line of reliable pikemen, or by cavalry charges, they're suckers for mounted archers. They're very numerous, but such a huge mass of infantry can't forage enough territory to keep themselves fed. So they have to keep moving or starve.

"Moreover, they're so primitive that their soldiers are not paid at all. They're expected to make their living by looting. If you can hold them in one spot long enough, they melt away by desertion. But don't underestimate their numbers and ferocity.

"Try to send agents into Burgundy to rouse the Burgunds against the Franks, who conquered them only a few years ago." He explained that the Burgunds were of East-German origin, like the Goths and Lombards, spoke a language much like theirs, and like them were primarily stock-raisers. Hence they did not get on with the West-German Franks, who were agriculturists when they were not devastating their neighbors' territory.

If there was going to be more war, Padway knew one invention that would settle it definitely in the Italo-Goths' favor. Gunpowder was made of sulphur, charcoal, and saltpeter. Padway had learned that in the sixth grade. The first two were available without question.

He supposed that potassium nitrate could be obtained somewhere as a mineral. But he did not know where, or what it would look like. He could not synthesize it with the equipment at hand, even had he known enough chemistry. But he remembered reading that it occurred at the bottom of manure-piles. And he remembered an enormous pile in Nevitta's yard.

He called on Nevitta and asked for permission to dig. He whooped with joy when, sure enough, there were the crystals, looking like maple sugar. Nevitta asked him if he was crazy.

"Sure," grinned Padway. Didn't you know? I've been that way for years."

His old house on Long Street was as full of activity as ever, despite the move to Florence. It was used as Rome headquarters by the Telegraph Company. Padway was having another press set up. And now the remaining space downstairs became a chemical laboratory. Padway did not know what proportions of the three ingredients made good gunpowder, and the only way to find out was by experiment.

He gave orders, in the government's name, for casting and boring a cannon. The brass foundry that took the job was not co-operative. They had never seen such a contraption and were not sure they could make it. What did he want this tube for, a flower pot?

It took them an interminable time to get the pattern and core made, despite the simplicity of the thing. The first one they delivered looked all right, until Padway examined the breach end closely. The metal here was spongy and pitted. The gun would have blown up the first time it was fired.

The trouble was that it had been cast muzzle down. The solution was to add a foot to the length of the barrel, cast it muzzle up, and saw off the last foot of flawed brass.

His efforts to produce gunpowder got nowhere. Lots of proportions of the ingredients would burn beautifully when ignited. But they did not explode. He tried all proportions; he varied his method of mixing. Still all he got was a lively sizzle, a big yellow flame, and a stench. He tried packing the stuff into improvised firecrackers. They went *fuff.* They would not go *bang*.

Perhaps he had to touch off a large quantity at once, more tightly compressed yet. He pestered the foundry daily until the second cannon appeared.

Early next morning he and Fritharik and a couple of helpers mounted the cannon on a crude carriage of planks in a vacant space near the Viminal Gate. The helpers had previously piled up a sandhill for a target, thirty feet from the gun.

Padway rammed several pounds of powder down the barrel, and a cast-iron ball after it. He filled the touch-hole.

He said in a low voice: "Fritharik, give me that candle. Now get back everybody. Way over there, and lie down. You too, Fritharik."

"Never!" said Fritharik indignantly. "Desert my lord in the hour of danger? I should say not!"

"All right, if you want to chance being blown to bits. Here goes."

Padway touched the candle flame to the touch-hole.

The powder sizzled and sparkled.

The gun went *pfoomp!* The cannon-ball hopped from the muzzle, thumped to earth a yard away, rolled another yard, and stopped.

Back went the beautiful shiny new gun to Padway's house, to be put in the cellar with the clock.

In the early spring, Urias appeared in Rome. He explained that he'd left the military academy in the hands of subordinates, and was coming down to see about raising a militia force of Romans, which had been another of Padway's ideas. But he had an unhappy, hangdog air that made Padway suspect that that wasn't the real reason.

To Padway's leading questions he finally burst out: "Excellent Martinus, you'll simply have to give me a command somewhere away from Ravenna. I can't stand it any longer."

Padway put his arm around Urias' shoulders. "Come on, old man, tell me what is bothering you. Maybe I can help."

Urias looked at the ground. "Uh…well…that is—Look here, just what *is* the arrangement between you and Mathaswentha?"

"I thought that was it. You've been seeing her, haven't you?"

"Yes, I have. And if you send me back there, I shall see her some more in spite of myself. Are you and she betrothed, or what?"

"I did have some such idea once." Padway put on the air of one about to make a great sacrifice. "But, my friend, I wouldn't stand in the way of anybody's happiness. I'm sure you're much better suited to her than I. My work keeps me too busy to make a good husband. So if you want to sue for her hand, go to it, with my blessing."

"You *mean* that?" Urias jumped up and began pacing the floor, fairly beaming. "I…I don't know how to thank you…it's the greatest thing you could do for me…I'm your friend for life—"

"Don't mention it; I'm glad to help you out. But now that you're down here, you might as well finish the job you came to do."

"Oh," said Urias soberly. "I suppose I ought to, at that. But how shall I press my suit, then?"

"Write her."

"But how can I? I don't know the pretty phrases. In fact, I've never written a love letter in my life."

"I'll help you out with that, too. Here, we can start right now." Padway got out writing materials, and they were presently concocting a letter to the princess. "Let's see," said Padway reflectively, "we ought to tell her what her eyes are like."

"They're just like eyes, aren't they?"

"Of course, but in this business you compare them to the stars and things."

Urias thought. "They're about the color of a glacier I once saw in the Alps."

"No, that wouldn't do. It would imply that they were as cold as ice."

"They also remind you of a polished sword blade."

"Similar objection. How about the northern seas?"

"*Hm-m-m.* Yes, I think that would do, Martinus. Gray as the northern seas."

"It has a fine poetic ring to it."

"So it has. Northern seas it shall be, then." Urias wrote slowly and awkwardly.

Padway said: "Hey, don't bear down so hard with that pen. You'll poke a hole in that paper."

As Urias was finishing the letter, Padway clapped on his hat and made for the door.

"*Hai*," said Urias, "what's your hurry?"

Padway grinned. "I'm just going to see some friends; a family named Anicius. Nice people. I'll introduce you to them some day when you're safely sewed up."

Padway's original idea had been to introduce a mild form of selective conscription, beginning with the city of Rome and requiring the draftees to report for weekly drill. The Senate, which at this time was a mere municipal council, balked. Some of them disliked or distrusted Padway. Some wanted to be bribed.

Padway did not want to give in to them until he had tried everything else. He had Urias announce drills on a voluntary basis, at current wages. Results were disappointing.

Padway's thoughts were abruptly snatched from the remilitarization of the Italians when Junianus came in with a telegraph message. It read simply:

> WITTIGIS ESCAPED FROM DETENTION LAST NIGHT.
> NO TRACE OF HIM HAS BEEN FOUND.
>
> (SIGNED)
>
> ATURPAD THE PERSIAN,
> COMMANDING.

For a minute Padway simply stared at the message. Then he jumped up and yelled: "Fritharik! Get our horses!"

They clattered over to Urias' headquarters. Urias looked grave. "This puts me in an awkward position, Martinus. My uncle will undoubtedly try to regain his crown. He's a stubborn man, you know."

"I know. But you know how important it is to keep things going the way they are."

"*Ja*. I won't go back on you. But you couldn't expect me to try to harm my uncle. I like him, even if he is a thickheaded old grouch."

"You stick with me and I promise you I'll do my best to see that he isn't harmed. But just now I'm concerned with keeping him from harming *us*."

"How do you suppose he got out? Bribery?"

"I know as much as you do. I doubt the bribery; at least Aturpad is considered an honorable man. What do you think Wittigis will do?"

"If it were me, I'd hide out for a while and gather my partisans. That would be logical. But my uncle never was very logical. And he hates Thiudahad worse than anything on earth. Especially after Thiudahad's attempt to have him murdered. My guess is that he'll head straight for Ravenna and try to do Thiudahad in personally."

"All right, then, we'll collect some fast cavalry and head that way ourselves."

Padway thought he was pretty well hardened to long-distance riding. But it was all he could do to stand the pace that Urias set. When they reached Ravenna in the early morning he was reeling, red-eyed, in the saddle.

They asked no questions, but galloped straight for the palace. The town seemed normal enough. Most of the citizens were at breakfast. But at the palace the normal guard was not to be seen.

"That looks bad," said Urias. They and their men dismounted, drew their swords, and marched in six abreast. A guard appeared at the head of the stairs. He grabbed at his sword, then recognized Urias and Padway.

"Oh, it's you," he said noncommittally.

"Yes, it's us," replied Padway. "What's up?"

"Well…uh…you'd better go see for yourselves, noble sirs. Excuse me." And the Goth whisked out of sight.

They tramped on through the empty halls. Doors shut before they came to them, and there was whispering behind them. Padway wondered if they were walking into a trap. He sent back a squad to hold the front door.

At the entrance to the royal apartments they found a clump of guards. A couple of these brought their spears up, but the rest simply stood uncertainly. Padway said calmly, "Stand back, boys," and went in.

"Oh, merciful Christ!" said Urias softly.

There were several people standing around a body on the floor. Padway asked them to stand aside, which they did meekly. The body was that of Wittigis. His tunic was ripped by a dozen sword and spear wounds. The rug under him was sopping.

The chief usher looked amazedly at Padway. "This just happened, my lord. Yet you have come all the way from Rome because of it. How did you know?"

"I have ways," said Padway. "How did it happen?"

"Wittigis was let into the palace by a guard friendly to him. He would have killed our noble king, but he was seen, and other guards hurried to the rescue. The guards killed him," he added unnecessarily. Anybody could see that.

A sound from the corner made Padway look up. There crouched Thiudahad, half dressed. Nobody seemed to be paying much attention. Thiudahad's ashy face peered at Padway.

"Dear me, it's my new prefect, isn't it? Your name is Cassiodorus. But how much younger you look, my dear sir. Ah, me, we all grow old sometime. Heh-heh. Let's publish a book, my dear Cassiodorus. Heigh-ho, yes, indeed, a lovely new book with purple covers. Heh-heh. We'll serve it for dinner, with pepper and gravy. That's the way to eat a fowl. Yes, three hundred pages at least. By the way, have you seen that rascally general of mine, Wittigis? I heard he was coming to call. Dreadful bore; no scholar at all. Heigh-ho, dear me, I feel like dancing. Do you dance, my dear Wittigis? La-la-la, la-la-la, dum de-um de-um."

Padway told the king's house physician: "Take care of him, and don't let him out. The rest of you, go back to work as if nothing has happened. Somebody take charge of the body. Replace this rug, and make the preparations for a dignified but modest funeral. Urias, maybe you'd better tend to that." Urias was weeping. "Come on, old man, you can do your grieving later. I sympathize, but we've got things to do." He whispered something to him, whereat Urias cheered up.

CHAPTER XV

The members of the Gothic Royal Council appeared at Padway's office with a variety of scowls. They were men of substance and leisure, and did not like being dragged practically away from their breakfast tables, especially by a mere civil functionary.

Padway acquainted them with the circumstances. His news shocked them to temporary silence. He continued: "As you know, my lords, under the unwritten constitution of the Gothic nation, an insane king must be replaced as soon as possible. Permit me to suggest that present circumstances make the replacement of the unfortunate Thiudahad an urgent matter."

Wakkis growled: "That's partly *your* doing, young man. We could have bought off the Franks—"

"Yes, my lord. I know all that. The trouble is that the Franks won't stay bought, as you very well know. In any event, what's done is done. Neither the Franks nor Justinian have moved against us yet. If we can run the election of a new king off quickly, we shall not be any worse off than we are."

Wakkis replied: "We shall have to call another convention of the electors, I suppose."

Another councilor, Mannfrith, spoke up: "Apparently our young friend is right, much as I hate to take advice from outsiders. When and where shall the convention be?"

There were a lot of uncertain throaty noises from the Goths. Padway said: "If my lords please, I have a suggestion. Our new civil capital is to be at Florence, and what more fitting way of inaugurating it is there than holding our election there?"

There was more growling, but nobody produced a better idea. Padway knew perfectly well that they didn't like following his directions, but that, on the other hand, they were glad to shirk thought and responsibility themselves.

Wakkis said: "We shall have to give time for the messages to go out, and for the electors to reach Florence—"

Just then Urias came in. Padway took him aside and whispered: "What did she say?"

"She says she will."

"When?"

"Oh, in about ten days, I think. It don't look very nice so soon after my uncle's death."

"Never mind that. It's now or never."

Mannfrith asked. "Who shall the candidates be? I'd like to run myself, only my rheumatism has been bothering me so."

Somebody said: "Thiudegiskel will be one. He's Thiudahad's logical successor."

Padway said: "I think you'll be pleased to hear that our esteemed General Urias will be a candidate."

"What?" cried Wakkis. "He's a fine young man, I admit, but he's ineligible. He's not an Amaling."

Padway broke into a triumphant gran. "Not now, my lords, but he will be by the time the election is called." The Goths looked startled. "And, my lords, I hope you'll all give us the pleasure of your company at the wedding."

During the wedding rehearsal, Mathaswentha got Padway aside. She said: "Really, Martinus, you've been most noble about this. I hope you won't grieve too much."

Padway tried his best to look noble. "My dear, your happiness is mine. And if you love this young man, I think you're doing just the right thing."

"I *do* love him," replied Mathaswentha. "Promise me you won't sit around and mope, but will go out and find some nice girl who is suited to you."

Padway sighed convincingly. "It'll be hard to forget, my dear. But since you ask it, I'll promise. Now, now, don't cry. What will Urias think? You want to make *him* happy, don't you? There, that's a sensible girl."

The wedding itself was quite a gorgeous affair in a semi-barbaric way. Padway discovered an unsuspected taste for stage management, and introduced a wrinkle he'd seen in pictures of United States Military Academy weddings: that of having Urias' friends make an arch of swords under which the bride and groom walked on their way down the church steps. Padway himself looked as dignified as his moderate stature and nondescript features permitted. Inwardly he was holding on tight to repress a snicker. It had just occurred to him that Urias' long robe looked amazingly like a bathrobe he, Padway, had once owned, except that Padway's robe hadn't had pictures of saints embroidered on it in gold thread.

As the happy couple departed, Padway ducked out of sight around a pillar. Mathaswentha, if she saw him out of the tail of her eye, may have thought that he was shedding a final tear. But actually he was allowing himself the luxury of a longdrawn "*Whew!*" of relief.

Before he reappeared, he heard a couple of Goths talking on the other side of the pillar:

"He'd made a good king, eh, Albehrts?"

"Maybe. *He* would, by himself. But I fear he'll be under the influence of this Martinus person. Not that I have anything specifically against Mysterious Martin, you understand. But—you know how it is."

"*Ja, ja.* Oh, well, one can always flip a sesterce to decide which to vote for."

Padway had every intention of keeping Urias under his influence. It seemed possible. Urias disliked and was impatient with matters of civil administration. He was a competent soldier, and at the same time was receptive to Padway's ideas. Padway thought somberly that if anything happened to *this* king he'd hunt a long time before finding another as satisfactory.

Padway had the news of the impending election sent out over the telegraph, thereby saving the week that would normally be necessary for messengers to travel the length and breadth of Italy, and incidentally convincing some of the Goths of the value of his contraptions. Padway also sent our another message, ordering all the higher military commanders to remain at their posts. He sold Urias the idea by arguing military necessity. His real reason was a determination to keep Thiudegiskel in Calabria during the election. Knowing Urias, he didn't dare explain this plan to him, for fear Urias would have an attack of knightly honor and, as ranking general, countermand the order.

The Goths had never seen an election conducted on time-honored American principles. Padway showed them. The electors arrived in Florence to find the town covered with enormous banners and posters reading:

VOTE FOR URIAS
THE PEOPLE'S CHOICE!

Lower taxes! Bigger public works!
Security for the aged! Efficient government!

And so forth. They also found a complete system of ward-heelers to take them in tow, show them the town—not that Florence was much to see in those days—and butter them up generally.

Three days before the election was due, Padway held a barbecue. He threw himself into debt for the fixings. Well, not exactly; he threw poor Urias into debt, being much too prudent to acquire any more liabilities in his own name than he could help.

While he kept modestly in the background, Urias made a speech. Padway later heard comments to the effect that nobody had known Urias could make such good speeches. He grinned to himself. He had written the speech and had spent all his evenings for a week teaching Urias to deliver it. Privately Padway thought that his candidate's delivery still stank. But if the electors didn't mind, there was no reason why he should.

Padway and Urias relaxed afterward over a bottle of brandy. Padway said that the election looked like a pushover, and then had to explain what a pushover was. Of the two opposing candidates, one had withdrawn, and the other, Harjis Austrowald's son, was an elderly man with only the remotest connection with the Amal family.

Then one of the ward-heelers came in breathless. It seemed to Padway that people were always coming to see him breathless.

The man barked: "Thiudegiskel's here."

Padway wasted no time. He found where Thiudegiskel was staying, rounded up a few Gothic soldiers, and set out to arrest the young man. He found that Thiudegiskel had, with a gang of his own friends, taken over one of the better inns in town, pitching the previous guests and their belongings out in the street.

The gang were gorging themselves downstairs in plain sight. They hadn't yet changed their traveling clothes, and they looked tired but tough. Padway marched in. Thiudegiskel looked up. "Oh, it's *you* again. What do you want?"

Padway announced: "I have a warrant for your arrest on grounds of insubordination and deserting your post, signed by Ur—"

The high-pitched voice interrupted: "*Ja, ja,* I know all about that, my dear *Sineigs.* Maybe you thought I'd stay away from Florence while you ran off an election without me, eh? *But* I'm not like that, Martinus. Not one little bit. I'm here, I'm a candidate, and anything you try now I'll remember when I'm king. That's one thing about me; I've got an infernally long memory."

Padway turned to his soldiers: "Arrest him!"

There was a great scraping of chairs as the gang rose to its feet and grasped its collective sword hilts. Padway looked for his soldiers; they hadn't moved.

"Well?" he snapped.

The oldest of them, a kind of sergeant, cleared his throat. "Well, sir, it's this way. Now we know you're our superior and all that. But things are kind of uncertain, with this election and all, and we don't know whom we'll be taking orders from in a couple of days. Suppose we arrest this young man, and then he gets elected king? That wouldn't be so good for us, now would it, sir?"

"Why—you—" raged Padway.

But the only effect was that the soldiers began to slide out the door. The young Gothic noble named Willimer was whispering to Thiudegiskel, sliding his sword a few inches out of the scabbard and back.

Thiudegiskel shook his head and said to Padway: "My friend here doesn't seem to like you, Martinus. He swears he'll pay you a visit as soon as the election is over. So it might be healthier if you left Italy for a little trip. In fact, it's all I can do to keep him from paying his visit right now."

The soldiers were mostly gone now. Padway realized that he'd better go too, if he didn't want these well-born thugs to make hamburger of him.

He mustered what dignity he could. "You know the law against duelling."

Thiudegiskel's invincibly good-natured arrogance wasn't even dented. "Sure, I know it. But remember. *I'll* be the one enforcing it. I'm just giving you fair warning, Martinus. That's one thing about—"

But Padway didn't wait to hear Thiudegiskel's next contribution to the inexhaustible subject of himself. He went, full of rage and humiliation. By the time he finished cursing his own stupidity and thought to round up his eastern troops—the few who weren't up north with Belisarius—and make a second attempt, it was too late. Thiudegiskel had collected a large crowd of partisans in and around the hotel, and it would take a battle to dislodge them. The ex-Imperialists seemed far from enthusiastic over the prospect, and Urias muttered something about its being only honorable to let the late king's son have a fair try for the crown.

The next day Thomasus the Syrian arrived. He came in wheezing. "How are you, Martinus? I didn't want to miss all the excitement, so I came up from Rome. Brought my family along."

That meant something, Padway knew, for Thomasus' family consisted not only of his wife and four children, but an aged uncle, a nephew, two nieces, and his black house slave Ajax and *his* wife and children.

He answered: "I'm fine, thanks. Or I shall be when I catch up on my sleep. How are you?"

"Fine, thanks. Business has been good for a change."

"And how is your friend God?" Padway asked with a straight face.

"He's fine too—why, you blasphemous young scoundrel! That will cost you an extra interest on your next loan. How's the election?"

Padway told him. "It won't be as easy as I thought. Thiudegiskel has developed a lot of support among the conservative Goths, who don't care for self-made men like Wittigis and Urias. The upper crust prefer an Amaling by birth—"

"Upper crust? Oh, I see! Ha, ha, ha! I hope God listens to you. It might put Him in a good humor the next time He considers sending a plague or a quake."

Padway continued: "And Thiudegiskel is not as stupid as one might expect. He'd hardly arrived before he'd sent out friends to tear down my posters and put up some of his own. His weren't much to look at, but I was surprised that he thought of using any. There were fist-fights and one stabbing, not fatal, fortunately. So—you know Dagalaif Nevitta's son?"

"The marshal? By name only."

"He's not eligible to vote. Well, the town watch is too scared of the Goths to keep order, and I don't dare use my own guards for fear of rousing all the Goths against the 'foreigners.' I blackmailed the city fathers into hiring Dagalaif to deputize the other marshals who are not electors as election police. As Nevitta is on our side, I don't know how impartial my friend Dagalaif will be. But it'll save us from a pitched battle, I hope."

"Wonderful, wonderful, Martinus. Don't over-reach yourself; some of the Goths call your electioneering methods newfangled and undignified. I'll ask God to keep a special watch over you and your candidate."

The day before the election, Thiudegiskel showed his political astuteness by throwing a barbecue even bigger than Padway's. Padway, having some mercy on Urias' modest purse, had limited his party to the electors. Thiudegiskel, with the wealth of Thiudahad's immense Tuscan estates to draw upon, shot the works. He invited all the electors and their families and friends also.

Padway and Urias and Thomasus, with the former's ward-heelers, the latter's family, and a sizable guard, arrived at the field outside Florence after the festivities had begun. The field was covered with thousands of Goths of all ages, sizes, and sexes, and was noisy with East-German gutturals, the clank of scabbards, and the *flop-flop* of leather pants.

A Goth bustled up to them with beer suds in his whiskers. "Here, here, what are you people doing? You weren't invited."

"*Ni ogs, frijond,*" said Padway.

"What? You're telling *me* not to be afraid?" The Goth bristled.

"We aren't even trying to come to your party. We're just having a little picnic of our own. There's no law against picnics, is there?"

"Well—then why all the armament? Looks to me as though you were planning a kidnapping."

"There, there," soothed Padway. "You're wearing a sword, aren't you?"

"But I'm official. I'm one of Willimer's men."

"So are these people our men. Don't worry about us. We'll stay on the other side of the road, if it'll make you happy. Now run along and enjoy your beer."

"Well, don't try anything. We'll be ready for you if you do." The Goth departed, muttering over Padway's logic.

Padway's party made themselves comfortable across the road, ignoring the hostile glares from Thiudegiskel's partisans. Padway himself sprawled on the grass, eating little and watching the barbecue through narrowed eyes.

Thomasus said: "Most excellent General Urias, that look tells me our friend Martinus is planning something particularly hellish."

Thiudegiskel and some of his gang mounted the speakers' stand. Willimer introduced the candidate with commendable brevity. Then Thiudegiskel began to speak. Padway hushed his own party and strained his ears. Even so, with so many people, few of them completely silent, between him and the speaker, he missed a lot of Thiudegiskel's shrill Gothic. Thiudegiskel appeared to be bragging as usual about his own wonderful character. But, to Padway's consternation, his audience ate it up. And they howled with laughter at the speaker's rough and ready humor.

"—and did you know, friends, that General Urias was twelve years old before his poor mother could train him not to wet his bed? It's a fact. That's one thing about me; I never exaggerate. Of course you *couldn't* exaggerate Urias' peculiarities. For instance, the first time he called on a girl—"

Urias was seldom angry, but Padway could see the young general was rapidly approaching incandescence. He'd have to think of something quickly, or there *would* be a battle.

His eye fell on Ajax and Ajax's family. The slave's eldest child was a chocolate-colored, frizzy-haired boy of ten.

Padway asked: "Does anybody know whether Thiudegiskel's married?"

"Yes," replied Urias. "The swine was married just before he left for Calabria. Nice girl, too; a cousin of Willimer."

"*Hm-m-m.* Say, Ajax, does that oldest boy of yours speak any Gothic?"

"Why no, my lord, why should he?"

"What's his name?"

"Priam."

"Priam, would you like to earn a couple of sesterces, all your own?"

The boy jumped up and bowed. Padway found such a servile gesture in a child vaguely repulsive. Must do something about slavery some day, he thought. "Yes, my lord," squeaked the boy.

"Can you say the word '*atta*'? That's Gothic for 'father.'"

Priam dutifully said: "*Atta.* Now where are my sesterces, my lord?"

"Not so fast, Priam. That's just the beginning of the job. You practice saying '*atta*' for a while."

Padway stood up and peered at the field. He called softly: "*Hai,* Dagalaif!"

The marshal detached himself from the crowd and came over. "*Hails,* Martinus! What can I do for you?"

Padway whispered his instructions.

Then he said to Priam: "You see the man in the red cloak on the stand, the one who is talking? Well, you're to go over there and climb up on the stand, and say '*atta*' to him. Loudly, so everybody can hear. Say it a lot of times, until something happens. Then you run back here."

Priam frowned in concentration. "But the man isn't my father! This is my father!" He pointed to Ajax.

"I know. But you do as I say if you want your money. Can you remember your instructions?"

So Priam trailed off through the crowd of Goths with Dagalaif at his heels. They were lost to Padway's sight for a few minutes, while Thiudegiskel shrilled on. Then the little Negro's form appeared on the stand, boosted up by Dagalaif's strong arms. Padway clearly heard the childish cry of "*Atta!*"

Thiudegiskel stopped in the middle of a sentence. Priam repeated: "*Atta! Atta!*"

"He seems to know you!" shouted a voice down front.

Thiudegiskel stood silent, scowling and turning red. A low mutter of laughter ran through the Goths and swelled to a roar.

Priam called "*Atta!*" once more, louder.

Thiudegiskel grabbed his sword hilt and started for the boy. Padway's heart missed a beat.

But Priam leaped off the stand into Dagalaif's arms, leaving Thiudegiskel to shout and wave his sword. He was apparently yelling, "It's a lie!" over and over. Padway could see his mouth move, but his words were lost in the thunder of the Gothic nation's Wagnerian laughter.

Dagalaif and Priam appeared, running toward them. The Goth was staggering slightly and holding his midriff. Padway was alarmed until he saw Dagalaif was suffering from a laughing and coughing spell.

He slapped him on the back until the coughs and gasps moderated. Then he said: "If we hang around here, Thiudegiskel will recover his wits, and he'll be angry enough to set his partisans on us with cold steel. In my country we had a word 'scram' that is, I think, applicable. Let's go."

"Hey, my lord," squealed Priam, "where's my two sesterces? Oh, thank you, my lord. Do you want me to call anybody else 'father,' my lord?"

CHAPTER XVI

Padway told Urias: "It looks like a sure thing now. Thiudegiskel will never live this afternoon's episode down. We Americans have some methods for making elections come out the right way, such as stuffing ballot boxes, and the use of floaters. But I don't think it'll be necessary to use any of them."

"What on earth is a floater, Martinus? You mean a float such as one uses in fishing?"

"No; I'll explain sometime. I don't want to corrupt the Gothic electoral system more than is absolutely necessary."

"Look here, if anybody investigates, they'll learn that Thiudegiskel was the innocent victim of a joke this afternoon. Then won't the effect be lost?"

"No, my dear Urias, that's not how the minds of electors work. Even if he's proved innocent, he's been made such an utter fool of that nobody will take him seriously, regardless of his personal merits, if any."

Just then a ward-heeler came in breathless. He gasped: "Thiu-Thiudegiskel—"

Padway complained: "I am going to make it a rule that people who want to see me have to wait outside until they get their breath. What is it, Roderik?"

Roderik finally got it out. "Thiudegiskel has left Florence, distinguished Martinus. Nobody knows whither. Willimer and some of his other friends went with him."

Padway immediately sent out over the telegraph Urias' order depriving Thiudegiskel of his colonel's rank—or its rough equivalent in the vague and amorphous Gothic system of command. Then he sat and stewed and waited for news.

It came the next morning during the voting. But it did not concern

Thiudegiskel. It was that a large Imperialist army had crossed over from Sicily and landed, not at Scylla on the toe of the Italian boot where one would expect, but up the coast of Bruttium at Vibo.

Padway told Urias immediately, and urged: "Don't say anything for a few hours. This election is in the bag—I mean it's certain—and we don't want to disturb it."

But rumors began to circulate. Telegraph systems are run by human beings, and few groups of more than a dozen human beings have kept a secret for long. By the time Urias' election by a two-to-one majority was announced, the Goths were staging an impromptu demonstration in the streets of Florence, demanding to be led against the invader.

Then more details came in. The Imperialists' army was commanded by Bloody John, and numbered a good fifty thousand men. Evidently Justinian, furious about Padway's letter, had been shipping adequate force into Sicily in relays.

Padway and Urias figured that they could, without recalling troops from Provence and Dalmatia, assemble perhaps half again as many troops as Bloody John had. But further news soon reduced this estimate. That able, ferocious, and unprincipled soldier sent a detachment across the Sila Mountains by a secondary road from Vibo to Scyllacium, while he advanced with his main body down the Popilian Way to Reggio. The Reggio garrison of fifteen thousand men, trapped at the end of the toe of the boot, struck a few blows for the sake of their honor and surrendered. Bloody John reunited his forces and started north toward the ankle.

Padway saw Urias off in Rome with many misgivings. The army looked impressive, surely, with its new corps of horse archers and its batteries of mobile catapults. But Padway knew that the new units were inexperienced in their novel ways of fighting, and that the organization was likely to prove brittle in practice.

Once Urias and the army had left, there was no more point in worrying. Padway resumed his experiments with gunpowder. Perhaps he should try charcoal from different woods. But this meant time, a commodity of which Padway had precious little. He soon learned that he had none at all.

By piecing together the contradictory information that came in by telegraph, Padway figured out that this had happened: Thiudegiskel had reached his force in Calabria without interference. He had refused to recognize the telegraphic order depriving him of his command, and had talked his men into doing likewise. Padway guessed that the words of an able and self-confident speaker like Thiudegiskel would carry more weight with the mostly illiterate Goths than a brief, cold message arriving over the mysterious contraption.

Bloody John had moved cautiously; he had only reached Consentia when Urias arrived to face him. That might have been arranged beforehand with Thiudegiskel, to draw Urias far enough south to trap him.

But, while Urias and Bloody John sparred for openings along the river Crathis, Thiudegiskel arrived in Urias' rear—on the Imperialist side. Though he had only five thousand lancers, their unexpected charge broke the main Gothic army's morale. In fifteen minutes the Crathis Valley was full of thousands of Goths—lancers, horse archers, foot archers, and pikemen—streaming off in every direction. Thousands were ridden down by Bloody John's cuirassiers and the large force of Gepid and Lombard horse he had with him. Other thousands surrendered. The rest ran off into the hills, where the rapidly gathering dusk hid them.

Urias managed to hold his lifeguard regiment together, and attacked Thiudegiskel's force of deserters. The story was that Urias had personally killed Thiudegiskel. Padway, knowing the fondness of soldiers for myths of this sort, had his doubts. But it was agreed that Thiudegiskel had been killed, and that Urias and his men had disappeared into the Imperial host in one final, desperate charge, and had been seen no more by those on the Gothic side who escaped from the field.

For hours Padway sat at his desk, staring at the pile of telegraph messages and at a large and painfully inaccurate map of Italy.

"Can I get you anything, excellent boss?" asked Fritharik.

Padway shook his head.

Junianus shook his head. "I fear that our Martinus' mind has become unhinged by disaster."

Fritharik snorted. "That just shows you don't know him. He gets that way when he's planning something. Just wait. He'll have a devilish clever scheme for upsetting the Greeks yet."

Junianus put his head in the door. "Some more messages, my lord."

"What are they?"

"Bloody John is halfway to Salerno. The natives are welcoming him. Belisarius reports he has defeated a large force of Franks."

"Come here, Junianus. Would you two boys mind stepping out for a minute? Now, Junianus, you're a native of Lucania, aren't you?"

"Yes, my lord."

"You were a serf, weren't you?"

"Well...uh...my lord ...you see—" The husky young man suddenly looked fearful.

"Don't worry; I wouldn't let you be dragged back to your landlord's estate for anything."

"Well—yes, my lord."

"When the messages speak of the 'natives' welcoming the Imperialists, doesn't that mean the Italian landlords more than anybody else?"

"Yes, my lord. The serfs don't care one way or the other. One landlord is as oppressive as the next, so why should they get themselves killed fighting for any set of masters, Greek or Italian or Gothic as the case may be?"

"If they were offered their holdings as free proprietors, with no landlords to worry about, do you think they'd fight for that?"

"Why"—Junianus took a deep breath—"I think they would. Yes. Only it's such an extraordinary idea, if you don't mind my saying so."

"Even on the side of Arian heretics?"

"I don't think that would matter. The curials and the city folk may take their Orthodoxy seriously. But a lot of the peasants are half pagan anyway. And they worship their land more than any alleged heavenly powers."

"That's about what I thought," said Padway. "Here are some messages to send out. The first is an edict, issued by me in Urias' name, emancipating the serfs of Bruttium, Lucania, Calabria, Apulia, Campania, and Samnium. The second is an order to General Belisarius to leave screening force in Provence to fight a delaying action in case the Franks attack again and return south with his main body at once. Oh, Fritharik! Will you get Gudareths for me? And I want to see the foreman of the printshop."

When Gudareths arrived, Padway explained his plans to him. The little Gothic officer whistled. "My, my, that *is* a desperate measure, respectable Martinus. I'm not sure the Royal Council will approve. If you free all these low-born peasants, how shall we get them back into serfdom again?"

"We won't," snapped Padway. "As for the Royal Council, most of them were with Urias."

"But, Martinus, you can't make a fighting force out of them in a week or two. Take the word of an old soldier who has killed hundreds of foes with his own right arm. Yes, thousands, by God!"

"I know all that," said Padway wearily.

"What then? These Italians are no good for fighting. No spirit. You'd better rely on what Gothic forces we can scrape together. Real fighters, like me."

Padway said: "I don't expect to lick Bloody John with raw recruits. But we can give him a hostile country to advance through. You tend to those pikes, and dig up some more retired officers."

Padway got his army together and set out from Rome on a bright spring morning. It was not much of an army to look at: elderly Goths who had supposed themselves retired from active service, and young sprigs whose voices had not finished changing.

As they cluttered down Patrician Street from the Pretorian Camp, Padway had an idea. He told his staff to keep on; he'd catch up with them. And off he cantered, *poddle-op, poddle-op*, up the Suburban Slope toward the Esquiline.

Dorothea came out of Anicius' house. "Martinus!" she cried. "Are you off somewhere again?"

"That's right."

"You haven't paid us a real call in months! Every time I see you, you have only a minute before you must jump on your horse and gallop off somewhere."

Padway made a helpless gesture. "It'll be different when I've retired from all this damned war and politics. Is your excellent father in?"

"No; he's at the library. He'll be disappointed not to have seen you."

"Give him my best."

"Is there going to be more war? I've heard Bloody John is in Italy."

"It looks that way."

"Will you be in the fighting?"

"Probably."

"Oh, Martinus. Wait just a moment." She ran into the house.

She returned with a little leather bag on a loop of string. "This will keep you safe if anything will."

"What is it?"

"A fragment of St. Polycarp's skull."

Padway's eyebrows went up. "Do you believe in its effectiveness?"

"Oh, certainly. My mother paid enough for it, there's no doubt that it's genuine." She slipped the loop over his head and tucked the bag through the neck opening in his cloak.

It had not occurred to Padway that a well-educated girl would accept the superstitions of her age. At the same time he was touched. He said: "Thank you, Dorothea, from the bottom of my heart. But there's something that I think will be a more effective charm yet."

"What?"

"This." He kissed her mouth lightly, and threw himself aboard his horse. Dorothea stood with a surprised but not displeased look. Padway swung the animal around and sent it back down the avenue, *poddle-op, poddle-op*. He turned in the saddle to wave back—and was almost pitched off. The horse plunged and skidded into the nigh ox of a team that had just pulled a wagon out of a side street.

The driver shouted: "*Carus-dominus, Jesus-Christus, Maria-mater-Dei,* why don't you look where you're going? *San'tus-Petrus-Paulusque-Joannesque-Lucasque...*"

By the time the driver had run out of apostles Padway had ascertained that there was no damage. Dorothea was not in sight. He hoped that she had not witnessed the ruin of his pretty gesture.

CHAPTER XVII

It was the latter part of May, 537, when Padway entered Benevento with his army. Little by little the force had grown as the remnants of Urias' army trickled north. Only that morning a forage-cutting party had found three of these Goths who had settled down comfortably in a local farmhouse over the owner's protests, and prepared to sit out the rest of the war in comfort. These joined up, too, though not willingly.

Instead of coming straight down the Tyrrhenian or western coast to Naples, Padway had marched across Italy to the Adriatic, and had come down that coast to Teate. Then he had cut inland to Lucera and Benevento. As there was no telegraph line yet on the east coast, Padway kept in touch with Bloody John's movements by sending messengers across the Apennines to the telegraph stations that were still out of the enemy's hands. He timed his movements to reach Benevento after John had captured Salerno on the other side of the peninsula, had left a detachment masking Naples, and had started for Rome by the Latin Way.

Padway hoped to come down on his rear in the neighborhood of Capua, while Belisarius, if he got his orders straight, would come directly from Rome and attack the Imperialists in front.

Somewhere between Padway and the Adriatic was Gudareths, profanely shepherding a train of wagons full of pikes and of handbills bearing Padway's emancipation proclamation. The pikes had been dug out of attics and improvised out of fence palings and such things. The Gothic arsenals at Pavia, Verona, and other northern cities had been too far away to be of help in time.

The news of the emancipation had spread like a gasoline fire. The peasants had risen all over southern Italy. But they seemed more interested in sacking and burning their landlords' villas than in joining the army.

A small fraction of them had joined up; this meant several thousand men. Padway, when he rode back to the rear of his column and watched this great disorderly rabble swarming along the road, chattering like magpies and taking time out to snooze when they felt like it, wondered how much of an asset they would be. Here and there one wore great-grandfather's legionary helmet and loricated cuirass, which had been hanging on the wall of his cottage for most of a century.

Benevento is on a small hill at the confluence of the Calore and Sabbato Rivers. As they plodded into the town, Padway saw several Goths sitting against one of the houses. One of these looked familiar. Padway rode up to him, and cried: "Dagalaif!"

The marshal looked up. "*Hails*," he said in a toneless, weary voice. There was a bandage around his head, stained with black blood where his left ear should have been. "We heard you were coming this way, so we waited."

"Where's Nevitta?"

"My father is dead."

"What? Oh." Padway was silent for seconds. Then he said: "Oh, hell. He was one of the few real friends I had."

"I know. He died like a true Goth."

Padway sighed and went about his business of getting his force settled. Dagalaif continued sitting against the wall, looking at nothing in particular.

They lay in Benevento for a day. Padway learned that Bloody John had almost passed the road junction at Calatia on his way north. There was no news from Belisarius, so that the best Padway could hope for was to fight a delaying action, and hold John in southern Italy until more forces arrived.

Padway left his infantry in Benevento and rode down to Calatia with his cavalry. But this time he had a fairly respectable force of mounted archers. They were not as good as the Imperialist cuirassiers, but they would have to do.

Fritharik, riding beside him, said: "Aren't the flowers pretty, excellent boss? They remind me of the gardens in my beautiful estate in Carthage. Ah, that was something to see—"

Padway turned a haggard face. He could still grin, though it hurt. "Getting poetical, Fritharik?"

"*Me* a poet? *Honh!* Just because I like to have some pleasant memories for my last earthly ride—"

"What do you mean, your last?"

"I mean my last, and you can't tell me anything different. Bloody John outnumbers us three to one, they say. It won't be a nameless grave for us, because they won't bother to bury us. Last night I had a prophetic dream…"

As they approached Calatia, where Trajan's Way athwart Italy joined the Latin Way from Salerno to Rome, their scouts reported that the tail of Bloody John's army had just pulled out of town. Padway snapped his orders. A squadron of lancers trotted out in front, and a force of mounted archers followed them. They disappeared down the road. Padway rode up to the top of a knoll to watch them. They got smaller and smaller, disappearing and reappearing over humps in the road. He could hear the faint murmur of John's army, out of sight over the olive groves.

Then there was shouting and clattering, tiny with distance, like a battle between gnats and mosquitoes. Padway fretted with impatience. His telescope was no help, not being able to see around corners. The little sounds went on, and on, and on. Faint columns of smoke began to rise over the olive trees. Good; that meant that his men had set fire to Bloody John's wagon train. His first worry had been that they'd insist on plundering it in spite of orders.

Then a little dark cluster, toppled by rested lances that looked as thin as hairs, appeared on the road. Padway squinted through his telescope to make sure they were his men. He trotted down the knoll and gave some more orders. Half his horse archers spread themselves out in a long crescent on either side of the road, and a body of lancers grouped themselves behind it.

Time passed, and the men sweated in their scale-mail shirts. Then the advance guard appeared, riding hard. They were grinning, and some waved bits of forbidden plunder. They clattered down the road between the waiting bowmen.

Their commander rode up to Padway. "Worked like a charm!" he shouted. "We came down on their wagons, chased off the wagon guards, and set them on fire. Then they came back at us. We did like you said; spread the bowmen out and filled them full of quills as they charged; then hit them with the lance when they were all nice and confused. They came back for more, twice. Then John himself came down on us with his whole damned army. So we cleared out. They'll be along any minute."

"Fine," replied Padway. "You know your orders. Wait for us at Mt. Tifata pass."

So they departed, and Padway waited. But not for long. A column of Imperial cuirassiers appeared, riding hell-for-leather. Padway knew this meant Bloody John was sacrificing order to speed in his pursuit, as troops couldn't travel through the fields and groves alongside the road at any such rate. Even if he'd deployed it would take his wings some time to come up.

The Imperialists grew bigger and bigger, and their hoofs made a great pounding on the stone-paved road. They looked very splendid, with their cloaks and plumes on their officers' helmets streaming out behind. Their commander, in gilded armor, saw what he was coming to and gave an order. Lances were slung over shoulders and bows were strung. By that time they were well within range of the crescent, and the Goths opened fire. The quick, flat snap of the bowstrings and the whiz of the arrows added themselves to the clamor of the Byzantines' approach. The commander's horse, a splendid white animal, reared up and was bowled over by another horse that charged into it. The head of the Imperialist column crumpled up into a mass of milling horses and men.

Padway looked at the commander of his body of lancers; swung his arm around his head twice and pointed at the Imperialists. The line of horse archers opened up, and the Gothic knights charged through. As usual they went slowly at first, but by the time they reached the Imperialists their heavy horses had picked up irresistible momentum. Back went the cuirassiers with a great clatter, defending themselves desperately at close quarters, but pulling out and getting their bows into action as soon as they could.

Out of the corner of his eye, Padway saw a group of horsemen ride over a nearby hilltop. That meant that Bloody John's wings were coming up. He had his trumpeter signal the retreat. But the knights kept on pressing the Imperialist column back. They had the advantage in weight of men and horses, and they knew it. Padway kicked his horse into a gallop down the road after them. If he didn't stop the damned fools they'd be swallowed up by the Imperialist army.

An arrow went by Padway uncomfortably close. He found the peculiar screech that it made much harder on the nerves than he'd expected. He caught up with his Goths, dragged their commander out of the press by main force, and shouted in his ear that it was time to withdraw.

The men yelled back at him: "*Ni!-Nist!* Good fighting!" and tore out of Padway's grip to plunge back in.

While Padway wondered what to do, an Imperialist broke through the Goths and rode straight at him. Padway had not thought to get his sword out. He drew it now, then had to throw himself to one side to avoid the other's lance point. He lost a stirrup, lost his reins, and almost lost his sword and his horse. By the time he had pulled himself back upright, the Imperialist was out of sight. Padway in his haste had nicked his own horse with his sword. The animal began to dance around angrily. Padway dug his left fingers into its mane and hung on.

The Goths now began to stream back down the road. In a few seconds they were all galloping off except a few surrounded by the Imperialists. Padway wondered miserably if he'd be left on this uncontrollable nag to face the Byzantines alone, when the horse of its own accord set off after its fellows.

In theory it was a strategic retreat. But from the look of the Gothic knights, Padway wondered if it would be possible to stop them this side of the Alps.

Padway's horse tossed its reins up to where Padway could grab them. Padway had just begun to get the animal under control when he sighted a man on foot, bareheaded but gaudy in gilded armor. It was the commander of the Imperialist column. Padway rode at him. The man started to run. Padway started to swing his sword, then realized that he had no sword to swing. He had no recollection of dropping it, but he must have done so when he grabbed the reins. He leaned over and grabbed a fistful of hair. The man yelled, and came along in great bucking jumps.

A glance back showed that the Imperialists had disposed of the Goths who had not been able to extricate themselves, and were getting their pursuit under way.

Padway handed his prisoner over to a Goth. The Goth leaned and pulled the Imperialist officer up over his pommel, face down, so that half of him hung on each side. Padway saw him ride off, happily spanking the unfortunate Easterner with the flat of his sword.

According to plan, the horse archers fell in behind the lancers and galloped after them, the rearmost ones shooting backward.

It was nine miles to the pass, most of it uphill. Padway hoped never to have such a ride again. He was sure that at the next jounce his guts would burst from his abdomen and spill abroad. By the time they were within sight of the pass, the horses of both the pursued and the pursuers were so blown that both were walking. Some men had even dismounted to lead their horses. Padway remembered the story of the day in Texas that was so hot that a coyote was seen chasing a jackrabbit with both walking. He translated the story into Gothic, making a coyote a fox, and told it to the nearest soldier. It ran slowly down the line.

The bluffs were yellow in a late afternoon sun when the Gothic column finally stumbled through the pass. They had lost few men, but any really vigorous pursuer could have ridden them down and rolled them out of their saddles with ease. Fortunately the Imperialists were just about as tired. But they came on nevertheless.

Padway heard one officer's shout, echoing up the walls of the pass: "You'll rest when I tell you to, you lazy swine!"

Padway looked around, and saw with satisfaction that the force he had sent up ahead were waiting quietly in their places. These were the men who had not been used at all yet. The gang who had burned the wagons were drawn up behind them, and those who had just fled sprawled on the ground still farther up the pass.

On came the Imperialists. Padway could see men's heads turn as they looked nervously up the slopes. But Bloody John had apparently not yet admitted that his foe might be conducting an intelligent campaign. The Imperialist column clattered echoing into the narrowest part of the pass, the slanting rays of the sun shooting after them.

Then there was a great thumping roar as boulders and tree trunks came bounding down the slopes. A horse shrieked quite horribly, and the Imperialists scuttled around like ants whose nest had been disturbed. Padway signaled a squadron of lancers to charge.

There was room for only six horses abreast, and even so it was a tight fit. The rocks and logs hadn't done much damage to the Imperialists, except to form a heap cutting their leading column in two. And now the Gothic knights struck the fragment that had passed the point of the break. The cuirassiers, unable to maneuver or even to use their bows, were jammed back against the barrier by their heavier opponents. The fight ended when the surviving Imperialists slid off their horses and scrambled back to safety on foot. The Goths rounded up the abandoned horses and led them back whooping.

Bloody John withdrew a couple of bowshots. Then he sent a small group of cuirassiers forward to lay down a barrage of arrows. Padway moved some dismounted Gothic archers into the pass. These, shooting from behind the barrier, caused the Imperialists so much trouble that the cuirassiers were soon withdrawn.

Bloody John now sent some Lombard lancers forward to sweep the archers out of the way. But the barrier stopped their charge dead. While they were picking their way, a step at a time, among the boulders, the Goths filled them full of arrows at close range. By the time the bodies of a dozen horses and an equal number of Lombards had been added to the barrier, the Lombards had had enough.

By this time it would have been obvious to a much stupider general than Bloody John that in those confined quarters horses were about as useful as green parrots. The fact that the Imperialists could hold their end of the pass as easily as Padway held his could not have been much comfort, because they were trying to get through it and Padway was not. Bloody John dismounted some Lombards and Gepids and sent them forward on foot. Padway meanwhile had moved some dismounted lancers up behind the barrier, so that their spears made a thick cluster. The archers moved back and up the walls to shoot over the knights' heads.

The Lombards and Gepids came on at a slow dogtrot. They were equipped with regular Imperialist mail shirts, but they were still strange-looking men, with the backs of their heads shaven and their front hair hanging down on each side of their faces in two long, butter-greased braids. They carried swords, and some had immense two-handed battleaxes. As they got closer they began to scream insults at the Goths, who understood their East-German dialects well enough and yelled back.

The attackers poured howling over the barrier and began hacking at the edge of spears which were too close together to slip between easily. More attackers, coming from behind, pushed the leaders into the spear points. Some were stuck. Others wedged their bodies in between the spear shafts and got at spearmen. Presently the front ranks were a tangle of grunting, snarling men packed too closely to use their weapons, while those behind them tried to reach over their heads.

The archers shot and shot. Arrows bounced off helmets and stuck quivering in big wooden shields. Men who were pierced could neither fall nor withdraw.

An archer skipped back among the rocks to get more arrows. Gothic heads turned to look at him. A couple more archers followed, though the quivers of these had not been emptied. Some of the rearmost knights started to follow them.

Padway saw a rout in the making. He grabbed one man and took his sword away from him. Then he climbed up to the rock vacated by the first archer, yelling something unclear even to himself. The men turned their eyes on him.

The sword was a huge one. Padway gripped it in both hands, hoisted it over his head, and swung at the nearest enemy, whose head was on a level with his waist. The sword came down on the man's helmet with a clang, squashing it over his eyes. Padway struck again and again. That Imperialist disappeared; Padway hit at another. He hit at helmets and shields and bare heads and arms and shoulders. He never could tell when his blows were effective, because by the time he recovered from each whack the picture had changed.

Then there were no heads but Gothic ones within reach. The Imperialists were crawling back over the barrier, lugging wounded men with blood-soaked clothes and arrows sticking in them.

At a glance there seemed to be about a dozen Goths down. Padway for a moment wondered angrily why the enemy had left fewer bodies than that. It occurred to him that some of these dozen were only moderately wounded, and that the enemy had carried off most of their casualties.

Fritharik and his orderly Tirdat and others were clustering around Padway, telling him what a demon fighter he was. He couldn't see it; all he had done was climb up on a rock, reach over the heads of a couple of his own men, and take a few swipes at an enemy who was having troubles of his own and could not hit back. There had been no more science to it than to using a pickax.

The sun had set, and Bloody John's army retired down the valley to set up its tents and cook its supper. Padway's Goths did likewise. The smell of cooking-fires drifted up and down pleasantly. Anybody would have thought that here were two gangs of pleasure-seeking campers, but for the pile of dead men and horses at the barrier.

Padway had no time for introspection. There were injured men, and he had no confidence in their ability to give themselves first aid. He raised no objections to their prayers and charms and potations of dust from a saint's tomb stirred in water. But he saw to it that bandages were boiled—which of course was a bit of the magic of Mysterious Martinus—and applied rationally.

One man had lost an eye, but was still full of fight Another had three fingers gone, and was weeping about it. A third was cheerful with a stab in the abdomen. Padway knew this one would die of peritonitis before long, and that nothing could be done about it.

Padway, not underestimating his opponent, threw out a very wide and close-meshed system of outposts. He was justified; an hour before dawn his sentries began to drift in. Bloody John, it transpired, was working two large bodies of Anatolian foot archers over the hills on either side of them. Padway saw that his position would soon be untenable. So his Goths, yawning and grumbling, were routed out of their blankets and started for Benevento.

When the sun came up and he had a good look at his men, Padway became seriously concerned for their morale. They grumbled and looked almost as discouraged as Fritharik did regularly. They did not understand strategic retreats. Padway wondered how long it would be before they began to run away in real earnest.

At Benevento there was only one bridge over the Sabbato, a fairly swift stream. Padway thought he could hold this bridge for some time, and that Bloody John would be forced to attack him because of the loss of his provisions and the hostility of the peasantry.

When they came out on the plain around the confluence of the two little rivers, Padway found a horrifying surprise. A swarm of his peasant recruits was crossing the bridge toward him. Several thousand had already crossed. He had to be able to get his own force over the bridge quickly, and he knew what would happen if that bottleneck became jammed with retreating troops.

Gudareths rode out to meet him. "I followed your orders!" he shouted. "I tried to hold them back. But they got the idea they could lick the Greeks themselves, and started out regardless. I told you they were no good!"

Padway looked back. The Imperialists were in plain sight, and as he watched they began to deploy. It looked like the end of the adventure. He heard Fritharik make a remark about graves, and Tirdat ask if there wasn't a message he could take—preferably to a far-off place.

The Italian serfs had meanwhile seen the Gothic cavalry galloping up with the Imperialists in pursuit, and had formed their own idea that the battle was lost. Ripples of movement ran through their disorderly array, and its motion was presently reversed. Soon the road up to the town was white with running Italians. Those who had crossed the bridge were jammed together in a clawing mob trying to get back over.

Padway yelled in a cracked voice, to Gudareths: "Get back over the river somehow! Send mounted men out on the roads to stop the runaways! Let those on this side get back over. I'll try to hold the Greeks here."

He dismounted most of his troops. He arranged the lancers six deep in a semicircle in front of the bridgehead, around the caterwauling peasants, with lances outward. Along the river bank he posted the archers in two bodies, one on each flank, and beyond them his remaining lancers, mounted. If anything would hold Bloody John, that would.

The Imperialists stood for perhaps ten minutes. Then a big body of Lombards and Gepids trotted out, cantered, galloped straight at his line of spears. Padway, standing afoot behind the line, watched them grow larger and larger. The sound of their hoofs was like that of a huge orchestra of kettledrums, louder and louder. Watching these big, longhaired barbarians loom up out of the dust their horses raised, Padway sympathized with the peasant recruits. If he hadn't had his pride and his responsibility, he'd have run himself until his legs gave out.

On came the Imperialists. They looked as though they could ride over any body of men on earth. Then the bowstrings began to snap. Here a horse reared or buckled; there a man fell off with a musical clash of scale-mail. The charge slowed perceptibly. But they came on. To Padway they looked twenty feet tall. And then they were right on the line of spears. Padway could see the spearmen's tight lips and white faces. If they held—They did. The Imperialist horses reared, screaming, when the lancers pricked them. Some of them stopped so suddenly that their riders were pitched out of the saddle. And then the whole mass was streaming off to right and left, and back to the main army. It wasn't the horses' war, and they had no intention of spitting themselves on the unpleasant-looking lances.

Padway drew his first real breath in almost a minute. He'd been lecturing his men to the effect that no cavalry could break a really solid line of spearmen, but he hadn't believed it himself until now.

Then an awful thing happened. A lot of his lancers, seeing the Imperialists in flight, broke away from the line and started after their foes on foot. Padway screeched at them to come back, but they kept on running, or rather trotting heavily in their armor. Like at Senlac, thought Padway. With similar results. The alert John sent a regiment of cuirassiers out after the clumsily running mob of Goths, and in a twinkling the Goths were scattering all over the field and being speared like so many boars. Padway raved with fury and chagrin; this was his first serious loss. He grabbed Tirdat by the collar, almost strangling him.

He shouted: "Find Gudareths! Tell him to round up a few hundred of those Italians! I'm going to put them in the line!"

Padway's line was now perilously thin, and he couldn't contract it without isolating his archers and horsemen. But this time John hurled his cavalry against the flanking archers. The archers dropped back down the river bank, where the horses couldn't get at them, and Padway's own cavalry charged the Imperialists, driving them off in a dusty chaos of whirling blades.

Presently the desired peasantry appeared, shepherded along by dirty and profane Gothic officers. The bridge was carpeted with pikes dropped in flight; the recruits were armed with these and put in the front line. They filled the gap nicely. Just to encourage them, Padway posted Goths behind them, holding sword points against their kidneys.

Now, if Bloody John would let him alone for a while, he could set about the delicate operation of getting his whole force back across the bridge without exposing any part of it to slaughter.

But Bloody John had no such intention. On came two big bodies of horse, aimed at the flanking Gothic cavalry.

Padway couldn't see what was happening, exactly, between the dust and the ranks of heads and shoulders in the way. But by the diminishing clatter he judged his men were being drawn off. Then came some cuirassiers galloping at the archers, forcing them off the top of the bank again. The cuirassiers strung their bows, and for a few seconds Goths and Imperialists twanged arrows at each other. Then the Goths began slipping off up and down the river, and swimming across.

Finally, on came the Gepids and Lombards, roaring like lions. This time there wouldn't be any arrow fire to slow them up. Bigger and bigger loomed the onrushing mass of longhaired giants on their huge horses, waving their huge axes.

Padway felt the way a violin string must the moment before it snaps.

There was a violent commotion in his own ranks right in front of him. The backs of the Goths were replaced by the brown faces of the peasants. These had dropped their pikes and clawed their way back through the ranks, sword points or no sword points. Padway had a glimpse of their popping eyes, their mouths gaping in screams of terror, and he was bowled over by the wave. They stepped all over him. He squirmed and kicked like a newt on a hook, wondering when the bare feet of the Italians would be succeeded by the hoofs of the hostile cavalry. The Italo-Gothic kingdom was done for, and all his work for nothing....

The pressure and the pounding let up. A battered Padway untangled himself from those who had tripped over him. His whole line had begun to give way, but then had been frozen in the act, staring—all but a Goth in front of him who was killing an Italian.

The Imperialist heavy cavalry was not to be seen. The dust was so thick that nothing much could be seen. From beyond the pall in front of Padway's position came tramplings and shoutings and clatterings.

"What's happened?" yelled Padway. Nobody answered. There was nothing to be seen in front of them but dust, dust, dust. A couple of riderless horses ran dimly past them through it, seeming to drift by like fish in a muddy aquarium tank.

Then a man appeared, running on foot. As he slowed down and walked up to the line of spears, Padway saw that he was a Lombard.

While Padway was wondering if this was some lunatic out to tackle his army single-handed, the man shouted: "*Armaio! Mercy!*" The Goths exchanged startled glances.

Then a couple of more barbarians appeared, one of them leading a horse. They yelled: "*Armaio, timrja!* Mercy, comrade! *Armaio, frijond!* Mercy, friend!"

A plumed Imperial cuirassier rode up behind them, shouting in Latin: "*Amicus!*" Then appeared whole companies of Imperialists, horse and foot, German, Slav, Hun, and Anatolian mixed, bawling, "Mercy, friend!" in a score of languages.

A solid group of horsemen with a Gothic standard in their midst rode through the Imperialists. Padway recognized a tall, brown-bearded figure in their midst. He croaked: "Belisarius!"

The Thracian came up, leaned over, and shook hands. "Martinus! I didn't know you with all that dust on your face. I was afraid I'd be too late. We've been riding hard since dawn. We hit them in the rear, and that was all there was to it. We've got Bloody John, and your King Urias is safe. What shall we do with all these prisoners? There must be twenty or thirty thousand of them at least."

Padway rocked a little on his feet. "Oh, round them up and put them in a camp or something. I don't really care. I'm going to sleep on my feet in another minute."

CHAPTER XVIII

Back in Rome, Urias said slowly: "Yes, I see your point. Men won't fight for a government they have no stake in. But do you think we can afford to compensate all the loyal landlords whose serfs you propose to free?"

"We'll manage," said Padway. "It'll be over a period of years. And this new tax on slaves will help." Padway did not explain that he hoped, by gradually boosting the tax on slaves, to make slavery an altogether unprofitable institution. Such an idea would have been too bewilderingly radical for even Urias' flexible mind.

Urias continued: "I don't mind the limitations on the king's power in this new constitution of yours. For myself, that is. I'm a soldier, and I'm just as glad to leave the conduct of civil affairs to others. But I don't know about the Royal Council."

"They'll agree. I have them more or less eating out of my hand right now. I've shown them how without the telegraph we could never have kept such good track of Bloody John's movements, and without the printing press we could never have roused the serfs so effectively."

"What else is there?"

"We've got to write the kings of the Franks, explaining politely that it's not our fault if the Burgunds prefer our rule to theirs, but that we certainly don't propose to give them back to their Meroving majesties.

"We've also got to make arrangements with the king of Visigoths for fitting out our ships at Lisbon for their trip to the lands across the Atlantic. He's named you his successor, by the way, so when he dies the east and west Goths will be united again. Reminds me, I have to make a trip to Naples. The shipbuilder down there says he never saw such a crazy design as mine, which is for what we Americans would call a Grand

Banks schooner. Procopius'll have to go with me, to discuss details of his history course at our new university."

"Why are you so set on this Atlantic expedition, Martinus?"

"I'll tell you. In my country we amused ourself by sucking the smoke of a weed called tobacco. It's a fairly harmless little vice if you don't overdo it. Ever since I arrived here I've been wishing for some tobacco, and the land across the Atlantic is the nearest place you can get any."

Urias laughed his big, booming laugh. "I've got to be off. I'd like to see the draft of your letter to Justinian before you send it."

"Okay, as we say in America. I'll have it for you tomorrow, and also the appointment of Thomasus the Syrian as minister of finance for you to sign. He arranged to get those skilled ironworkers from Damascus through his private business connections, so I shan't have to ask Justinian for them."

Urias asked: "Are you sure your friend Thomasus is honest?"

"Sure he's honest. You just have to watch him. Give my regards to Mathaswentha. How is she?"

"She's fine. She's calmed down a lot since all the people she most feared have died or gone mad. We're expecting a little Amaling, you know."

"I didn't know! Congratulations."

"Thanks. When are you going to find a girl, Martinus?"

Padway stretched and grinned. "Oh, just as soon as I catch up on my sleep."

Padway watched Urias go with a twinge of envy. He was at the age when bachelors get wistful about their friends' family life. Not that he wanted a repetition of his fiasco with Betty, or a stick of female dynamite like Mathaswentha. He hoped Urias would keep his queen pregnant practically from now on. It might keep her out of mischief.

Padway wrote:

Urias, King of the Goths and Italians, to his Radiant Clemency Flavius Anicius Justinian, Emperor of the Romans, Greetings.

Now that the army sent by your Serene Highness to Italy, under John, the nephew of Vitalianus, better known as Bloody John, is no longer an obstacle to our reconciliation, we resume discussion for terms for the honorable termination of the cruel and unprofitable war between us.

The terms proposed in our previous letter stand, with this exception: Our previously asked indemnity of a hundred thousand solidi is doubled, to compensate our citizens for damages caused by Bloody John's invasion.

There remains the question of the disposal of your general, Bloody John.

Though we have never seriously contemplated the collection of Imperial generals as a hobby, your Serenity's actions have forced us into a policy that looks much like it. As we do not wish to cause the Empire a serious loss, we shall release the said John on payment of a modest ransom of fifty thousand solidi.

We earnestly urge your Serenity to consider this course favorably. As you know, the Kingdom of Persia is ruled by King Khusrau, a young man of great force and ability. We have reason to believe that Khusrau will soon attempt another invasion of Syria. You will then need the ablest generals you can find.

Further, our slight ability to foresee the future informs us that in about thirty years there will be born in Arabia a man named Mohammed, who, preaching a heretical religion, will, unless stopped, instigate a great wave of barbarian conquest, subverting the rule both of the Persian Kingdom and the East Roman Empire. We respectfully urge the desirability of securing control of the Arabian Peninsula forthwith, that this calamity shall be stopped at the source.

Please accept this warning as evidence of our friendliest sentiments. We await the gracious favor of an early reply.

by

Martinus Paduei, Quaestor.

Padway leaned back and looked at the letter. There were other things to attend to: the threat of invasion of Noricum by the Bavarians, and the offer by the Khan of the Avars of an alliance to exterminate the Bulgarian Huns. The alliance would be courteously refused. The Avars would make no pleasanter neighbors than the Bulgars.

Let's see: There was a wandering fanatical monk who was kicking up another row about sorcery. Should he try to smother the man in cream, as by giving him a job? Better see the Bishop of Bologna first; if he had influence in that direction, Padway knew how to make use of it. And it was time he cottoned up to that old rascal Silverius…

And should he go on with his gunpowder experiments? Padway was not sure that this was desirable. The world had enough means of inflicting death and destruction already. On the other hand his own interests were tied up with those on the Italo-Gothic State, which must therefore be saved at all costs…

To hell with it, thought Padway. He swept all the papers into a drawer in his desk, took his hat off the peg, and got his horse. He set out for Anicius' house. How could he expect to cut any ice with Dorothea if he didn't even look her up for days after his return to Rome?

Dorothea came out to meet him. He thought how pretty she was.

But there was nothing of hail-the-conquering-hero about her manner. Before he could get a word out, she began: "You beast! You slimy thing! We befriended you, and you ruin us! My poor old father's heart is broken! And now you've come around to gloat, I suppose!"

"*What?*"

"Don't pretend you don't know! I know all about that illegal order you issued, freeing the serfs on our estates in Campania. They burned our house, and stole the things I've kept since I was a little girl—" She began to weep.

Padway tried to say something sympathetic, but she flared up again. "Get out! I never want to see you again! It'll take a squad of your barbarian soldiers to get you into our house. *Get out!*"

Padway got, slowly and dispiritedly. It was a complex world. Almost anything big you did was bound to hurt somebody.

Then his back straightened. It was nothing to feel sorry for oneself about. Dorothea was a nice girl, yes, pretty, and reasonably bright. But she was not extraordinary in these respects; there were plenty of others equally attractive. To be frank, Dorothea was a pretty average young woman. And being Italian, she'd probably be fat at thirty-five.

Government compensation for their losses would do a lot to mend the broken hearts of the Anicii. If they tried to apologize for treating him roughly, he'd be polite and all, but he didn't think he'd go back.

Girls were okay, and he'd probably fall one of these days. But he had more important things to worry over. His success so far in the business of civilization outweighed any little failures in personal relationships.

His job wasn't over. It never would be—until disease or old age or the dagger of some local enemy ended it. There was so much to do, and only a few decades to do it in; compasses and steam engines and microscopes and the writ of habeas corpus.

He'd teetered along for over a year and a half, grabbing a little power here, placating a possible enemy there, keeping far enough out of the bad graces of the various churches, starting some little art such as spinning of sheet copper. Not bad for Mouse Padway! Maybe he could keep it up for years.

And if he couldn't—if enough people finally got fed up with the innovations of Mysterious Martinus—well, there was a semaphore telegraph system running the length and breadth of Italy, some day to be replaced by a true electric telegraph, if he could find time for the necessary experiments. There was a public letter post about to be set up. There were presses in Florence and Rome and Naples pouring out books and pamphlets and newspapers. Whatever happened to him, these things would go on. They'd become too well rooted to be destroyed by accident.

History had, without question, been changed.

Darkness would not fall.

L. Sprague de Camp's
Great Leap of Imagination

By Alexei and Cory Panshin

The science fiction short stories and the science articles that de Camp wrote during 1938 and 1939 helped to replace Techno Age emotionalism with a new tone of rationality and good humor. They made a strong case for the legitimacy, value and power of human nature. And they tended to suggest that immediate human survival and advancement would not come by way of evolution, which was a slow, gradual, long-term process that could be trusted to take care of itself, but rather through scientific progress, the cumulative mastery of universal operating principles.

Useful, even essential, as this early work was, however, de Camp's most original and significant contribution would come in the novels and short novels that he began to write both alone and collaboratively for *Unknown*, the new companion magazine of *Astounding*.

This second magazine, which started publication in March 1939, was the true measure of John Campbell's breadth and subtlety. It was the culmination of Campbell's early editorial experiments with SF form and content.

Unknown would be to *Astounding* something of what *All-Story* had once been to *Argosy*—a less dignified, less responsible and less respectable sibling. A place for SF writers to have some fun without being held to strict account for it.

In outward appearance, *Unknown* would seem not to be a magazine of science fiction at all—at least not science fiction as Hugo Gernsback might reckon it. Instead, it presented itself as a magazine of traditional fantasy, printing stories about gods, witches, genies, devils and gnomes.

But this appearance would be deceiving. To the degree that the fiction printed in *Unknown* might honestly be called a kind of fantasy, it was fantasy written as though it were a variant form of modern science fiction. The "magic" in *Unknown* would not be based upon *spirit*, as in traditional myth. Instead, it would come to be regarded as another kind of science, the result of the operation of alternative underlying operating principles—which L. Sprague de Camp and his collaborator Fletcher Pratt would call "the laws of magic."

In fact, many of the stories printed in *Unknown* would bear little or no resemblance to traditional spirit-based fantasy. Rather, they would be contemporary SF stories with some impossible twist or odd assumption.

When Campbell received a good story that did not observe the strict parameters of plausibility and subject matter that he was attempting to establish in *Astounding*, it was highly convenient for him to be able to term the story "fantasy" and print it in *Unknown*.

Since Campbell was drawing from a common pool of manuscripts, there might at times appear to be a certain degree of arbitrariness in his decisions as to just what story would appear in which magazine. At least some of the stories that he published—de Camp's invading alien story "Divide and Rule," for instance—might as easily have appeared in one place as the other.

But in Campbell's mind, there was an essential formal distinction between his two magazines. And to aid his writers in their conceptions, he would tell them explicitly: "'I edit two magazines, *Astounding* and *Unknown*. For *Astounding* I want stories which are good and logical and possible. For *Unknown*, I want stories which are good and logical.'"*

What this meant in practice was that the special business of *Astounding* was stories of the future and outer space—the mainstream of science-fictional possibility. And the province of *Unknown* was variant realities.

Within the context of the times, it was *Astounding* that was the vastly more important magazine. *Astounding* was engaged in the serious business of bringing the future of man into being. *Unknown* was just fun and games.

But beyond the immediate moment, *Unknown*—which would only last for four years and thirty-nine issues—would have a considerable importance of its own. In *Unknown*, a basis would be made for perceiving traditional fantasy and pulp magazine science fiction as being different

---

*   Campbell's distinction between *Astounding* and *Unknown* is cited by Theodore Sturgeon in Earl Demp, ed., *The Proceedings; Chicon III* (Chicago: Advent, 1963), p. 122

aspects of a larger SF. And, as the first presentation of SF not just as a literature of *change,* but of *alternate possibilities, Unknown* would be a portent of coming things in SF just as surely as *The Steam Man of the Prairies* had been a forehint of *The Time Machine* and *The Skylark of Space.*

Of all Campbell's writers, it was L. Sprague de Camp who found the freedom of *Unknown* most necessary and most congenial. De Camp suffered from one great inhibition in producing stories for *Astounding*—the "science fiction" published in *Astounding* was supposed to be possible, and the rational side of de Camp took this injunction with the utmost seriousness. But this meant that de Camp was not able to write about time machines or faster-than-light travel, since in his scientific heart-of-hearts he didn't believe that either of these irrational modes of travel would ever be possible.

Way back in *The Skylark of Space,* E.E. Smith might have his venturers casually dismiss Einstein and zoom away toward the stars at supralight speed, saying, " 'Einstein's Theory is still a theory. This distance is an observed fact.'" But de Camp, the new Atomic Age man of reason, debunker of Techno Age credulity, was utterly incapable of this sort of imaginative recklessness.

And because he couldn't see how to leap lightly from here to there, de Camp was never fully at home writing about either the future or outer space. His strict imaginative scruples kept his science fiction stories in *Astounding* comparatively limited and Earthbound.

Ah, but for de Camp stories thought of as "fantasy" and written for *Unknown* were crucially different from stories of "science fiction" meant for *Astounding.* Stories for *Unknown* were not *expected* to be possible—and this set de Camp's imagination free.

As one example, operating according to the standards of *Astounding,* de Camp would never have been able to imagine "The Gnarly Man," his story of a prehistoric man coping easily with the challenges of the modern world. By what *possible* means, pray tell, might a Neanderthal man survive for 50,000 years, never aging? Certainly none that de Camp the rational man of science knew. But writing in the context of *Unknown,* he was permitted to posit that his prehistoric bison hunter had been physiologically altered by a (purely conventional) stroke of lightning, and then get on with the pure fun of imagining how modern people might react to him, and he to them.

Unknown gave de Camp a license to take great leaps of the imagination—which he was then expected to develop logically and rigorously. John Campbell couldn't have devised an imaginative formula more perfectly suited to the nature and knowledge of this particular writer.

So it was, then, that in a story like *Lest Darkness Fall* (*Unknown,* Dec 1939), the de Camp who could not in all conscience write about science fiction time machines felt free to assume yet another lightning-bolt-of-convenience—"the granddaddy of all lightning flashes"—as a device to send his protagonist, archaeologist Martin Padway, back in time to a crucial moment in Western history, the final fall of Rome. Then, from that point, de Camp could play the game of *what if* and proceed to write a novel about the application of universal operating principles to the needs of an earlier moment and the transplantation of scientific progress into the past.

It was *Lest Darkness Fall* that firmly established L. Sprague de Camp as the star writer of *Unknown.* The obvious model for this story was Mark Twain's *A Connecticut Yankee in King Arthur's Court* (1889). *Lest Darkness Fall* might be thought of as an attempt to take *A Connecticut Yankee* and do it *right*—that is, in Atomic Age terms.

In both of these stories, contemporary protagonists are transferred to the past through unlikely accidents. Twain's man is sent back through time as the result of a blow on the head from a crowbar in the hands of a dissident worker, while de Camp's is sent to the past by that humungous bolt of lightning. The point of arrival in both cases is Europe in the Sixth Century A.D., the eve of the Dark Ages. And the aim of both of these modern men becomes to alter the past.

But at that point, the two books diverge subtly but significantly.

Twain's Boss, Hank Morgan, is a man of the Techno Age, a maker of tools and engines and a superintendent of labor. He's a guy who knows how to build machines and keep men in line. His natural impulse is to take the half-historical, half-legendary world he has entered and whip it into shape. Since it is what he knows how to do, he will make guns and railroads and electric lights and set out to turn Arthurian Britain into a facsimile of Nineteenth Century America whether the yokels and peasants like it or not.

But because the story of King Arthur as we know it simply doesn't go that way, eventually he must be slipped a sleeping draught by Merlin which has the effect of returning him to his own time. In the end we have to take all that comes between the blow on the head (which comes before the beginning of the narrative proper) and the sleeping potion at the end as some sort of dream or hallucination.

De Camp, however, was the active beneficiary of all the stories of travel in time and dimension written in the fifty years since *A Connecticut*

Yankee—even though he himself might spurn Wellsian time machines of nickel and ivory and crystal as scientifically impossible. And at the very outset of *Lest Darkness Fall*, before the crucial bolt of lightning strikes, he has an Italian professor set forth a very Wells-like theory of time as a tree with many branches:

> "I was saying all these people who just disappear, they have slipped back down the ... trunk of the tree of time. When they stop slipping, they are back in some former time. But as soon as they do anything, they change all subsequent history.... The trunk continues to exist. But a new branch starts out where they came to rest."

Thus, pure device of convenience though that stroke of lightning may be, we do have a basis of argument for taking it seriously as a time travel device. And when Martin Padway finds himself transferred to a known historical period—a declining Rome in 535 A.D., ruled by an Ostrogothic king and about to suffer invasion by Justinian's brilliant general, Belisarius—it isn't a dream and he isn't going to just as suddenly find himself back in the Twentieth Century. He's in Rome for real, and he's there for good.

What is more, he isn't condemned to complete futility by what our history books say did happen then. He has some assurance that by the actions he chooses to take, he can alter the course of history. It is within his power to create a whole new reality if he is clever and able enough.

Unlike Twain's Techno Age Boss, who perceives the Sixth Century Britons as no better than children or animals, Martin Padway is an Atomic Age democrat who sincerely likes and respects the people he has fallen among. De Camp being de Camp, these various Italians, Goths, Vandals, Syrians, Jews, Greeks and such are presented as familiar, normal, decent, fallible human beings not very different in nature from ourselves.

What distinguishes Padway from them is not that he is some sort of superior human being, higher on the evolutionary ladder than they, but rather his comparatively greater degree of knowledge and objectivity. He is forearmed by knowing something of history as it would have been without him. And he is also a man of scientific training, an heir of the past few centuries of Western scientific progress.

Padway's impulse isn't to attempt to re-create the Twentieth Century in Sixth Century Rome, erecting skyscrapers beside the Colosseum. Indeed, he doesn't for an instant believe that such a thing would be possible. But he is deeply aware of the pivotal nature of the moment in which he finds himself:

He was living in the twilight of western classical civilization. The Age of Faith, better known as the Dark Ages, was closing down. Europe would be in darkness, from a scientific and technological aspect, for nearly a thousand years. That aspect was, to Padway's naturally prejudiced mind, the most, if not the only, important aspect of a civilization.

Almost inevitably, then, it occurs to Padway to wonder: "Could one man change the course of history to the extent of preventing this interregnum?"

It's as though Padway were some special sort of doctor brought to the bedside of this ailing culture to give it a shot of what it needs the most. That isn't an instant, inappropriate modernity, but rather transplants of appropriate inventions and techniques from the Middle Ages and the Renaissance, stuff that may serve to start up the machinery of scientific progress.

So it is that Padway introduces Arabic numerals, horse harnesses, distilling, the telescope, semaphore telegraphy, paper and printing, a postal system and schools. When he proposes this last, he says frankly, " 'I'm going to have things taught that really matter: mathematics, and the sciences, and medicine. I see where I shall have to write all the textbooks myself.' "

Of necessity—there is that invasion by the armies of the Eastern Roman Emperor Justinian to consider—Padway does become involved in military and political activities like Twain's Hank Morgan, but he sees these only as means. He says: " 'The end is things like the telegraph and the presses. My politicking and soldiering may not make any difference a hundred years from now, but the other things will, I hope.' "

And by the end of the story, he has grown convinced that he has been successful. Whatever befalls him, these things he has introduced are now too widespread and well rooted to disappear. History has been changed. Darkness will not fall—at least not on this one new branch of the tree of time.

"L. Sprague de Camp's Great Leap of Imagination" is adapted from Alexei and Cory Panshin's Hugo winning study of science ficiton, *The World Beyond the Hill.*

THE DEADLY MISSION OF
PHINEAS SNODGRASS

FREDERIK POHL

This is the story of Phineas Snodgrass, inventor. He built a time machine.

He built a time machine and in it he went back some two thousand years, to about the time of the birth of Christ. He made himself known to the Emperor Augustus, his lady Livia and other rich and powerful Romans of the day and, quickly making friends, secured their cooperation in bringing about a rapid transformation of Year One living habits. (He stole the idea from a science-fiction novel by L. Sprague de Camp, called *Lest Darkness Fall.*)

His time machine wasn't very big, but his heart was, so Snodgrass selected his cargo with the plan of providing the maximum immediate help for the world's people. The principal features of ancient Rome were dirt and disease, pain and death. Snodgrass decided to make the Roman world healthy and to keep its people alive through twentieth-century medicine. Everything else could take care of itself, once the human race was free of its terrible plagues and early deaths.

Snodgrass introduced penicillin and aureomycin and painless dentistry. He ground lenses for spectacles and explained the surgical techniques for removing cataracts. He taught anesthesia and the germ theory of disease, and showed how to purify drinking water. He built Kleenex factories and taught the Romans to cover their mouths when they coughed. He demanded, and got, covers for the open Roman sewers, and he pioneered the practice of the balanced diet.

Snodgrass brought health to the ancient world, and kept his own health, too. He lived to more than a hundred years. He died, in fact, in the year A.D. 100, a very contented man.

When Snodgrass arrived in Augustus's great palace on the Palatine Hill, there were some 250,000,000 human beings alive in the world. He persuaded the principate to share his blessings with all the world, benefiting not only the hundred million subjects of the Empire, but the other one hundred millions in Asia and the tens of millions in Africa, the Western Hemisphere and all the Pacific islands.

Everybody got healthy.

Infant mortality dropped at once, from 90 deaths in a hundred to fewer than two. Life expectancies doubled immediately. Everyone was well, and demonstrated their health by having more children, who grew in health to maturity and had more.

It is a feeble population that cannot double itself every generation if it tries.

These Romans, Goths, and Mongols were tough. Every 30 years the population of the world increased by a factor of two. In the year A.D. 30, the world population was a half billion. In A.D. 60, it was a full billion. By the time Snodgrass passed away, a happy man, it was as large as it is today.

It is too bad that Snodgrass did not have room in his time machine for the blueprints of cargo ships, the texts on metallurgy to build the tools that would make the reapers that would harvest the fields—for the triple-expansion steam turbines that would generate the electricity that would power the machines that would run the cities—for all the technology that 2,000 subsequent years had brought about.

But he didn't.

Consequently, by the time of his death conditions were no longer quite perfect. A great many were badly housed.

On the whole, Snodgrass was pleased, for all these things could surely take care of themselves. With a healthy world population, the increase of numbers would be a mere spur to research. Boundless nature, once its ways were studied, would surely provide for any number of human beings.

Indeed it did. Steam engines on the Newcomen design were lifting water to irrigate fields to grow food long before his death. The Nile was dammed at Aswan in the year 55. Battery-powered streetcars replaced oxcarts in Rome and Alexandria before A.D. 75, and the galley slaves were freed by huge, clumsy diesel outboards that drove the food ships across the Mediterranean a few years later.

In the year A.D. 200 the world had now something over twenty billion souls, and technology was running neck-and-neck with expansion. Nuclear-driven ploughs had cleared the Teutoburg Wald, where Varus's bones were still mouldering, and fertilizer made from ion-exchange mining of the sea produced fantastic crops of hybrid grains. In A.D. 300 the world population stood at a quarter of a trillion. Hydrogen fusion produced fabulous quantities of energy from the sea; atomic transmutation converted any matter into food. This was necessary, because there was no longer any room for farms. The Earth was getting crowded. By the middle of the sixth century the 60,000,000 square miles of land surface on the Earth were so well covered that no human being standing anywhere on dry land could stretch out his arms in any direction without touching another human being standing beside him.

But everyone was healthy, and science marched on. The seas were drained, which immediately tripled the available land area. (In 50 years the sea bottoms were also full.) Energy which had come from the fusion of marine hydrogen now came by the tapping of the full energy output of the Sun, through gigantic "mirrors" composed of pure force. The other planets froze, of course; but this no longer mattered, since in the decades that followed they were disintegrated for the sake of the energy at their cores. So was the Sun. Maintaining life on Earth on such artificial standards was prodigal of energy consumption; in time every star in the Galaxy was transmitting its total power output to the Earth, and plans were afoot to tap Andromeda, which would care for all necessary expansion for—30 years.

At this point a calculation was made.

Taking the weight of the average man at about a hundred and thirty pounds—in round numbers, 6×10^4 grammes—and allowing for a continued doubling of population every 30 years (although there was no such thing as a "year" anymore, since the Sun had been disintegrated; now a lonely Earth floated aimlessly towards Vega), it was discovered that by the year 1970 the total mass of human flesh, bone, and blood would be 6×10^{27} grammes.

This presented a problem. The total mass of the Earth itself was only 5.98×10^{27} grammes. Already humanity lived in burrows penetrating crust and basalt and quarrying into the congealed nickel-iron core; by 1970 all the core itself would have been transmuted into living men and women, and their galleries would have to be tunneled through masses of their own bodies, a writhing, squeezed ball of living corpses drifting through space.

Moreover, simple arithmetic showed that this was not the end. In finite time the mass of human beings would equal the total mass of the Galaxy; and in some further time it would equal and exceed the total mass of *all* galaxies everywhere.

This state of affairs could no longer be tolerated, and so a project was launched.

With some difficulty resources were diverted to permit the construction of a small but important device. It was a time machine. With one volunteer aboard (selected from the 900 trillion who applied) it went back to the year 1. Its cargo was only a hunting rifle with one cartridge, and with that cartridge the volunteer assassinated Snodgrass as he trudged up the Palatine.

To the great (if only potential) joy of some quintillions of never-to-be-born persons, Darkness blessedly fell.

THE APOTHEOSIS OF
MARTIN PADWAY

S. M. STIRLING

"T his is the *right* vector," the computer insisted.

"If you say so," Maximus Liu-Peng replied. *Insolent machine,* he added to himself. *Still, there's something fishy here. Some sort of temporal loop?*

Luckily, the passengers were too occupied oohing and ahing at the screens to notice the interplay. The big holographic displays around the interior of the compartment showed a blinking succession of possible cities, all of them late-sixth-century Florence; cities large, small, burning, thriving, an abandoned one with a clutch of Hunnish yurts...

They wavered, then steadied to a recognizable shape; recognizable from maps, from preserved relics four hundred years old, and from the general appearance of an Early Industrial city.

Classical-era buildings sprawled across a set of hills with a river winding through it, all columns and marble around the squares and squalid tenements elsewhere; old temples had been converted into churches; city walls torn down and replaced by boulevards and parks; and a spanking-new railway station on the outskirts had spawned a clutch of factories with tall brick chimneys and spreading row housing for the workers.

"How quaint!" gushed somebody's influential cousin, officially an observer for the Senatorial Committee on Anachro-Temporal Affairs.

Maximus controlled his features. Several of the scholarly types didn't try to hide their scorn; either safely tenured, naive, or both. A coal-black anthropologist cleared her throat with a *hrrrump.*

"You're certain this is our *own* past?" she said.

The operator's poker experience came in handy again. "That's a"—*bloody stupid question*—"moot point, *Doctore Illustrissimo,*" he said. "It's definitely a past with Martinus of Padua in it. There are no other lines within several hundred chronospace-years that show a scientific-industrial revolution this early. Quantum factors make it difficult"—*fucking meaningless*—"to say if it's *precisely* the line that led to us."

"But will *He* be here?" an archbishop said.

That required even more caution. "Well, Your Holiness, that's what we'll have to find out. This *is*—" he pointed to the July 14, 585 A.D. readout "—the traditional date of the Ascension."

"I am not worthy to witness a miracle," the cleric breathed. "Yet that is why we have come—"

"We're here to find final proof of the Great Man theory," a historian answered, and they glared at each other. "Not to indulge in superstition. It's only natural that primitives, confronted with one of history's truly decisive individuals, should spin a cocoon of myth as they did with Alexander or Manuel—"

"Nonsense," the anthropologist said. "Martinus was merely there at the right time. Socioeconomic conditions were obviously—"

"I just drive this thing," Maximus muttered as the argument went into arm-waving stalemate, and checked the exterior deflector screens. It wouldn't do to have any of the natives see them floating up here....

Lieutenant Tharasamund Hrothegisson, *hirdman* in the Guards of Urias III, King of the Goths and Italians and Emperor of the West, looked carefully at each man's presented rifle as he walked down the line.

Then he called his troop to attention, drew the long *spatha* at his side, turned to face his men and stood at parade rest, with the point of the blade resting lightly on the pavement between his feet. The street was flat stones set in concrete—nothing but the best for the capital of the Romano-Gothic Empire!—but not too broad, perhaps thirty feet from wall to wall counting the brick sidewalks.

"All right, men," he said, raising his voice. "This shouldn't be much of a job. Wait for the word of command, and if you have to shoot to kill, shoot low."

There were nods and grins, quickly stifled. Tharasamund had spoken in Gothic; that was still the official language of the army—though nowadays only about a fifth of the men were born to Gothic mothers, even in a unit of the Royal Guards, and that was counting Visigoths. There were plenty of Italians, other Romans from Hispania and Gaul and North Africa, Burgunds, Lombards, Franks, Bavarians, Frisians—even a few Saxons and Angles and Jutes, a solitary Dane, and a couple of reddish-brown Lyonessians from beyond the western sea.

None of them were unhappy at the thought of taking a slap at a city mob, though, being mostly farmers' sons or lesser gentry themselves. Good lads, but inclined to be a bit rough if they weren't watched.

"Deploy in line," he said, looking back over his shoulder at the guns for a moment.

There were two of them: old-fashioned bronze twelve-pounders, already unhitched from their teams and pointing forward. *And may God spare me the need to use them*, he thought. They were obsolete for field use, but as giant short-range shotguns with four-inch bores they were still as horribly efficient as they'd been in the Second Greek War, when they were a monstrous innovation and surprise.

The soldiers trotted quickly to make a two-deep line across the street, identical in their forest-green uniforms and cloth-covered steel helmets. The city was quiet—far too quiet for Florence on a Saturday afternoon, even with the League playoffs sucking everyone who could afford it out to the stadium in the suburbs. The wind had died, leaving the drowsy warmth of an Italian summer afternoon lying heavy; also heavy with the city smells of smoke and horse dung and garbage. The buzzing flies were the loudest sound he could hear, save for a distant grumbling, rumbling thunder. Shopkeepers had pulled down their shutters and householders barred window and door hours ago.

"Load!"

The men reached down to the bandoliers at their right hips, pulled out cartridges and dropped them into the open breeches. They closed with a multiple *snick-snick-snick*.

"Fix bayonets!"

The long sword-knives went home below the barrels with another grating metallic rattle and snap.

"Present!"

The troops advanced their rifles with a deep-throated *ho!* That left a line of bristling steel points stretching across the street. With any luck…

Tharasamund took off his helmet and inclined his head slightly to one side. *Yes, here they come*, he thought.

He replaced the headpiece and waited, *spatha* making small precise movements as his wrist moved, limbering his sword arm. The first thing he saw was a man in the brown uniform of the city police. He was running as fast as he could—limping, in fact—and blood ran down his face from a scalp bare of the leather helmet he should have worn. When he saw the line of bayonets, he stopped and started thanking God, Mary, and the saints.

"Make some sense, Sathanas fly away with you," Tharasamund snapped.

He was a tall, rangy, blue-eyed man a few years shy of thirty himself, with a close-trimmed yellow beard and mustaches and shoulder-length hair a shade lighter, but his Latin was without an accent—better than the rather rustic Tuscan dialect the policeman spoke, in fact. Still, his uniform and Gothic features calmed the Italian a little. They represented authority, even in these enlightened times of the career open to talents.

"My lord," he gasped. "Patrolman Marcus Mummius reporting."

"What's going on?"

"My lord, the Carthage Lions triumphed!"

Tharasamund winced. "What was the score?" he asked.

"Seventeen-sixteen, with a field goal in sudden-death overtime."

Oh, Sathanas take it, he thought, restraining an impulse to clap his hand to his forehead and curse aloud.

The Florentine mob *hated* losing, even when times were good—which they weren't. When times were bad, they were as touchy as a lion with a gut ache. For some reason they thought being the capital city entitled their team to eternal victory, and this was just the sort of thing to drive them into a frenzy. Particularly with defeat at the hands of an upstart team like the Carthage Lions, only in the League a few years—North Africa hadn't been part of the Western Empire until the war of 560, twenty-five years ago.

"We tried to keep everything in order, but when the Carthaginian fans stormed the field and tore down the goalposts, the crowd went wild. They would have killed all the Lions *and* their supporters if we hadn't put all our men to guarding the entrances to the locker rooms. Then they began fighting with all the men from other cities, shouting that foreigners were taking all the best jobs, and—"

"Sergeant, give this man a drink and patch him up," Tharasamund said, ignoring the Italian's thanks as he was led away.

There were thousands of out-of-towners around for the playoffs, plenty of material for a riot with the bad times of the last year—the papers were calling it a *recession*, odd word.

The first spray of hooligans came around the corner two hundred yards south, screaming slogans, banging on shop shutters with rocks and clubs. *They* were wearing leather helmets, the sort actual footballers used, but painted in team colors and with gaudy plumes added, and the numbers of their favorite players across their chests.

Their noisy enthusiasm waned abruptly as they saw the soldiers; then a deep baying snarl went up, and they began to edge and mill forward towards the line of points.

Tharasamund winced. That was a *very* bad sign.

"I've been too successful for too long," Martinus of Padua said as he lit a cigarette and leaned back for a moment in his swivel chair, looking at the neat stacks of paper that crowded his marble-slab desktop.

"On the other hand, consider the alternative," he told himself.

His voice was hoarse with age and tobacco smoke; the precise Latin he spoke was a scholar's, but it bore the very faint trace of an accent that was—literally—like none other in the whole world. He'd been born Martin Padway, in the United States of America during the first decade of the twentieth century, but even he hardly ever thought of himself by that name anymore; it had been fifty-two years since he found himself transported from Benito Mussolini's Rome to the one ruled by Thiudahad, King of the Goths and Italians, 533 A.D.

He gave a breathy chuckle; the city fathers of Padua had even erected a monument to his supposed birth in their fair town, and it attracted a substantial stream of tourists. Quite a lucrative little business, all built on a linguistic accident—any native Latin speaker would hear *Padway* as *Paduei*, "of Padua." The chuckle became a rumbling cough, and he swore quietly as he wiped his lips with a handkerchief. The years had carved deep runnels in his face, leaving the beak of a nose even more prominent, but he still had most of his teeth, and the liver-spotted hands were steady as he picked up a file from the *urgent* stack.

He took another drag on the cigarette, coughed again, flipped the file open and read:

Item:

The East Roman armies looked like they'd finally broken the last Persian resistance in Sogdiana, what Padway mentally referred to as Afghanistan.

Damn. I was hoping they'd be pinned down there fighting guerrillas forever. The way the Byzantines keep persecuting Zoroastrians and Buddhists, they deserve it. Plus the Sogdians are even meaner than Saxons. Oh, well. Might be good for trade if they settle down peacefully.

The East Roman Emperor Justinian was even older than Martin Padway, and he'd never stopped hating the Italo-Gothic kingdom—what had become the reborn and expanded Empire of the West. The more it grew, the more bitter his enmity. Despite the fact that he personally would have been long dead without the doctors Padway had supplied, and never would have beaten the Persians or pushed the Byzantine frontier far north of the Danube without the gunpowder weapons and telegraphs and steamboats his artisans had copied from the models Padway had "invented."

That made absolutely no difference to Justinian's intensely clever but even more paranoid mind; he probably thought he'd have done it all anyway if Padway hadn't shown up. Or even more.

Maybe his grandnephew will be more reasonable. The old buzzard can't last forever…can he? Note to State Department: get the spies working double-time to see if the Byzantines start shifting troops west to the Dalmatian frontier. He'd love to take another slap at us.

Item:

Riots between pagan and Christian settlers had broken out again in Nova Eboracum, over in Lyonesse; what in another history had been called New York.

Maybe I was a bit too clever there.

Diverting the Saxon migrations from Britannia to the Americas had taken care of their land hunger and gotten a lot of inveterate pirates out of the Channel. It had even introduced them to the rudiments of civilization, since the new colonies were more firmly under the Empire of the West's control than the North Sea homelands.

What it hadn't done was lessen their love of a fight; "Saxon" meant something like "shiv-man," and the tribal ethnonym was no accident. These days they were just using different rationalizations, stubborn Wodenites bashing enthusiasts for the White Christ and vice versa and the Britanno-Roman and Gallo-Roman and Iberian settlers rioting against them all.

The current financial crisis didn't help either. People here just weren't used to the idea of market fluctuations—bad harvests and famine, yes, the trade cycle, no. FDR hadn't been able to cure the one at home, and Padway hadn't found any way to do it here either, except spread a little comfort money around and wait.

Note to Royal Council: send a couple of regiments to Lyonesse. Not ones with a lot of Saxons or Frisians in the ranks. Push the troublemakers up west of Albany into the frontier townships and give them all land grants.

Then the transplanted Saxons could take out their pugnacity on the Indians. The British Empire had used that trick with the Scots-Irish, in Ireland and America both.

Item:

The Elba Steel Company was complaining about competition from the new mills in the Rhineland. *Nothing much I can do about that*

Italy just didn't have much basis for heavy industry, and now that the Rhone-Rhine canal and railway were working…But the Elba Company *did* have a lot of important Italian and Gothic aristocrats on the board of directors. *They* had pull in the House of Lords. Plus he'd advised many of them to put their serf-emancipation compensation money into Elba stock, back when. Italian industry had spent a generation or two booming, because it was the only game around. Now the provinces were starting to catch up and all the established balances were shifting.

Wait a minute. We'll throw them some government contracts, and they can use the profits to tempt some of the new Gallic and Britannic steel firms to agree to cross-shareholdings. That would ease the transition—and keep those important votes sweet.

Item:

Down in Australia—

A knock came at the door, and his secretary Lucilla stuck her head through. "Quaestor," she said, having always refused to call him "excellent boss" like everyone else. "Your granddaughter is here."

"And it's my *birthday,* Grandfather!" Jorith said, bursting through and hurrying forward. He rose—slightly painfully—and returned her enthusiastic hug.

His daughter's youngest daughter was just turned eighteen. She took after her father's side of the family in looks; he was the third son of King Urias I. She was nearly up to Padway's five-foot-six, which made her towering for a woman of this age and area, with straight features, long dark-blonde hair falling past her shoulders, and bright green eyes.

Actually, she reminds me of her father's mother, Padway thought. *Just as gorgeous a man-trap, and just as smart. Doesn't have Mathaswentha's weakness for lopping off people's heads, though.*

At one point, he'd come within an inch of marrying Mathaswentha himself. Urias' uncle Wittigis had tried to marry her by force, during the first Byzantine invasion, a few months after Padway was dropped back into Gothic-era Rome; as a princess of the Amaling clan, she made whoever married her automatically eligible for the elective Gothic monarchy. That was one reason he'd pushed the Goths into accepting a pure eldest-son inheritance system; it cut down on succession disputes.

Padway had rescued Mathaswentha from a forced marriage at the very altar, and for a while he'd been smitten with her, and vice versa.

Brrrr, he thought; the memory of his narrow escape never failed to send a chill down his spine. Luckily he'd wised up in time, and had had Urias on hand—a Goth smart enough and tough enough to keep that she-leopard on a leash, and a good friend of Padway's.

Gentle, scholarly Drusilla had been much more the American's style.

"Pity your parents couldn't get back from Gadez," he said, feeling slightly guilty.

The truth was he'd never much liked his daughter Maria. That was unjust. It wasn't *her* fault that Drusilla had died in childbirth. He'd tried to be a good father anyway, but between that and the press of business, she'd mostly been raised by relatives and servants. Jorith was the delight of his old age.

And doesn't she know it, he thought indulgently.

They walked out together through the Quaestor's Offices, her arm linked around his left elbow. He was slightly—resentfully—conscious of the fact that she was walking slowly and ready to catch him if he stumbled, despite the cane he used with his right hand. He was in his mid-eighties now. Moving hurt. He'd spent nearly six decades back here, and he wasn't that spry, brash young archaeologist anymore.

Not even the same person, really. A few weeks ago he'd tried to make himself *think* in English, and found it horrifyingly difficult.

I should be grateful, he thought, as they walked down corridors past offices and clerical pools, amid a ripple of bows and murmurs. *I'm not senile or bedridden.* Or dead, for that matter. And he'd done a lot more good here than he could have in his native century; nobody who'd seen a real famine close up, or what was left of a town after a sack by Hun raiders, could doubt that.

He ignored the quartet of guards who followed, hard-eyed young men with their hands on the hilts of their swords and revolvers at their waists. *They* were part of the furniture. Justinian and assorted other enemies would *still* be glad to see him go. He chuckled a little as they came out into the broad marble-and-mosaic foyer of the building.

"What's so funny, Grandfather?" Jorith said.

"That there are still men prepared to go to such efforts to kill me," Padway said.

"That's *funny?*" she said, in a scandalized tone.

"In a way. If they'd killed me right after I arrived here, they might have accomplished something—from their point of view; stopped me from changing things. It was touch and go there, those first couple of years. It's far too late, now…"

"But not too late for the theatre," Jorith said. "It's a revival of one of your plays, too—*A Midsummer Night's Dream*…what are you laughing at *this* time, Grandfather?"

"There's nothing here," the archbishop fretted.

"Well, the Cathedral wasn't built until the 700s," the historian pointed out with poisonously sweet reasonableness.

The field wasn't empty, strictly speaking. There was a big two-story brick building, so new that the tiles were still going on the roof. The rest of it was trampled mud, wheelbarrows, piles of mortar and brick and timber and boards, and a clumsy-looking steam traction engine.

"But why should…marvelous are the works of the Lord," the archbishop said. "If His Son could be born in a stable, a saint can rise to heaven from a building yard."

"We're redirecting traffic, my lord," the policeman said, walking up to the door of the carriage.

"What for?" Padway said. *Mustn't get testy in my old age*, he thought. *And it was a pretty good performance.* Thank God for a good memory; he'd managed to put down something close to Shakespeare's text.

"There are rumors of riots," the policeman said, sweating slightly. Nobody liked having the Big Boss suddenly turn up on their beat when something was going wrong. "Riots among the football spectators, my lord."

"Oh. Well, thank you, Officer," Padway said. As the carriage lurched into motion, he went on: "I keep outsmarting myself."

Jorith giggled. "Grandfather, why is it that all the other politicians and courtiers are dull as dust, but you can always make me laugh?"

It does sound funnier in Latin, he thought. Plus he'd gotten a considerable reputation as a wit over the past fifty years by reusing the clichés of the next fifteen hundred years. He chuckled himself.

And Drusilla swooned over things like parting is such sweet sorrow, *too.* That brought a stab of pain, and he leaned out the window of the carriage.

"What I mean," he went on, "is that I introduced football to quiet people down. Didn't think anyone could get as upset about that as they did over chariot races."

"I've never seen the point, myself," Jorith said. "Polo is much more exciting."

Padway grinned to himself. The Gothic aristocracy had taken to *that* like Russians to drink. In fact, they'd virtually reinvented the game themselves, with a little encouragement and some descriptions from him.

They remind me of horsy country-gentleman-type Englishmen, he thought, not for the first time. *Particularly now that they've taken to baths and literacy.*

They were out of the theatre crush now, the carriages moving a little faster as they moved downhill. The clatter of shod hooves on pavement was loud, but at least most of them had rubber wheels these days, which cut down on the shattering racket iron-clad ones made on city streets. He stopped himself from making a mental note to look into how automobile research was coming.

Leave it to the young men, he thought.

There were enough of them coming out of the universities now, trained in the scientific worldview. In the long run, it would be better *not* to intervene anymore, even with "suggestions." There were enough superstitions about "Mysterious Martinus"; he wanted the younger generation to learn how to think rationally, and for themselves.

He smiled, thinking of the thrill he'd had the first time a young professor had dared to argue with him about chemistry—and the whippersnapper had turned out to be right, and Padway's vague high-school recollections wrong, too. And after that...

Jorith was smiling at him indulgently. He blinked, realizing he'd dozed off, lost in half-dreams of decades past.

"Sorry," he said, straightening on the coach's well-padded seat, wincing a little at the stiffness in his neck.

"You deserve to be able to nap when you feel like it, Grandfather," Jorith said. "It's a sin, the way you work yourself to a nub, after all you've done for the kingdom. Why, I remember only last month, how everyone cheered in the Senate when you made that speech—the one where you said we had nothing to fear but fear itself—"

A short crashing *baaammm* rang out ahead. Padway's head came up with a start, the last threads of dream slipping away. He knew that sound of old—was responsible for it being heard a millennium or so early.

Rifles, firing in volley...

"*Fire!*" Tharasamund said reluctantly.

The sound of fifteen rifles going off within half a second of each other battered at his ears. The front rank reloaded, spent cartridges tinkling on the pavement, and the sergeant bellowed:

"Second rank, volley fire present—*fire!*"

Dirty-white powder smoke drifted back towards him, smelling of rotten eggs and death. Ten yards away the crowd milled and screamed, half a dozen lying limply dead, twice as many more whimpering or fleeing clutching wounds or lying and screaming out their hurt to the world. The rest hesitated, bunching up—which meant a lot of them were angry enough to face high-velocity lead slugs.

"*Cease fire!*" he said to his men, with enough of a rasp in it to make them obey. To the mob, he went on in Latin.

"Disperse! Return to your homes!" he called, working to keep his voice deep and authoritative, and all the desperation he felt out of it. "In the

Emperor Urias' name!"

"Down with the Goths!" someone screeched. "Down with the heretics! *Dig up their bones!*"

"Oh-oh," Tharasamund said.

That was call to riot, an import from Constantine's city....The religious prejudice was home-grown, though. Most Goths were still Arian Christians—heretics, to Orthodox Catholics—and the Western Empire enforced a strict policy of toleration, even for pagans and Jews and Nestorians, and for Zoroastrian refugees from Justinian's persecutions.

I hate to do this. They're fools, but that doesn't mean they deserve to he sausage meat. Drunk, half of them, and a lot of them out of work.

"Clear firing lanes!" he rasped aloud.

The soldiers did, shuffling aside but keeping their rifles to the shoulder to leave a line of bright points and intimidating muzzles facing the crowd. The artillerymen stepped aside from their weapons—they'd recoil ten feet each when fired, on smooth pavement—with the gun captains holding the long lanyards ready. Those four-inch bores were even more intimidating than rifles, if you knew what they could do.

"Ready, sir," the artillery noncom said. "Doubled-shotted with grape."

Tharasamund nodded. "Disperse!" he repeated, his voice cutting over the low brabbling murmur of the crowd. "This is your last warning!"

He heard a whisper of *Why give them any fucking warnings?* but ignored it; there were some times an officer was wise to be half-deaf.

The noise of the crowd died down, a slow sullen quiet spreading like olive oil on a linen tablecloth A few in the front rank tossed down their rocks and chunks of brick, turning and trying to force their way back through the crowd; the slow forward movement turned into eddies and milling about. He took a long breath of relief, and felt the little hairs along his spine stop trying to bristle upright.

"I should have stayed home in Campania and raised horses," he muttered to himself. "But no, I had to be dutiful..."

He half-turned his head as he sheathed his sword; that let him catch the motion on the rooftop out of the corner of his eye. Time froze; he could see the man—short, swarthy, nondescript, in a shabby tunic. The expression of concentration on the man's face as he tossed the black-iron sphere with its long fuse trailing sputterings and blue smoke...

"*Down!*" Tharasamund screamed, and suited action to words—there was no time to do anything else.

Someone tripped and fell over him; that saved his life, although he never remembered exactly what happened when the bomb fell into the open ammunition limber of the twelve-pounder.

"What was *that?*" Jorith exclaimed, shock on her face.

Neither of them really needed telling. *That* was an explosion, and a fairly big one. The driver of the carriage leaned on the brake and reined in, but the road was fairly steep here—flanked on both sides by shops and homes above them. Padway leaned out again, putting on his spectacles and blinking, thankful that at least the lens grinders were turning out good flint glass at last. Then another blast came, and another, smaller and muffled by distance.

"Goddamn that bastard Justinian to *hell,*" he growled—surprising himself by swearing, and doing it in English. Normally he was a mild-mannered man, but...

"Grandfather?" Jorith said nervously; she wasn't used to him lapsing into the mysterious foreign tongue either.

"Sorry, kitten," he said, then coughed. "I was cursing the Emperor of the East."

Her blue eyes went wide. "You think—"

"Well, we can produce our own riots, but not bombs, I think," Padway said. "Dammit, he can try and kill *me*—he's been doing that for fifty years—but this is beyond enough."

Shod hooves clattered on the pavement outside. One of the bodyguards leaned over to speak through the coach's window.

"Excellent boss," he said. "There are rioters behind us. We think it would be best to try and go forward and link up with the soldiers we heard ahead, and then take the Equinoctal Way out to the suburbs. There will be more troops moving into the city."

"As you think best, Hermann," Padway said; he'd commanded armies in his time, but that was forty years ago and more, and he'd never pretended to be a fighting man. He tried to leave that to the professionals.

Tharasamund shook his head. That was a bad mistake; pain thrust needles through his head, and there was a loud metallic ringing noise that made him struggle to clap hands to his ears. The soft heavy resistance to the movement made him realize that he was lying under several mangled bodies, and what the sticky substance clotting his eyelashes and running into his mouth was. He retched a little, gained control with gritted teeth and a massive effort of will, and pushed the body off. Half-blinded, he groped frantically for a water bottle and splashed the contents across his face while he rubbed at his eyelids. The blood wasn't quite dried, and the flies weren't all that bad yet; that meant he hadn't been out long. A public fountain had broken in the blast, and water was puddling up against the dam of dead horses and men and wrecked equipment across the road.

As he'd expected, what he saw when he *could* see properly was very bad. Nobody looked alive—most of the bodies weren't even intact, and if one of the field guns hadn't taken some of the blast when both limbers went off, he wouldn't be either. Nobody but the dead were here—a tangle of the mob around where the last of his soldiers had fallen. All the intact weapons were gone, of course, except for his sword and revolver; he'd probably looked too thoroughly like a mangled corpse to be worth searching by men in a hurry. The fronts of the shops on either side were smashed in by the explosion and by looters completing the work; a civilian lay half in and half out of one window, very thoroughly dead.

"Probably the shopkeeper," Tharasamund muttered grimly, his own voice sounding muffled and strange. The pain and the ringing in his ears were a little better, but probably he'd never have quite the keenness of hearing again.

That was another score to settle, along with the cold rage at the killing of his men. He staggered over to the fountain and washed as best he could; that brought him nearer to consciousness. The first thing to do—

He hardly heard the coach clatter up, but the sight brought him out into the roadway, waving his sword. That brought half a dozen pistols in the hands of the mounted guards on him, and a shotgun from the man beside the driver. The men were in civil dress, country gentleman's Gothic style, but they were a mixed lot. Soldiers or ex-soldiers, he'd swear; from the look of the coach, some great lord's personal retainers. None of them looked very upset at the carnage that was painting the coach's wheels and the hooves of their horses red…best be a little careful.

"Tharasamund, Captain in the *Kunglike-hird*, the Royal Guard," he snapped, sheathing the blade. "I need transport, and I call on you to assist me in the Emperor's name."

"Straight-leg, we don't stop for anyone," the chief guard said—he had a long tow-colored mane, a thick bull-neck, and an equally thick growling accent in his Latin: Saxon, at a guess. "The only thing I want to hear from you is how to get our lord to someplace safe."

Tharasamund looked around. He could hear distant shouting and screams and the crackle of gunfire. That meant they were *loud*. And he could see columns of smoke, too. It might be an hour—or four or five—before enough troops marched in from the barracks outside town, between the built-up area and the royal palace, to restore order. Someone had screwed up royally; he'd be surprised if there wasn't a new urban prefect soon.

Not that that will be much consolation to the dead, he added to himself.

He was opening his mouth to argue again—he had to get back to regimental HQ, to report this monumental ratfuck, and get some orders—when a young woman leaned out of the half-open carriage door.

Not just any young woman. Her gown and jewels were rich in an exquisitely restrained court fashion, but that face would have stopped him cold if she were naked—*especially* if she were naked. His gesture turned into a sweeping bow.

Wait a minute. They said their lord, not their lady.

The girl's eyes widened at the sight ahead, and she gulped. Then she fought down nausea—he felt a rush of approval even in the press of emergency—and looked at him. There was a faint feeling like an electric-telegraph spark as their eyes met, gray gazing into blue, and then she was looking over her shoulder.

"Grandfather," she said, in pure upper-class Latin. "There's been a disaster here."

"There's been an attack on Imperial troops here," Tharasamund said firmly, pitching his voice to carry into the interior of the vehicle. "I must insist, my lord—"

It seemed to be a day for shocks. The man who leaned out in turn, bracing himself with a grimace, certainly looked like a grandfather. Possibly God's grandfather, from the wrinkles; he'd never seen anyone older and still alive. The pouched eyes behind the lenses and big beak nose were disconcertingly shrewd. It was a face Tharasamund had seen before, when his unit was on court duty; anyone who saw magazines and engravings and photographs would have recognized it as well, these past two generations and more.

Martinus of Padua. Quaestor to three Emperors of the West; kingmaker, sorcerer or saint, devil or angel—some pagans thought him a god—and next to Urias II, the most powerful man in the world. Possibly more powerful. Emperors came and went, but the man from Padua had been making things happen since Tharasamund's grandfather was a stripling riding to his first war, when the Greeks invaded Italy in Thiudahad's day.

Tharasamund saluted and made a deep bow. "My apologies, my lord. I am at your disposal." He managed a smile, a gentleman's refusal to be disconcerted by events. "And at yours, my lady."

"Jorith Hermansdaughter, noble captain," she said, a little faintly but with courtly politeness. A princess, then, and the old man's granddaughter.

This *definitely* took precedence over his own troubles....

Ouch, Padway thought, pushing his glasses back up his nose and giving thanks, for once, for the increasing shortsightedness of old age. He'd seen worse, but not very often.

"Captain, pleased to see you," he said. "What happened here?"

"My lord," the young man said crisply. He looked suitably heroic in a battered way, but it was a pleasure to hear the firm intelligence in his voice. "A detachment of my company was ordered by General Winnithar of the Capital City garrison command to suppress rioters in aid to the civil power. We were doing so when a bomb thrower dropped a grenade into the ammunition limber. I suspect the man was a foreign agent—the whole thing was too smooth for accident."

As he spoke, another explosion echoed over the city. Padway nodded, looking like an ancient and highly intelligent owl.

"Doubtless you're right, Captain. Do you think the Equinoctal Way will be clear?"

Tharasamund made a visible effort. "It's as good a chance as any, my lord," he said. "It's broad—rioters generally stick to the old town. And it's the best way to get to the garrison barracks quickly."

Broad and open to light, air and artillery, Padway thought—a joke about the way Napoleon III had rebuilt Paris, and part of his own thoughts over the years planning the expansion of Florence.

"Let's go that way," he said. "Hengist, head us out."

"I never wanted to have adventures," Padway grumbled. "Even when I was a young man. *Certainly* not now."

Jorith looked at him and gave a smile; not a very convincing one, but he acknowledged the effort.

"This is an adventure?" she said. "I've always *wanted* adventures—but this just feels like I was walking along the street and stepped into a sewer full of big rats."

"That's what adventures are like," Padway said, wincing slightly as the coach lurched slowly over something that went *crunch* under the wheel and trying not to think of what—formerly who—it was, "while you're having them. They sound much better in retrospect."

The young guardsman—Tharasamund Hrothegisson, Padway forced himself to remember—chuckled harshly.

"Oh, yes," he said, in extremely good Latin with only the faintest tinge of a Gothic accent, then added: "Your pardon, my lord."

Jorith looked at him oddly, while Padway nodded. He might not have been a fighting man himself, but he'd met a fair sample over the years, and this was one who'd seen the elephant. For a moment youth and age shared a knowledge incommunicable to anyone unacquainted with that particular animal. Then a memory tickled at Padway's mind; he'd always had a rook's habit of stashing away bits and pieces, valuable for an archaeologist and invaluable for a politician.

"Hrothegisson…not a relation of Thiudegiskel?"

The young man stiffened. Officially, there had been an amnesty—but nobody had forgotten that Thiudegiskel son of Thiudahad had tried to get elected King of the Goths and Italians instead of Urias I, Padway's candidate; or that he'd gone over to the Byzantines during the invasion that followed and nearly wrecked the nascent Empire of the West.

"My mother was the daughter of his mother's sister," he said stiffly. "My lord."

That didn't make him an Amaling, but…

"Ancient history, young fellow. Like me," he added with a wry grin. "What are you doing, by the way?"

The young Goth had gotten up and was examining the fastenings of the rubberized-canvas hood that covered the carriage.

"I thought I'd peel this back a bit at the front, my lord—"

"You can call me Boss or Quaestor or even sir, if you must," Padway said. He *still* wasn't entirely comfortable being my-lorded.

"—sir. I'd be of some use, if I could see out."

"Not all the way?"

"Oh, that would never do," Tharasamund said. "You're far too noticeable… sir."

Tharasamund finished looking at the fastenings, made a few economical slashes with his dagger, and peeled the soft material back from its struts, just enough to give him a good view. Warm air flowed in. "Uh-oh," he said.

I know what uh-oh *means,* Padway thought. *It means the perfume's in the soup…or the shit's hit the fan.*

"Give me a hand," he snapped.

Something in his voice made the two youngsters obey without argument. Grumbling at his own stiffness and with a hand under each arm, he knelt up on the front seat and looked past the driver and guard.

"Uh-oh," he said.

"It's in the soup, right enough, excellent boss," Tharasamund said.

One advantage of Florence's hilly build and grid-network streets was that you could see a long way from a slight rise. The view ahead showed more fires, more wreckage…and a very large, very loud mob about half a mile away, milling and shouting and throwing things. Beyond that was a double line of horsemen, fifty or sixty strong. As they watched, there was a bright flash of metal, as the troopers all clapped hand to hilt and drew their *spathae* in a single coordinated movement to the word of command. A deep shout followed, and the horses began to move forward, faster and faster....

"Oh, that was a bad idea. That was a *very* bad idea," Tharasamund muttered.

Sensible young man, Padway thought.

A big man on a big horse waving a sword and coming towards you was an awesome spectacle; scores of them looked unstoppable. Armies had broken and run from the sheer fear from the sight, including one memorable occasion when Padway had been in command, trying to make a mob of Italian peasant recruits hold a pike line against charging Byzantine heavy cavalry.

The problem was...

The horsemen struck. Sure enough, the front of the mob surged away in panic, trying to turn and run. The problem was that there were thousands of people behind them, and they *couldn't* run. There wasn't room. The swords swung down, lethal arcs that ended in slashed-open heads and shoulders, but the horses were slowing as they moved into the thick mass of rioters. Horses were all conscripts, with an absolute and instinctive fear of running into things, falling, and risking their vulnerable legs.

A line of brave men with spears could stop any cavalry ever foaled. A mass of people too big to run away could do the same, in a messy fashion, by sheer inertia.

Padway shifted slightly, keeping his body between Jorith and the results, and noticed that Tharasamund did the same. People stopped running as the horses slowed; they turned, started to throw things, yelled, waved their arms. The cavalry horses were bolder than most of their breed, but they backed, snorting and rolling their eyes; a few turned in tight circles, caught between their riders' hands on the reins and an inborn need to run away from danger. The rain of bits of stone and iron and wood grew thicker; a soldier was pulled out of the saddle....

And at the rear of the mob, a purposeful-looking group was turning towards the carriage halted at the top of the hill.

"Guards cavalry," Tharasamund said tightly. *They never did know anything but how to die well. Though I grant they* do *know how to do that.*

He looked at Padway, back at the white, frightened, determined face of the girl, then at the mob. "Obviously, there are agitators at work," he said, "not just hungry rioters sparked off by a football game."

Padway nodded. The Saxon chief of his guardsmen bent down from the saddle and pointed to a narrow alleyway.

"That way, I think," he growled. "Liuderis, Marco, get that cart and set it up."

The coachman turned the horses' heads into the narrow, odorous gloom of the alley. The guardsmen grabbed a discarded vendor's pushcart, dumped out its load of vegetables in a torrent of green, and pulled it into the alleyway after the carriage before upending it. Most of them crouched behind it, drawing their pistols.

"We'll hold them here," Hengist said grimly. "Excellent boss, you and this gentleman—" he nodded to Tharasamund "—and the young mistress get going."

Gray eyes met blue, and Tharasamund nodded sharply. Padway seemed about to protest, and the Saxon grinned.

"Sorry, excellent boss, that's not an order you can give me. My oath's to keep you safe—obedience takes second place."

Hengist slapped the rump of the rear horse in the carriage team, leaping back to let the carriage lurch by in the narrow way. Tharasamund lifted a hand in salute, then used it to steady Padway; the Quaestor sat down heavily, sighing. Jorith helped him down, and braced him as they lurched across cobbles and then out into rutted dirt.

Think, Tharasamund, the soldier told himself. They weren't out into the country yet, and wouldn't be for half an hour, but the buildings were very new, some still under construction. No people were about; with a holiday and then a riot there wouldn't be, and this area had few residences, being mostly workshops.

He looked back; nothing to see, but then came a snarling brabble of voices, and a crackle of pistol fire. *By Christ and His mother that's a brave man*, he thought. *And true to his oath. Saxons may not be civilized but they're stubborn enough.*

Jorith looked behind them as well. "Is that—" she said, and swallowed.

Tharasamund nodded. "Yes, lady. They can hold them quite a while, in that narrow way. Not many rioters will have firearms, and there can't be many agents of the Greek emperor. Just enough."

She shivered. "It sounds…different, in the epics. Last stands."

Padway mumbled something in a language Tharasamund didn't recognize, though a couple of the words had a haunting pseudo-familiarity, sounding like oaths. For a moment he thought the old man was dazed, and then he spoke sharply—loud enough for the coachman to hear.

"If any of you get out of this, and I don't, take a message to the king and Council: this means Justinian thinks he's ready for a showdown. I should have—never mind."

There was a mutter of assent. *The Quaestor is a brave man too, in his way,* Tharasamund acknowledged. *He's thinking of the Kingdom's welfare.* And, from the way his eyes darted her way, his granddaughter's.

An idea blossomed. "Sir, I have an idea. Some of those men who turned our way were mounted, and they've identified this coach. What we need to do is to get you to a place of safety for a few hours, until the city's brought back to order. Do you see that half-built whatever-it-is on the hill up ahead? We can..."

"This doesn't look much like what I'd anticipated," the archbishop said, peering at the wide screen.

Maximus snorted. He wasn't an expert, but he *had* scanned the briefing. This was the beginning of the Wars of Reunification; what did the cleric expect, a festival with wreaths and flowers and incense?

The pilot's long nose twitched. There would be incense down there, all right, of a type he'd seen on previous expeditions. Things burning; people too, possibly. That sort of thing happened, if you went this far back. For a long time to come, too.

"There!" he said aloud, and everyone crowded up behind him; he ran a hand through a light-field to make sure nobody tripped a control by mistake. "There, that's *him!*"

The screen leapt, magnification increasing as the computer obeyed his intent—that was a virtue of the more modern types; they did what you wanted them to do, not just what you told them.

A carriage drawn by four matched black horses galloped out of an alley and turned westward, swaying as the coachman stood on his seat and lashed them with a whip. The overhead cover had been partly cut away; Maximus froze a portion of the screen to show the face of an old man. The computer helpfully listed the probability of this being the man they were after. It was as near unity as no matter. This was also the earliest era when photographs of famous men were available, and enough had survived into modern times to be digitized.

Somebody made a half-disgusted sound. "He's so...so *ugly,*" one said. The archbishop made a reproving sound. Maximus nodded, agreeing for once. It wasn't the man's fault that regeneration therapy wouldn't be invented for another two hundred years, or perfected for three. One thing time travel taught you was how fortunate you were to be born in the tenth century A.D.

"And he's stopping!" the historian cried. "I wonder why?"

Maximus hid another snort, and swung the viewpoint. "At a guess, most learned one, because those cutthroats are after him, and he's planning on hiding before they get here."

"Are you sure this is a good idea, Captain?" Padway said.

The young Goth shrugged. "No, sir," he said, helping the older man down from the carriage. "But they ought to follow the coach. It's much more visible."

Padway wheezed a chuckle as they hurried into the unfinished building, around the heaps of sand and bricks and timber; it was always nice to meet a man who didn't promise more than he could deliver. The carriage spurred off, making a great show of haste but not moving as fast as it might. He made two mental notes: one to see that the coachman got something, if he made it out of this, and another to put in a good word for Captain Tharasamund. He'd had a *lot* of experience judging men, and there were never enough good ones around.

The first floor of the building was an echoing vastness smelling of raw brick and new cement, with a concrete slab floor, thin brick walls, and cast-iron pillars holding it all up. A lot of timber was piled about, and a rough staircase led to the second story. Tharasamund and Princess Jorith half-lifted Padway up the stairs and propped him against a pile of sacks of lime mortar; then the Gothic soldier ran to a window, standing beside it and peering out through boards nailed over the unfinished casement.

"Oh, Sathanas take it," he said.

"They didn't follow the coach?" Padway asked.

"Most of them did. Two mounted men are turning in here, and a crowd of what look like ruffians after them. My apologies, sir," he finished, with bitter self-reproach.

"You took a chance. I agreed. If you bet, you lose sometimes."

Tharasamund saw Padway's eyes flick to Jorith's face and then away. His own lips compressed. *Damned if I'll let a mob get their hands on a royal princess*, he thought. *But by all the saints, what can I do about it?*

Fighting was the only thing that came to mind. Tharasamund had a healthy opinion of his own abilities in that line, but fighting off what looked like fifty or sixty men wasn't in the realm of the possible, even with a narrow approach and slum scum on the other side.

"Do what you can, then," he said to himself, looking around.

He had six shots in his revolver, and three reloads in his belt pouches....

He heard voices below and set himself. One of the men he'd seen riding came into view, urging his followers on, a short muscular-looking fellow in respectable but drab riding clothes, with a neatly trimmed black beard. The Goth let the long barrel of his revolver drop over his left forearm, squeezed....

Crack. The man toppled backward, screaming, and then screaming that his leg was broken—screaming in Greek. An educated man's dialect, but a native speaker's, as well. There were such folk in the Western Empire— parts of southern Italy and much of Sicily spoke Greek as their first language—but he would have bet his father's lands against a spavined mule that the man had been born not far from Constantinople.

Tharasamund dodged back as someone emptied a pistol at him; probably the other Greek. Whoever he was, the shooter started exhorting his men to attack; "Gothic heretics" and "two hundred gold crowns for their heads—each" seemed to be about equal inducements. It took a while, and he thought he knew the reason when he heard hasty sawing and hammering sounds.

"They're building a mantlet," he said grimly. At the confusion in the young woman's eyes, he went on: "A wooden shield, the sort they used to use in sieges. Wouldn't do them much good against a rifle, but a few layers of thick planks will turn a pistol ball."

Jorith raised her head. "I know I can rely on you, Captain," she said quietly. Tharasamund winced; he knew what she relied on him to do, and he didn't like it.

Well, that's irrelevant, he thought. *You'll do it anyway, and make it quick.*

Then her eyes went wide. "What's that you're leaning against, Grandfather?" she asked.

"Mortar," Padway said, raising a curious white brow.

"Lime," the girl said. "In the old days, during sieges, didn't—"

"They threw quicklime on men climbing siege ladders," Tharasamund half-whooped, with a strangled shout to keep the rioters and foreign agents below in the dark.

Padway moved himself aside, grinning slightly. Tharasamund moved towards the pile of sacks; Jorith halted him with an upraised hand.

"Wait," she said, and whipped off a gauzy silk scarf. "Those gauntlets will protect your hands, but your face—"

He bowed his head, and she fastened the thin cloth across his face like a mask; with the fabric close to his eyes, he could see out of it well enough. Then he worked, dragging the rough burlap sacks over towards the stairwell, carefully avoiding exposing his body to sight from below.

"Let's see," he muttered. "I'll stack them up here"—he made a pyramid of four, carefully weakening the lacing that held each sack closed at the top—"at the back of the stairwell, so they'll be above and behind anyone coming up the stairs. My lady Jorith? I'm afraid I'll need you to push."

He tried to keep his voice light, but there was a grave knowledge in the way she nodded.

"You up there!" a voice called. "Send us the old man, lay down your weapons, and we'll let you go!"

"And we can believe as much of that as we want to," Tharasamund called back. "No, thank you. Here's our deal: if you run now, before the troops come, I won't shoot you in the back."

"You'll be dead before then, you whipworthy barbarian!" the voice snarled. "You and your drab and the sorcerer too! *Take them!*"

The stairs were steep; Tharasamund had to go down on his belly to reach the upper one without exposing more than his eyes and gun hand. The mantlet—it was a door, with layers of planks nailed across it—came staggering upward. The hale Greek stood behind, firing over his men's heads to keep the Goth's down; he was half-concealed behind an iron pillar, and had his weapon braced against it.

Tharasamund swallowed against a dry throat and ignored him, ducking up to shoot at the feet of the men carrying the wooden bracer instead. Most of the shots missed. The targets were small and moving, and he had to snap-shoot in an instant, with no careful aiming. At last one hit, and the mantlet wavered and stalled as a man fell backward squalling and clutching at a splintered ankle.

"*Now, Jorith!*" he shouted.

The girl had lain down behind the sacks, with her slippered feet braced against them. She shoved, and they wavered and toppled forward. Momentum took over, and the sacks tumbled down. Acrid white dust billowed in choking clouds, and Tharasamund reflexively threw an arm across his face, coughing. One of the toughs behind the mantlet looked up and shouted, gesturing frantically—and his comrades followed the pointing arm, which was the worst possible thing they could have done.

Screams sounded sweetly, and strangled curses. The mantlet was thrown aside to crash on the hard cement floor beneath, and men ran—up out of the cloud of alkaline dust, or down and away from it. The Goth grinned behind his protecting face mask as he bounded erect and drew his *spatha*. A man staggered up the stairs, coughing and wheezing, his eyes already turning to bacon-rind red.

He swung a club. Tharasamund skipped neatly over it and lunged, his point skewering down over the thug's collarbone; muscle clamped on it, and he put a booted foot on the other's chest and pushed him back onto his fellows. More cursing and crashing; then two came forward, with their handkerchiefs held over their mouths. Both had swords, and one even had some idea of what to do with it. For a long minute it was clash and clatter and the flat unmusical rasp of steel on steel, and then the Goth sheered off half a face with a backhand cut.

"*Ho, la, St. Wulfias!*" he shouted exultantly, then found himself coughing again; some of the dust had gotten through the silk, and his eyes were tearing up as well.

Jorith came up beside him and offered a flask. He drank; it was citron water, and he used some to wash his eyes as well. The acid in it stung, but it would be better than leaving lime dust under his eyelids.

"Saw them off, sir," he wheezed to Padway, and Jorith clapped her hands and rose on tiptoe to kiss him. At another time, he would have paid more attention to that, but…

"For now," Padway said. "But if Justinian didn't send idiots, and his *agentes in rebus* usually are fairly shrewd, they'll—"

The noise below had mostly been bellowing, cries of pain and shrieks of *I'm blind!* and departing footfalls as many of the strong-arm squad decided there were better things to do in a riot-stricken city than have quicklime poured over their heads.

Now a crackling sound arose as well. All three looked at each other, hopelessly hoping that someone would deny that the sound was fire. When smoke began to drift up from between the floorboards, no doubt at all was left.

"Captain," Padway said.

"Sir?"

"I'm going to give you an order," he said. "You're not going to like it, but you're going to do it anyway."

"Sir—"

"Grandfather—"

"Take Jorith and get out of here," Padway rasped. "No, shut up. I'm an old man—a very old man—and I haven't six months to live anyway."

Jorith went white, and Padway waved a hand and then let it fall limp. "Didn't want to spoil your birthday, kitten, but that's what the doctors say. My lungs. Maybe I shouldn't have sent that expedition to find tobacco....I've lived longer than I ever had a right to expect anyway. Now get out—they won't have enough men to chase you, not when they see I'm not with you. I put my granddaughter in your hands. That is your trust."

A racking cough, and a wheeze: "*Go!*"

Tharasamund hesitated, but only for an instant. Then he brought his sword up in a salute more heartfelt than most he'd made, sheathed it, and put a hand on Jorith's shoulder as she knelt to embrace her grandsire.

"Now, my lady," he said.

She came, half-stunned, looking back over her shoulder. Tharasamund snatched up a coil of rope, made an end fast, looked out to the rear. Padway had been right; there were only two men out there, and they backed away when they saw the tall soldier coming down the rope, even hindered with a woman across his shoulder. He landed with flexed knees, sweeping the princess to her feet and drawing steel in the same motion.

"Follow me…and *run*," he said.

"No!" He turned, surprised that she disobeyed. Then he stopped, forgetting her, forgetting everything.

Light speared his eyes, and he flung up a hand and squinted. Light, not the red of flames, but a blinding light whiter than the very thought of whiteness in the mind of God. In the heart of it, a brazen chariot shone mirror-bright, turning gently with a ponderous motion that gave an impression of overwhelming weight—it must be visible to all Florence, as well.

The roof of the building exploded upward in a shower of red roofing tile and shattered beam, and through it he could see a form rising.

It was Martinus Paduei. It could be nobody else. Borne upward on a pillar of light…

Dimly, he was aware of the remaining rioters' screaming flight, followed by their Greek paymaster. He was a little more aware of Jorith beside him, tears of joy streaming down her face as she sank to her knees and made the sign of the cross again and again. He sank down beside her, holding up his sword so that it also signed the holy symbol against the sky. The light was pain, but he forced his eyes open anyway, unwilling to lose a moment of the sight.

There was a single piercing throb of sound, like the harp of an angel taller than the sky and the light was gone, leaving only the fading afterimages strobing across his vision.

"He was a saint!" Jorith sobbed. "Oh, Grandfather—"

"Yes," the young man said. "I don't think there's much doubt about that now. He *was* a saint."

He looked down into the girl's face and smiled. "And he told me to take care of you, my lady Jorith. We'd better go."

Martin Padway opened his eyes, blinking. For a long moment he simply lay on what felt like a very comfortable couch, looking at the faces that surrounded him. Then two thoughts sent his eyes wide:

I don't hurt. That first. All the bone-deep aches and catches were *gone*, all the pains that had grown so constant over the years that he didn't consciously notice them. Yes, *but* how *I notice them now they're gone!* he thought.

The second thought was: *They're all so* young*!* There were a round dozen men and women, every color from ebony-black to pink-white via a majority of brown that included several East Asian types. But none of them looked over twenty; they had the subtle signs—the flawless fine-textured skin, the bouncing *freshness* of movement—that were lost in early adulthood. It was far more noticeable than the various weirdnesses of their clothing.

Behind them were what looked like movie screens showing aerial shots, or various combinations of graphs and numbers, all moving and in different colors.

"Time travelers, right?" he said. *After all, I know time travel is possible. I've had going on fifty years to get used to the concept.*

One man—young man—gave a satisfied smile. "Instant comprehension! Just as you'd expect from a superior individual. I told you that the Great Man theory—"

He seemed to be talking upper-class sixth-century Latin, until you noticed that his lip movements weren't quite synchronized with the words and there was a murmur of something else beneath it.

Fascinating, Padway thought. *And that's an academic riding a hobbyhorse, or I was never an archaeologist.* Evidently some things were eternal.

Some of the others started arguing. Padway raised a hand:

"Please! Thank you very much for saving my life, but if you wouldn't mind a little information…"

"Yes, excellent sir," another man said—he was in a plain coverall, albeit of eerily mobile material. "From four hundred years in your future. We are—well, mostly—a study team investigating a crucial point in history… your lifetime, in fact, excellent sir."

"Four centuries in which future?" Padway said. "Gothic Rome, or my original twentieth? Twentieth century A.D.," he went on, to their growing bewilderment.

There was a long moment of silence. Padway broke it. "You mean, you didn't *know?*" he said.

The argument started up again, fast enough that Padway caught snatches of the language it was actually in, rather than the who-knew-how translation. His mind identified it as a Romance-derived language; something like twentieth-century Italian, but more archaic, and with a lot of Germanic loan words and other vocabulary he couldn't identify.

A slow, enormous grin split the ancient American's face. "Fifty years," he murmured.

Fifty years of politics and administration and warfare and engineering. None of them his chosen profession, just the things he had to do to survive and keep the darkness from falling. If this bunch were from only four centuries ahead in the future *Padway* had made, he'd done that, with a vengeance; they were from the date that in Padway's original history had seen the height of the Vikings.

He'd kept the darkness at bay, and now...now he could go back to being a research specialist. The grin grew wider.

Better than that, he'd actually get to *know how things turned out!* Making history was all very well, but he'd always wanted to read it more.

TO BRING THE
LIGHT

DAVID DRAKE

King Amulius' herdman (whose name is said to be Faustulus) found the infants and brought them home to raise....When the youths [Romulus and Remus] grew up, they made a habit of attacking bandits [herdsmen of Numitor, King Amulius' brother]....The bandits ambushed the youths while they were performing a religious rite. Romulus escaped, but Remus was captured....Numitor recognized the youths as his grandchildren. They wove a plot against Amulius...and killed him.

Livy: Ab urbe condita, Book I

Numitor gave Romulus and Remus everything that was necessary to found a city....Some say Remus yielded leadership of the colony to Romulus, but with resentment....Whereupon Celer...stuck Remus with a mattock and killed him.

Dionysius of Halicarnassus: Roman Antiquities, Book I

Flavia Herosilla leaned on the bronze balcony railing and craned forward to get a better look at the placard which the wagon-driver's attendant held over the snarling tigers. "Egypt?" she read aloud. "That's nonsense! There aren't any tigers in Egypt! If the emperor doesn't have better generals than he has geographers, Rome won't last another thousand *days*, much less years."

"Well, I suppose they're talking about the port of entry on the Red Sea, then down the Nile and by ship to Rome," said her host, Gnaeus Julius Maternus. "India isn't part of the Empire."

Herosilla snorted. "Neither is Dacia, not really," she said. "But there's supposed to be a Dacian display coming later in the day."

Maternus had extensive shipping interests which paid (among other things) for this mansion on the Palatine Hill. The high balcony, facing the Sacred Way with the Forum on the left, was the perfect location from which to watch the parades Emperor Marcus Julius Philippus—Philip the Arab—was giving to mark the Thousandth Anniversary of the Founding of Rome.

Herosilla frowned thoughtfully and added, "I wonder if the Dacian display will have the traditional Sarmatian wagons with painted frames?"

Following the caged tigers were a dozen men whose leader waved a placard reading GUARDIANS OF THE NUBIAN FRONTIER. The dark-skinned men had bushy hair into which ostrich plumes were woven, adding to their already amazing height. Their shields were naturally-patterned oxhide, and their spearheads seemed to be hammered out of pig iron.

"If that's what's guarding Egypt from the south," Maternus said, "then I'm thankful Rome's grain supply comes from Africa now.

"I suppose the emperor's picking the most colorful troops for the festival," Herosilla said. She lived most of the year in Cumae on the Bay of Naples, so she could afford to be philosophical about the chance of bread riots among the Roman poor. "There are wonderful opportunities for an ethnographer here."

"Perhaps you should write a monograph," Maternus said, shaking his head. He looked up at the clouds. The sky rumbled though there was no immediate sign of rain.

On the broad Sacred Way, a dozen armored horsemen blew a cacophony on silver-mounted horns. Behind them was a convoy of caged hippopotami, one to a wagon. The hippos would soon die along with the tigers and thousands of other animals in the arena, as part of the month-long festivities.

"My goal is to know rather than to teach," Herosilla said. She was thirty years old and already—in her well-justified opinion—the finest mind of her day. "Although the emperor could do worse than have me for a teacher."

She gestured at the parade route. A squad of horse archers interspersed the procession of hippos. "For example, I know that the best authorities follow the dating of Eratosthenes. The real thousandth anniversary won't be for another two years."

Maternus began counting. The gold and polished stones of the several rings he wore on each finger winked in the wan sunlight. Finally he gave up. "What would the founding date be according to the Christian reckoning, then?" he asked.

"Have you added that superstition to your ridiculous list as well?" Herosilla asked with curl of her lip. Her face had the chiseled beauty of a statue. Men had told her often enough that she was as hard as marble; but for that, it depended on the man. "Since you ask, though, it would be 751 BC."

The calculation had been easy for her. She'd learned the Indian method of counting, using a zero.

"One can't be too careful, my dear," said Maternus. "What I'm really looking for is one that'll let me take it with me."

He lifted two fingers without looking behind him. A slave wearing a silk tunic as fine as Herosilla's own put a bite-sized fishball in the corner of her master's mouth.

Maternus chewed, grinned at Herosilla, and continued, "Of course one reason Philip probably chose the earlier date because he can't be sure he'll still be emperor in another two years. Recent history makes a depressing study, and I must say—"

He glanced at the grim sky again.

"—those clouds provide no good omen for him."

"Don't spout superstitions even you can't believe," Herosilla said tartly. "As for your real point, the state of the empire—the things that happen on the frontiers needn't bother a truly civilized person. Now of course I'd rather be reading in my villa at Cumae, particularly since I agree with you that it looks like a storm coming. But these celebrations are a unique event for which a true scholar is willing to undergo the discomfort of a trip to Rome."

Next in the procession, dark-skinned pygmies led a pair of—were they deer or oxen? Herosilla had never seen anything like them. The beasts' hides were a dun that was almost purple, with horizontal stripes on the haunches. The long necks suggested kinship to the giraffes that would doubtless be following soon.

"Your problem, my dear," Maternus said in a voice that was hard beneath the banter, "is that you're *always* a scholar. You should remember occasionally that you're a woman."

"Oh, I assure you I'm aware that I'm a woman, Maternus," Herosilla snapped. "I just don't choose that to be a factor in my relations with you. You're an amusing enough companion and your house has an excellent view of the procession route, but that's all. If you need another lesson in what I mean by, 'No,' however—"

"Peace, my dear, peace!" Maternus said, holding his palms forward. "I'm still bruised from the other evening."

"One of the men who had no reason to doubt my femininity," Herosilla said with a satisfied smile, "was a Bactrian wrestler whom I kept for a time. I learned *quite* a number of useful things from him."

She returned her attention to the parade. Egyptian slaves in cotton breechclouts carried pallets with models of the Sphinx and the Pyramids. The men must have been miserably cold, dressed like that in the middle of February in Rome. Perhaps they were giving thanks that they were only part of the display, not the slaughter to come in the Colosseum.

"Of course," Herosilla said thoughtfully, "any date is really guesswork. All the stories say gods were involved in the founding of Rome—which means all the stories are fantasies."

"Oh come now, my dear!" Maternus said. "It's bad enough that you sneer at other people's gods. Now you're blaspheming your own! This is really too much."

"They're *not* my gods," Herosilla said. "They're not anybody's gods because they don't exist. Isn't that a simple enough concept for you to understand?"

Maternus sucked in his lips and shook his head in disapproval.

"Well, what will you take for proof, then?" Herosilla said. She heard her voice rising with the frustration that she felt so often, an intelligent woman in a world of credulous fools.

She raised her clenched fist to the heavens. "You there! Gods!" she shouted. "If any of you really exist, I demand you strike me down this instant!"

A big drop of rain whacked the railing. The bronze rang in echo. The hair on Herosilla's neck prickled.

The thunderbolt an instant later was all the light and noise in the universe, focused on a single point.

Herosilla's vision pulsed. Her nostrils were full of the sulphurous stench of burned air. She didn't think she'd lost consciousness but she wasn't sure.

For a moment she wasn't even sure she was alive.

The veils of throbbing color thinned slowly. The roar that filled her ears was her own blood; that began to subside also. Beneath Herosilla's palms was dirt mixed with pebbles and coarse grass, not the smooth mosaic floor of Maternus' balcony.

She was aware of figures or at least shadows that moved and gabbled words at her. There was a sudden consciousness of pain: burning sensations from her arms, ankles and around her throat where her gold filigree necklace hung.

Her *jewelry* was blisteringly hot. Now that the reek of the lightning had dissipated somewhat, she could smell her hair singeing around her jeweled diadem.

Herosilla shouted and jumped to her feet, shaking the anklets of gold chain away from her flesh. She stripped off her armlets: double-headed snakes with ruby eyes. All she could do about the necklace was bend forward to let as much of the metal as possible hang away from the white skin of her breast. She'd never be able to release the catch in a hurry. In fact she didn't even remember how it worked; that was a task for her maids.

The world came into focus around Herosilla.

She stood on a hill. The oak tree beside her had been struck by lightning so recently that the stump still burned. Splinters of the upper trunk smoldered in a circle thirty feet in diameter. A dead sheep lay at the edge of the blasted area with its stiff legs in the air. Other sheep faced Herosilla, their jaws working in a sideways motion as regular as the drip of raindrops from a gutter.

Two muscular young shepherds flung themselves on the ground. They were grunting something at her.

By the stars! The shepherds were calling her, "*Goddess*," in the most barbarous Latin Herosilla had ever heard in her life!

"Get up, you idiots," Herosilla snapped. She was dizzy and completely disoriented. There were no buildings in any direction unless the beehive of rocks a little higher on the hill was a shelter of some kind. "I'm not a goddess!"

Lightning flashed; Herosilla flinched involuntarily. The bolt struck one of the hills across the valley. Rain came in a rush, making the tree stump hiss and kick out clouds of steam.

Just a moment ago, Maternus' slaves had been waiting with a furled rain canopy. Now they'd vanished along with every other aspect of the mansion. "Where on earth are we?" she said to the shepherds.

The taller, leaner man turned his head slightly so that he could look up at Herosilla without breaking his neck. He spoke a connected sentence. His stockier fellow watched Herosilla silently.

For a moment the sound was merely a series of grunts; then the syllables fell into focus in Herosilla's mind. "Say that again," she directed.

"We're watching the king's sheep in the north pastures," the shepherd repeated obediently.

Their accent wasn't barbarous, it was *archaic*! The lightning bolt had somehow flung her to the countryside so far from Rome that the peasants still spoke Old Latin. Herosilla couldn't imagine how the *flinging* had been accomplished—much less how she'd survived it—but it was all perfectly natural. Like volcanos and earthquakes, excessive humors of one sort or another caused disruptions in the earth. There was no need to invent gods for the cause...

"Very well, my good men," Herosilla said, shifting her speech as well as she could into the archaic dialect. "You may rise, now."

She'd never expected that her studies of the ancient Laws of the Twelve Tables would help her communicate in the present day. Perhaps all peasants spoke Old Latin? Now that Herosilla thought about it, she didn't recall ever before having spoken to a peasant.

The men got up hesitantly. They weren't quite as young as Herosilla first thought, but she'd seen gladiators who weren't so lithely muscular. Perhaps she should have visited the country earlier, and by more orthodox means.

"Goddess?" said the broader-built shepherd, though the stars knew neither man was wispy.

"Stop calling me a goddess," Herosilla said firmly. Given her consistent failure to rid her wealthy peers of vain superstition, she choked off a lecture on the nonexistence of gods that these rural louts wouldn't even be able to understand. "Now, take me to your supervisor."

The men spoke to one another in voices too low for Herosilla to make out what they were saying. 'King' in their usage obviously meant the man who owned the land and perhaps owned the shepherds as well. Even if these louts were technically free, they were so unsophisticated that she felt it was better to deal with their immediate superior instead of demanding the shepherds lead her to the manor house themselves.

"We will take you to our father, goddess," the stocky man said. He held himself straight, throwing out a chest that a sculptor could have used to model Apollo. Each shepherd wore a tunic of coarse wool and, in place of a cape, a whole fleece with the hind legs tied around his neck. Their legs were bare. For footgear they had crudely-shaped pieces of hide in which the soles and uppers were the same single thickness.

"Don't call me goddess," Herosilla repeated with a sigh. "You may call me lady or mistress. Either is proper. Now, let's not delay further while the rain falls."

The taller shepherd gave a penetrating whistle. The bellwether, a grizzled ram which might be as old as the man himself, blatted in reply and set off toward the south. Three baked clay rods hung around his neck. They clacked as he moved, guiding the remainder of the herd.

The shepherds bowed deferentially to Herosilla and walked to either side of her as they followed the ram. "It's clear proof of my high station that the lady appeared to me," the stocky man said to his brother as though Herosilla wasn't between them.

"She appeared to both of us," the taller brother replied. "And also to ten tens of sheep. They're sheep of high station, belonging to the king as they do. Perhaps she was sent to them."

The stocky brother snorted angrily. Conversation lapsed.

Herosilla started to shiver. The rain was cold on clothing that was never intended to be waterproof; and the walk also gave her time to think about what had happened to her...and how much worse it could easily have been.

The village was at least a dozen round huts with walls of woven twigs plastered with mud—wattle and daub. Brushwood laid on the roofs prevented high winds from blowing away the thatch. Among the outbuildings was an open-fronted shed in which women milked ewes from flocks whose herdsmen had returned before Herosilla's pair.

Perhaps there were more dwellings; she couldn't be sure because of darkness and the complete disorder of the village layout. Certainly there was nothing of any size or built of stone—unless you wanted to count the sheep pen made by laying rocks on top of one another without mortar.

The area between huts was a waste of mud and sheep dung except where the soil had been trampled down to bare rock. There were no proper streets.

"Dad!" Herosilla's taller companion called. "We've a lady here brought by a lightning bolt!"

"She's a messenger sent to me by Mars!" his brother said. He raised his voice even louder, perhaps hoping volume could compel belief.

Heads turned as soon as the brothers spoke. When the folk outside saw Herosilla in her silks and jewelry, their excited babble drew others from the huts.

"I'm a gentlewoman of Cumae, visiting Rome for the celebrations," Herosilla said crisply. "My arrival here is a purely natural phenomenon, nothing to do with gods. I want you to take me to your master immediately. I'll see to it that you're all well rewarded."

The rain had stopped. A full moon began to edge into the gap between clouds. She'd been sure—she'd *thought*—the moon had been in its last quarter the night before...

The brothers and Herosilla stopped in front of a hut no different from the others. The opening cut in one sidewall for a window was shuttered. There was no hole in the roof peak. Smoke from the fire within seeped through the thatch and lay like a cloud over the brush roof weights.

An old man hobbled from the hut, leaning on a staff and the arm of a woman who was possibly somewhat younger. The other villagers stood close but didn't crowd Herosilla and her guides. The brothers' 'dad' was the supervisor or at least first among equals in the community.

"Oh, she's Greek!" the woman with 'dad' said. Switching to that language she went on, "Lady, I am Acca and this is my husband Faustulus. We make you welcome."

To Herosilla's further amazement, Acca spoke with an Ionic accent rather than the simplified common dialect. Homer might have sneered at Acca's diction, but he wouldn't have had any difficulty understanding what she was saying.

"Ah!" said Faustulus in the same archaic Latin that his sons used. "We've had traders come through here from time out of mind, mistress, but never a Greek *lady* before."

"I—" Herosilla began. She'd planned to explain that she wasn't Greek. She realized the effort would be pointless. All Herosilla cared about was returning to civilization: her books, her circle of learned friends; her home and the wink of waves on the Bay of Naples. If these yokels wanted to think she was Greek, so be it.

She spoke the language, of course. Half of Rome's population, Emperor Philip included, came from the east of the empire and spoke more Greek than Latin. Any educated person had studied the *Iliad* and *Odyssey*, so Acca's dialect provided no difficulties.

Why on earth would the villagers equate traders with Greeks, though? Had the lightning cast her all the way down the toe of Italy to where families traced their ancestry to Greek settlements centuries older than Rome's expansion into the region?

"I really need to see your master," Herosilla said. Cold, exhaustion and the shock of *whatever* had happened struck her suddenly humble. "But may I buy some dry clothing? I'll pay whatever you ask."

"We'll have to hold a council on this," somebody rumbled from the crowd.

"Yes, yes, you hold your council," Acca snapped, "but I'll take this lady inside for something warm to put on and put in her besides. You'd like a bite of food, wouldn't you, dearie?"

"Yes," Herosilla said. She almost staggered at the thought of food. She hadn't realized how hungry she was until Acca spoke. "Yes, I really would. I'll pay you—"

"Tush! Why speak of pay when there's been no honor so great to the village in the time folk have pastured their flocks here?" Acca said, drawing Herosilla after her into the hut. The interior was dark and smoky, but the warmth was wonderfully comforting.

"You're not a goddess, you say, lady," Acca said. "But do you speak for the gods like the Sibyl of Samos does?"

"No, I'm a scholar," Herosilla said. She thought about the question and asked, "Why do you say, 'the Sibyl of Samos', woman? If you're going to mention one of the ten sibyls, why didn't you say, 'the Sibyl of Cumae'? Cumae is much nearer."

"Oh, is there a sibyl in Cumae now?" Acca said in surprise. "There didn't used to be."

Acca stoked the fire with a stick of brushwood. By the light of fresh flames she rooted in one of several wicker hampers. The only other furnishings were the low bed and a loom on which she was weaving a strip of wool banded by selecting naturally colored yarn.

"My best," Acca said with pride as she brought out a tunic. "I wear it to town on market days."

Herosilla couldn't see how the coarsely-woven garment differed from the one her hostess wore now, but it looked warm and dry which was all the recommendation required at the moment. Herosilla spread her arms, then realized that she didn't have a maid to dress her. "Oh," she said in embarrassment. "I..."

Acca nodded knowingly. "First we'll feed you," she said, switching back to careful Greek. "Then I'll help you change. You've come from Chalcis, I shouldn't wonder?"

She set the tunic on the hamper and took a shallow wooden bowl from a shelf. Tools and bundled vegetables hung from the roof beams. The shelves held utensils and more wooden dishes, but the only pottery was the earthenware pot on the fire and a small jug with a tawny glaze and a simple geometric design. Absurd as it seemed to Herosilla, the jug seemed to be kept as a showpiece rather than for use.

"I'm, ah..." Herosilla said. "I live in Cumae, actually."

Cumae had been settled by colonists from Chalcis in Greece; by legend, shortly after the Trojan War, but certainly in the distant past. Why would anybody think a Greek lady came from a backwater like Chalcis now, though?

"You're so lovely that I thought you were from Chalcis," Acca said as she dipped a horn spoon into the pot. She filled the bowl with steaming porridge and handed it to her guest. "There's many fine ladies there, I'm sure."

Herosilla paused for a moment, then realized she was meant to slurp the meal with the aid of her fingers. She was too hungry to protest.

Outside, male voices rose in the rhythmic patterns of oratory. Apparently one facet of civilized society held true here: not even sex intrigued males as much as the sound of their own voices.

"I lived in Cumae for a time," Acca said in a wistful tone. "That was long ago when I was young, though."

She stepped behind her guest and carefully untangled the saffron-colored shawl as Herosilla ate. "Oh, what wonderful cloth! Could you teach me to weave like this, lady?"

Herosilla blinked. She wasn't sure how to answer without insulting a woman whom both decency and self-preservation demanded she treat well. "I couldn't weave these myself," she said. "Someone else made them. This is delicious porridge, Acca."

The porridge *was* remarkably tasty. It seemed to contain primarily millet and cheese, with no spices but a chopped onion and the natural pungency of ewe's milk. Herosilla would have turned up her nose at the dish at a dinner party, but hunger made her willing to find excellence in simple things.

"Such lovely clothing," Acca said, relapsing into Latin as she fondled the silk, "We can't hang it to dry until the morning."

"That will be fine," Herosilla said. Grimacing, she urged more of the thick porridge toward her mouth with her fingertips. She thought of asking for bread, but she hadn't seen any sign of an oven outside the house. "Can you get my necklace off?"

"Oh, may I?" Acca said, touching the catch. "Such *lovely* things."

Herosilla let the hut's warmth penetrate her muscles as Acca removed her clothing and ornaments. If Herosilla closed her eyes, she could imagine that she was in her study with a charcoal brazier beside her, preparing to write an account of her translation from Rome to this village. Lightning, an aspect of the element of fire, had rent the air—a denser element—as air itself bubbles violently through water...

The borrowed tunic itched terribly, the more so because Herosilla's skin was still damp, but it was an improvement on wet silk. She put down the bowl, looked for a water dish to wash her fingers—and licked them instead, feeling terribly uncomfortable.

The male voices outside continued to drone. "What are they discussing, anyway?" Herosilla asked.

"Why, you, lady," Acca said in surprise. "Nothing so important has ever happened to our village before!"

"I should have known," Herosilla said. "Well, I'd better join them or they may never get around to choosing someone to lead me to the manor house. Do you have a wrap for me?"

Dealing with this village reminded her of the time she'd had to walk in mud when her carriage threw a wheel on a rural track. A process as simple as raising one foot, then the other, took three times as long as it would on civilized pavement. Perhaps mud conditioned every aspect of peasant life.

Her back and shoulders covered by a fleece that was even filthier than the ones the brothers wore, Herosilla ducked out of the hut. About twenty men sat on stones around a fire built near Faustulus' hut. The village women squatted behind them, and children down to the age of toddlers stood at the back.

The shorter of Herosilla's guides was standing as he spoke. When she appeared he gestured and said, "Behold, the god-sent messenger who proves the grandeur of my destiny!"

"Nonsense!" Herosilla said. "I just need someone to take me to the landowner. To your king, that is, or his steward if the king's not in residence at the moment."

Villagers moved out of the way as she strode to a place to the right of

Faustulus. The man beside the leader jumped over the fire itself to make room.

The taller brother stood. "It's my right to guide her."

"I—" said the other.

"You took the lambs to town for the last feast," the taller man said. "It's my *right*."

"For pity's sake!" Herosilla snapped. "I'm perfectly willing to pay both of you. So long as I've one guide, I don't care if you all come. I'll reward the whole village, those who come with me and those who stay."

"It's not that, lady," another man said. Toothlessness distorted the dialect to the point Herosilla could barely understand his words. "With both the boys gone at the same time, what if we're attacked? It's not safe."

"Sit down, both of you," Faustulus ordered with the weary tone of repetition. "Roscio still hasn't spoken."

A man with short legs and long, hairy arms hopped at once to his feet but then waited, glancing diffidently at the brothers. They glared at each other for a further moment, then sat down in unison.

Roscio began to speak. He waved his arms in a fashion that seemed to have nothing to do with the emphasis in his voice. As best Herosilla could tell, the man was talking about a great battle in his youth. He appeared to be in his midtwenties now.

It struck Herosilla as she looked around the circle that there were only three real men in the gathering: Faustulus and his sons. The other males could have been molded from the surrounding mud. The brothers had fire inside, and their father had at least the warmth of coals beneath the crippling pain of his arthritis.

Most of the villagers watched Herosilla sidelong. The young woman standing behind the stocky brother glared straight at her. Herosilla hadn't seen such hatred in another's face since the morning she corrected a grammarian's derivation of the word 'rich' (it really meant 'well-manured') in front of several wealthy patrons.

There was a rustle as Acca squatted behind Herosilla. Roscio continued to maunder; now he was talking about the time somebody had threatened him with a rock.

Herosilla leaned back and whispered, "The woman across the fire with the sour expression. Who is she?"

Acca put her lips to Herosilla's ear. "That's Ganea," she said. "Jealous, I shouldn't wonder. She and my boy have an understanding. But I think what he understands isn't quite what she does."

Herosilla looked at the stocky youth. Ganea glowered threateningly and put a hand on his shoulder. He swatted it off. His eyes measured Herosilla like a side of mutton.

Herosilla's nose wrinkled. "Ganea needn't worry," she whispered.

"Aye, I know that," Acca said. "But the girl's young and hasn't learned that some women are interested in more that what a man's got hanging between his legs. Though that too."

Herosilla blinked, then nodded. "Yes, that too," she said. She'd always claimed to appreciate plain speaking, but it was nonetheless disconcerting to hear it from a near stranger.

Roscio finally finished. Ran out of words, at any rate. He looked around in puzzlement. The man seated next to him tugged his tunic; Roscio sat down hard.

Faustulus planted his staff in front of him and levered himself upright with the strength of both arms. Acca braced her husband midway in the process, then stepped back.

"We all know there was trouble with Numitor's herdsmen before my boys got their growth," Faustulus said without preamble. "And we know that since then there's been trouble the other way, with Numitor's folk showing splints and bandages any time their flocks get too near our grazing."

He paused. There was a chorus of, "Aye, that's so," and, "Just what I said." Given the length of time the council had been sitting, Herosilla would have been amazed if there was anything that *hadn't* been said at least once.

"That's well and good," Faustulus continued, "but there's us and there's all the men in the three other villages besides. Are you going to tell me that Numitor's going to run us all off if both the boys are gone for a day or two? Is that all you are, sheep yourselves?"

"It's not like we're afraid," said the man to the other side of Herosilla. "It's just, you know, we need somebody to lead. And you don't get around so good any more."

The stocky brother jumped up. "If there's no more manhood here than that," he said, "then Mars strike me if I'm going to stay any longer! I'm going to town with the lady messenger tomorrow. The only question you all can decide is whether I bother to come back. The *only* question!"

He crossed his arms and stood with lowering fury. The man beside him, the rural equivalent of a rich man's toady, cheered.

The taller brother had risen also. "It's my right, so I'll go," he said and crossed his arms in turn.

"Well, one day," muttered the man beside Herosilla.

"*Maybe* one day," Roscio said. "Could be two, easy could be two."

"Are we all agreed, then?" Faustulus said in a voice that was nearly a growl. "Will anyone stand to say he's afraid to spend a day in the pastures without one of my boys to hold his hand?"

"Oh, let them go," a man said. "But it don't make sense, *I* say."

"It's decided," Faustulus said. He turned to his taller son and continued, "Remus, you'll guide our lady guest to Alba in the morning to see the king. Romulus, since you're so set on going you may; but the next trip to town is your brother's again."

Herosilla tried to stand. She stepped on the hem of her borrowed tunic. She toppled backward and would have fallen if Acca hadn't caught her.

"Romulus and Remus?" she said. "Is this the Palatine Hill?"

"Well, our village is Palatium, lady," the taller brother—Remus!—said. He looked puzzled by her sudden question. "I guess you could call the hill the Palatine, sure."

"By the stars!" Herosilla said.

The lightning had indeed thrown her a long way. The distance, however, was through time rather than space.

"By the very *gods*."

"All praise to the gods who rule men's lives," Faustulus said, in what he thought was agreement with his guest.

Herosilla sat on the roots of a pine, looking down over the moonlit plain where some day the Circus Maximus would seat a quarter million Romans watching horse races. There wasn't a single horse in present-day Palatium. Presumably there were a few in the royal town of Alba.

A thousand years. A thousand years.

The villagers must all be asleep by now. The occasional gust no longer brought snatches of speech as folk chewed over the marvelous events of the day. The arrival of a Greek woman from Cumae was as amazing to them as the truth was to Herosilla herself.

A thousand years.

Footsteps crunched behind Herosilla. She stood and turned, stepping around the tree. Romulus was walking down to where Herosilla had gone to think after awareness of the situation struck her like a second thunderbolt.

She could easily have gotten home from some rural valley outside Rome. There was no way back from the past, except as bones.

"No one believed me when I told them my destiny," Romulus said. "They didn't laugh to my face, but I knew what they were thinking. Now they have to believe."

"I'm not—" she said. But Romulus was right: he *was* destined for greatness. It just had nothing to with what had happened to Flavia Herosilla, gentlewoman and scholar.

"I'm the son of Numitor's daughter," Romulus said. "The king is my granduncle. Some day I'll be king myself, but a great king—not a worm like Amulius!"

"The king's brother Numitor is the rightful king?" Herosilla asked. She'd always assumed the stories of the founding were legend; that they had no more reality than similar tales of Olympus or Thule, written by folk to whom the truth would only have been a hurdle to leap in the course of their fictions. "Amulius ousted him?"

"What?" said Romulus. He was a tall man; only in the company of his brother would he have looked stocky. "Really? I wouldn't have thought Amulius had the backbone. The gods told you this?"

Herosilla opened her mouth, then closed it again. She'd never understood how a king who'd let his brother depose him had gained the manhood decades later to take his throne back. But then, she hadn't believed any part of the legend.

"But you and Remus are Rhea's twin sons, aren't you?" she asked.

"Oh, not him," Romulus said scornfully. "He's just a shepherd like the rest of them here, Faustulus' son by Acca. But *I'm* the son of Mars, just as Rhea claimed. The king said Rhea's son had died with her in childbirth, but really he had me set out on a hillside because he was afraid. Faustulus found me and brought me here to be suckled with his own son."

Facts were all Flavia Herosilla had ever cared about. The thunderbolt had destroyed her previous certainties along with all other aspects of her former life. Parts of the legend passed to her down a thousand years were perhaps true; other parts were certainly wrong. Romulus couldn't rationally be sure about things that had happened before he was born… but perhaps a god really *had* whispered them in his ear! She couldn't prove otherwise.

The only thing Herosilla could be sure of now was that she stood on a hilltop and the winter wind was cold.

"So you see I'm descended from a god also," Romulus concluded. "Therefore it's proper that you and I should mate." He put his hand on her arm.

"What?" said Herosilla. She backed away. "Don't be an idiot!"

Romulus laughed with the confidence of a strong man fully conscious of his power. He caught Herosilla by the arm again, above the elbow.

"Goddess you may be, but I'll bet you're a woman as well. Don't try to run or you'll get hurt and spoil your part of the fun."

Herosilla knew better than to run. She stooped, caught Romulus' unloaded ankle, and twisted as he tried to shift his weight. He went over her back and hit the rocky slope with a crash and a bellow.

Herosilla started toward the huts at a brisk pace, stooping once to grab a handful of dirt to throw in Romulus' eyes when he caught her. It was mud rather than dust or fine sand, but it would have to serve. From the sounds behind her the big man had rolled some way while stunned from landing on his head.

Acca, Remus, and several others trotted from the village. The moon behind Herosilla's back lit them brightly. "Lady?" Acca called.

"I'm here!" Herosilla said.

"We heard you…" Remus said doubtfully. Romulus, panting like a blown horse, caught up to them.

"Your brother slipped," Herosilla said. "I was coming for help."

She turned. Romulus looked at her with slitted eyes. There was a dark blotch on his forehead. "That's right," he muttered. "But I didn't need help."

Herosilla threw down as much of the dirt as she could and tried to wipe off the sticky remainder between her palms. She wondered what served the village for a water supply. Puddles, she feared.

"I'd like to sleep now," she said. "Is there a bed I could use?"

"Ours, lady," Acca said. "My husband and I will give you our house and sleep with our sons."

"If you wouldn't mind, Mistress Acca," Herosilla said, her eyes on the lowering Romulus, "I'd prefer that you remain with me tonight."

"I'm going to bed," Romulus said. "We'll get an early start for town."

"Why of course, lady," Acca said.

Romulus stalked up the path, pushing aside villagers who didn't get out of his way in time.

In her own day Herosilla had visited the villas of wealthy friends around Lake Albana, twelve miles from Rome. That hadn't prepared her for the experience of hiking to the region over a track surfaced in mud and sheep dung. The only vehicles in Palatium were wheelbarrows. There wasn't a mule or donkey to ride, much less a horse. The risk of being carried in a litter by herdsmen who'd never done anything of the sort before was greater than the discomfort of walking.

But the discomfort was worse than anything Herosilla'd experienced since she spent her first and only sea voyage leaning over the ship's railing and wondering whether it wouldn't be preferable to drown.

"That's it?" she said as they reached the top of the hill. She'd thought the huts glimpsed from the bottom of the long final climb from the lakeside were Alba's outskirts: the shanties beyond the walls occupied by poor people.

There were no walls. There was no more street plan than there had been in Palatium. Muddy tracks meandered between hovels much like those of the village. A few had a stone foundation course; a few had a small courtyard separated from its neighbors by a fence of twigs woven on a frame of vertical posts. Some houses were oval and perhaps contained two rooms instead of one, but they were the exceptions.

"Makes you feel cramped, doesn't it?" Remus said, mistaking Herosilla's shudder. "They've got tens of tens of tens of people here. It's too much."

"A real king would have a real city," Romulus said. "Like Troy, with stone walls. And think of how great Agamemnon was in Mycenae, to have conquered Troy!"

"Men aren't meant to live like that," his brother retorted. "Wars are because folk go mad when they're pressed too tight. They act like rats in a basket."

The first spikes of winter-sown grain showed in the fields below Alba. The town's immediate vicinity was cultivated; the pastures were around outlying communities like Palatium because live animals could be driven a greater distance than vegetable crops could be hauled over what passed for roads.

Children and dogs played in the streets. A few women sat on their lintels, talking and spinning yarn between their palms. They watched the visitors. One of them called a knowing greeting to Romulus, but for the most part their eyes were on Herosilla's saffron shawl. It was the only item of her own clothing that she'd dared bring on the muddy track.

A horn blatted from deeper into town. "We're here on market day," Remus explained. "That's the signal that the king is ready to hear petitions in the forum."

"Better if we'd gotten here sooner," Romulus said. "It can't be helped now."

"It couldn't be helped at all unless you were willing to carry me on your back," Herosilla snapped.

Both brothers had been surprised at the slow pace she set them, though Remus had been more polite in his comments. The ability to stride swiftly through muck had never been a virtue Herosilla thought to cultivate. Now she felt unreasonably angry at herself for that failure.

"There's no great hurry," Remus said. "Amulius would want to see her even if it weren't his petition day."

For all that, Remus moved faster through the twisting streets. Herosilla quickened her step despite fiery pains in both shins. The brothers led her by half a stride, clearing obstacles with their spearshafts or shoulders regardless of complaints from townsfolk.

Despite herself, Herosilla was expecting Alba's forum to have some kinship with the forum of a town of her own day. No commemorative arches or statues of leading citizens, but a covered porch for market days in bad weather and at least a few stone buildings.

This forum was a wide junction of the streets feeding it. That would have been greater praise if the streets had been more than dirt alleys. There were several hundred people present, some of them crying the remainder of their produce at reduced prices. Most of the citizens were indistinguishable from the shepherds of Palatium, though a few of the wealthier sort wore dyed cloth and metal or amber jewelry.

On one side of the forum was a compound surrounded by a log stockade. Two spearmen with bronze breastplates, plumed helmets, and large round shields guarded the gate. Across the forum was a similar stockade, marginally smaller.

"That's the king's palace," Remus said, nodding to the first compound. "The other's Numitor's. He's an envious little toad."

If Romulus disagreed with the description of the man he claimed as grandfather, he didn't do so aloud. "Come on," he muttered. "Let's get to the front."

The gate of the royal compound swung inward, opening. The stockade enclosed four or five buildings much like those in the rest of town. Amulius lived with guards and servants, maybe even courtiers if the term could be applied; but he lived in conditions very like those of Alba's other three thousand or so residents.

The horn sounded twice from within the compound. Four more guards and several attendants walked through the gate accompanying a man in his sixties who wore an embroidered purple robe.

One of the attendants carried a cow horn with a wooden mouthpiece; another held a wooden staff with knob of carved ivory; and the third had a folding stool which looked similar to the senatorial chairs of Herosilla's day except for being wood rather than ivory. The gate guards fell in at the end of the procession, leaving the stockade open behind them.

The brothers led Herosilla to the front of the crowd with the same strong-arm technique that had cleared the route through town. Citizens bleated at being shoved aside, but when they saw who was responsible they merely muttered about 'wild men from the hills.'

Herosilla smiled wryly. The folk of this day saw gradations in a culture which was from her viewpoint as uniform as a mud puddle. To the townsfolk, the shepherds were uncouth thugs who couldn't be expected to understand civilized norms.

The attendant spread the legs of the stool. As he did so, the gates of the other compound opened. Two spearmen with helmets but no shields or breastplates led out a man in a blue cloak. A group of blue-clad servants already at the front of the crowd opened space for the newcomers.

"Numitor," Remus whispered.

"So I gathered," Herosilla said.

Amulius sat on the stool, careful not to overbalance. He was somewhat overweight, while his brother was as thin as an aging weasel. The staffbearer raised his arms and said, "Citizens of Alba, your king is now—"

"King Amulius!" Romulus boomed as he stepped forward. "I bring you the messenger sent me by the gods in a lightning bolt. She—"

"Seize that man, Amulius!" Numitor cried. "And his brother too! They're the leaders of the bandits who've been attacking my herdsmen!"

"Seize me yourself, Numitor!" Remus said. He faced the king's brother, holding his spear held upright with the point down. Though not directly threatening, Remus could rotate and throw his weapon in a fraction of a second.

The crowd was already backing away. Amulius' guards moved in front of the king and raised their shields. From their shelter he cried, "Stop this! Stop this right now!"

The staffbearer leaned down and spoke in the king's ear. Numitor's guards raised their spears. Numitor touched their arms, restraining them.

"Citizens of Alba!" the staffbearer said. "There is inviolability for all during the king's petition time. Put down your weapons."

"Another time," Numitor said. He hadn't flinched during the confrontation, though he must have known as Herosilla did that Remus was strong enough to strike his target even if that meant the spear went through a guard first. "Let's hear the messenger of the gods, shall we?"

"King—" Romulus resumed, turning his own spear butt-down again.

"I can speak for myself," Herosilla said, stepping in front of Romulus. That brought her almost in contact with the king's guards. She prodded the shepherd with her elbow to back him up. "King Amulius, I am Flavia Herosilla, a gentlewoman of...of another place."

'Rome' would mean nothing. Saying she came from Cumae wouldn't dispose the king to help her.

Amulius leaned forward and tapped his guards to move them aside. He peered at Herosilla without expression.

"Lightning struck an oak tree in the storm yesterday and she appeared," Remus said. "We saw her, my brother and me, while we were herding your sheep."

"She's proof of my high destiny," Romulus put in. Nobody seemed to pay any attention. Even in Alba they'd probably heard the claims often enough.

Amulius and his attendants bent their heads together for a moment whispering, their eyes on Herosilla. The king sat up again and said, "Are you claiming to be an oak dryad, then?"

"Nothing of the sort!" Herosilla said. "I'm a gentlewoman, a noble of my own country. I—"

Spectators laughed. Herosilla realized she was dressed for the most part as a peasant and was filthy from the journey besides.

Amulius' eyes narrowed in puzzlement. The staff-bearer whispered to him again. "Well, what is it you want from me, woman?" the king said.

"I—" Herosilla said. She paused, stunned when her mind burst through the wall it had raised to protect her from the full horror of her situation.

She wanted to return to civilization. There *was* no civilization. Rome didn't exist. Athens and the other cities of Greece would scarcely be intellectual centers in this age. Writing was a new art, and literature was limited to drinking songs and oral renditions of Homer.

Should she go to Egypt, the source of so many of the beggars clogging the streets of Rome in her day?

Or should she simply open a vein and end this misery?

Herosilla stiffened. Weakness was the worst of vices; worse even than ignorance. "King Amulius," she said in a firm voice. "Provide me with a house and servants. There are many things I can teach you."

The laughter was louder this time. Amulius grinned; his staffbearer said something to him in a normal voice, but the crowd's merriment hid the words.

"Are you a goddess after all, then?" the king said when the noise had died down. "Only, I thought goddesses would be able to speak proper Latin."

Everybody laughed again.

"Of course I'm not a goddess, you witless clods!" Herosilla shouted. That she could speak their barbarous dialect even with an accent made her a marvel of her own time—but this wasn't her time. "I'm Flavia Herosilla, one of the most learned persons of any age, let alone this swamp of mud and boorishness! You should provide me with the basic amenities because I'm the closest thing to civilization that you'll ever see!"

The laughter finally ended. Romulus and Remus edged close to either side of her, disconcerted by the turn of events.

Herosilla doubted anyone in the crowd had heard her outburst. It wouldn't have made any difference if they did. Amulius was a worm, not a man who might have had her executed for telling him the blunt truth.

"Well, Flavia Herosilla," Amulius said with false geniality. "I suspect you can get something for that shawl you're wearing. As for the rest of your needs..."

He gestured toward Romulus. "You men. You're the sons of Faustulus, my herdsman at Palatium, aren't you?"

"You know we are," Romulus growled, too angry to claim heavenly parentage.

"Since you found her," the king said, "I give you full responsibility for her. She'll no doubt teach you many things. Now, is there other business to come before me?"

Herosilla turned and walked away. She was blind with rage. Citizens moved out of her way, but Remus put a hand on her arm to stop her before she collided with a house at the far end of the forum. The brothers were beside her, wearing troubled expressions.

"The ignorant *fools*," Herosilla said.

"They didn't see you come from the lightning," Remus said. "If I hadn't been there myself..." He shrugged.

"I would have believed!" Romulus said.

"You'd believe the sun rises in the west if you thought it would prove you were king!" Herosilla snapped. Open anger immediately made her feel better. She tossed her head, shaking the cobwebs loose from her brain.

Amulius and his advisers were ignorant fools, but that had been true of most people in Herosilla's own day. She was a fool herself to have thought the situation would be better during the barbarous past. The question before her was what to do now?

Her clothing and jewelry was unique and doubtless valuable in this age. Unfortunately, no one in Alba—and perhaps no one in Italy—had sufficient long-term capital to pay the amount Herosilla would need to live the remainder of her life in reasonable comfort. Any ruler who did have that wealth probably had also the will and ability to take the items by force from a friendless stranger.

She supposed she could live in Palatium on the villagers' charity. She visualized the prospect: she couldn't imagine any existence that would be more dreary and miserable. There didn't seem—

"So you two own her, huh?" said an unfamiliar voice. Herosilla looked around. A local man had walked over to the brothers. He wore an iron ring on his right index finger and a russet cloak over a tunic with a patterned border. The garb and his fat belly marked him as one of Alba's leading citizens.

"Go away," Romulus said.

"Now, don't be hasty," the fat man said. He was clean-shaven, but his bushy mustache flowed into his sideburns. "I was hoping we could do business. I think she might clean up into something interesting."

He gripped Herosilla's jaw with a thumb and forefinger to turn her face in profile. She slapped his hand away in amazement.

The man chuckled. "Now, she'd have to stay in Palatium," he continued. "My wife would—"

"You moronic pig!" Herosilla shouted. She kicked at the man's crotch. The purse hanging from his belt got in the way. Nearby citizens turned to watch the commotion. "You fat cretin! I'd fling myself off the Tarpeian Rock before I'd let you touch me!"

The local backed away, then turned. A heavily-built woman wearing a mantilla of imported lace trotted out of the crowd. She made a beeline for him. The man began mouthing excuses, but they obviously weren't going to do him any good.

"We'd better get out of here," Remus said somberly. "I want to get home before dark. I don't trust Numitor if we give him time to prepare something."

"I'd like to see him try," Romulus said. His voice rasped like a file cutting iron.

The three of them strode through Alba in silence. When they reached the path down to the lake and home, Remus said, "Lady?"

"Yes," Herosilla said.

"I was wondering..." Remus said. "What is the Tarpeian Rock?"

"Why," Herosilla said in amazement, "it's the outcrop on the Capitolium where—"

She stopped. The story of Tarpeia betraying Rome to the invading Sabines hadn't occurred yet. There wasn't a city to betray.

"I'll show you some day," Herosilla said. After a moment she went on, "I can see that if I'm to live in civilized surroundings, I'm going to have to create them myself. Which I will!"

The vermin in the bed she shared with Acca didn't keep Herosilla from getting to sleep, nor did the bustle of the shepherds taking out their flocks awaken her in the morning. Only when the sun found a gap in the clouds and streamed past the hut's half-closed door did she rouse from dreams as sharp-edged as the walls of a Greek temple.

Herosilla straightened her legs and groaned. She ached in every muscle, even those she wouldn't have thought had anything to do with walking.

Acca opened the door fully. "Are you up, dearie?" she said. "I have some breakfast for you here."

Herosilla thrust her feet into her own sandals. They wouldn't have lasted a mile of the journey to Alba, but the loose-fitting local products she'd worn instead—hide *wrappers*, really—rubbed blisters in several places. She stumbled out to join her hostess.

Acca handed her a wooden mug of beer and an ashcake made from left-over porridge cooked all night on a flat rock beside the fire. Herosilla thought she could get used to the beer in time. There was nothing in Palatium to drink except beer or water, and she didn't trust water from the shallow well near the sheep pen.

There was probably wine in Alba; certainly there would be in Cumae. It wasn't Herosilla's first priority, but she'd see to it in time.

"It didn't go as you'd hoped, the boys told me," Acca said as Herosilla began to eat. None of the other women joined them, though most watched Herosilla as they continued with their own tasks. Ganea, Romulus' doxy, glared briefly before she went back to chopping vegetables against a treetrunk split to form a flat surface.

Herosilla dipped the ashcake into the beer to soften it. "Not yet," she said. "It will eventually."

She looked around the straggling village. She hadn't paid it much attention before; hadn't been here in daylight except a snatch the previous morning before she set out to Alba with the brothers.

Drainage ditches would be fairly easy. Paving or at least stepping stones shouldn't be difficult either. Improvements to the water supply were trickier, but hollowed logs could bring adequate clean water from a distance. She wasn't an engineer, but her studies in natural philosophy provided a basic awareness of slope and flow.

Herosilla swallowed the bite she was chewing and said, "Tell me about your sons. Is Faustulus really their father?"

Acca looked around to see if any villagers were nearby. She said, "I suppose I'd better tell you about myself. Most of those who knew are dead or they've forgotten…"

She stared at the backs of her spread hands. "It was a long time ago."

Herosilla dipped more ashcake and waited.

"I was betrothed to Faustulus as a girl," Acca continued, raising her eyes to Herosilla's. "But a trader came by, a Greek like you. Not so fancy as you, lady, but...I'd never seen clothes like he wore, and he had lovely bronzeware on his donkey."

"I understand," Herosilla said. She didn't, really; her own affairs—in all senses—had been arranged after a cold balancing of costs and benefits. She'd seen the normal cycle of passion and disaster often enough in others, though.

"So I went to Cumae with him for a year," Acca said in a quiet, calm voice. "That's where I learned to speak Greek, lady. But when he went home to Chalcis, I, well, he didn't take me. I came back to Palatium and Faustulus married me as if nothing had happened."

She added fiercely, "He's a *good* man."

"Ah!" said Herosilla at what she thought was a light dawning. "So the boys weren't really suckled by a wolf. 'She-wolf' is just the slang your people used for prostitute."

"What?" Acca said. She frowned. "I'd never heard that."

The older woman's mouth opened in amazement as the implications sank in. "You mean you think I'm a whore because I spent some time with the wrong man? Oh, lady! Is it like that with your people?"

Herosilla thought of the morals of her age. Of her own morals, for that matter; though she'd never considered that what she chose to do with her own body was a moral question.

"No," she said. "I certainly didn't mean that. I apologize for giving the impression that I did."

Acca smiled wryly. "Though I've been lucky," she admitted. "There's few enough husbands who wouldn't have thrown the business in my face a time or two when we argued. Faustulus is a good man."

"I see that," Herosilla said. This time she meant the words as more than a placeholder to entice a story from the embarrassed teller.

"Anyway, Faustulus took a flock to Alba a few days after I gave birth," Acca continued. "Gave birth to *his* son—it was a year and more since I'd come back from Cumae. There was a babe, a little boy, left to die by the lakeside. Faustulus couldn't let that happen, he's too soft hearted. He brought it to me to raise with our own."

She shrugged. "What could I say, lady? When he'd been so kind to me? We've brought them both up the same with no differences between them."

"Was Numitor's daughter Rhea the mother?" Herosilla asked.

Acca dipped her chin in denial. "Rhea and her baby died at the birthing," she said. "I knew the midwife. There's some believe that Numitor was more than the child's grandfather, if you catch my drift."

She looked toward the distant horizon, thinking about the past. "The mother of the child my husband found was just some girl who got into trouble and took the only way out. I was lucky it wasn't me, off in Cumae."

"But it's still true that Romulus isn't your son?" Herosilla prodded gently.

"Romulus?" Acca said. "Oh, no, he's our son all right. It was Remus that my husband found by Alba."

The old woman shook her head in amusement. "I've never understood where Romulus gets his notions. The only thing special about his father—"

Her tone hardened.

"—is that Faustulus is a better man than any other I've met!"

The afternoon rain had passed; the sky to the west was clearing enough to let reddened sunlight through again. "They're coming," said Acca. "That's Grayleg, my boys' ram."

Herosilla turned. She'd been sketching a drainage plan in the soft ground, using a long stick so that she didn't have to bend. If she listened carefully she could hear sheep and a faint clatter that could have been the bellwether's neck rattle, but it was hard to believe Acca could identify the sound as that of a particular ram.

"Mostly my boys are the last in," Acca said with quiet pride. "In case there's trouble with Numitor, you know. But because of tomorrow they're coming in early."

Sheep came over the crest of the hill behind the brothers' gray ram, as Acca had predicted. Romulus and Remus walked at the back of the flock.

Remus played a simple tune on a reed pipe. Wax stopped the bottom of the single tube; he varied the notes by opening or closing holes in the shaft with his fingertips.

Ganea ran to Romulus and ostentatiously kissed him. Remus stuck the pipe through his sash and called, "I see you're able to move today, lady. Last night we weren't sure."

"I'm in perfectly fit condition," she said sharply. "Walking through mud was an unfamiliar exercise, but I assure you I'll adapt."

The women of the village were taking the sheep in charge. Ganea tried to hold Romulus with her, but he shook her curtly from his arm and walked over to see what his brother and Herosilla were discussing.

"If I'm to live in Palatium, as it appears that I am for a time," Herosilla said, including Romulus with her eyes, "then I intend to pay my way by improving the life of everyone in the community."

She allowed herself a self-deprecating smile. "My own included, of course. Tomorrow we can start with detailed planning of the drainage route I've sketched to direct waste and rain water away from the village."

Other herdsmen were bringing in their flocks. Pressure in their udders made the fresh ewes eager to be milked, and the other sheep were too strongly group conscious to hang back from a general movement.

"We can't do it tomorrow, lady," Romulus said. His tone suggested that he didn't like to get orders from females, even females he thought might be divine.

"You two and your father are the leaders of the community," Herosilla said, "and he can't walk the ground. I don't expect you to do the digging by yourselves, but—"

"It's not that, lady," Remus said apologetically. "The two of us with Roscio and Celer have a religious rite tomorrow we call the Lupercal. We run—"

"I know what the Lupercal is," Herosilla snapped. "Who do you think—"

She caught herself. The brothers thought she was a foreigner who wouldn't understand a fertility rite unique to their village—nude men, Luperci, running around the Palatine daubed with the blood of a sacrifice to ensure the success of the Spring lambing season.

"Ah," she said. "I, ah—" the word 'apologize' caught in her throat. "I'm familiar with the Lupercalia, that is."

Another piece fell into place in the legends of a thousand years later. "Oh!" Herosilla said. "But you can't run the Lupercalia tomorrow. Numitor's men will attack you while you're unarmed!"

"Is she on about the future again, Romulus?" asked Celer, the toady Herosilla had noticed the day before. Returning shepherds were joining the brothers after handing their flocks over to the women.

"Go talk to your sheep, Celer," Remus said. "You may know something a sheep'd be interested in hearing."

He turned to Herosilla and continued more gently, "Lady, we've lived with Numitor's threats for a long time. We can't hide all day because we're afraid of him."

"Listen to what I'm saying, you numskull!" Herosilla said. "Numitor *is* planning to ambush you. No buts, ifs, or maybes. You can't run the Lupercal, period."

"You've seen this, lady?" Romulus said. He was frowning, though perhaps as much at Herosilla's tone as at what she was saying. "Or your god whispered it in your ear?"

"I read it!" Herosilla said. "I—"

Her own mind put her suddenly more on the defensive than anything these yokels could say. She'd always believed the accounts of Rome's founding were legends or worse, fictions invented by historians of later centuries to inflate the genealogies of rich patrons in their own day. There was obviously some truth in the legends; she had the evidence of her own eyes as proof.

That didn't mean that every detail—the attack on the Luperci, for example—was accurate. Even if the story was basically true Herosilla couldn't be sure the attack would occur this year rather than next year or ten years in the future.

Unless of course a god or gods was controlling events, using Flavia Herosilla as a pawn. That thought made her *very* uncomfortable.

"What's reading, Romulus?" Roscio asked.

What an age, what a *world*! "An activity for which you are wholly unsuited, Roscio," Herosilla said aloud. "Like childbirth!"

"Well, we appreciate your concern, lady," Remus said in obvious embarrassment. "We'll come look over the drainage with you in the next few days. Right now we've got things to get ready for the morning."

The brothers turned away, drawing the remaining shepherds with them. Celer said something that made several others laugh. Remus didn't smile; nor, more surprisingly, did Romulus.

The moon lit the tops of reeds growing below Herosilla, where the Forum would be. The broad valley would be a swamp during the winter rains until the Cloaca Maxima, the Great Sewer, was built to drain it in a century or so.

Beyond the Forum Herosilla could see the corner of the Capitoline Hill from which the Tarpeian Rock jutted. During the Republic murderers were flung to their death from the outcrop. The emperors had substituted more refined methods of execution.

She didn't turn when she heard footsteps behind her. The slope before her was steep enough that death for herself and her attacker would be the probable result if she launched herself outward. Either outcome would satisfy her in her present state of mind. Herosilla tensed, waiting for the hands to grip her shoulder.

"I brought you some supper," Remus said.

"I'm not hungry," Herosilla said. She relaxed. She realized that she *was* hungry, very hungry. Frustration always increased her appetite.

Remus seated himself and handed her an ashcake with a slab of cheese.

"I've got beer in a skin here," he said. "Mom's keeping some broth warm back at the hut."

Herosilla nibbled at the cheese. The cake was too hard to chew unsoftened. Perhaps if she held a sip of beer in her mouth…

"Even if you're right about Numitor, lady…" Remus said. He laced his fingers together and stared across the valley so that he didn't have to meet her eyes. "And I don't say you're not. But the strongest men in the village owe it to the gods to run the rite."

Herosilla swallowed a bite of cheese. "There are no gods," she said. "There *is* Numitor and chances are there'll be an ambush. I'm not so confident about the details though—like the fact you survive!"

"There are gods here, lady," Remus said quietly. "I don't know about your country."

He turned his troubled face toward her. "Lady, if there's a bad lambing season Amulius won't starve. He'll just eat less meat with his bread. But we here in the hills depend for our very life on the half the increase that's ours. We don't have grain except what we trade lambs for to the farmers at Alba. What our women raise in their plots won't keep the whole village alive over the winter. We *have* to honor the gods properly."

Herosilla smiled bitterly. "Remus," she said, "do you believe that events just happen or do you think men make them happen?"

Remus pursed his lips. He was a strikingly handsome man, a lean Mercury to his brother's muscular Apollo.

"Well, lady," he said. "I've always thought the gods set up the pattern and we mortals pretty much run or fall depending on how well we follow it. My brother, now, he thinks the gods have chosen him to make a pattern."

He shrugged and gave her a wry smile. "My brother has great dreams," he said. "For a city bigger than anywhere else in the world. All built of stone, like traders say they do in Greece. Is that true, lady?"

"Most places in Greece, yes," Herosilla said. Even in this day, she supposed. For a region as rocky as Greece, there was very little choice.

"For myself," Remus continued, "I think even Alba's bigger than a city ought to get. So many people cramped together like that, it brings out the wrong things in them."

He grinned, cheerfully this time. "Though after the Lupercal, we'll look into this drainage you want. I never found there was anything romantic about mud either."

Herosilla laughed and rose to her feet. She'd come to a decision. She was still a little stiff from yesterday's exercise, but with Acca's help she'd be able to repeat the hike to Alba the next morning even if she had to crawl the last of the way.

"Walk me back to the village," Herosilla said, offering the shepherd her arm.

"Lady?" he said, but he obediently took her arm.

"Remus," she said, "I respect your attitude, but for myself I'm unwilling to imagine a world without the greatness of—of its greatest city."

"Chalcis, lady?" Remus said.

"Not Chalcis," she said crisply as they walked slowly along a path sheep had worn to the bedrock. "You will run the Lupercal because your gods direct you to do so. And I will do what I need to do according to the forces directing me."

Herosilla pursed her lips and added, "Which I must admit are looking more and more like gods."

She squeezed Remus' arm. It was a good, strong arm. Remus was a lad who had possibilities that the right woman could bring out.

"Hoy, child," Acca said. Walking to Alba at the best speed Herosilla could manage hadn't winded the older woman, even though she was the one carrying the bundle of clothing along with food and drink for the trip. "Are you Tertia?"

The little girl rocking an infant in a wicker cradle in front of a house dipped her chin solemnly. "I'm Quartilla, Aunt Acca," she said.

"Well, run tell your mother I'm here with a friend and we're going to change clothes in your house," Acca said. "I'll watch the—"

She peeked into the cradle and lifted the covers.

"—boy while you're gone." She nodded to Herosilla. "Go on inside. Clodia's probably with her sister-in-law and the new baby."

The house was similar to those in Palatium, though the inner walls had been whitewashed. There was a hanging lamp in the form of a bronze griffin which Herosilla would have been proud to find a place for at her villa in Cumae. A shield, a spear, and a helmet of hardened leather stood against one wall.

Besides shutters, the two windows had grates of thick withies to maintain security while allowing air to circulate in hot weather. Herosilla remembered Remus' comment about cities encouraging the worst in men.

She began to take off her borrowed village garb. Acca came in a moment later, carrying the cradle. The infant remained asleep or at least quiet.

"Oh, lady, your skin is as fine as the cloth you wear," Acca said in amazement. She was seeing her guest undressed for the first time by daylight. She set the bundle of silk clothing on the bed frame and untied it with sure fingers.

Herosilla hadn't had a bath or a bed free of vermin in the past three days of exercise and exposure. She thought of how a woman of her time and class would rate her now and shook her head sadly.

Acca wasn't a trained maid, but she had good hands and there was light to work by. Besides, the audience wasn't going to be as fastidious as a gathering of upper-class Roman women.

Herosilla dressed quickly, then put on her jewelry. Her earlobes were still tender; lightning had heated the wires hot enough to blister. She hung the earrings anyway. Garnets and faceted gold beads dangled from the lowest of the three tiers. The effect was spectacular enough to be worth minor pain.

Acca stepped back to view the completed result. "Oh, lady," she whispered.

"Let's go," Herosilla said curtly. She smiled with satisfaction nevertheless. She'd have liked to view herself in a mirror, but Acca's reaction was really a better way to judge how she looked to the folk with whom she'd have to deal.

Acca led; Herosilla couldn't have hoped to find her way through this warren. The streets were crowded. Because it wasn't market day Alba had fewer visitors from the outlying villages, but the local women generally worked in the street before their houses rather than going to the forum. Acca didn't have her sons' brute strength, but she cleared a path for her guest without overmuch delicacy.

Citizens gasped and stared when they saw the shimmering silk and jewelry. Herosilla smiled again.

The guards outside Numitor's compound were the same pair who'd attended him at the royal audience. As before, they weren't fully armed like the guards across the forum. Amulius, though a spineless fool, wasn't so great a fool that he didn't preserve *some* marks of his superior status to his brother.

"You there!" Herosilla said to the taller guard. She needed to pick one, and they didn't wear indications of rank. "I'm here to see your master Numitor."

"Nobody can go in today," the guard said nervously. He'd never supposed an apparent goddess would appear before him. He looked to his partner for support.

The other guard edged a little farther away. He acknowledged Herosilla's presence only by sidelong glances. Folk in the Forum drifted closer to watch in awe. The guards at the royal compound were interested also, but they didn't leave their posts when citizens blocked their view.

"You will *not* keep me out, you rural simpletons," Herosilla said in a venomous tone. "Your only choice is whether you willingly admit me to give your master the information about the ambush he's waiting for; *or* I enter over the lightning-blasted ashes of your bodies. Do you understand?"

"She's the messenger?" the shorter guard asked, trying to look at his partner without letting his eyes fall on Herosilla. His question answered Herosilla's doubt about whether this was the correct year.

"Sorry, lady," the taller guard muttered. He pushed the gate fully open as he stepped aside. "We were expecting Talpus."

Herosilla strode into the compound. It held four two-room huts. Female servants prepared food in front of one. The women glancing up from their weaving beside the next were better dressed; the fat one wearing bronze armlets was most likely Numitor's wife. Across the compound, a third hut had a litter of tools and spearshafts leaned against it, though none of the male servants or other guards were present.

That left the other as Numitor's dwelling. Herosilla walked through the open door and surprised Numitor talking to an attendant with white hair and a sour expression. Both men jumped up.

The hut's front room contained an ornate bronze tripod supporting a brazier. The charcoal was laid but not lighted; apparently the locals didn't consider the day chilly enough to require heat.

A pair of large jugs with geometric designs stood to either side of the door into the bedroom beyond; shelves displayed half a dozen drinking bowls on edge so that the figures in black glaze could be seen. One of the bowls had the characters' names written in Greek above the figures: Herakles and the centaur Cheiron.

The names were written backwards. The illiterate artist had copied them out as he would have any other design element, but he hadn't realized that the order of the letters was significant. It didn't matter to the owner either: he was just proud to own an item with writing on it.

"Guards!" Numitor shouted.

"Stop blustering, you fool," Herosilla said. "I'm your only chance of getting the kingship that you want more than you do your right arm. Shut up and listen or I'll walk across the street to your brother."

"I'll get—" the attendant muttered as he stepped toward the door.

Numitor caught his arm. "Wait a moment," he said. His eyes didn't leave Herosilla.

She smiled coldly. "Now," she said. "You've set an ambush for the men from Palatium as they run the Lupercal. I suspect you'll capture Remus and some of the others but not Romulus. None of that matters. What matters is what we do next."

The attendant blinked at 'we'.

Numitor said, "Who told you that?" His voice was deadly.

"Would you be happier if I said the lightning told me?" Herosilla snapped. "I told you to shut up and listen. If you try to bring enough of your own men into Alba to unseat your brother they'll be noticed. The citizens may not have much affection for Amulius, but they know you're a vicious little snake. They'll resist and you'll lose."

"You're a very interesting woman," Numitor said softly.

"Instead, I'll use the herdsmen from Palatium and the nearby communities to deal with your problem," Herosilla said. "After that, I'll—"

"They're Amulius' men," the attendant protested.

Herosilla's earrings clinked as she turned her head quickly. "They're *my* men, so far as you're concerned," she said.

"I don't see how you can achieve that," Numitor said thoughtfully. "But then, I don't suppose I need to understand. Since I'll have no involvement in the entertainment if it fails. That is correct, is it not?"

"Quite correct," Herosilla said. Numitor was one of the most unpleasant men she'd ever met, but he was clearly not stupid.

"And I suppose you'll want some position for yourself if you succeed?" Numitor said. He glanced through the doorway toward the women's quarters across the compound. "Well, I suppose that can be arranged also."

"That is not what I want in return," Herosilla said in an icy voice. She didn't bother to state her loathing for Numitor: he was observant enough to read it in her expression.

"What you will do, as much for your own safety as because I require it," she continued, "is send a colony from Alba to where Palatium now stands. The sons of Faustulus will head the new community. Alba's bursting at the seams, besides which at least some hundreds of the citizens are going to be direct threats to your rule if you don't get rid of them. You'll solve both difficulties this way."

"A *very* interesting woman," Numitor repeated, this time in a musing tone. "When would you expect this…change in government, we'll call it… to be achieved?"

Herosilla sniffed. "In ten days or so. I'll send my men into Alba over a few days to stay with friends and kin here. Too much haste could arouse suspicion. In two market days, let's say."

She turned and looked through the doorway. Numitor's fat wife was staring into her husband's dwelling, nervously twisting one of her armlets.

"Of course," Herosilla added with her back to the men, "you'll have to release the Luperci you've captured this morning. I'll need them to lead the assault."

There was commotion at the gate of the compound. A man in a torn tunic entered and ran to Numitor's dwelling. Leaning on the doorpost he gasped, "We caught three of them, but one of those damned brothers got away!"

Blood spattered the messenger's tunic. He didn't have an open cut, though his left cheek was swollen from a blow. He paid no attention to Herosilla despite having to look past her to see Numitor. "Servius wants to know what to do with the ones we've got?" he added.

"Release them to me," Herosilla said. "Talpus here can lead me to where they're being held. I'll return with them to Palatium."

"Huh?" the messenger said as his eyes focused on Herosilla for the first time.

"Yes," Numitor said. He smiled like a weasel moving toward its prey. "Do as this one says, Talpus."

Herosilla smiled back at him. Numitor's attendant and the messenger looked at them in fear and horror.

The bonfire in the center of Palatium was stoked high as a beacon for herdsmen coming in from the surrounding communities, but it hadn't illuminated the track up the hill's steep southern face. Herosilla stumbled repeatedly during the climb; once she would have fallen except for Remus' quick hand on her shoulder.

Acca and the three shepherds hadn't had any difficulty. Even Roscio, half delirious from the pain of the broken bone in his right forearm, plodded surefootedly through the dark.

There were scores of men around the fire; perhaps as many as a hundred. A fellow Herosilla didn't recognize turned at the sound of the returning Luperci and cried, "It's an attack!"

"No, we're coming home!" Remus shouted. "And if you ever want to see *your* home again, Balthus, you'd better not aim that spear at me!"

Remus had been clubbed unconscious, but the bloody bandage around his head was the only present sign of the attack. He spoke and moved like a man in perfect health.

Romulus pushed through the crowd of assembled shepherds. "Remus?" he said. "We were coming to get you."

"You were coming to have your heads lopped off," Herosilla said, pitching her voice to carry. "What did you think was going to happen when you attacked Alba, you dimwit? There's five townsmen for every one of you, and I shouldn't wonder if they had better weapons besides."

Romulus scowled like the start of an avalanche. "Women don't understand these things," he said.

"This woman understands quite well," Herosilla said. "Which is why you're going to do this my way instead of cocking it up again. I can't afford a failure."

She'd changed back to peasant garb before leaving Alba, so she didn't have silk and ornaments to over-awe the gathered herdsmen. The climb up the Capitoline would have wrecked the fine clothing anyway.

"I've been wondering, brother," Remus said. His tone was reasonable, but he spoke loudly enough that he could be heard well into the crowd of armed herdsmen. "How is it you happened to be a hundred strides behind the rest of us when Numitor's men attacked? You're usually a better runner than that. Is it because you believed the lady's warning?"

"I turned my ankle at the start," Romulus said. His voice dropped in volume with every syllable. "I was coming to get you. You can see that."

"Then let's listen to what the lady has to say," Remus said loudly. "After all, *she* rescued us from Numitor's men."

"Sure, we'll listen," his brother agreed, mumbling now. "I don't see there's much to talk about since you're all free."

"Come," Herosilla said, striding toward the bonfire in the correct expectation that the men would jump out of her way. It put the seal on her dominance of the assembly. "I want to sit down, and I want all of you to hear."

The closest thing to seats in Palatium were the stones set around the fire for village councils. Herosilla took one that was a hand's breadth higher than the others. She needed not only rest for her legs but also the effect she would gain by standing again. Romulus and Remus seated themselves to either side of her.

Faustulus was across the circle. He gestured to the fire and ordered, "Let it burn down. No one else will be arriving tonight."

Herosilla waited for the assembly to settle around her. Most of the men were strangers. Local shepherds whispered to their neighbors, telling them who the lady with the strange accent and manner was.

The only women present were those from Palatium, and they kept very much to the fringes. War was men's work; though women were the second booty after sheep.

In clear, ringing tones trained by declamations to groups much larger than this one, Herosilla said, "We are going to put Numitor on the throne of Alba."

The shepherds buzzed. "We are going to do that," Herosilla said, ripping through the amazement the way a sickle saws grain, "because Numitor has enough intelligence to give us what we want. If Amulius had the wit the gods gave to sheep, he'd have put his brother out of the way ages ago."

Faustulus lurched unsteadily to his feet. "Lady!" he cried. "We're Amulius' men, all of us here."

"Are you?" Herosilla said. "Is that what you believe?"

She stood and pointed to her right. "Remus, when Numitor would have seized you the other day, was it Amulius or your own right arm that preserved you?"

She turned and pointed to Romulus on her other side. "Romulus, when you gathered men to free your brother, did you bother to ask Amulius for help? No, you expected to have to fight *all* the men of Alba, because you knew the king's spine is as soft as wax in the August sun!"

Her tone was harsh and hectoring. The shepherds had never heard a trained voice before. It stunned them the way sight of Herosilla's finery had blasted the wills of those she needed to impress in Alba.

Herosilla swept her eyes around the assembly. "If your children were starving this winter, would Amulius feed them? Though you know his table never lacks for the meat you raise! If this Amulius owns your souls, then indeed the gods have sent me to the wrong place. I was meant to go to a land of men, not ewes!"

As a scholar, she sneered at the notion of deities. When she fought—verbally or in other fashions—she used any weapon she thought would be effective.

Herosilla paused, letting the murmurs die down. Before she could resume, Remus said, "Lady?"

She nodded curtly to him. Remus remained seated, but everyone in the village could hear his voice.

"Lady," he said, "all you say about Amulius is true. But how can we trust Numitor after we've made him king?"

"An excellent question," Herosilla said, directing her cold smile to the full audience. "When we've succeeded, you and your brother will lead a colony of the citizens of Alba who hate Numitor worst. You'll found a new town right here in company with the folk of Palatium and the other villages on these hills, brought together in such strength—"

The crowd gasped with a sound like surf on gravel. Romulus jumped to his feet.

"—that Numitor won't be able to touch you!"

Herosilla crossed her arms. No one could have shouted over the shocked babbling. Trying to do so would have made her ridiculous.

The brothers looked at her from either side. After a moment, Romulus began to smile.

The sun was still a finger's breadth below the eastern horizon, but a few early comers were arranging their wares in Alba's forum. The owner of a fish stall bartered with a herdsman's wife as she hung skeins of naturally colored wool on a tripod of sticks.

Servius, the chief of Numitor's guards, opened one leaf of the gate enough that Herosilla could slip out. Servius himself stayed, hidden.

Herosilla stalked across the forum in brisk majesty. The fishmonger, then the wool seller, turned and gaped.

The guards at the king's gate didn't notice Herosilla until she was halfway toward them. They stiffened. One lifted his spear, then leaned it against the stockade behind him as if embarrassed by his initial impulse.

Herosilla wore her festival garb. The predawn halflight didn't show her to best effect, but the glinting, shimmering adornment still provided a more-than-regal effect in this drab age.

"Oh cursed man!" Herosilla said. She pointed her left arm toward one of the guards: limb and index finger made a single threatening line. "Open the gates that I may warn your master of the doom that awaits him!"

"The king will hear petitions after midday," the other guard said. His shield was a heavy concave round of wood with a bronze facing. He twitched it forward slightly as if he were about to meet the shock of an enemy charge.

Herosilla lowered her left arm. Her right hand continued to grip the hanging end of her shawl. "Fool!" she said. "Do the gods wait on man's convenience to voice their warnings? Will you send your master screaming to the Underworld because you didn't choose to break his sleep? The death you bring him will be a sleep never broken, you blasphemous yokels!"

The guards looked at one another; neither found an answer in his fellow's face. "Mistress," said the one who'd spoken before, "we can't let you in. If Amulius didn't flay us, his chamberlain Oscus would. *Please,* mistress."

"Then send for Oscus," Herosilla said flatly. She put her left hand on her hipbone and flared the elbow out akimbo.

"Right," said the other guard in relief. "Let him sort it out. Boy!"

"Sir?" peeped a small voice from the other side of the gate.

"Get Oscus here right now," the guard snarled. "I don't care if you have to drag him by his pecker!"

"Yes sir," the boy said. The words faded slightly as he sprinted across the compound.

Herosilla waited, as still as a statue. She faced the closed gate with a grim scowl. The guards fidgeted to either side of her glare.

Nothing happened for several minutes. Stars faded in the eastern sky. There were sounds within the compound: footsteps, a querulous objection, and finally the crossbar rasping through the shackles that held it.

The gate leaves swung inward. A man in his tunic stepped into the opening. He was the attendant who'd carried Amulius' staff during the audience. He held a crimson sash in his hand, but he hadn't managed to tie it around his waist.

"What in the name of Jupiter is this—" he said.

Herosilla swung her right arm. There was a rock the size of her fist in the tip of her shawl. It struck the chamberlain in the middle of the forehead, felling him in the gateway like a sacrificed lamb.

"Hell and Death!" a guard shouted. He seized Herosilla with his right hand; the shield bound his left. She elbowed him reflexively. The blow clanged on his bronze breastplate and her arm went numb.

"Attack!" the other guard cried. "We're being attacked!"

Herosilla bit the hand of the guard holding her. He batted her against the stockade, once and again as she continued to struggle. Her sight dimmed. The other guard was trying to close the gate, but the chamberlain's body lay in the opening the way Herosilla had planned. The guard bent to drag Oscus clear, still bellowing a warning.

Herosilla heard a loud clang. The man holding her grunted and let go. She fell into a sitting position, her back against the stockade.

Romulus rammed his spear with both hands into the remaining guard's back. His bronze armor made the spearhead chirp, but it couldn't stop a thrust with the shepherd's full strength behind it. Remus, his spear already bloody, jumped the body and led dozens of bellowing herdsmen into the royal compound.

Herosilla tried to get up. The guard who'd held her lay across the hem of her tunic. He'd knocked off his helmet when he fell against the stockade wall, showing his bald patch.

She tugged the tunic free. The man made a faint gurgling sound. Only his fingers moved, clasping and unclasping on nothing. Blood oozed from the hole in his backplate.

Shepherds milled in the forum. Those nearer the front of the attack blocked the gateway to Amulius' compound. Numitor and his own six guards, fully armed with breastplates and shields, came from their stockade in close formation. Citizens appeared, then vanished into their houses to arm themselves and wait nervously.

"Let me through," Herosilla said to the back of a shepherd in the gateway. She gripped his shoulder to steady herself. His forearm was splinted.

The man turned; he was Roscio. "Lady!" he said, "Here, make way for the goddess!"

Using the butt of the spear in his good hand, Roscio forced a path for both of them through the confusion. A shepherd trying to hold in his intestines lurched against Herosilla as he plodded toward the gate. A woman was screaming.

The crowd parted. Celer came from the king's house, ducking under the low doorway. He wore a looted helmet.

"Where's Amulius?" Herosilla demanded. "Is he dead yet?"

Remus, then Romulus, came out of the dwelling. They dragged Amulius between them. Romulus held a straight-bladed sword that he'd taken from a guard.

Amulius was naked. His eyes were wild, and there was a fresh gash on his left cheek.

"Why isn't he dead?" Herosilla said shrilly. "Even a cowardly worm like that is too dangerous to let live now! Do I have to do everything for you?"

For a moment she viewed the scene from high above her body. The spell of dizziness passed.

The brothers stared at her. "No," Romulus said. "You don't."

He stabbed Amulius in the chest. The king screamed and gripped the blade with both hands in a vain attempt to prevent the iron from grating deeper through his ribs. The edges cut his hands, but he didn't let go until blood gushed from his mouth and his body collapsed in spasms.

Herosilla was above her body again. She sneered at the clumsy blow. Romulus was a herdsman, unfamiliar with swords. Flavia Herosilla had hundreds of times watched experts in the arena.

"Now I'll go outside and tell the people that justice has been done," she heard her mouth say. "The heaven-born twins have removed the usurper Amulius and set the real elder brother, Numitor, in his rightful place as King of Alba."

And by the end of the month, even the folk who'd grown up with Numitor and Amulius would believe the story...

The moon in its first quarter rode in and out of the clouds. If Herosilla squinted she could imagine that the sheen of the boggy pasture was marble rather than standing water and that the shadowy trees were the columns of the great public buildings that would someday surround the Forum.

This time she recognized the firm steps coming down the track behind her. "Tonight I ate before I came," she called without turning her head.

"I know," Remus said. "There's wolves here occasionally, and you're not really familiar with the path in darkness. Although—"

She heard the smile in his voice; not quite a chuckle.

"—I suppose you will be before long."

"Come sit," she said, patting the smooth stone beside her.

"I was planning to wait up by the cypress," Remus said. "I just wanted to tell you I was here so that you didn't think I was spying."

"Sit," Herosilla repeated. "It's a good place to think. I've been wondering if Aeneas was real too."

Remus lowered himself onto the seat with the careful grace of a cat relaxing. "Aeneas?" he said.

She smiled wryly. She said, "Nobody you've heard of, then. He was a Trojan hero who was supposed to have founded a colony here after the fall of Troy four hundred years ago. Four tens of tens of years."

Remus shook his head. "Four tens of tens," he said. "It's hard to believe anybody knows what happened so long ago."

He turned his face toward her and added, "It's because you can read that you know about these things?"

"I suppose so," Herosilla said. "I know a lot of things that aren't true as well. Since I came here last month I've had a hard time deciding which things belong in which category."

Remus laughed, then sobered slowly. "It'll be good having our own grainfields with the new colony," he said after a time. "I'm not sure that I'm going to like living in a city of six hundred people, though. It'll take some getting used to. At least we'll be able to get the drainage right."

"You'll have more power," Herosilla said, watching her companion to see how he would react. "Real power. The ford here is the best route across the river for many miles. You can grow wealthier than Numitor ever thought of being."

"I'm not my brother," Remus said; an observation rather than a gibe. "Living as a free man among free men is…"

He looked directly at her again. That he desired Herosilla was as clear as the fact he had no intention of acting on that desire unbidden. "I was going to say 'enough'. But I honestly can't imagine anything better."

Herosilla didn't speak for a moment. She'd met very few people whom she really liked, and there were fewer still natural gentlemen. To find both rarities combined in a shepherd from a barbarous village was as remarkable as the lightning bolt that had transported her here.

A very handsome shepherd, besides.

"Remus," she said briskly. "Do you ever worry about dying? Of being killed?"

"No," he said with a dismissive shrug. "Oh, I expect it'll happen. I'm not one to start trouble, but often enough somebody else will and I'm not going to stand back, either. A man can't worry about that, though. Not and live like a free man."

"Much as I thought," Herosilla said. She patted his arm. "Help me up," she directed. "We'll go back to the village now."

As they rose, as graceful as a pair of panthers, Herosilla added, "And since you're not going to worry about keeping yourself alive, I'll take care of that too. Along with the drainage."

The colony celebrated its first night on the Palatine with mutton and vast quantities of beer. It seemed to Herosilla that at least half the settlers ate and drank more like mourners at a funeral feast than in joyous anticipation of the future.

The moon was full again. Flavia Herosilla had lived in this age almost exactly one month. The location was nearly the same as well: the brothers had decided to place the settlers' temporary shelters on the broad pasture at the north side of the hill rather than clustering them around the existing houses of Palatium.

Herosilla thought of looking for the oak that lightning blasted when she arrived; she decided the sight would depress her even more. Besides, several families were probably using the stump to support one end of their lean-tos.

She'd been alone during most of her former life. Now she was lonely: there was no one in this age with whom she shared more than a month's worth of memories.

"Mistress Herosilla?" Romulus said, coming out of the shadows. Dozens of small cookfires burned among the warren of shelters, but at any distance the vagrant light they threw was more distorting than an aid to vision.

"Leader?" called a burly man coming from the other direction. He wore a cape with a patterned border, marking him as a person of wealth. "Can I speak to you? I'm Gaius Helvius and I've got a pottery workshop."

"*Co*-leader," Herosilla said.

"Co-leader," Romulus agreed with a nod. He looked over the other man and added with a slight frown. "Are you a member of the colony, Helvius?"

"We'd like to be," Helvius said nervously. He was wringing his hands beneath his cape. "I wasn't going to come, you know, not and live in a field for, well, the gods know how long. But the wife and I talked this morning and with Numitor king…well, can you take another household, us and my slaves?"

"Always glad to have another citizen, Gaius," Romulus said. "We'll be making the allotments at the assembly tomorrow, so you're not even late."

He turned his back on the potter to end the conversation. Helvius babbled thanks anyway, then scurried into the darkness.

"There's a hut on the knoll," Romulus said to Herosilla, nodding toward the drystone building she remembered from the evening she arrived. "Will you walk up there with me where we can talk without people interrupting?"

"Yes, all right," Herosilla said after a moment's consideration. The beehive structure was slightly above the camp, but it was well within the distance she could shout if there was trouble. "But we'll stay outside."

"Whatever you want," Romulus said curtly. He led the way up the track worn by generations of sheep. Herosilla followed, stumbling occasionally but better able to stay with him than she would have been a month before.

Sheep rubbing themselves on the shelter's lower layers had worn the stones smooth. Tufts of wool fluttered from crevices and the air breathed the warm, slightly sweetish odor of lanolin. Herosilla could see and hear more of the encampment's sad bustle than she had when she stood on a level with it.

"You don't like me, do you, lady?" Romulus said bluntly.

She sniffed. "No, of course not," she said. "Why should I like you? You're a boor, a braggart, and you tried to rape me. Nonetheless, I want the same thing you do: a city here that will become the greatest the world will ever see. You—your presence, your vision—is necessary for that dream to succeed."

Romulus nodded. He didn't appear to be offended by her equal frankness. Though pride got in the way of his thinking on occasion, Herosilla knew Romulus was far more than a stupid shepherd.

"And you do like my brother," Romulus said. "That's true too, isn't it?"

"As a person?" Herosilla said. "Yes, I rather do. He has just as much will and intelligence as you do, though he directs it differently. Do you know, he says he wants to learn to read?"

She smiled ruefully. "Not that there's a great deal to read in this age."

She heard the rustle behind her. Thick cloth covered her head before she could turn. She tried to strike backward but Romulus snatched her feet into the air.

Herosilla hit the ground hard. The impact knocked the air from her lungs; the cloth was smothering her. She stabbed with her fingers and tore flesh.

"Death take you, Celer!" Romulus snarled. "Get her arms!"

Callused hands twisted Herosilla's wrists together. She tried to shake the bag away from her head. A fist hard enough to drive tent pegs slammed the pit of her stomach.

For a moment Herosilla's consciousness was a red glow hovering close to black. She felt herself being moved; the movement stopped. Hands stuffed a wad of raw wool in her mouth, then tied a strip of cloth at the back of her neck to keep the gag in place.

A figure knelt over her, silhouetted against the low door arch. She was in the herdsman's shelter; hints of moonlight came through chinks in the stones.

"Listen to me, lady," Romulus said. He paused to control his breathing. "I can't trust you not to turn the crowd against me at the assembly in the morning. You'll wait here until it's decided who rules the colony. If you've been quiet, you'll be released with no harm done...but if you try to raise a fuss, well, Celer's going to be right outside. He'll hear you before anybody else does, and he'll cut your throat."

Herosilla's ankles were bound; her wrists were tied behind her to a peg hammered into the hard dirt floor, She tried to kick Romulus. He chuckled and backed out of the hut.

The men thrust a thick bundle of brushwood into the opening, closing it more effectively than a door. Flavia Herosilla, scholar and gentlewoman of Rome, was alone with her thoughts.

The horn blew a second summons across the camp. Herosilla had pulled her wrist peg from the ground instants before the initial warning at dawn. There was light enough to read by now, and she was well on the way to getting her hands free.

"Citizens of a new city!" Romulus shouted in the meadow below. "Citizens chosen by the gods to rule a new future!"

Attaching Herosilla's wrists to a peg had been a mistake. The bindings were strips of half-tanned goat hide, too tough and flexible for her to have worn through against the interior walls if she'd been left to thrash around the hut. She'd gained a minuscule purchase on the main knot when she got the peg out by working it in a circle, though her wrists bled and her hands were numb.

Romulus let the rustle of excitement die down. Either he was a natural orator or he'd learned from Herosilla's performances. "This new community is the seed of the greatest city in the world," he continued. "Greater than Troy, greater than Knossos when Minos was king!"

Herosilla's fingertips gently teased the outer coil of leather. It was a job for care and delicacy, not desperate tugging that would only draw the loops tighter.

"We will be a new kind of city," Romulus said. He certainly had the lungs to address a large crowd. Now that Herosilla thought about it, she supposed that was true of most shepherds, accustomed to bellowing information across valleys to their fellows. "Open to anyone who can contribute to our benefit, whatever they may have been or done somewhere else."

A coil came loose. Herosilla picked the ends of the strap free, then twisted her wrists slightly to relax the inner loop.

She could hear low voices outside the hut. Celer was talking to someone. She hadn't yet determined a plan for the next stage of her escape, but this would complicate it.

"The man who may have been a slave or an outlaw in another community," Romulus boomed, "can be a valued fellow-citizen to us! My brother and I were threatened with outlawry by the court of the usurper Amulius!"

"No!" Remus said. "No, that's not what we'll do!"

"Wait your turn, brother!" Romulus said.

"This is my turn," Remus said. His voice was a carrying tenor in contrast to his brother's thunderous baritone. "No decent man wants to live in the company of robbers and runaways!"

Herosilla's hands were free. She ignored the pains lancing along her fingers as she scrabbled to remove the gag. She'd controlled her reaction to the gag for as long as there was no choice, but the chance to remove it now drove her frantic.

"It's my destiny to found a great city!" Romulus said. "You all heard Lady Herosilla, the messenger of the gods, say so. I am the son of Mars!"

Herosilla pulled the bandage from her face and spat out the wad of wool. She almost fainted with relief from the choking sensation.

Someone spoke again outside. The faggot in the door opening rustled as if kicked.

"Alba's already too large!" Remus said. "We're six hundred now, the right size for a community where everybody knows and trusts his neighbors."

"The lady said both of you were sons of Mars, Romulus," called a voice from the crowd.

"I don't know that I want a gang of cutthroats in the next house either!"

somebody else shouted. "Say, where is the lady, anyway?"

Somebody outside pulled on the brush. The faggot was stuffed tightly against the stone; sticks crackled against the stones.

Herosilla's fingernails nibbled at the strap binding her ankles. Even with her hands free, the tight knot wouldn't loosen easily.

"Lady Herosilla probably went back to the gods now that she's delivered her message!" Romulus said.

The assembly was dissolving into uproar. The colonists weren't a single community yet, and the rules of precedence in council hadn't been set.

The faggot slid all the way out. Ganea knelt and crawled through the opening.

"You thought your fine clothes and jewels would take him from me, didn't you?" she said in a voice that rasped like sand on stone. "But you were wrong, *lady*. And *he* was wrong, thinking he could hide you away safe!"

She had a bloody knife in her right hand.

"I'll let you have him!" Herosilla said, letting her voice rise into a shrill falsetto to project false terror. She backed away. The hut was too low to stand in.

"Bitch!" Ganea said and slashed at Herosilla's face. Herosilla caught the knife wrist in both hands and pivoted on her left buttock. Ganea flew past Herosilla's shoulder, straightening from her kneeling posture until her forehead hit the wall with a hollow clunk.

Ganea's body shuddered and went limp. Her breath drew in with a loud snore. Herosilla leaned over the body to get the fallen knife.

The assembly's shouted arguments merged into a shout from hundreds of throats. "Let them fight!" a man screamed in a brief silence. "Let the gods decide!"

Herosilla sawed methodically at the strap holding her ankles. Her hands tingled. When the blood wiped off, the edge of the blade gleamed white from recent sharpening.

The crowd bellowed again. Words of joy or concern wove a delicate counterpoint around the bloodlust of the main audience.

The strap parted. Herosilla crawled out of the hut, holding the knife by her side so that it couldn't be snatched by anyone waiting outside.

Celer lay on his back. His eyes and mouth were open, and his throat had been slashed to the backbone. Blood was a gummy pool beneath his shoulders; it no longer drained from the wound.

Herosilla stood, using her left hand on the hut to steady herself. Her feet felt as if they were resting on hot coals. She walked around shelter to look down on the assembly.

Romulus knelt over Remus and was choking him. Beside them was a small altar made of turf squares laid dirt-side up. They'd been preparing to burn an offering to consecrate the new settlement. Nearby were a mattock and the small, straight-bladed shovel that cut the turfs.

"Sons!" Faustulus called from the front row of spectators. He was crying. Two men, neither of them from Palatium, held the old man back. "My sons!"

Remus bowed his back. His long legs came up together and scissored around his brother's waist. Romulus gave an inarticulate cry as he went over backward to slam his head and neck on the ground. The crowd howled, sensing the kill.

"Remus!" Herosilla said. "Don't kill him!"

Remus rolled onto all fours and scrambled to his brother. Romulus tried to rise. The impact had left him groggy.

Remus seized him by the throat and banged his head down again. Remus' back and shoulder muscles bulged as he began to strangle his brother. The spectators inhaled instinctively. Romulus' arms and legs thrashed without direction.

"Remus!" Herosilla cried in the hush. "We *need* him! The future needs him!"

Remus looked up, over his shoulder. "Remus, we need him!" she repeated.

Romulus' hand touched the mattock's haft. He swung it up and caught his brother's skull a ringing blow with the side of the iron tool.

Remus sprawled sideways, blood streaming from the cut in his scalp. Herosilla started down the slope. She was still too stiff to run, even in daylight.

Romulus stood, swaying. His head was bowed. He rotated his grip on the mattock so that the cutting edge was aligned for the next stroke. Remus lay face down. His arms moved slightly as though he was trying to gather strength to rise.

"Romulus, stop!" Herosilla said. "You've won, but you'll die if you kill your brother."

Romulus looked at her. His face was distorted but unreadable. "Why?" he said in a snarl. "Will the gods strike me down, lady?"

"No," Herosilla said. She threw down the bloody knife. It stuck quivering in the soil at her feet. "But I will."

Romulus continued to look at her. He was twice her size and armed. He laughed.

The laughter rang false. His brother's handprints were livid on his throat.

"He can't stay here," Herosilla said. The crowd was silent. "He'll come with me to Cumae. You'll have your city, your Rome. But you won't have his life."

"Take him, then!" Romulus said. "But if I see him again—"

He drove the blade of the mattock haft-deep into the ground.

"—I'll split his skull!"

"Yes," Herosilla said. She knelt beside Remus and dabbed at the cut in his scalp. Faustulus and Acca joined her; Acca held a skin of wine.

"I dare say there'll be other people who can read and write in Cumae even now," said Flavia Herosilla, once a gentlewoman of Rome. She gave Acca a vague smile. "Cumae can use a Sibyl to foretell the future, don't you think, Acca?"

CPSIA information can be obtained
at www.ICGtesting.com
Printed in the USA
BVOW06*0327061117
498631BV00010B/10/P

9 781612 422268